HER NAME IS

Mariah

HER NAME IS

Mariah

MIMA

HER NAME IS MARIAH

iUniverse books may be ordered through booksellers or by contacting:

iUniverse
1663 Liberty Drive
Bloomington, IN 47403
www.iuniverse.com
1-800-Authors (1-800-288-4677)

Because of the dynamic nature of the Internet, any web addresses or links contained in this book may have changed since publication and may no longer be valid. The views expressed in this work are solely those of the author and do not necessarily reflect the views of the publisher, and the publisher hereby disclaims any responsibility for them.

Any people depicted in stock imagery provided by Thinkstock are models, and such images are being used for illustrative purposes only. Certain stock imagery © Thinkstock.

ISBN: 978-1-4917-6361-2 (sc)
ISBN: 978-1-4917-6362-9 (e)

Library of Congress Control Number: 2015904619

Print information available on the last page.

iUniverse rev. date: 3/27/2015

Acknowledgements

I would like to thank Mitchell Whitlock for working his magic on the back cover of *Her Name is Mariah*. I'm very fortunate to have a great friend who is also a terrific writer!

I would also like to thank my mother for her love and support, as well as Virginia Doyle for taking my photograph for the back cover.

As always, I want to thank everyone who has taken the time to write a review, share a Facebook or Twitter post or supported my career…and last but not least…

…here's one for the misfits, the nonconformists and for those who never quite fit in. This one's for you!

Chapter one

Things are often not as they appear to be. It is an unfortunate lesson that most will learn at some point in their lives, often replacing their naivety and innocence with distrust and skepticism. Some learn this difficult lesson in college, often following a defunct relationship while others do so shortly after starting their first job, quickly accepting that the rat race consists of many frayed edges. Mariah Nichols came to this realization at a much younger age; she was five.

It happened in a beautiful house that sat in the residential area of a quiet, Ontario town. It was inside the walls of a bungalow that was surrounded by perfectly manicured lawn, with a large oak tree displayed in the front yard. The modest house was reasonably new and well maintained; a dog-ear fence embracing the property and beautiful flower garden full of Black eyed Susan's. Those who took notice saw the children merrily run outside to play in the fresh snow every winter and the boy occasionally played basketball in the summer, while the little girl blew bubbles and skipped rope. It appeared to be the perfect family.

And really, who would ever think that everyone in the house was miserable: but they were.

The mother was a beautiful Russian immigrant, with an ivory complexion and huge chocolate colored eyes that communicated her innocence since first arriving in Canada years earlier. She had only been a young girl of 18, her father encouraging her to move and marry abroad in order to escape the dismal financial situation in their own family. Although it hadn't felt right to wed a mere stranger in another country, she trusted and respected her family's opinion when they insisted that her future husband was a good person. Although this Canadian man was slightly older than the Russian beauty, her father was certain it was a positive sign because it indicated he was more financially stable and mature than someone her own age. Her mother claimed that the combination of getting married to a handsome man and living in a new country was very exciting and a wonderful opportunity, something she should appreciate.

Her name was Polina and although she knew her parents meant well, it would quickly become clear that they were wrong.

Rather than introducing his new wife to friends and help her understand Canadian culture, Polina's husband thrusts her into a new world and showed no compassion regarding her fears or concerns. Since he was more interested in working long hours then crashing in front of the television, she was left feeling isolated, like she was his housekeeper during the day and whore at night. He demonstrated impatience when she was not able to understand various aspects of her new country and intolerance, often depicting every word she mispronounced and insulting her Russian upbringing whenever the opportunity presented itself. This wasn't the friendly, welcoming Canadian culture that her parent's had described.

With the birth of their first child a year later, Polina quickly fell into a depression, feeling scared and alone, with little knowledge on how to bring up a child. She often cried with her newborn son, feeling completely helpless. Secluded and living in misery, she insisted on going on the pill immediately after (to which, her husband seemed apathetic) but an error seven years later and Polina miserably found herself pregnant again.

The father was hopeful about the second child because he felt Polina attempted to keep his son away from him, often speaking to the boy in Russian and insisting that bringing up a child was 'a mother's duty'. She grew angry every time he tried to help until finally, he stopped. Maybe the next baby would be different.

No, he thought to himself, the next baby *will* be different.

His marriage to the stunning, young Russian hadn't turned out as he had hoped. Polina was much different once arriving in Canada than she had been in their many conversations before her move. It was almost as if he had signed up for one thing – then got another. In fact, one of his friends would joke that it was his own fault for 'shopping in a catalogue for a woman'. It angered him because he hadn't seen his wife as a product or a desperate, last measure to marry that his friends were suggesting. In fact, it wasn't something he had planned.

His name was Frank Nichols and he considered himself to be just a normal, average man. He studied business at university, got a great marketing job at a soft drink company and played by the rules. After falling desperately in love with an emotionally unavailable woman in his mid-twenties, he later made many attempts to get back into the dating game until his mid-thirties, when he finally decided it was a dead end road and began to look outside the country. Frank was discouraged. He was a simple guy who hadn't crazy expectations in life. He didn't want to be a rock star. He wasn't trying to be the richest man in the world. Frank just wanted a normal, stable and happy life with a wife and children.

At first, Polina seemed to be that missing piece of the puzzle: and then she wasn't. Although he discovered hints of vulnerability and love in the young Russian's eyes, they were brief and rare. She seldom communicated with him and her demeanor was as cold as ice. He gave her anything she wanted and yet, Polina showed no appreciation or respect in return.

The couple's second child did not bring happiness to their marriage. In fact, the baby brought more stress. And for all the times Frank stared into the little girl's big, brown eyes and truly wanted to keep the family together as one unit, the truth was that he couldn't deal with the increasing hostility in his marriage. He waited until his daughter was five before deciding to leave his wife.

The neighbors were surprised to see the marriage end. They had been so happy – hadn't they? It was an attractive couple with beautiful children, living in a modern, reasonably sized home. On the outside, it did appear to be ideal for those who strolled by on their evening walks, casually peaking in the windows from afar and making assumptions about the people inside.

The little girl with the big, brown eyes grew to idolize her brother. He was an angel in her heart. Always so patient and understanding, she knew he loved her more than anyone in the world. Meanwhile, their mother's behavior only grew more erratic after Frank Nichols left their home and moved to another city. It was supposedly for work, but the children knew better.

Polina and Frank's children were very close. The little girl even confessed to her brother that she didn't think their mother loved her. He calmly listened to her concerns and remained silent, biting back the truth that threatened to escape his lips. His sister didn't have to know that their father chose to name her after a former girlfriend – the one that 'got away' – and that this piece of painful truth had stabbed through Polina Nichols' heart and created a bitterness that was unlikely to fade away.

His name was Anton and it was one of two secrets he kept from his sister.

At age 13, Anton decided to buy a second hand bass guitar and join a neighborhood band. They weren't very good, but it didn't stop them from talking about their rock star dreams - the fame, the fortune, the girls – and Anton would smile and follow the lead of the other boys, as if he shared their fantasies. But it wasn't the truth. He hadn't joined the band because he wanted to be rich and famous, in fact Anton was much like his father and had modest dreams. And it wasn't for the girls either, although with an attractive face and dark curls, he already had their attention. In fact, Anton's desire to learn bass and join this band was for one reason only. He had a huge crush on the lead singer. And the singer was a boy.

Had Anton's parents known his secret, it wouldn't have gone very well. They often spoke poorly of the homosexual lifestyle, especially his dad, who laughed at it as if it were a weakness. His mother believed it was wrong and disgusting, often shaking her head at any gay references on television or in movies. Not that there were many at that time.

He pushed it down where no one could see it. Just trying to fit in and be one of the guys. He even dated a girl at 14 and lost his virginity to her. But it wasn't who he was and he felt bad when ending the relationship shortly after their only encounter. Anton could see he broke her heart, but he couldn't tell her that their sexual relationship only reinforced what he already knew; he was gay.

At least he thought he was gay. After having sex with his girlfriend, it occurred to Anton that he was curious about what she looked like naked and had wanted to touch her body. She fascinated him, but not necessarily in a sexual way. It was subtle things like how she dressed, wore her makeup or even the way she walked in high heels that impressed him. She was one of the prettiest girls in school and while other boys were aroused by her curves, Anton was transfixed. It was kind of like when his sister looked at a fashion magazine and commented on the pretty models, how she liked their lipstick or shoes. She didn't do that, Anton considered, cause she was attracted to the women in the magazine. No, his sister did that because she wanted to *be* the women in the magazine.

And that was when Anton realized that his secret was much more complicated and confusing than he thought. It wasn't just that he was gay; it was that he wanted to be a girl. He felt on the inside what he saw in those glossy magazine images.

The shoplifting started slowly. He would steal a tube of lipstick or an eyeliner pencil. Eventually, Anton stole a bra off a neighbor's clothesline one afternoon when he knew they were away. He gathered all the feminine things that exhilarated him and hid them in a secret place. Other 14-year-old boys hid porn. Anton hid fake pearls and high heel shoes.

It wasn't difficult to experiment with women's clothing and makeup. His mother was rarely home after the divorce, didn't go in his room and assumed that her son was straight. After all, he had had a girlfriend and did 'normal' guy stuff. But it was an act. As soon as she was out of the door and his sister wasn't around, Anton practiced putting on eyeliner and drawing eyebrows that resembled that of Madonna and Marilyn Monroe.

He hated himself for being this way and would sometimes stop for a week or two, but eventually, Anton would look at photographs of beautiful models and fantasized about walking in stilettos and to express his femininity. It wasn't that he just wanted to dress like a woman. It wasn't that he wanted to be a woman. It was that he *felt* like a woman. His body told one story while his heart told the complete opposite.

But he told no one. He knew his secret would be met with ridicule and misunderstandings. Then one day, he had no choice.

Anton managed to hide the secret from everyone for a couple of years. He was 15, almost 16 when his sister arrived home early from a neighbors' one day, to find him wearing a full face of makeup. He swiftly grabbed a washcloth to remove it, but it was too late.

"Anton, why are you wearing makeup?" Her innocent voice asked the question he had so many times asked himself. She was so young, only eight years old and nervously hovered in the doorway of his room, her head tilted as she bit her lower lip. She was obviously too young to be exposed to the entire truth but he knew that lying would forever cause a tear in their bond and wasn't there also a part of himself that longed for the opportunity to expose his secret? Even if it were only a fragment, wouldn't it be better than hiding everything?

"Can you keep a secret?" Anton asked as he grabbed a cloth and hastily began to remove the makeup, then suddenly stopped. No! If he was going to do this he couldn't tell her the truth while erasing the evidence of it the same time. "You have to promise to never tell anyone. Not mom, dad or anyone."

"I will keep your secret forever, Anton." Her eyes lit up while a soft wrinkle formed on her forehead. Although she originally resembled their father, he could now see her morphing into a younger version of their mom, with her porcelain skin and delicate features. "And ever and ever. I promise." She placed her tiny hand over her heart – or at least where she thought her heart was – then made a crossing signal with her finger. "Cross my heart and hope to die."

"Don't hope to die." It was a lame attempt of teasing her, but she continued to stare at him with serious eyes. Anton sighed and searched for the best words to explain something very complicated. If it were this hard to expose the truth to a little girl who loved him, how would he ever tell anyone else? "The truth is that I like wearing makeup."

"I thought only girls and clowns wore makeup." She sauntered into the room, her fingers lingering on the wall as if in fear of no longer being on solid ground. She was so tiny due to being a finicky eater, always wearing pink either in clothing or hair accessories; her dark, blonde hair was pulled back in a very loose ponytail. "I don't understand."

"Come 'mere," Anton waved his hand toward his chest. "Let me fix your hair."

A smile lit up her face and she bounced across the room and sat beside him on his bed. He quickly worked to readjust her ponytail while she wrinkled her face in a frown. She hated having anyone touch her hair.

"*Usually*, only girls and clowns wear makeup," He began to speak while stretching the elastic and wrapping it around her shoulder length hair. "But sometimes boys do too, it's just not as often and a lot of people don't understand."

"Do you understand?" she asked, reminding him of the strength of their connection. Had she sensed that Anton was as confused as she was at that moment?

"No," He gently replied as he finished her hair. "Honestly, I don't."

"I don't always understand why I do things either." She attempted to be very adult as she sat back on the bed and crossed her legs. "But you're the best brother ever, even if you like girl stuff like makeup."

Anton felt a sense of relief fill his heart. Maybe most people didn't know his truth and maybe he didn't fully understand it himself, but his little sister accepted and loved him. And that was something.

Her Name is Mariah, and this is her story.

Chapter two

Underneath every secret is a fear of exposure. Often that same fear becomes as large as the secret itself: it is nurtured and it grows until one day it blooms into a self-fulfilling prophecy. That's when the shit hits the fan.

Mariah was much too young to understand this concept and didn't foresee how anyone would learn that her brother liked to dress up as a lady. With her childlike naivety and innocent nature, she fully accepted his choice without giving it much of a second thought. A few times she had almost let it slip in front of their mother, but always caught herself in time. Mariah was very careful to protect her brother, just as he always had for her. She had no intentions of telling Anton's secret and unless he did, well… how else would anyone know?

But things happen. Little girls have their hearts broken even before they understand what it means. Sometimes it happens when someone they love expresses disappointment in them or when a parent leaves the family home permanently: Mariah had already experienced both these situations, but neither compared to the day she arrived home to discover that her brother was gone.

She walked in the door to find her mother sitting in the living room, alone, with a drink in hand. Her mascara and eyeliner were escaping the corner of each eye, caught up in the soft lines that were forming on what was once smooth, pure skin. Anger had stolen away her delicate smile and replaced it with etched lines that Mariah thought was the result of a permanent frown. Her hair was pulled back in a messy ponytail while her frail figure was lost in an oversized hoodie and sweat pants.

Her head turned, she showed no interest in her daughter's arrival home, but swallowed the last of her drink. Mariah didn't bother to say hello, but headed toward the hallway and Anton's room.

"You won't find him," Her mother bellowed before she had a chance to get there. Mariah noted signs of self-satisfaction in her mother's voice but ignored it. Her words were sharp, attacking her like daggers flying freely through the air. Although she logically attempted to convince herself that Anton was merely out for the afternoon, somehow she knew differently.

As she slowly turned back around before heading down the hallway, Mariah considered that some of her brother's trademark items had been missing from the living room. Perhaps his jacket or backpack was with him, but Anton's music magazines weren't on the coffee table, the sketch he drew in art class had been removed from the living room wall and both pairs of his shoes were gone from beside the door. Stepping further into the living room and toward the kitchen, it quickly became apparent that any evidence that her brother had ever lived there was missing.

Her heart raced steadily and Mariah felt her throat tightening, all moisture was zapped from her mouth and lips as she rushed toward his bedroom, ignoring his mother's repeated reminder that Anton was not there. Upon pushing the door open, she felt her legs grow weak and tears burning her lids as she saw only a stripped bed, empty dresser and desk in his room. Everything else was gone. There wasn't even a sock, a shoe or book left in his closet. The window was opened and a set of simple, blue curtains swayed in the breeze, as if to freshen a tainted room.

"Anton!!!!!!" Mariah wanted to scream, but his name came out more like a wounded cry, as she ran out of his room and back toward the living room. "Where is Anton? What have you done to Anton??"

"He's gone." Her mother showed no compassion, as her eyes grew even colder than ever before and her entire face seemed to become tighter. "Dead to us."

"HE'S DEAD?" Mariah screamed and instantly felt hot sweat gathering over her chest and underneath her arms. Tears sprang from her eyes and dripped down her chin. Suddenly she was shaking uncontrollably, her teeth chattering and her legs felt weak beneath her.

Polina didn't move from her chair, but watched her daughter collapse on the floor, in hysterical tears. "He is not dead you dramatic fool, but he may as well be, as far as I'm concerned. I wouldn't feel shame if he was dead."

"What?" Mariah asked weakly and confused by what was going on. Was her brother gone? Why was his room empty? What has happened to him?

"Your brother is no longer living with us," Her mother finally started to explain, rising to walk toward the bottle of vodka sitting on the kitchen counter. Pouring some in her glass, followed by some anonymous bottle of red juice, she mixed the drink and returned to her chair. "I asked him to leave after discovering his dirty little secret. Did he not think I would find out that he wore women's clothing? That he wore makeup and dressed like a drag queen? I am ashamed to be his mother."

Mariah rose from the floor. Her tears were no longer falling and although she felt weak, the nine year old courageously walked across the floor and stood in front of her mother. It didn't matter how much this woman frightened her or how sad she was at that moment, Mariah had to be brave for Anton. He would tell her to not let anyone scare her.

"Where did he go? Where is all his stuff?" Her voice suddenly sounded more like that of an adult, rather than the innocent little girl that entered the house that afternoon. And when her mother didn't answer, she took a deep breath and raised her voice. "I *said where* did you put his stuff?"

Her mother's cold glare was the same as usual, but this time, there possibly was more disinterest as she continued to hastily drink, as a small drop of the red mixture fell on her hoodie. "I threw it out with him. I got rid of everything. I don't want to have any memory of that boy."

"*What?*" Mariah felt more tears forming in her eyes and a sharp pain in the center of her chest. "Why did you do that?"

"I told you, he's dead." Her words were calm, as if nothing unusual had taken place that day. "He is gone. I don't want him in my life anymore. He brought me shame."

Instinctively, Mariah rushed into the kitchen and found several of her brother's things in the garbage. Clothing, personal items and on the very top sat the ripped sketch that had previously hung proudly on the living room wall. She stood in silence for a moment, trying to process everything.

Her brother was no longer living with them. Their mother had discovered that he liked to dress up like a girl. Everything he owned was either in the garbage or out of the house. Their mother wished he were dead.

Closing her eyes momentarily, her tiny body took in another deep breath and Mariah looked down at her hands. Her short fingernails were freshly polished a scarlet red, something Anton had done for her the evening before, as the two sat and talked about their day, after Polina Nichols went out with a friend. He had commented on how she had dainty, ladylike hands that other girls would envy and Anton insisted that she should always be proud of her beauty, never allow anyone to put her down. Mariah had giggled at the mere notion of anyone being jealous of her, but Anton was insistent that the day would come and he couldn't wait.

Was he really gone forever?

Opening and closing both hands, she watched the red nail polish continually disappear when hid within the closed fist of her hand. She licked her lips and swallowed back the many emotions that she felt enclosed inside her, knowing that any sign of vulnerability was what her mother wanted to see. It made her feel powerful whenever anyone else was sad, as if crying or being kind was a weakness. Anton explained that some people were just like that and it was important to never show that they had the upper hand.

"You will thank me someday," Her mother suddenly piped up again; her words were now slurred and somehow sounded more vulgar than moments earlier. Mariah turned and gave her a cold stare and felt anger slowly building inside her, growing with every passing second. "We don't need a faggot living in this house."

Mariah didn't know what that word meant, but she was aware it was derogatory in context. She remembered when a kids at school said it one day in the schoolyard and was abruptly pulled into the principal's office, so it was definitely something bad. She didn't want to hear her mother call Anton a bad name.

"Don't call him that!" Mariah screamed, feeling a tension crawling up her body. "Don't call Anton bad names!"

"Bad names?" Her mother's head fell back and she laughed. "Bad names? You have no idea what a bad name is, little girl. I call your brother a faggot because he is one! He dresses like a woman that is not normal. You wouldn't believe the things I found in his room after I threw him out. Disgusting! Makeup, women's lingerie – who was he trying to be sexy for, can you tell me that? What do you know? Did he have a little boyfriend over while I was out?"

Mariah had never felt such anger in her life. She hadn't even been aware it was possible to feel such rage, such intense fury toward another human being, that she wanted to hurt them. Mariah did not fully understand why her brother wanted to be like a girl but she also didn't understand why it mattered. Why did that make him less of a person to their mother? Why did she suddenly hate him, based on that one fact?

"*Stop* saying that," Mariah's voice held such raw power that it greatly resembled that of someone much older. She felt the blood rushing to her face, as Mariah's heart pounded excitedly causing an electricity to flow through her veins. "I *love* Anton." She paused for a moment, breathing erratically, much like someone who had just completed a race. Her mother continued to look unmoved by the conversation; more interested in the drink she was about to finish. "But I *hate* you."

These words clearly stung and for a brief moment, she could sense the hurt it caused her mother. But almost as quickly as sorrow filled her eyes, it was replaced by seething anger. "Don't you say that to your mother or you will be on the street with him."

"I *HATE* you!" She roared through the house, filling up every room with her wrath and without giving it another thought, she rushed toward her mother and with one quick movement, Mariah slapped her across the face.

Her mother grabbed her arm and Mariah felt pain shoot through her wrist, as Polina stood up and roughly threw her daughter against the wall. A framed picture of the family fell to the ground, the glass breaking while Mariah felt like the air in her body had been sucked out and she couldn't breath. She was certain of her death, gasping and fighting for some air, she finally managed to squeeze some into her lungs while her mother started to scream.

"You are an ungrateful, little brat!" Her mother bellowed, throwing her empty glass across the room, hitting a nearby wall and shattering into a million little pieces. "I should kick you out too! Put you on the street, just like your brother. Maybe you can find your father and live with him and his whore."

Somehow managing to center herself, Mariah felt her body grow weak after being aggressively pushed against the wall. She wanted to curl up in a corner and cry, but who would care? Anton was already gone. She had no one else to look after her now. Except, she decided, herself.

"I will go to the neighbors," Mariah heard herself rush to reply. Anton would tell her to not let their mother get the best of her and she wanted to say whatever would make him proud. In that moment, she *needed* to do and say whatever he would've done, had the tables been turned. How many times had he rushed to her defense? "I will tell them you threw me out. They will call the police on you."

Her mother looked stunned and fell silent.

Mariah knew that more than anything her mother couldn't stand to be judged. She worried about what neighbors thought and wanted to represent an image of someone they should respect. It would look poorly on Polina's image if her nine year-old child told everyone what kind of mother she really was: how she drank too much, kicked out her son and was abusive to her daughter. If she had learned nothing else from her mother, it was how to manipulate people to do what she wanted or in this particular case, what was necessary.

Many times, Mariah would relive this scene in her mind and only as an adult had she realized that something pivotal changed in her that day. The loss of her brother along with the hatred of her mother had caused Mariah to grow up instantly and leave her childhood sobbing on the living room floor. Polina Nichols had taken the one person from her life that really loved and nurtured her and once that person is removed from anyone's life, are they really ever the same person again?

Mariah did not know why her mother seemed so detached but assumed that since her birth was long after Anton's that perhaps it was because she had been an unwanted mistake. It was the story she told herself over and over again, assuming it to be the truth. It was the only thing that made any sense.

The house was quiet when Mariah slid under the covers that night. Knowing that her mother had passed out, she finally felt safe to cry for her brother.

Where are you, Anton? Are you safe? Do you miss me like I miss you?

Staring at the ceiling, she eventually stopped crying. Her eyes and throat were dry, but she didn't care. Mariah knew she would see Anton again. He'd want her to be strong and tell her to not let their mother hurt her. A smile attempted to curve her lips but didn't quite make it because as much as Mariah was certain that her brother would once again be a part of her life, she was also certain that one day she would get even with her mother.

Chapter three

It has been said that people can get used to anything. A child living in a cold shack knows nothing of sleeping in a warm mansion. A child who has little to eat knows nothing of a four-course meal. A child who has an emotionally disconnected mother knows nothing of comfort and nurturing: and that child has no choice but become self-sufficient and independent at a very young age.

Mariah Nichols saw her world change after her brother left. The first thing she noticed was the silence.

Polina didn't feel that her daughter was really in need of a babysitter. After all, the nine year-old was responsible so it wasn't like leaving a baby home alone. It was too expensive and bothersome to find childcare for when she was at work or socializing, so it made more sense to just 'see' how things went when Mariah was by herself. She didn't feel that there was much chance of anything going wrong in such a quiet neighborhood; so just let the girl learn to be responsible.

And although she was scared, Mariah wouldn't admit it. She bravely came home to the quiet house and broke the silence by turning on the television. Afternoon soap operas were an intriguing form of entertainment because they often centered on strong, yet dysfunctional families. Mariah related. But most of the time it was simply background noise to keep her company while she did her homework.

Late at night, she would turn off the television, double check that the front door was locked and go to her room. While most little girls in her situation would've feverishly prayed to be protected inside those four walls, Mariah didn't believe in God. She instead shut off her bedroom lights and turned on her music. It always made her feel safe.

Her favorite band was Metallica. She listened to them during infrequent car trips with her father, since it was his favorite band too. The melody combined with the powerful voice of James Hetfield, helped create a protective barrier that gently surrounded Mariah through many evenings of her childhood. The aggressive songs ironically helped her to relax and sleep, almost as if the famous rock band were physically in the house, standing guard to protect the lost little girl. It gave her the strength she needed.

Anton played a parental role with his sister and not only introduced her to good study habits, he also taught her some practical life skills. She could do her own laundry, wash the dishes, and even prepare some basic meals like soup, toast or boiled eggs. This was a good thing since her mother was rarely home to cook.

Occasionally Polina would make a 'family' meal but that didn't really happen unless she wanted to impress a new boyfriend. Mariah assumed that preparing a tasty dinner and being a good mother must've impressed these men since it was the only time her mother made such efforts.

The guys her mother brought home were usually kind of weird. Some were really nice to her and others barely noticed that she was even in the room. Sometimes these strange men would stay the night and Mariah would find one in the bathroom or the kitchen first thing in the morning. It made her very uncomfortable. She missed her family – her real family and longed for the days when both her brother and father were still at home. It wasn't always great, but it was something.

Mariah's dad rarely contacted her after the separation. He abruptly moved to a new city and eventually started a relationship with another woman. There was talk of an engagement. Polina often made snide remarks about how he went off to replace his family and Mariah wanted to ask her dad if that was true but feared how he would answer, so she didn't. But when he stopped calling on a regular basis, it was hard to believe that her mother hadn't been right.

But the person she really missed was her brother. Anton didn't call for months after getting kicked out and Mariah had started to lose hope he would ever call again. Where was he now? Was he going to be okay? Did he think about her? So many questions and fears plagued her mind until one day, the unexpected happened. The phone rang after school and Mariah discovered her brother's voice on the other end of the line.

"Anton!" Mariah exclaimed, and suddenly felt tears form in her eyes. It was the first time she allowed herself to cry since the night he left. "Anton, I miss you. Can you come back now? Please! Just tell mommy that you don't dress like a girl anymore. I won't tell her if you still do." She finished her plea with long sobs and she collapsed on the floor, grasping the telephone with both hands.

"Calm down, baby girl." Her brother's soothing voice seemed to have a sedating effect on Mariah. She played with the phone cord with one of her fingers while scratching off a nail polish stain on her jeans, with the other one. "Is mom home?"

Glancing toward the door, Mariah replied. "No, she's almost never home."

"Are you okay? Does she leave you home a lot?"

"Yes, but I don't care." Mariah spoke dramatically. "I hate her! She made you leave. I want to go with you."

"I'm sorry Mariah, but that's just not possible. You have to stay there with mom," Anton spoke softly and she could hear a gentle muffle of voices in the background.

"Where are you?"

"I'm staying with some friends," He replied. "Um, we're actually moving to Montreal."

"Montreal?" Mariah thought for a moment. "You're leaving here?"

"Yes, it's kind of a long story, but I decided that I needed a change in environment." Anton spoke slowly, as if carefully choosing his words. "Someday when you are older, you can come to see me."

"I want to see you now," Mariah felt fresh tears burning her eyes and she abruptly used her sleeve to wipe them away. "I hate her. I can't stay here now. She hates me too."

"Mariah, I really wish I could." He paused for a moment. "Have you talked to dad?"

"Yeah."

"Does he know I'm gone?"

"Yeah."

"Did you ask if you could stay with him for awhile?" Anton probed.

"No, he met someone else and stuff," Mariah didn't want to get into it. She knew their father wasn't a possibility and simply didn't want to discuss it further. She just wanted to have her brother back. Period. "Besides, I want to go where you are, can you please let me? I'll be good."

"Mariah, it's just not that simple." Anton 's words were gentle and gave her comfort, even if he wasn't saying what she wanted to hear.

Their conversation ended shortly afterward with him making Mariah promise him that she would follow their old routine: dinner, homework and TV time and bed by nine. He made her promise that she'd work hard to keep her marks up and Anton assured her that he'd be monitoring the results. He made her promise to be careful when home alone and to be wary of any men that their mother brought over, always pushing a chair in front of her bedroom door at night so no one could get in. He made her promise a lot of things that night and Mariah agreed to follow each of them to the letter. And she would.

Anton assured her that he would call again as soon as he could. If their mother were to ever answer, he'd hang up. If Mariah answered and their mother was there, she was to pretend that he was a charity looking for money and abruptly end the call. Mariah didn't have to be told that she'd be in trouble if her mother learned that they were talking at all. She had been forbidden to talk to her brother while living under that roof.

But Anton wouldn't call again for a long time. In fact, months went by and eventually years. Mariah constantly feared that something was wrong. Why hadn't he been in touch? Did he forget about her too? What if he got hurt or even worse, what if he were dead? Would they ever talk again? She felt so alone, so helpless.

A million things crossed her mind daily, but her childlike sense of optimism helped to carry her through.

Mariah kept all the promises she made to Anton. She was an excellent student and spent most of her spare time reading library books. Her focus was learning and she had a specific interest in reading Psychiatry Today, in hopes of better understanding her own family. For this reason, teachers took a special interest in her while her own parents were clearly living lives that were not only separate from one another, but from their daughter as well.

Life can be lonely without friends, but Mariah was able to make one in seventh grade. Up until that point, various girls flitted through her life, but none really had an interest in connecting with her. And chances are that Emily Thomas wouldn't have even become her friend, had the two not been placed together in order to work on a presentation for health class.

The 14 year-old girls were gifted intellectually, if not socially, but shared an interest in television programs, music and excitedly talked about boys they thought were cute. They formed a habit of going to Mariah's house most days after school and doing homework together while watching soaps that Emily wasn't allowed to view at home.

It was during one of these study sessions that her brother finally phoned again. Hitting the mute button for the latest episode of *Days of our Lives*, Mariah's eyes briefly met her friends as she rushed to answer the ringing phone.

"It's probably that Rick guy in English that has the huge crush on you," Emily teased Mariah, whose only response was to roll her eyes and grin. Neither girl had any experience with dating at that point, but teased each other as if they did.

"Shut up!" Mariah pretended to be angry and threw a pillow at Emily before grabbing the phone. "Hello?"

"Mariah?" His voice caused her face to soften and tears to burn her eyes. Seeing the concerned look on Emily's face, she quickly blinked them away.

"Anton." She said his name as she sat on the couch and pulled her legs close to her body. Emily had a look of understanding on her face because she knew the story about Anton – not the real story, but the fact that Mariah's older brother had moved out and the two rarely talked. Emily quickly rose from the chair and pointed toward Mariah's room, to indicate leaving in order to give them privacy. "Oh my God! I thought I would never talk to you again. I've missed you so much. Are you doing okay?"

"I'm fine," He assured her, but she couldn't help but wonder why he took so long to call. "There's just been a lot of stuff going on and I wanted to get my life together before I called you again."

"It's been a long time." Mariah couldn't help but point out as she stared at her toe sticking from the hole in heavy, gray socks. It was March and they suffered unseasonably low temperatures for days. "I was scared."

"I'm really sorry, Mariah." He sounded slightly subdued and took a deep breath. She could hear people talking in the background. "I called a couple of times and mom answered so I hung up, but still, that's no excuse."

"Did you end up going to Montreal?"

"Yes, I've been here for a few years."

Since we last talked.

"Are you really okay, Anton?"

"I'm great, Mariah. I've just been so busy here." He explained and she noticed that a door shut in the background and there were no more voices on his end of the line. "I really miss you so much. I want to try to go back and see you someday but I don't know if mom will let me."

"She's never around, she wouldn't even notice if you were living here," Mariah glibly commented. "She barely knows I'm here."

"Is she okay with you?"

"The same."

"And school?"

"In the top of my grade."

"Wow! I'm so impressed." His voice lifted in pleasure and she felt warmth of praise run through her body. "I'm very proud of you, Mariah. You know you will be so much more than what this pathetic family brought us up to be. Don't ever let mom get you down."

"I won't, Anton."

"Finish school, keep getting those grades." He insisted and she could picture his warm eyes staring into her own in that moment. "It's going to be okay. We're going to be okay."

"I know." Mariah agreed, even though she wasn't so sure. Lately she was getting more and more creeped out by her mother's boyfriends, especially now that Polina drank on a more regular basis. She wouldn't tell that to Anton though. He would just worry too much. Mariah could handle herself.

"You've made it this far and once you finish school, you can come stay with me. We'll get through it together."

And that was all she needed to hear. Mariah felt like his words could carry her through the most horrific storm because she knew that at the end of the line, he would be waiting for her with open arms. Everything would be okay.

This time they ended their conversation with an exchange of emails and a promise it wouldn't take years for Anton to call her again.

"You have to promise," she said at the end of their conversation. "Please don't scare me like that again. I just want to know that you're okay."

"I'm better than okay, Mariah." She heard laughter in his voice. "Hey, I'm supposed to be looking after you, not the other way around."

"I think we need to look after one another." Mariah corrected him. "I can't wait to see you again, big brother."

"It will happen soon enough." He assured her.

In the end, it was later than Mariah hoped and sooner than Anton anticipated.

# Chapter four

C haos is a normal state for some people.

Mariah was in regular contact with her brother but generally speaking, little changed over the next couple of years. She continued to live a very separate life from her mother. In a way, it was preferred over a forced relationship that meant nothing. But there were times when she had to face how unusual it was to be so disconnected from both her parents.

It was when Mariah went to Emily's house that she recognized how her own home life was so dysfunctional. Family dinners, watching television together or having any kind of an emotional connection was a foreign concept in the Nichols' household. She had no curfew, no rules and no monitoring. Although slightly jealous of the connection within Emily's family, she couldn't help but feel slightly superior because she had so much freedom.

Polina Nichols used their house as a home base while Mariah's father was in the picture even less. His second family was blossoming in a way his first never had, so chances were good he wanted to forget his original marriage disaster. He paid for Mariah's driving lessons, school expenses and was made generous child support payments, but that is where their relationship ended. Occasionally, they would share an awkward phone call, but those were few and far between.

And while Emily often commented that Mariah was lucky to not have parents 'always nosing in' her life, she also showed signs of concern for her friend. Wasn't it weird to not see half of her family? Was she scared or sad? Lonely? Where was her mother all the time?

To each of these questions, Mariah would merely give an apathetic shrug. It was what it was.

Teachers praised her for having excellent marks. Female classmates thought she was a weirdo and, other than Emily, all avoided her. On the other side of the spectrum, male classmates were attracted to Mariah but found her much too intimidating to approach.

Not that she cared; Mariah couldn't understand why the other girls were so obsessed with high school boys. Sure, it was empowering to have their attention, but she certainly wouldn't cry herself to sleep if the cutest guy in school didn't think she was pretty. Her fantasies about boys didn't include promise rings and dates to the prom. She had no illusions that this would be a part of her future – that was for other girls, the same kind who gushed over celebrities and dreamed of their wedding day. It was really silly. They just lived in a dreamland.

Informed and intelligent people are more realistic about the world. They soaked up large amounts of information before coming to a logical conclusion. In that respect, Mariah was probably much more open minded than most people her age but especially her best friend, Emily. Having come from such a dysfunctional family, it was natural for her to see that things were often much more complicated than they appeared.

Emily, on the other hand, saw things in a more black and white perspective. In fact Mariah was surprised by how judgmental and conservative she became over the years. Once soft spoken and sweet, Emily formed a bitter edge to her personality that was less pleasant. It seemed to intensify after going to a religious camp the previous summer. It was really kind of weird.

For example, Mariah didn't think much about her classmates, one way or another but Emily was extremely critical. She was quick to condescendingly insist that certain students were 'sluts' while others were 'nice' girls and Mariah noted that it appeared to have more to do with what they were wearing, than their actual reputation. She gently commented that perhaps things weren't quite as they appeared, but Emily was pretty persistent about her point of view. Mariah decided it was easier to let it go.

Then Emily decided that abortion was wrong and wanted to join various protests in order to vocalize her opinions. It made sense that a young woman who was brought up in the Catholic Church would stand by such a belief. Mariah privately disagreed but decided it wasn't worth debating and remained silent.

And then one day, the topic of homosexuality came up for discussion.

Not surprisingly, as per Emily's conservative values, she felt it was wrong to be gay and considered it to be 'gross' and 'disgusting.' She insisted it was often a symptom of some much bigger problem or an unusual form of rebellion, sort of a way of saying 'fuck you' to society by going against the grain and entering a gay relationship.

Mariah silently listened to her theory and thought it was rather far-fetched but didn't comment. The last thing she would do is to admit her brother fell in this category because she loved him too much to not stand up for him. On the other side of things, she really needed a friend and therefore didn't want to do or say anything that rocked the boat.

But she was still pissed off. Very, very pissed off.

It was in Mariah's blood to keep secrets that might put her in the position of being judged. After all, her mother had done the same by attempting to build a facade to impress the neighbors and now, Mariah was doing the same thing in order to keep a lone friend. But unlike the misery that Polina Nichols attempted to hide in order to appear to be a normal, her daughter was hiding some very different kinds of secrets.

To begin with, at 16 Mariah wasn't the virgin waiting for the perfect guy, as Emily believed her to be. Not that she slept around, but there was a college guy that she had a sexual relationship with that was mutually satisfying, if not monogamous or serious. In fact, she was pretty tainted with the idea of ever forming a serious love connection and while girls like Emily dreamed of finding their prince and living happily ever after, Mariah thought it was totally bullshit. Love was an exaggerated idea that people bought into and nothing she had ever seen or experienced convinced her that it was real.

But she did like sex. She was curious and when opportunity with a college boy introduced itself, Mariah grabbed it. He was the one who took her virginity, taught her everything she wanted to know. He also introduced her to porn.

And while she recently listened to Emily rant about how wrong 'dirty movies' were and how 'grossed out' she was after discovering a collection on her older brother's computer, Mariah realized that perhaps her friend's sibling might actually have something in common with her.

His name was Edward and he wasn't anything to write home about, but he was kind of cute, tall, with floppy curls and an awkward expression on his face whenever the two met in the family's house. He spent a lot of time alone in the room and upon learning about his extensive porn collection, Mariah innocently asked. "Oh, what does he watch? You mean like *Playboy* stuff or the weird kind they talk about in school?"

"It was so gross," Emily rolled her eyes and covered her mouth, as if about to vomit. "There was stuff with two girls with fake boobs, doing stuff to one another. That was the one on the screen when I went into the room. And when I glanced through his movies, they were all dirty." Pushing a strand of hair out of her eyes and showing what Mariah considered over-dramatized teenaged girl's expression. "Oh, and there was like stuff with groups and girls playing with themselves. I just couldn't believe it. Mom would freak if she knew! I don't want to get him in trouble, but I don't think he should be objectifying women like that. We aren't just here to be some guy's plaything cause he's horny or whatever. You know?"

Mariah prided herself on not letting out a smile on the many occasions she wanted to react. She had a poker face and it was something inherited from her mother and it came in handy. "Do you think guys think about us doing those things to them?"

Watching the expression on Emily's face was absolutely priceless.

"Oh, gross!" She shivered. "Don't get me wrong, I want to have sex someday, but not with some horn dog just looking for a booty call or whatever."

Mariah gave a sympathetic nod and didn't reply. There were definitely some things that Emily didn't need to know.

One night as Mariah was leaving, she ran into Edward outside. He was alone, shooting hoops and gave her a shy smile as she walked down the front steps. It sparked the memory of an earlier conversation about how Emily felt her brother was on his way to hell for watching porn. This was after commenting on how a homosexual classmate was 'disgusting' and 'abnormal'. All these thoughts were brewing in her head as she approached him.

"Can I talk to you?" Mariah spoke directly to Edward, who appeared stunned, if not slightly bewildered by her attention.

A few minutes later, Mariah watched as Emily's brother bolted inside the house to get the car keys, awkwardly rushing out the door while yelling something about giving Mariah a drive home. Practically tripping on the steps, he was flustered when he reached the car and briefly made nervous eye contact with Mariah who gave him a confident smile.

The two were barely back at her empty house, when Mariah was leading him into her bedroom and showing him that the real thing, was always better than anything he watched on adult websites.

It wouldn't be the last time she would do something completely out of spite, but it was the first. Someday, when the moment was right, she would make sure Emily found out the truth – but not yet. As they said, revenge was a dish best served cold.

By the time Mariah was almost 17, she was self-assured in her brains, looks and sexuality. Confident that no one could win a battle against her, she was ready to take on the world. And the first person she wanted to avenge was her mother. Mariah hadn't forgiven her for kicking Anton out and had spent many hours considering how to get even.

Several options had crossed her mind, but none of them felt just right. After all, how could she hurt a heartless woman? What could she take away from her? But everyone has a weak point; it was just a matter of finding out what it was.

Mariah thought a lot about what did matter to Polina Nichols. There wasn't really much. She cared about what people thought. She cared about money. She cared about being desirable to men.

Polina created the impression that she was a poor, Russian immigrant who was broken hearted after her husband left, followed by her son. In fact, she had lead people to believe that Anton had gone to live with his father. Mariah's mother sang the single mother song, implying she was forced to work a couple of jobs in order to pay the bills. If only they knew that Anton was kicked out for being gay, that Frank Nichols made substantial child support payments each month and left, cause she was a bitch. Polina actually only worked one job and socialized as much as possible. But how could Mariah turn this around without looking like either a liar or just a vindictive teenaged daughter?

But if you patiently wait, there comes a day when life presents you with the answers to a question that had been hovering in the eaves for much too long. Everything has its time and place.

It happened at Mariah's 17th birthday. Her mother, on a whim, decided to throw her 'baby girl' a party. It was quite an unusual move for the almost absent mother so Mariah was naturally suspicious. Then again, her mom was prone to make impulsive decisions and often with no rhyme or reason.

When the day arrived, Mariah was on high alert, suspicious of this sudden interest in her birthday. Emily was the only friend she had at the party, the rest were friends of Polina and neighbors. She assumed that was the angle all along, to give the impression she was the mother of the year by throwing the party, then using it as her own social activity. Lovely.

Seething in anger, Mariah hid her emotions with a poker face, occasionally glancing in her mother's direction. Polina was having a lively conversation with neighbors and friends, the 'belle of the ball', Mariah thought spitefully. On the other side of the room, she sat with Emily and attempted to carry on a conversation, while grabbing snippets of the exchange her mother was involved in. She had to figure out a way to get even with Polina. If only there were a clue about the best way to do so or a way she could embarrass her at this party. After reading tons of psychological books, she figured her mother to be very insecure, manipulative and a narcissistic so it shouldn't be too difficult.

But halfway through the party, Mariah had her answer. It was when an attractive, Spanish man with warm, brown eyes and a light caramel complexion walked in the door and looked in her direction. He had a seductive smile that would've even had Emily wet, something Mariah considered while glancing at her friend, who seemed equally caught up in the latest guest to Mariah's party.

"Who is *that*?" She whispered and at the same time, being quite obvious in her interest. She leaned in so close to Mariah that the scent of her bubble gum lingered in the air. "He is so hot. Like, movie star hot."

"Yeah?" Mariah made a conscious effort to hide her interest. There were a variety of reasons for this. First of all, she didn't want Emily to know that any guy really captivated her. Second, she didn't want any guy to know that they really captivated her. But mostly, she didn't want her mother to suspect that Mariah saw him as anything more than 'an old, creepy man', which is how she often described her mother's boyfriends.

As if on cue, her mother swooped in and grabbed the young man by the arm and pulled him in the opposite direction as Mariah.

A thin smile spread across her lips.

Bingo.

 *Chapter five*

"I think my brother has a crush on you," Emily said with a giggle, a few days after Mariah celebrated her 17th birthday. The two were at a local coffee shop, each enjoying their chosen beverage as Emily spied on a cute boy that was working behind the counter. Mariah suspected that this was the real reason for her friend's sudden interest in mochas, but kept this thought to herself.

"Oh me?" Mariah grinned and avoided making eye contact with her friend, choosing instead to glance at an odd poster displaying a happy couple sharing a milkshake. She could feel her cheeks growing warm as flashes of a few random, erotic moments between her and Edward raced through her mind. She certainly couldn't allow Emily to guess that anything was going on between them, partially because she couldn't lose her only friend, but mostly because there was something exhilarating about sneaking around.

Emily, however, mistook Mariah's flustered reaction to indicate that she was simply embarrassed by the realization. "Yeah, I know, he's gross," She shook her head and rolled her eyes to the heavens, then casually glancing at the boy behind the counter for the millionth time. "I just get the impression that he likes you, but don't let that make you uncomfortable when you come by the house. Just as an FYI."

"Don't worry about it." Mariah tried to brush it off, pushing a strand of dark, blonde hair from her face and glancing out a nearby window, before returning her gaze to Emily. "I hadn't noticed."

And that was a lie. Of course she had noticed but figured that like Emily, the entire family just assumed Edward had a crush on his sister's friend. No big deal, really. No one had any reason to think otherwise and he was experiencing a no strings attached sexual relationship, so she doubted that Emily's brother would utter a word.

Mariah had zero interest in a real relationship. Watching her mother's never-ending parade of disastrous love affairs was enough to turn her off the concept of love, regardless the romantic fantasies Emily had danced through her head. It was very clear that having feelings for someone was another way of handing over your self-esteem on a platter and Mariah was much too smart to allow that to happen.

At least it was understandable in Emily's case. After all, her parents had a good relationship and she was still young and very inexperienced in life. Mariah was sometimes envious of her naivety since her own childhood appeared to end at a very young age. It was difficult to not resent her mother. Of course, Mariah's survivor instincts kicked in and everything had been fine: but it still wasn't right.

Then again, Polina Nichols was clearly a train wreck. She chased after men, centered her life on meeting one and put her entire being in relationships, rather than trying to evenly distribute her heart. But Mariah had long figured out that her mother was just one of those pathetic women that needed a man in order to feel whole. Something was missing inside her and she used both men and alcohol, in attempts to compensate. It just didn't work.

"Hey, wouldn't it be funny if your brother came home for a visit and had a crush on me?" Emily's eyes were full of innocent pleasure, reminding Mariah that the only way she'd continued this friendship was to go with the flow. Obviously she couldn't reveal that her brother had a fondness for wearing more feminine clothes than Emily and only ever told her about a crush on a singer named Luke. "I never saw a picture of your brother, is he cute?"

"Yes," Mariah replied with confidence, knowing that she wasn't lying this time. He was very handsome, looking much like their father, with shiny, black hair and eyes were as dark as the night skies. His complexion was darker than Mariah's and his smile was warm, full of sincerity. "But he is quite a bit older than us. He's 24."

"Does he have a girlfriend?"

Mariah hid her grin with a large mouthful of coffee and shook her head. "I don't think so."

Actually, she knew little about her brother's personal life. He didn't talk about the fact that he was thrown from their family home because he was transgender. Then again, was that even the proper term? Was it offensive at all? Mariah wished she could ask him these questions and more, but somehow felt limited, as if his private life was not to be shared. She assumed he was gay, but wasn't sure if he continued to dress in women's clothing. Maybe it was an experiment at the time or a sexual fetish. Her own introduction to porn had shown that there was a lot of things that turned people on and they weren't even sure why.

"Does he live on his own or is he still with your dad?" Emily finished her drink and pushed the empty mug aside. Clasping her hands together, she was attentively listening to Mariah. "I remember he used to live with your dad, right?"

"No, he's on his own."

Mariah rarely talked to her father anymore. The calls became less and less frequent. It was almost as if he wanted to completely forget his old life and merely move forward into the next one. It should've hurt her, but it didn't. In fact, she felt nothing at all.

But wasn't that strange?

"It must be weird to have half your family living in different places." Emily observed, but only seemed slightly involved in the conversation, which made Mariah feel less guilty about the secrets she hid from her. "Do you ever see them?"

"Not really," Mariah confessed and finished off the rest of her coffee. "I mean, my dad has been gone since I was seven so I barely can remember him and my brother has been in Montreal for a long time too."

"But really, he's only 24. It couldn't have been that long."

Mariah had no intentions of telling her under what circumstances her brother left. "Oh, well five years feels like a long time when you are close to someone." Feeling her stomach suddenly overcome with a burning sensation that went with the lies, she started to move to the edge of her chair. She had mislead Emily into believing that her parents had a bitter divorce that created a break even with her own brother, who chose their dad's side over Polina's and that's why they hardly were in touch in earlier years. "Want to get out of here?"

"Sure," Emily agreed and grabbed her purse, taking another glance at the guy behind the counter. It was very obvious that he was ignoring her. "This is a cool place, we will have to come back again." She said the words more in his direction than Mariah's; something that would've annoyed her, had she been feeling better but instead, she just ignored it.

Mariah arrived home to find a small, red car in the driveway, next to her mother's sedan. She glanced in the window as she walked by and noticed a drug store bag on the passenger side. Noting that the living room curtains were closed, she stopped to inspect things a little farther. It was smart to be prepared, maybe she could learn about the person inside her house a little before entering.

The contents of the bag appeared to be some kind of weird, super powerful vitamins. Judging by the graphics on the container, they were marketed toward men, not women. There was also a package of gum, razor blades and she couldn't quite see, but was that a box of condoms in the back? Mariah made a face and hoped that she wasn't about to walk into some kind of encounter in the middle of the living room. After all, the curtains weren't usually closed this early on a Saturday afternoon: unless her mother was really hung over.

The car - both on the inside and out - appeared to be meticulously cleaned, with no empty coffee cups on the floors, not a smidgen of dirt on the exterior and no stains on the seats. Interesting.

She hesitated before opening the door of the house and walking inside. At first, she didn't notice anything until glancing in the living room. The attractive Spanish man - the same guy who had crashed her birthday party - was now lying on the couch. Fully clothed and with his leather jacket on, he appeared to be asleep. Her mother was nowhere in sight.

Suddenly, his long eyelashes fluttered and the stranger, with the really clean car, was looking at her. Appearing awkward under her gaze, he quickly jumped into a sitting position and gave her a self-conscious smile. He flashed a perfect grin, his teeth looking like something out of a whitening toothpaste ad. He was quite muscular under the jacket and she immediately noticed his friendly eyes.

"Hi." He gave a shy wave and glanced toward the hallway, as if indicating that was where Polina could be found. "You must be, Mariah? The birthday girl?"

"Well, when it *was* my birthday," Her voice chose a seductive tone and she took a deep breath, pushing her breasts out, knowing that the pink tank top she wore under her jacket was somewhat shear. His eyes traveled down her body and almost as if he caught himself, he quickly looked away and stood up.

"Your mother is just getting ready to go out and she said it would be okay if I took a nap."

"Sure," Mariah said and finally moved in his direction, hoping she took her time preparing her caked on makeup and found some clothing to cover her bone-thin figure. "That's fine."

"So, you just turned 17?" She noted a slight accent that hadn't been as apparent when he first spoke. "I didn't have an opportunity to talk to you at the party"

"Yes," Mariah tilted her head slightly to the side and hid her contempt for Polina. Of course, she wasn't about to introduce such an attractive man to her daughter. "That's unfortunate, but better late than never."

"I'm Teo," He sounded relieved that the conversation was finally starting to flow and reached out to shake her hand. She obediently did so, noting how warm and soft his palms were and Mariah couldn't help but wondered if he was attracted to her, as she was to him. It didn't matter that he was clearly older, he couldn't have been more than thirty, she guessed.

"Mexican?" She squinted as if attempting to analysis his face and she felt him let go of her hand. "Am I right?"

"Columbian," He somehow seemed impressed with her guess, even though it was wrong. "Columbia is in-

"South America, I know." Mariah smiled and nodded. There was power in beauty, but there was even more in brains. She made a point of absorbing all the information she could in order to have a heads up against most women here age. "Are you my mom's boyfriend?"

"No, I mean.. ah, we work together," He stuttered on with an explanation and the fact that he seemed to be pulling away from the mere possibility was probably a good sign for Mariah, if not her mother. "We are just going to a work function tonight."

"Sounds fun," Mariah said and gestured for him to sit on the couch and she did the same. "So you work with her at the store?"

"Not directly," He replied. "I'm a regional sales director and I-

"Oh, I see Mariah is keeping you company," Polina smiled with her scarlet lips, if not her eyes, as she entered the room, interrupting their conversation. She wore a short, fitted dress that would've looked fantastic, had she any shape. Weren't Spanish men attracted to curves? "How lovely, I don't believe I had the opportunity to introduce her the other night."

"Oh, that is fine," Teo gestured toward Mariah with admiration in his eyes. "We were just getting acquainted now. She is clearly a very bright, young woman. She must get that from you, Polina."

Mariah wasn't sure which one of them grimaced more, but her mother was the first to cover it with a smile.

"That's lovely." She started to walk toward the door while chirping, "but we must get going, Teo or we will be late."

Just like an obedient dog, he rose from the chair and trotted along behind her. Before heading out the door, he turned around and gave a quick wave. "It was wonderful meeting you, Mariah."

"As it was you."

Chapter six

Bitterness is like a fire. The calm, rational person will contain it and be certain that it never got out of hand, recognizing the damage it can do. They know that flames can expand rapidly, searing through all that is in its path and in the end, everything is lost and nothing is gained. Fire can hurt and destroy lives. But then again, so can bitterness.

Mariah Nichols never forgave her mother for kicking Anton out of the house and in fact, her anger only intensified. Forgiveness wasn't even an option. Perhaps if Polina Nichols had shown any regret or change of heart regarding her original decision, it would've been different. But even years after the fact, she refused to speak of Anton and when she did, it was in such unpleasant and cruel terms that Mariah's anger only grew from the subtle flicker within a nine year-old child, to a full-blown fire of a 17 year old woman.

Not that anyone had thought of Mariah as a child in years. In fact, few even thought of her as a teenage girl. She had the curves and lustrous beauty of an adult woman. She didn't wear clothing that was a trademark of adolescent attire, nor did she apply her makeup like an inexperienced young lady. Mariah took great care in her presentation and dialogue in order to represent a more mature version of her. Even Polina appeared a little taken aback by her youngest child. But yet, there was nothing in her appearance that could be criticized. She didn't dress provocatively or go heavy on her makeup, but quite the opposite.

It wasn't just her physical facade that convinced people she was older than her actual age. Her demeanor in general expressed that of a confident woman, someone who was self-assured and fearless. And when she spoke, her words were carefully chosen, rarely throwing in any stumble words, such as 'ah' or 'like'. She spoke slowly, carefully enunciating each word and always made eye contact with whomever she spoke. It wouldn't have mattered if it were the CEO of a company or a bum on the street, she would've given them her full attention and didn't do things like roll her eyes, grimace or express any negativity.

Not to suggest her thoughts were pure. In fact, quite the opposite, but her stoic expression never gave anything away.

For this reason, it was an honest mistake that she was thought to be much older than her 17 years. Men hit on her, thinking she was at least 25 while she was rarely asked for identification at the movies, liquor stores or in bars. And to Mariah, this made perfect sense. After all, hadn't she been forced to grow up quickly? Regardless of her actual age, she felt that life had advanced her development at a much faster pace.

There was nothing in her presentation that suggested a teenage girl remained. Not even her bedroom showed the usual teenage signs. She didn't have posters on her wall, clothing on the floor or dishes on the nightstand. Mariah kept her room exceptionally clean. In fact, it was rare to even see school books in full view and her makeup and clothes were mostly from upscale retailers.

Of course, her mother rarely gave Mariah money to purchase luxuries. Occasions such as her birthday and Christmas were one of the few times Frank Nichols contacted his daughter and guilt often lead him to send large checks to replace his presence in her life. She also took two after school job - one at the local library and the other at an expensive clothing retailer. It was a far cry from most 17 year-old jobs, which often included greasy fast food restaurants and shady convenience stores that were robbed on a regular basis. That wasn't something that Mariah would even consider.

Her supervisors adored her. Always arriving to work on time, staying late if needed, she became a model employee. She knew her work face and put it on before every shift.

Emily was still a friend, but there was definitely a change in their relationship. Where there had been an unspoken knowledge that Emily had been the stronger of the two, somewhere along the lines, she stepped back and allowed the obvious queen to reign. She didn't question any of Mariah's decisions (the few she was made aware of) and accepted her place in their relationship.

In fact, nearly everyone did. Mariah hadn't realized it at first, but when she did, it was a power she would never let go.

And it was a power she would use.

No one knew it but Mariah had a secret. It was something people would never believe had they known, but she was very careful to not allow this to happen. It was something she wasn't permitted to do and honestly, she wouldn't even tell if she could. And that secret was that Mariah was a mortal vampire.

Not to be confused; she wasn't a glowing, garlic fearing vampire that had fangs and wasn't able to handle the light of day. In reality, those creatures didn't exist. They were a myth with as much validity as Santa Clause or the Easter bunny. In the real world, there were two kinds of vampires. Immortals that were few and far between, the kind that lived forever and ran the world under the aliases of CEOs, scientists, politicians and other powerful forces in the world. They were the ones who kept all vampires in line and went to great lengths to keep their secret.

The other kind of vampires was mortal and much more common, although still a very small percentage of the population. Unlike the immortals, the mortal vampires had a normal lifespan, could get sick, die or do pretty much the same as other people. They also had significantly less power and didn't have to go to such lengths to hide their secret. Sure, they couldn't tell people, but they also didn't have to move from place to place every few years, starting a new life, for fear of being found out. Immortals could not really have any long-term attachments.

But all vampires had a few things in common.

First of all, they had much stronger senses than the average person. They were able to see things at a greater distance, much better than anyone with 20/20 vision. Their sense of smell was, at times, overwhelming, allowing a vampire to smell vulgar odors such as decomposing garbage down the street or the fragrant scent of a flower garden, across the road. They had such a concentrated sense of taste that sugar and salt repulsed them, often they were not able to eat any processed food, but stuck mostly to fresh, organic cuisine – which in turn allowed them to keep slender, strong and with a beautiful complexion, hair and nails. Their sense of hearing allowed them to hear words, music and noise at a greater frequency, that was often more disruptive than pleasant. And of course, there was their sense of touch. This is the one that got new vampires in trouble because it intensified their physical encounters and unlike the other four senses, it had few unpleasant side effects. Well, unless one considers having a stronger physical reaction to touch an inconvenience. It created such powerful carnal desires that most would've preferred to tolerate the distastefulness of the other four senses. Mariah was one of these people.

In fact, Mariah barely struggled with the other four senses the way most new vampires did and instead focused on the positive. And in this case, the positive was the pleasurable sensations that one felt when their sense of touch was enhanced to a whole new level. One vampire actually compared it to taking Ecstasy and then having a night of exhilarating sex. It really had kept Mariah's attention focused and allowed her to get over the original 'hump' associated with the change over.

It also caused her to unleash her desires a little more liberally. She finally kind of got the guys who were ready, willing and able to hook up with any random girl and even tell lies in order to get in her pants. Mariah had moments where she would've told someone she was attracted to that they were the sun, moon and stars in order to enjoy the pleasures of her new identity. Fortunately for her, she rarely had to go to such lengths to have those she wanted cave to her needs.

All this aside, there was also the issue with blood. Apparently this was one of the few truths about being a vampire, those who fell under this category did need a certain amount in order to sustain their bodies. Not to suggest that they were bloodsucking savages, but merely needed it to maintain a balance. And Mariah mostly found hers through willing sexual partners. Of course, she did have to be very careful when selecting them, but if this wasn't viable, there was also an underground store that supplied blood to vampires called VP, or Vampire Plus.

Without a regular supply of blood, vampires would simply feel weak, depressed and almost as if the light of their soul had been dimmed. It was not unusual for someone to be a vampire and not know, often writing off depression, tiredness and seeking medication for it. In fact, someone could live their entire lives as a vampire and never even know why they didn't feel 'right'. Some of these people instinctively would crave things like rare steak, but it did little to help out. Only human blood had everything needed to fulfill a vampire.

Mariah hadn't known she was a vampire in the beginning. It was with the man she had been having a casual fling with on and off for years, that had changed her without consent. Fortunately, she hadn't been angry about it because it was quite disapproved of to change someone over in a casual way. But when he told her about the transformation, she knew it to be true because she noted the changes he described in her body very shortly afterward. The person who changed someone into a vampire was expected to stay by her side for weeks after the transformation, but Mariah didn't want or need this to happen. In fact, it was something she grew used to very easily. After all, Mariah was familiar with sudden life changes. How would this be any different?

But she did have questions. One day while lying in bed with the man who had created her new status, she inquired about a specific, but an unusual scent that she had noticed since becoming a vampire. She described it as sweet, tantalizing and explained how it drew her in almost hypnotically.

"That's a virgin." He replied. Mariah was lost in thought. "It is the forbidden fruit for us, unless they are of age. But then again, it's rare you even smell them unless they are past puberty. Before that they kind of give off a weird smell, you wouldn't enjoy it. Their blood is so pure and clean, it's like drinking the freshest water."

"Interesting." She replied with a mild interest. And then something else occurred to her. "Is that why you wanted me a few years ago?"

But she already knew the answer. Hadn't he bitten her a few times, writing it off as passion driven hickeys? According to him, this time he had 'slipped' and now she was a vampire. He didn't explain how it was done, but Mariah preferred to not know. At the time, it seemed irrelevant.

But her powers could be used to her advantage. And it would be used to her advantage.

Her mother had been spending more and more time with the man, who had insisted to Mariah, they were merely coworkers. But she knew differently. She had noticed things that aren't necessarily obvious to others.

Her senses were at an all time high and it was clear that something was brewing between her mother and Teo. And unlike most before him, he was a good person. They appeared to be happy together. Taking things slow... really slow and doing very sweet things like going on picnics and limiting their physical encounters to a few kisses and almost innocent touching. Mariah knew cause her newfound hearing allowed her to listen to their conversations from another room. They wanted to wait till the time was right.

Except that Mariah intended on intervening.

And it started when Teo came to the door one afternoon. With flowers in hand, he insisted it was a surprise visit and that he hoped Polina was home. Mariah smiled sweetly, stepped aside and invited him in. She told him that her mother was in bed with a migraine. This was true. However, her mother's 'migraines' were actually hangovers. That part, Mariah didn't bother to mention.

Once inside and alone with Mariah, he didn't have a chance.

Chapter seven

"Mariah?" Anton Nichols appeared hesitant when he opened the door to his sister for the first time in years. Mixed feelings surged between the two of them and took a minute for Mariah to register that she was really in Montreal and standing in front of her brother. She felt a hesitation between them, but just long enough to carefully inspect him, remembering the 16-year-old boy that she had last seen. Anton's face had lost some of its luster now exhibiting signs of aging, such as fine lines around his eyes and lips while the original roundness had drained out, leaving his cheeks sunken and pale. Even Anton's eyes seemed to lose some of their original glimmer, slightly darker and more piercing than she remembered.

Standing tall and slender, his physique resembling that of a teenage boy. It was oddly as if his head and body didn't match: that was actually one of the first things that caught Mariah's attention. But after sizing him up for those original – although brief seconds - she quickly pulled him into an emotional hug.

"Anton, I missed you so much." She felt one of the few tears slip from her eyes since he was originally kicked out of the family home. Few things warranted crying since that horrific day, so Mariah rationed her tears very carefully. In fact, the only time liquid seeped her eyes was usually in the bitter cold of winter, when a few drops escaped from behind the lids.

She finally let go of her grasp on him, but only after being interrupted, when the man across the hallway exited his apartment. Mariah turned around just in time to recognize a look of surprise on the stranger's face, mixed with intrigue. Grinning to herself, she wondered if he thought she was Anton's girlfriend. He couldn't have been further from the truth.

The two entered his apartment carrying her luggage and safely closed the door behind them. Wiping another tear from her eye, Mariah removed her beige trench coat, inspecting the compact apartment that would be her temporary home. In fact, a glance into the bathroom and bedroom proved that the entire place was extremely small, barely enough room for furnishings and yet, Anton had somehow made the entire place look cozy.

The living room and kitchen area were practically on top of one another, while bright light shone through a large window, creating a sense of warmth that was comforting and homey. In fact, the entire room seemed to be filled with white objects, from the appliances in the kitchen to the throw over the sofa bed and Buddha statue on the shelf.

"I love it, Anton." Mariah said and she continued to study his face, noting that shoulder length hair was pulled back in a thin ponytail. When she arrived that day, she hadn't been sure who would meet her at the door. In preparation for the possibility that her brother may have embraced his femininity and chose to live as a woman, was always a possibility. Although she was still learning, Mariah had done a lot of research and understood that some men who dressed as women were considered transgender, sometimes even going through both hormone treatments and surgeries in order to become their true selves. It was still very confusing to her, but she intended to gently approach the topic with Anton in the future. "I just can't believe I'm here with you."

"I can't either," His warm, brown eyes expressed vulnerability and he moved in to hug her once more, this time more tightly. "I can't tell you how happy I am to see you again."

"The feeling is mutual." Mariah felt choked up in a way that only her brother would be able to create in her. No one else could. She would make sure of that. "I feel like I'm home again."

They parted and he gave her a sad smile.

"But don't worry, I won't overstay my welcome." She let out a little laugh and he shook his head.

"That's quite all right, I would love to have you here. If anything," He paused for a moment, gesturing around the room. "This might be a little too small for you."

"It's fine." Mariah's voice was soft, almost childlike. Her smile had never felt so real, unlike the many times she would only react how she thought was necessary in the particular situation. "I can't believe that you're grown up, you look so much like dad."

"I could say the same for you expect, you actually look a lot like mom." His words had no ill intent, but managed to drop Mariah from the cloud she was floating on to abruptly hit the ground. Nothing could have deflated her natural high faster than hearing any reference to their mother.

Noting the look on her face, Anton quickly picked up where he left off. "I mean that as a compliment, Mariah. Regardless of what you think of our mother, she was a very beautiful woman, especially when she was younger. It doesn't mean you are like her, in fact, I don't think you could be anything like her."

"I won't forgive her for what she did to you." Mariah moved toward the couch and sat down, while Anton quickly joined her. "She was a horrible mother to us both and in the end, she kicked me out too, so I guess that says everything, doesn't it?"

"Yeah, about that," Anton leaned back on the couch, a curious expression on his face. "You never did explain that on the phone. Every time I asked, you just said you'd tell me another time. Was it because you were at your friend's house and you couldn't talk?"

Mariah merely grinned. That would be putting it mildly.

"I did something terrible to our mother and she kicked me out. I admit it was wrong and it was something I wanted to do in order to hurt her," Mariah suddenly felt reluctant to share the details with her brother. Before arriving, she had planned to spill the beans, but now, something was causing her to hesitate. Mariah sensed that he wouldn't approve or accept the entire story, so perhaps she would just water it down.

But that was impossible. Anton knew her far too well.

"Did you steal a man from her?" He grinned while playfully pretending to scold her at the same time. "Cause what people thought of her and her love life was all she cared about when I was still home. Unless things have changed since that time."

"No, no they haven't." Mariah paused for a moment, perhaps to stall but also trying to remember back. "Was mom really like that way back then too? I thought it was just over the years?"

"No, you were just too young to notice back then," Anton's expression became slightly more serious. "Mom was out every night of the week. She went to single events at bars, for coffee with friends, that kind of thing. I think at the end of the day, her main goal was to find a man. I remember seeing that kind of self-help, tacky love books in her room. I think that's all she cared about."

"She certainly didn't care about us." Mariah grumbled and was surprised at the anger exhibited through her voice. Judging by the look on his face, she wasn't sure if he felt the same. "Come on, don't tell me you forgive her for what she did."

"Mariah, sometimes you just got to let things go. They only end up hurting you." Anton spoke with kindness, not judgment. His face was so peaceful and relaxed that she was envious and yet, slightly irritated at the same time. Had she held all this anger toward her mother for years, only to learn that Anton had forgiven her for the past? "I know you probably don't want to hear that, but it's true. Anger will destroy you if you let it. You can't harbor it."

"Where is this coming from?" Mariah was slightly taken aback. Although they usually didn't get into very deep conversations on the phone or the Internet, she still hadn't expected him to be so 'live and let be' about everything. Then again, had he ever really been vengeful, even when he still lived at home? "How could you not be angry with her for tossing you out?"

"She's a miserable person, I will give you that." Anton shook his head in defeat. "And that's something we cannot change. But we also cannot let it ruin our lives either. It's her decision to be resentful of dad or angry over my sexuality, that's her choice, but it's not right that we adopt her attitude too. That makes us as bad as her."

"Are you saying that I've adopted her attitude?" Mariah couldn't believe her ears. Was he really trying to excuse their mother's behavior? It was unbelievable to her.

"No, I didn't say that Mariah." Her brother spoke clearly, placing his hand on her arm. The small gesture seemed to calm her down and suddenly fill her with shame. "I would never judge you, but I don't want you to turn into her either and if you harbor anger, you will."

"I'm not like her, Anton." Tears sprung from her eyes and she suddenly feared that her brother would be ashamed of her when he found out the truth. Originally she had envisioned them together, laughing over what she had done, but now, this clearly wasn't going to happen. "I'm strong. She's so weak. That's why she was just some mail order bride."

"We don't know that." Anton insisted. "And even if dad did bring her from Russia in order to marry her, I don't think it was that cut and dry. There is a lot of poverty in Russia and some families want to find a way out for their children. Granted, it probably isn't ideal, but people sometimes do desperate things. We just don't know and we shouldn't assume." He took a deep breath. "If anything, it was dad who had the upper hand in this situation, not mom. He was older, wealthier and that's something you have to consider too. I'm not making excuses for anyone, I'm just telling you that things are often much more complicated than they seem."

"But she didn't have to be hateful to us." Mariah spoke with shame in her voice; fearful of what Anton would think when everything came out. "Maybe it's because she is Russian."

"No, see, you can't do that either." Her brother shook her head. "I've met a lot of Russians since leaving home and it's not fair to paint the entire country with the same brush. In fact, most were very kind to me, especially once they found out that I also spoke some Russian. They are a very unique culture and I see some of that in you. I do mean that in a positive way."

"What do you mean?" Mariah suddenly felt naive for knowing nothing of her own ancestry. Her mother refused to talk about her old life. In fact, other than teaching Anton Russian while he was a child, she made little reference to her home country.

"Well, Russian women are generally very beautiful and ladylike, just as you have turned out." Anton spoke with such smoothness that his compliments almost felt even more meaningful. Mariah lighted up with pleasure as he continued. "They are very feminine, I can't really explain it, but they're really, very lovely women. I've met several and I liked them."

"I don't know if that is true, Anton," Mariah felt her defenses fall around her brother. He could make her smile, unlike almost everyone else in her world. "But I do appreciate it."

"It is true." He spoke sincerely and tapped his fingers on her leg. "So, what did you do? Flirt with mom's new boyfriend? Piss her off? Did you guys have a huge blow out fight? Obviously, you must have if she kicked you out, right?"

Mariah wasn't even sure where to begin her story or if there was any way to tell it that wouldn't make her look like a horrible person, but she couldn't lie to Anton. As much as it would've served her purpose to do so, she just couldn't do it.

"Anton, you said you don't judge?"

"Of course not." He laughed at her as if she was a silly girl. "You know I won't judge you."

"Well, you might," Mariah started her first of many confessions. "Especially after you hear what I just did."

Chapter eight

I t was the look that she dreaded. Even on the plane earlier that day, cramped between two other passengers, Mariah felt a combination of suffocation and anxiety as she thought about what she would say to Anton. How could she possibly confess her actions and still manage to avoid the possibility of disappointment and shame in her brother's eyes. He had been the one person who believed in her, so how could Mariah let him down now?

True, she had done most of what he asked of her years earlier. She finished high school with top honors, managing to show a great deal of maturity by getting two jobs and always remaining rational, careful not to submerge herself into the lake of teenage drama and absurdity. She hadn't dressed in an overly sexual way in order to get attention and rarely drank, didn't take drugs and had no interest in partying. In fact, everything Mariah did had some sort of reasoning involved. She wasn't an overly impulsive person, but someone who calculated every move well in advance.

And that's how she ended up sleeping with Teo, her mother's love interest. She hadn't done it on a whim. It wasn't the result of a drunken evening or an accidental meeting at a social event, Mariah had planned it all along. In fact, from the very moment that she recognized this man as her mother's possible weakness - a vulnerable spot on her usual heartless repertoire- she quickly began to zone in and put her plan together. She seduced Teo.

It was the only way that Mariah would ever create the same excruciating pain that her mother had bestowed onto her years earlier, when she threw

Anton out. Her brother had landed on his feet, but he just as easily could have died on the street. That was of no concern to Polina Nichols. It was about how the situation affected her and fuck everyone else. Well then, Mariah had decided, it was time to put her on the receiving end of being of being screwed over. When she was alone with neither of her children in her life, a husband long gone and a new boyfriend who lusted after someone much younger, perhaps their mother would finally get what she deserved.

Unfortunately, that required her to confess everything to her brother and that was something Mariah hadn't looked forward to at all. It was the look in his eyes as she told him how she had purposely seduced the attractive Columbian over time; an 'accidental' touch here and there, sexual innuendos when her mother was not around, answering the door in particular articles of clothing (or without a bra) and pretending to be embarrassed when she discovered it was him on the other side. She had been careful and monitored his response to each and every thing she did, testing his reaction in order to see what to do next or just how far she could push it. As it turns out, she could push it pretty far.

Mariah recognized that Teo had mixed feelings about his relationship with Polina Nichols. She could sense it and wasted no time targeting the vulnerable and moving in for the kill. Being a vampire and having sharp senses only made it a little easier because she knew he wanted her as much as she wanted him. She could even smell it.

And it happened sort of how she would later tell the story, but she would never quite confess the entire thing to anyone. There was an insecure part of her, a side of Mariah that had a conscience and it feared that by the cruel intentions of taking away someone from her mother's life that some sort of karma would actually turn around and do the same to her. And so it was for that reason that she felt it was necessary to put a different spin on the story, depending on whom she talked to about it and what she thought that person would respond to the most.

With Emily, she had tearfully 'confessed' to maybe sending her mother's 'friend' the wrong message and how he was making her nervous. When Mariah's mother later learned the truth about the affair and kicked her out, she would craft a story about how an 'old, creepy man' had attempted to rape her, but Polina Nichols had read the situation wrong and as a result, kicked her virginal daughter out of the house. Since Emily was already aware of their tense relationship, it wasn't a surprise turn of events and she showed no hesitation about pleading with her own parents to allow Mariah to stay with them until graduation. Having been a respectful, intelligent young woman in their home, they agreed to Emily's appeal and left thinking very poorly of Polina Nichols.

Meanwhile, Emily's brother Edward had no issues with Mariah in the house. Despite the fact that their casual thing had gone cold over the months, it would quickly pick up late at night, as the rest of the house slept. Since she shared a room with Emily, Mariah knew her friend was a heavy sleeper so it was easy to wander away to see her brother, who was in the basement. He wasn't the best lay ever – he was definitely no Teo – but Mariah loved the rush of sneaking around, hoping not to get caught.

At the same time, her mother's boyfriend Teo was actually 'Tom" when Emily heard the stories. After all, it might create suspicion if her mother's gross, old pedophile man was actually the hot, young Columbian that Emily was drooling over the night of Mariah's birthday party.

Anton would learn more of the truth than Emily, but there were still a few things Mariah would cautiously hold back. She would tell him about the seduction, she made on Teo, how the two had an encounter and Polina Nichols would find out and immediately kick out Mariah, just as she had done to Anton many years earlier. He knew that it was out of vengeance that his sister plotted the entire scheme and resentment fueled her every move.

What he didn't know was that Mariah was very attracted to Teo and that his mature age had proven to bring a whole new dimension to their tryst. While she appreciated his experience, he appreciated her youth. Their time together wasn't just a one-time fling, but an ongoing affair.

The little she did tell Anton brought on a look of disappointment and Mariah felt her face burning under his eyes: she quickly looked away. He was the only person who made Mariah question her own judgment and moralities. And although it was probably best that everyone had someone in his or her lives that would stand as a moral compass, it sometimes caused some resentment toward the person who made them feel judged. It was ironic, knowing that you were in the wrong and being angry with someone who would point that out, but it was also human nature to act out of some level of fear and although Mariah saw herself as someone who was scared of nothing, perhaps her biggest fear would be discovering that this was actually not true.

"Mariah... I'm not sure what to say." Anton shook his head in disbelief. Did she detect a slight French accent in his voice? It did make sense, considering he lived in a Montreal for a number of years, but she had assumed accents had more to do with how you were brought up and not what you encountered. It made her wonder how many other influences had changed her brother over the years because even in their short time together that day, she already felt as though he was a different person than the brother who had left at the age of 16. Did he think the same of her? Especially now that she confessed everything that she had done to their mother?

"You don't have to say anything." Her voice was small, like a child and her eyes jumped around the room, doing all they could to avoid his face.

"I just... I just don't want to think that you did this in order to get revenge for what mom did to me." He seemed hesitant to say the words. "Not to suggest that I'm the center of the world either." Anton let out a self-conscious laugh and his dark eyes seemed to melt into a pool of compassion that eased her.

Realizing that it was his own guilt that was probably fueling this reaction, Mariah jumped in to reassure him. "Oh no, Anton. No, no," She reached out and touched his arm, her lips curved into a loving smile. "I didn't just do this because of what mom did to you, I did it for what she did to *us*. She destroyed our entire family. She was cold and horrible to dad and he left. She was homophobic and cruel to you and she hated me and I don't know why."

Anton glanced away in silence.

"I brought myself up, Anton. She did nothing for me." She took a deep breath. "I was alone. She was never a mother."

Sensing that Anton was in her corner again, Mariah smiled and jumped forward to hug him, attempting to change the subject.

"You are so thin Anton," She addressed her original thoughts upon arriving. "Are you eating okay?"

"Yes, I am." He seemed to quickly brush off her question and embraced her back. "So what did you do for money after she kicked you out?"

Pulling away from Anton, Mariah sighed and ran her fingers through her hair. "I called dad. He just stopped sending the money to her house and sent it to me instead. Plus, I was working some with school, that kind of thing."

And Teo bought her a lot of things, such as her expensive clothing and shoes, but she wasn't about to confess that secret.

Anton appeared to be satisfied with her answer and nodded his head in understanding. "At least she didn't fight dad on that."

"How could she? She knew an adult had sex with her minor daughter and she threw me out. She didn't have a leg to stand on."

Shaking his head, he looked down at his feet. "I really don't think you should have done that, Mariah. You were playing with fire."

"It's done and finished. My life in Ontario is over." Mariah found hope shining through her. "My new life in Montreal is just beginning. I get to be with my real family again."

"I agree." Anton's face was suddenly full of light as the sun shone through the window, illuminating his entire being in a way that would make her always remember that moment. It was probably the closest the siblings would be in the upcoming days.

Mariah would soon find out that she wasn't the only one keeping secrets. There were just some things better told in person and there are some other things that should never be shared at all.

# Chapter nine

It wasn't the easiest topic, but it was getting easier. People's reactions could never be predicted and they were usually a result of preconceived notions, inaccurate information and their own personal fears. This wasn't something Anton understood at first, as he made a clumsy attempt to deliver the news and then personalized every verbal or physical reaction that appeared negative. For a while, he got angry. And then he would get depressed.

Now he knew that it was generally better to ease into his news. Slowly. Smoothly. Gently. People had to be handled with kid gloves and once you decided to cater to their fragile concept of how the world should be - as opposed to how it actually was – they tend to get over the hump of it and relax. That's usually when they started to ask questions. Some were directed in a sensitive manner while others were not. In the beginning he found them to be draining, partially because of his own fears, but that was getting easier too.

After moving to Montreal, Anton assumed that he'd meet other people in the gay community who understood and supported his lifestyle. He had been wrong. Although he found a great deal more encouragement than he had in his hometown, he was still a little surprised to find some homosexuals to be apathetic toward him and Anton was never sure if it was simply a personal thing, or perhaps those particular people were wrapped up in their own complex concerns.

And it was complex. Being straight was simple. You didn't have to gently approach the topic, attempting to get a sense of whom you could or couldn't tell. You didn't have to break it to the people in your life, especially family. You didn't have to worry about society's biases or fight for your rights. You didn't have to worry about getting attacked by a stranger just for the simple fact that you preferred to have same sex relationships. Sure, everybody had their problems – Anton totally got that – but he felt that straight folks kind of took things for granted.

When he first arrived in the city, Anton actually offended a very brash lesbian when he compared the straight and gay community to that of a house or homeless cat. What he was attempting to explain was that a house cat was slightly pampered, not having to worry about food or danger but simply being loved unconditionally. An outdoor cat on the other hand, always had to be on high alert to any dangers or dubious characters in their path. Although some people would genuinely want to help them out, distrust had been instilled and was never far away.

The woman he gave this theory to was furious. Her face turned an inflamed purple and she snapped, "I don't want to be compared to a fucking cat!"

He nervously attempted to backtrack, fumbling over his words and feeling very alone in that moment. She simply shook her head and turned her attention to someone else.

But in his mind, that's how Anton felt. Possibly it had as much to do with being kicked out of his home and couch surfing for over a year but Anton felt himself comparable to a stray. He later considered that was just a dismal reflection of him at the time. Oh well, you live and you learn.

Things slowly came together over the years. Anton went through a series of dead end jobs until getting work at a high-end retailer while simultaneously working toward his GED. It wasn't easy, but he did it. Next, he worked up the ranks of his company and finally had a management position. He lived frugally and saved every penny he could and worked each day with one goal in mind. And someday, he would achieve it.

But would Mariah understand?

It was a bit surreal when she arrived at his door. Not that it had been a complete surprise because they had previously arranged her move to Montreal. She didn't have much to bring and shipped a few, small boxes ahead of time, but it still felt strange sitting across from her as an adult.

It was surprising to learn what she did to their mother. Not that he could judge her actions. It was just difficult to recognize her as an adult woman, let alone one who could so easily manipulate and hurt those around her. He had long ago forgiven their mother, deciding that she was living in a prison of misery and had no interest in finding her way out. Holding a grudge against her for kicking him out and saying such cruel things as he left that day would only hurt him, not her. That was what he believed in. He wanted a life of peace and not of conflict. Especially when it could be avoided.

But Mariah clearly wasn't at the stage yet and he certainly wasn't going to judge. Everyone had a journey and obviously his sister had held anger for Polina's actions toward herself and Anton. It was touching that she loved him so much, but he certainly didn't want his sister to hold so much fury in her heart and hoped that distancing herself would help to ease those troubled waters.

"Mariah, I have something that we need to discuss." He paused, noting the warmth of her brown eyes as she tilted her head slightly; her face seemed to soften for the first time since arriving. Perhaps the anger had lifted and was replaced by love and the two siblings shared a smile. "When I came to the door earlier today, did you notice how the man across the hallway appeared surprised? Kind of like he saw something he hadn't expected?"

"Yes," Mariah's plump lips curved into a smile and he observed her perfect features, slightly jealous of her natural beauty. He wondered if Mariah was aware of all she had. A glow spread over her face and she let out a small, girlish giggle that showed that despite her talk, there was still a child inside of her. "I assumed he thought you were gay and probably wondered why you were hugging this strange woman." She shrugged. "Not that gay men never hug women, I don't mean it that way, I just-

"That's not why, Mariah." He hadn't meant to cut her off, but couldn't hear her go on with that train of thought. He had to tell her before losing his nerve. She was the one person who had always accepted him unconditionally and it would break his heart if she suddenly changed her mind. Mariah was his only family. He deeply needed her acceptance.

"I don't understand." She spoke softly. "Is everything okay?"

"He reacted strangely," Anton pushed through his nerves and his queasy stomach to confess the truth. "He reacted strangely because he isn't used to seeing a man in this apartment."

Mariah looked slightly confused, her mouth fell open as if words were hanging from her lips but weren't ready to leave.

"I dressed like this today because I didn't want to shock you after all this time." He felt his heart race frantically as a burning sensation spread throughout his stomach. "Mariah, I don't normally.. I mean I don't usually dress like a man."

Her eyes seemed to grow with each word but he saw no judgment and that eased his fears. As much as he always told himself that it didn't matter what anyone thought of him, deep down, Anton knew that sometimes it really did.

"I normally dress in women's clothing and I wear makeup." Anton hand reached over his shoulder to touch a smooth piece of hair that fell down his back. "I know you remember me dressing in women's clothing as a child, but I don't know if you're aware that it didn't stop when I left home. In fact, it increased a little at a time until I just had to face who I am."

"Actually, no." He cut himself off and studied his hands. "I feel like I am making light of this whole situation. It wasn't really as simple as all that." Tears burned in the back of his eyes and relief flowed through him when Mariah reached out and took his hand. Suddenly pulling him into a strong hug, she was silent at first and when she finally spoke, it was the soothing voice he had waited years to hear in person.

"Remember the first time we had this discussion, Anton. You told me you liked to wear makeup?" Mariah slowly let him go and watched him as he wiped away a stray tear, as he began to nod. "And I said I didn't care because I loved you regardless? That's still very true."

He felt a huge lump in his throat and was unable to speak, but allowed her to take over the conversation.

"Are you trying to tell me you are transgender?" She continued to hold his hand, her fingers gently clasping around his hand. Watching him nod his head, she did the same. "I know, Anton. I guess I've always known or assumed, but I wasn't sure if I should bring it up. I didn't know if I had a right to ask."

"Okay." He managed to croak out the words as his nose began to run and he grabbed a nearby tissue. He had heard a reference to something being a huge relief off someone's chest, but until that moment, had never experienced it. He felt as though an enormous weight had fallen from his body, replaced by a sense of freedom.

"And if I hadn't arrived here today, you would be wearing what?"

Taking a deep breath and wishing to get back to his normal voice, Anton barely whispered the answer. "I would be dressed like a lady. I would be wearing makeup and I'd spend a half an hour on my hair."

Mariah laughed. "Okay, you're a little more high maintenance than me."

He couldn't help but laugh too. "You have the advantage of being a natural beauty as well as a natural woman. There's a huge difference."

"I don't judge you, Anton. I really just want you to be happy." She hesitated for a moment. "I mean, I don't understand everything like how the dating thing works or if you dress like a woman for work."

He nodded slowly. "I dress in lady's wear for work."

"They know?"

"They know." He nodded and wiped away the last tear. "They're very supportive. I'm very lucky to work for such a forward thinking company."

"That's awesome, honey." Her voice was gentle and soothing.

"It is. Most people can't tell." He took a deep breath. "It's just such a normal way to live for me now that today, just rolling out of bed and not doing any of that preparation for the day, actually feels weird. I just, it feels right to me, Mariah. I don't feel like I'm a male. I feel like I was born in the wrong body. I guess it would be like you waking up everyday as a male, and then suddenly looking in the mirror to discover a woman looking back at you. There's just a discontent. It's like something isn't right and it's so incredibly hard to explain, but I took a really hard look inside myself to come to this point. It wasn't something I did casually and I spent a lot of time wishing to be different. God, I wished to just be a normal, gay man. That would have challenges in itself without a man, who feels like a woman and is attracted to men."

Mariah giggled. "I'm not laughing at you honey, that just sounds so confusing."

"It is." He seemed to relax now, getting more comfortable and open with Mariah. "And it's weird cause when I meet someone else who is the same, it's such a relief just to know you are not alone. You know what I mean?"

"You aren't alone, Anton." Mariah spoke firmly.

"I know." He clasped her hand tightly. "But I also know it must be hard for you to understand."

"It is a little difficult to wrap my brain around, yes, but it's not like you just sprang this on me today. We had a similar conversation when I was a kid and I've had time to process it and research this kind of stuff, cause I wanted to understand."

"I love you for that." Anton smiled.

"I love you because you are you." Mariah replied. "And I wouldn't want you to be any other way."

# Chapter ten

It's human nature to fantasize about how situations will turn out. Who hasn't had a daydream about an upcoming event, making several attempts at guessing how everything will fall into place. We gain comfort from 'knowing' the future and somehow think it will prepare us for whatever comes along on our path.

Unfortunately, we're usually way off either because we have over romanticized or created an illusion out of fear, rather than reality.

Mariah had imagined her reunion with Anton over and over again. She knew there would be some tender moments, especially when her brother first opened his apartment door. She was right to assume he'd have a quaint, little apartment in an older, Montreal, building that would be comfortable, yet display lots of character. She knew that upon talking in person, the two would pick up where they had left off years earlier. It was almost perfect.

But there was something she hadn't counted on. And that was learning her brother wanted to have a special operation that would transition his life as a male, to one of a woman.

It wasn't a complete shock. Sure, Mariah wasn't blindsided. Still, there was a big difference between altering his appearance and altering his body and although she supported his decision, a part of her felt uncomfortable with the idea of one day, having to say good-bye to 'Anton' forever, after he went through the final stages of the procedure. Even though he'd be the same soul, physically he would be a whole new person. It would feel kind of strange.

But she didn't dare share these feelings with Anton. The last thing she wanted was for him to think that he didn't have her support. Of course she supported her brother in making this change because she was aware of how much it meant to him. There was simply no question of her loyalty and devotion, however, it was still a lot to process.

But Anton knew this fact. He assured her it would take awhile to get used to the change, but on the plus side, he was just in the beginning stages and therefore she would have time.

"We can go through this together." Anton assured her with a begging smile. "Even though this is something I want, obviously it's still a huge change for me too."

"Are you scared?" Mariah had bluntly asked him.

"I'm terrified." He replied and didn't attempt to hide his vulnerability. "But sometimes it's the things that scare us the most that are the most worth it in the end."

Although it was not even close to being the same, Mariah could kind of relate. Having become a mortal vampire months earlier, she was aware of how it isn't easy to adapt to significant changes to your body. Clearly their situations were worlds apart and she couldn't even share her secret with Anton, but it was easy to understand how it was to be in a body that didn't quite fit. Although the early stages of her personal transformation were easy, the weeks that followed proved to be slightly more difficult.

As it turns out becoming a vampire wasn't as glamorous as all the books and movies made it out to be and in fact, it wasn't even close to being the same. For example, she struggled with her intense senses and found it hard to explain to people why she no longer ate processed food, especially those full of sugar and salt or why the smell of bakery items made her want to barf. Her altered senses made this impossible to consume what was socially acceptable and in fact, the food she once enjoyed. It often made her seem pretentious and difficult to get along with, when in fact she couldn't tell them the real reason for her reactions. Eventually it just became easier to play the role of a food snob that causes people to roll their eyes.

At a certain point, Mariah thought it was easier to ignore the fact that she was a vampire and just do her own thing. However, it became abundantly clear that even if she tried, it simply wasn't happening. She was on this commitment for life and her body wouldn't allow her to neglect her natural instinct for blood.

She rarely had contact with the one who changed her and didn't resent him for his weakness. It had been a careless error, but this was one incident where Mariah held no grudge. Eventually everything would even out, she assumed. It hadn't been too difficult in the beginning and chances were good, it would improve over time.

Of course, she still needed blood and she could easily access it through the Internet to arrive in her post office box each week. A small tube, she merely hid it in a tampon wrapper and put it in the back of the box. No one would see it there.

Anton admitted that he had started the gender reassignment process by talking to a psychologist who had to evaluate whether or not he was a candidate for the surgery. Having just completed this phase, he was now entering the 'scary' stuff, which had already started with the required hormone therapy. Since Mariah's brother was already living as a woman – by regularly dressing in lady's apparel, wearing makeup, adopting feminine mannerisms and grooming habits – he was consistently making great efforts to work toward his end goal. Apparently taking hormones could make him edgy and he heard horror stories about how they had a very intense emotional impact.

"Picture puberty times ten!" He waved his hands around dramatically then stopped and shrugged. "Well, it might not be that bad, but I guess it can be rough. I'm actually a little nervous."

"And when do you get the actual... surgeries?" Mariah had a rough idea what that entailed and although she supported her brother, she was worried about any possible complications. Although Anton assured her it was safe and he would be fine, a part of her remained unsettled about the entire process. But again, she didn't want to speak up and tell him how she felt in case he misinterpreted it as her being against the procedure.

"That won't be for awhile. The hormone therapy takes some time, but on the plus side, Montreal is considered one of the best places in the world to have this surgery performed." He seemed to brighten up with this last comment. "I couldn't find better people to help me with this transition."

Mariah asked various questions, but at the end of the day, she couldn't shake the terrible feeling about Anton's decision. Perhaps she was simply worrying too much, afraid that something would go wrong. He had recommended that she accompanied him to some of his future appointments and perhaps at that time, she would feel more at ease. It was probably just a little too fresh she decided then let it go.

The upcoming days moved quickly as Mariah attempted to familiarize herself with Montreal. Although she often gave the impression of the cool, confident and fearless young woman, the truth was that this new city scared her. It was the first time she had lived anywhere except for her childhood hometown and although Anton was quite sensitive, he forgot that everything was still pretty new to her and if she had to get from point A to B, Mariah needed very specific instructions on how to do so without getting lost. It was frightening, but exhilarating at the same time.

Although Anton stayed home for a couple of days to spend time with her, he quickly returned to his usual routine. Mariah was slightly taken aback the first time he walked out of his bedroom wearing a beautiful, lady's pantsuit, in full makeup and with his hair styled. Even though she anticipated and respected it, Mariah found it difficult to digest. Still, she couldn't deny that if it were a stranger on the street, she never would've guessed it was a man underneath the clothing.

"It's a lot to take in, isn't it?" Anton sensed her shock, but remained casual, clearly comfortable in his own skin. In fact, he seemed much more confident than he had the day she arrived, when he was dressed in masculine clothing. "I can completely understand if you feel weird."

"I won't lie," Mariah sat on the couch, where she had been sleeping. Although Anton insisted that it opened as a bed, she simply thought it would crowd up the room and inconvenience him more than necessary.

"It's a little strange for me. And I don't mean any disrespect in saying that, it's just hard for me to get used to be around you at all, let alone…" Mariah's voice trailed off.

"In drag?" He joked while Mariah barely smiled, unsure of how to react.

"It's really okay. I understand. It'll get easier for you."

"It will." She assured him while finally taking a moment to take him in more carefully. "You really do a magnificent job. Honestly, you look more like a woman than I do." Mariah spoke respectfully, sincerely meaning her comment. In fact, she was certain that even though he hadn't started hormone therapy yet, that she could see that the transition had already started to take place. But then again, Anton had always been very petit for a man, not overtly masculine compared to most of the guys Mariah knew.

"It's not easy, I had a lot to learn." Anton stopped and gave her a generous smile. "I still see all the things that don't look feminine enough and of course, my voice isn't there yet."

"It'll get there." Mariah assured him. "It's actually pretty convincing. So, this might seem like a weird question, but when you are dressed... I mean, when you are, um..."

"Like a woman?" He showed understanding, knowing how difficult this situation must be for his sister. "Don't worry about picking your words carefully with me. You know I'm not going to be offended, Mariah."

"I know but at the same time, I don't want to seem disrespectful." She confessed. "I don't want you to think I'm being insensitive, especially if I still reference you as a man."

Anton shook his head, a collection of perfectly styled curls moved beautifully like something out of a shampoo commercial. "If I feel you are being disrespectful, I'll tell you. You can call me Anton. I don't see how that is offensive. I know it's a confusing time cause it's a transitional period. Soon you will be used to seeing me like this everyday." He struck a pose and Mariah couldn't help but to giggle.

"Okay, thank you." She smiled. "I was going to ask if you would prefer I call you a different name but I wasn't sure how to ask. It feels weird calling you 'Anton'." She used a very masculine voice and they both giggled. "You know, cause you aren't really him anymore."

"You're right, I'm not." Her brother nodded. "Just call me Ana. And if you spell it, I prefer only one 'n'."

"Okay, Ana with only one 'N'." She nodded while curling up in her blanket. "From now on I will stick with Ana all the time, till you go full blown woman." She teased.

Rising from her seat, wearing old yoga pants and sweatshirt she hugged what was her brother at birth, but now in transition to become her sister. "I'm proud of you for being so brave."

Chapter eleven

It started off sweet. It really did. Over a bottle of wine, Anton explained to Mariah how his intrigue with dressing in women's clothing had transformed into something more – the moment he knew that it wasn't just about a fetish, but something deeply ingrained in his personality – that was when the entire world opened up to him. Everything changed from that day on and he finally knew what he had to do.

He talked about spirituality and how 'life' had brought him to a very low point, but how the soul could always be counted on to rise above everything. Mariah noticed that her brother rarely got into specifics, but made reference to 'good' and 'bad' times and she felt it wasn't her place to ask. Perhaps there were periods of his life that he simply didn't want to relive.

Anton pointed out a beautiful painting of a butterfly in his apartment and said that it was symbolic of transformation. He was entering a phase of rebirth and the picture was a constant reminder that he would need to be very strong for the upcoming months. Mariah felt a twinge of concern as he spoke, sensing that maybe her brother wasn't quite ready for the challenges he was about to face. Pushing her concerns aside, she gently reminded him that he had her support.

It was a lovely evening and one she would recall with fondness. But rather than being an indication of what was coming up next, instead this night was merely a distraction from real life. Although Mariah was very intelligent and graduated with impressive marks, she was still very young and didn't realize that researching a topic and living it were two very different things. Although she had done a lot of research on transgender, homosexuals and since her move to Montreal, sex reassignment surgery, it was really just facts. Things were often much more complicated than emotionless details and when you are young and inexperienced, it can be hard to wrap your brain around.

In Mariah's mind it was simple. She would get a job and apartment, then when the time was right, Anton would start hormone treatment and eventually have his surgeries. She made a conscious decision to let go of her anger toward their mother, to move forward with a great attitude and have an open heart and mind. Both she and Anton didn't have to end up being like their parents. They would survive again.

But life wasn't simple. It wasn't meant to be. What would be the point if everything worked out perfectly, as it usually did on television or in Hollywood movies? In the real world, it was pretty easy to judge until you were in a challenging position. And then, it was a whole other thing.

Anton was excited that his hormone treatment was about to begin. It was the first, real step he would be making toward his goal to transform into a woman and to finally feel like his body and heart were on the same page. He spoke emotionally on that particular evening, telling Mariah that he would soon be able to experience the person he was always meant to be. His body would show physical signs of femininity, allowing him to comfortably transform into 'Ana' even before the surgeries. He spoke of it the same way Mariah would talk about climbing into a warm bath after a long, exhausting day.

In reality, it was nothing like that at all. Rather than blossoming beautifully into his femininity, Anton instead turned from a confident, cheerful person, into an emotional basket case in a very short period of time. The hormone treatment was much more concentrated than either of them had expected. Mariah found herself walking on eggshells, never sure when her brother would yell at her for leaving a dirty dish on the counter and then break out in tears, begging forgiveness and saying how much he loved her.

The doctor warned that the treatment would create similar results as going through puberty all over again, although much more intense. It was awful. Mariah grew edgy and unsure of the best way to deal with her brother and she didn't fully understand. Even during her worst PMS days, she hadn't experienced anything quite so disruptive.

In the beginning, Anton seemed to get angry a lot, but eventually it just fizzled out into full fledge depression. There were days he was incapable of going to work because the pressure of his job and life. He was quickly drowning in a pool of his own expectations.

Mariah tried to understand. She really tried. Of course the amount of hormones he was given would be enough to drive anyone over the edge, but at the same time, how could she help? Everything she did and said seemed to be wrong. For example, if she referenced Anton as a 'him' or her 'brother', sometimes he would explode, insisting that he was going through hell to become a woman so she should at least respect him enough to refer to him in the feminine. But then there were times when she did that that Anton would flip out and say something like, "I'm obviously not a woman yet, so must you rub it in?"

She was always wrong and there were days Mariah wanted to suggest that the process was probably not worth it, since it was making her... sibling so miserable. There were times when Anton flew into a rage and started screaming that Mariah saw glimpses of their mother. Anton had a similar coldness in his eyes, emotionally ravished and disconnected. It truly made Mariah nervous and sometimes she wondered if living with her brother was a good idea.

But seeing Anton curled up in the corner of the couch, tearfully talking about how depleted and frustrated he felt softened Mariah's heart. She couldn't be like their parents and leave when he was at his lowest point. It really wasn't fair. After all, she didn't know the hell he was going through and in the end, feelings of guilt would become overwhelming.

But Mariah did need a break. Her own problems weren't about to go away, as she attempted to help Anton. She was still very new to the city and was attempting to learn the transit routes, various streets and location of specific businesses, as well as trying to navigate through the French culture. Her social life was a bust and for a randy vampire, that caused some issues. Not to mention the fact that she needed a new job.

Although she had originally gotten a job at the same company as her brother, Mariah's instincts were telling her to get out before Anton's emotional outburst overlapped into his work life. Fortunately, another high-end boutique in the downtown area was hiring and she used her magic to get the job. It was only part time but she would prove herself quickly, she always did.

Unfortunately, Anton saw this move as a personal slight.

"So I recommended you, *highly* recommended you and now you're quitting?" Anton said, his arm swinging around dramatically, while the collar of his shirt fell aside to show a bra strap underneath. He was already talking about having a breast augmentation and his recent obsession was permanently removing body hair. Mariah had attempted to make a 'welcome to being a woman' joke, but it was not appreciated. As the weeks went by, he was definitely showing various signs of the femininity he desired, but his emotions continued to run high.

"I just thought it would be better. This way I can work up in a new company and people can't say that it's favoritism." Mariah spoke calmly and she thought, logically as well. And although she didn't want to tell Anton, she preferred the clothes in this little boutique. Created by a very talented young woman, she wanted to teach her latest employee about the elegant world of fashion.

"Who gives a fuck what people think?" Anton shot back at her.

"I'm not saying I care, but I just thought it would make things less awkward if I went somewhere else." She replied while Anton appeared to ignore her. Grabbing his leather jacket and handbag, Anton... Ana, flew out the door. As much as her brother looked and spoke like a woman, Mariah still had some trouble referencing him as a woman, even in her thoughts.

Taking a deep breath and dropping her face into open hands, Mariah sunk further into the chair and shook her head. She truly wanted to do everything in her power to help Anton become Ana but living with someone who is an emotional wreck was starting to wear thin. Mariah had no problem helping with the transition; but she did have a problem with was living with another version of her erratic, lunatic of a mother.

What she needed was a break from the craziness of her new life.

What she needed was to escape.

What she needed was to get laid.

Having not met anyone yet - partially because Anton's melodramas were draining her spare time - she decided the best way to handle this situation was to call Teo. He was a possible diversion and only person she continued contact with after her move from Ontario.

"Hey beautiful Mariah," He flirted and she felt as though he was smiling at her, even though it was through the phone. A slight echo combined with the sound of a radio in the background indicated that he was in his car. "I'm glad to see that you haven't completely forgotten me, now that you are officially a Montrealer."

"How could I ever forget you," She felt her spirit perk up with the sound of a familiar voice. It was moments like this that she questioned if moving to Montreal was the right thing, especially with all the drama from her brother. "So how are things?"

"Since you moved? Lonely." He replied with slightly less zeal in his voice. "Life is boring without you around."

"I bet." She felt her confidence restored by his comment.

And then. "Your mom quit."

"She quit?" Mariah suddenly felt herself hit reality again. "*Now* she quits?"

"I know I figured that when she stayed after... well, you know, she found out about us, that she wouldn't be leaving. But she gave her notice a couple of weeks ago." He replied in a matter of fact voice. Unlike Mariah, Teo clearly had some regrets about their affair and sincerely felt bad for hurting Polina. Mariah did not. "She went, to some other store, I think? I'm really not too sure."

"Anyway," Mariah quickly changed the subject, suddenly tired of her family members draining her energy. "I was wondering if you would like to come see me sometime."

"Of course, mi querido." She could hear the smile in his voice and Mariah did the same from the other end of the line. "Do you have your own place yet?"

"No, still at my brother's apartment, although probably not much longer."

There was laughter on the other end of the line. "Why? You two had a fight?"

"Something like that." Mariah grinned, wondering how she would ever explain this situation to Teo. He had no idea that her brother was gay, let alone transgender. "I think I need my own space."

"I would like to get into your space." His comment was seductive and it made her want him even more.

"I would like that too." She flirted back. "I need a... vacation from my brother, even just a weekend away from him. There's a lot of... drama going on here and I think I just need to... regroup."

"Regroup?" Teo's let out a seductive laugh. "You have only been there a short time. Are you already regretting your move? I can help you prepare to return, if you wish?"

For a moment, Mariah considered his offer. Would it be better if she just left? There were many times that she felt Anton would prefer that she wasn't around. Perhaps he was attempting to send her messages through his outburst that indicated he wanted to be alone? Then again, if she left town now, would that make her neglectful when Anton needed her the most? She felt torn.

"I don't know. My brother really needs me now. I would feel terrible if I were to just walk out on him.

"I really need you right now," Teo bluntly remarked, his voice was husky and she felt an increased sensation throughout her body. Perhaps a distraction would help her get back on track and she would be in a better position to support her brother. Maybe she could talk to Teo about this situation? Maybe-

"Hey, what are your plans for this weekend?" Teo interrupted her thoughts, his voice started to cut out. "Maybe I can take a short vacation to Montreal, just to get away for a couple of days. Are you available now?"

A smile arched Mariah's lips and she felt her body respond to this question before her lips had a chance to move.

"I'm free."

"Perfect. I will go see you." He continued to cut out and finally they had to hang up, but only after he assured Mariah that her weekend would refuel her engine.

Chapter twelve

Some people are very talented manipulators. They have the ability to see into a situation and the people involved, seeping through until they discover the weakness that lies beneath the surface and then quickly slink in to make their move. There is a certain amount of arrogance involved and often the manipulator stops hoping for things to turn their way but instead, expects it. And as long as everything works to their liking, all is fine with the world.

Teo came to see Mariah that weekend. Now in a new city, she noted that he seemed more comfortable being seen with his barely legal, 18 year old lover. Not that it really mattered in Montreal, where hardly anyone knew either party. It was easy to be lost in the crowd and get caught up in her new surroundings.

The two went out to dinner and did some shopping but spent most of the weekend in Teo's hotel room. It was the perfect balance for Mariah and she was disappointed when it came to an end. Not just because she missed the companionship of the young Columbian, but because she wasn't looking forward to returning to Anton's apartment. Mariah was never sure what she'd walk into and for that reason, preferred to enter the apartment alone.

However Teo insisted he help bring her bags upstairs when they arrived on a late Sunday afternoon, even though Mariah had done everything in her power to discourage him. She hadn't volunteered much information about her brother and felt it was best to keep Teo on a need to know basis.

He didn't have to know that Anton was on the pathway to sex reassignment surgery and when all was said and done, Mariah didn't feel her brother needed to meet Teo either. It wasn't like their relationship was going anywhere and it was just too complicated to really explain everything to each side – especially when Anton seemed to assume that it was one of her girlfriends coming to visit that weekend.

"Just in case my brother is home, I want to warn you that he's a little.. ah," Mariah wrinkled her nose and tapped her finger on her head. It wasn't a fair assessment of Anton, considering he was taking a crazy amount of hormones and wasn't truly his true self. She just thought it would be enough to discourage Teo from hanging around for too long.

"Loco?" A sexy grin spread over Teo's face. He truly was a handsome man, but unfortunately, Mariah wasn't looking to fall in love. It just wasn't going to happen.

"Loco." She leaned in and quickly kissed his lips. "You can come in though, if you want-

"Actually, I'm just going to help you upstairs and then I've got to take off and catch my flight." He started to get out of the car and then stopped. "Are you sure you're going to be okay staying here. I mean, if your brother is acting strangely-"

"Yes." Mariah smiled. "I promise I'll be okay."

"It just sounds like maybe it would be in your best interest to get your own place." He commented as the two got out of the car and he reached in the backseat for the gifts he bought her. She picked up her purse and the overnight bag on the other side. "I know it's none of my business, but you were clearly very stressed when I got here on Friday night."

"I think you took care of my stress this weekend." She grinned and winked at him as they headed inside the building. "Don't worry about me. I can take on anything."

She also hadn't been drinking enough blood and knew it was important to get back on track. Mariah had been told stories of new vampires being suicidal because they weren't having an adequate supply and didn't want to get to that point. She already had enough stress in her life.

The one who turned her recently was in contact with Mariah. He feared that she was just becoming accustomed to her new status and feared that a switch in cities may create extra stress, causing her to be more vulnerable. Mariah insisted she was fine.

He also told her of apartment buildings springing up throughout the country that catered to only vampires. Currently, there was one Vancouver, Calgary and soon to be in Toronto. Obviously, they weren't advertised as such, but only allowed vampires to move in. They were soundproof buildings that were designed purposely to fit the lifestyle of an ultra sensitive vampire, so they could live in comfort. The idea intrigued Mariah and she wondered if they would eventually come to Montreal. That would be the ideal situation.

As promised, Teo carried her bags upstairs and didn't go into the apartment in case her 'loco' brother happened to be around. He wasn't shy to give her a passionate kiss outside the door, his hand sliding down her waist and greedily grabbing her ass while he pulled her closer to his body. Feeling her own breath increase as his fingers slid down her hips and between her legs, he suddenly let her go when the man across the hallway walked out of his apartment. Appearing flustered, the neighbor quickly looked away and rushed toward the stairway.

Feeling pleasurable sensations flowing to her more delicate areas, she couldn't have cared less who watched her getting off in the middle of the hallway, but Teo was less of an exhibitionist as he moved away from her. "I should be going."

"He won't come back and no one is near." Mariah begged. She closed her eyes and listened carefully. Nope. There was no indication that anyone was even on the floor. Except, of course, maybe her apartment.

Fuck

"Come on Teo, there's no one around and-

"And I'm not getting arrested for having sex in public." He grinned as he moved in and gently added, "But I will kiss you again."

She planned to get everything she could out of that kiss. Leaning against him, relieved she was wearing a thin, flowing skirt and no underwear, she felt his hand automatically rolled over her ass and back between her legs. Hearing her breathe increase, he pushed her back against the wall and changed his hands to the front of her skirt and more importantly, right where she wanted it.

Mariah felt her heart race at the possibility of someone showing up, just as she was getting off to the rough strokes of Teo's fingers. They worked aggressively, while her nipples grew harder, sending farther sensations throughout her body. Their mouths were still fused together as she felt her pleasure heighten to the unmistakable prelude to an orgasm and suddenly she felt the relief she craved.

Teo glanced around self-consciously and loosened his grip, as dark eyes searched her face, as if he wanted to ask a question but he remained silent. Finally, he said. "I should go."

"Okay." Mariah nodded and noting the wet spot on the front of her skirt, quickly found a way to carry her bags that it wasn't noticeable.

Not that it mattered much. Once in her apartment, it was pretty clear that Anton was very wrapped up in his own torments to notice and any desires she felt in the hallway, were quickly washed away.

Maybe this is the antidote to lust.

Seeing him curled up on the couch, she hadn't taken notice at first as she sauntered by with her bags. But then, something stopped her. It was his face. Anton had a huge black eye and two small cuts on his right cheek.

"Oh my God! What in the hell happened to you?" Mariah dropped down on the couch beside him, her bags falling to the floor. Gently, she put her hand on his face, but he turned his head, shaking it away.

"It happens sometimes. Just when I'm out and stuff." His voice was weak and yet, very feminine at the same time. He was dressed in black leggings and a simple, pink T-shirt. It still felt weird watching her brother going through these transformations, but she was starting to get used to it. "I mean, not super often, but it does happen."

"What happens? People randomly attack you?" Mariah prepared to create the story in her mind. Of course, gay bashing! Some insecure, hick would attack her brother, angry with him for being different. It caused rage to build inside of her and she anxiously bit down on her lip.

"It's not like that, Mariah." Anton seemed a lot mellower than he had been in days, but still not his usual self. He went on to explain that sometimes he went to the bar. And sometimes he went to gay bars and got bored, then moved on to 'straight' bars. And sometimes straight men hit on him, thinking he was a 'real' woman'. And sometimes things got carried away when people were drinking and when these particular men found out the truth about Anton, things didn't go so well.

"Oh." Was all Mariah could say and wondered how she would feel if she was hitting on a handsome man at a bar all night, only to find out it was a woman going through the transformation. She doubted it would come down to violence, but men were very different that way. She wanted to suggest that maybe he should be careful about misleading anyone but didn't want to offend him in any way, especially when his emotions were already on edge. It was best not to stir the pot so she hugged him instead.

Things grew increasingly uncomfortable as the days went by. Anton started to have more people around and although most were extremely friendly to Mariah, others were indifferent or rude. It made her worry what her brother was saying behind her back and suddenly, their strong connection was feeling not as it once had. It was weird and unexpected. He was a stranger to her with each passing day.

That was when she started to seriously consider moving out. Not that the idea hadn't been on the agenda previously, but perhaps she was overstaying her welcome. However, when she casually mentioned it to Anton one night, thinking he would jump at the idea, she was shocked to learn that he hated it. In fact, much to her surprise, he started to cry.

"I just thought that maybe you needed your own space. I mean, you got a lot going on, maybe you need room to breathe." She tried to show him as much compassion as possible but lately, it was wearing thinner by the day. Especially when she learned that his main interest in her staying with him had more to do with the financial aspect of things, rather than the love of family. It was like a kick in the teeth, especially considering, Anton was probably the only person she truly loved.

"So, you want me here to help pay the bills?" She asked skeptically.

"Well, obviously, I want you here for your support too. But if you could stay on just a little longer, it would be a huge help. It would mean a lot to me," He gave her the same sad, pathetic eyes, she often used to manipulate and Mariah felt her stomach tie up in knots. "It's just so expensive to go through this, things I hadn't even thought of before I started."

Mariah silently nodded.

Unfortunately, she wasn't making enough money to really consider moving and often had to take from her savings when extra expenses

popped up. She wanted to find a way to make more money and quickly –
but, doing what?

It was interesting, but she recalled a lecture from her high school
guidance counselor about listing your skills and talented when deciding on
a job. What were her skills? What talents did she have that made her stand
out against the crowd? Most jobs required degrees, but if she returned to
school, it would be difficult to justify moving out of her brother's place.
First she would have to be financially independent and then, Mariah would
look for her own apartment.

But she couldn't tell Anton yet. He would be furious. She had to find
a second job and start squirrelling away money.

And then one day it hit her as she walked by a popular business. There
was something she would be good at and could make some quick money.
Perhaps everyone did have a talent after all and her ability to charm men
would be the icing on the cake. Mariah had found her answer.

Chapter thirteen

Living with a diva is never fun. They are demanding and temperamental. Everything is a drama and what isn't a drama, is just 'boring' and not worth their time. And speaking of time, there was only one clock in the universe and it apparently centered their every schedule and whim. It is not enjoyable.

Mariah's temporary resolve to this issue was to stay away from the apartment as much as possible. Fortunately, that worked out nicely with her plans to move out because it required her to take on another part time job in order to save some cash. Of course, there weren't many jobs where you could get ahead in the short term. Sure, you could work hard at a company and slowly move up the ranks, but Mariah was a little more interested in instant gratification, so she was more drawn to tip-driven industries since it came down to how much effort she put in it. And a girl didn't need a straight brother to tell her that strip bars are an ideal place to earn cash fast.

Although sexuality open, Mariah didn't think she was quite ready to jump on stage and start swing around a pole just yet, but perhaps she could work as a waitress? Unaware of what was the more upscale venues, Mariah did some research both online and by asking a party girl from work before reluctantly approaching her brother for his opinion. Of course, Mariah was abundantly clear that she had no intentions on being a stripper, although she somehow was left feeling that the look of concern on his face was insincere. Then again, maybe she was just paranoid?

"There are a few around Saint Catherine's street," He replied while examining himself in a small, hand held mirror and only appearing to be half involved in their conversation. He was becoming very obsessed with his appearance; fearful that he was still looking 'too masculine' even though Mariah explained to him that it would take some time before everything fell into place, it didn't stop him from staring at every inch of his face obsessively. "But why a strip bar? Why not just a regular club or even better yet, waitress at a sports bar?"

It was a reasonable question and one that she had to scramble to answer. She certainly wasn't about to tell her brother that she was considering the possibility of doing more than serving a few drinks in the future. A girl had to be smart.

"I don't think they would tip as well. I just thought if I worked as a waitress at a strip club, maybe I would do better. And the entire stripper thing doesn't bother me." She casually mentioned and finally decided that it was time to finish this topic and move on. "So do you know any that have a good reputation?"

"I think there is one place called Hot Spring Waters." He continued to look in the mirror as he spoke and avoided eye contact. This was becoming the norm and although Mariah expected changes during this process, it never occurred to her that Anton's personality and heart would become so cold. "It sounds sketchy, but it's known to be classy beside some of its competition."

"Hot Spring Waters it is," She rose from her seat and headed toward his computer to check out the location on a map so she could look into dropping off a resume. Already thinking about what kind of seductive outfit she would wear to do so, she mindlessly said. "Thank you, Anton."

"What the fuck, Mariah?" She watched her brother throw the mirror down on the couch beside him as tears welled up in his eyes: angry tears. Shaking his head as if she had just done the vilest thing, she noted how his makeup was absolutely perfect and had he not been such an asshole lately, Mariah would have confessed this fact to him. Wearing all pink clothing, she wondered if it was overcompensating for his insecurities. "I told you before that I don't want to be called that anymore. I'm ANA now and you have to remember to start calling me that. I'm already looking into getting it legally changed and...."

Mariah blanked out at this part of the conversation. She had heard it all before, every time she did or said something that made reference to the previous life of her brother. It wasn't out of disrespect that she did this, but simply because it was difficult to change old habits. But when she attempted to explain this to Anton – or Ana – it never went over very well.

"Look, I'm sorry," She cut in and took a deep breath. "You've been 'Anton' to me for 18 years. You can't expect me to suddenly wipe that away in a few weeks and start calling you by a new name. It's not quite that easy."

"Well, you're going to have to get used to it," He snapped. Jumping up, Anton flew into his room and loudly slammed the door. This new habit of having the last word and dramatically, leaving the room was becoming a little tired. In fact, she often wanted to remind ah... Ana that she was doing a disservice to the transgender community by acting like a diva, but figured that would be opening a whole new can of worms.

Just let it slide, Mariah. Get another job and get the fuck out of here.

Mariah fantasized about having her own place. To having privacy again and not have to deal with constant tension, decorate how she wished and invite company to visit whenever she wanted. Maybe she could start dating again, regain a social life. Right now, it was just very difficult.

The strip club thing didn't turn out as she had wished. Sure, the club manager thought Mariah would be a great 'candidate' for Hot Spring Water but not as a bartender or waitress. He had some other ideas in mind. But after a meeting the persuasive young woman, the manager agreed to take her as a bartender in training, but he was still insistent that she could make 'loads of cash' by 'doing the backrooms', indicating the private dances that took place in the VIP room.

Todd Bettan was not the dirty perve that most would expect when meeting the owner of a strip bar. He was a businessman, plain and simple. He talked numbers and that told Mariah that they were on the same page. Bettan didn't hide the fact that his customers paid through the nose from the moment they enter the club until they walked out, but insisted that they got their money's worth.

"I only hire the best girls." He made direct eye contact with Mariah. His eyes were such a weak shade of blue that they almost appeared to be faded in color. Todd Bettan wore a tan suit, white shirt and no tie. Perhaps slightly overweight, his face was flushed, as if he spent a little too much time in the sun. Overall, he appeared to be a family man, with a photo of him, a woman and two children on his desk. "It's a strip bar and people think we're all dirty. I get it. But I want them to see that we're a little better than the average and that's what keeps bringing people back."

Mariah nodded solemnly. "I have no doubt."

"So what I'm suggesting to you is that you come in, help out with this or that, learn some bartending. But at the end of the day, the money is the VIP room, the table dances, private parties and that kind of thing. I kind of see the main stage as more of an advertisement cause some money gets thrown at those girls, but just a few bucks here and there. The real money comes from my clientele when someone specific grabs their attention because they want more of that personal experience with her and well, boys will be boys, right?"

"Boys will be boys." Mariah nodded confidently for a woman who hesitated to even enter the club a half hour earlier. It turned out that just like the way vampires were portrayed on televisions, strip clubs also weren't always represented accurately by the media. In many ways, it was just another bar. The staff was friendly, not scary or sketchy. The customers were pretty average; some were more involved in their own conversations and only occasionally glanced at the beautiful woman on the stage. Creepy old men weren't leering at her from the bar. It wasn't what Mariah had expected nor did it feel very intimidating.

"Hey," He put his hands up in the air. "I'm a boy too, I know how men think and that's why I try to keep it classy. We want a specific customer at Hot Springs, not the horny college kids with only $40 in their pocket. In fact, we almost try to discourage that age range cause they get drunk and it becomes a fucking mess in five minutes." He hesitated for a moment to take a bottle of water from a small fridge beside his desk and offer Mariah one. She quickly shook her head no. "What we want here are the lawyers, the politicians, the businessmen, the celebrities floating through town, that kind of thing. We don't want the troublemakers or the people with no money. It's as simple as that."

Mariah nodded, considering his ideas to be quite reasonable. "I have to say, I'm impressed with your management style." She sat up a little taller in her chair, fearing that she was slumped over. "At least from what you described."

"You never danced?" He asked skeptically. "You just seem so comfortable with this so I assumed you had been down this road before?"

"No." Mariah smirked.

"That's too bad. You could make some serious cash." He spoke honestly with a hesitant smile on his face, as if he was waiting for Mariah to change her mind. "You're young, but not too young. A lot of my customers like that kind of thing."

"I'm keeping my options open." Mariah figured she would at least give him that much. "I'm not from Montreal so at least I won't have to worry about anyone I know wandering in."

"Very unlikely if you aren't from this town. I'm not saying it doesn't happen, but I've been sitting in this chair for awhile and you aren't the first girl to share that concern with me." He shrugged. "You know, it's so busy here and we have a lot of dancers, the nights are rotated, people are drunk, some come in and only stay awhile or get caught up with one particular girl and never even see anything else around them. I'd have to say that if that is your biggest worry, you're probably safe and honestly, if you look out and see someone you know it's also possible to throw on a wig or something. In fact, some of the girls look a hell of a lot different here when they walk out at the end of the night, then when they are on that stage." He pointed toward the door. "I had one girl who had some dirt bag ex hassling her here one night about a year ago. She walked out past him in a wig and a ton of makeup later on, he didn't even recognize her."

"Wow, really?"

"Look, I could write a book, Mariah." He pointed toward his head. "I got lots of stories up here. But that's not important." He moved ahead in his chair and faced her head on. "If you want a job here, you got it. If you are more comfortable on the floor than the stage, you got it. But I guarantee you that after a week or two, you'll change your mind."

Chapter fourteen

I nnocence is lost everyday and sometimes it's replaced by something remarkable, but quite often, it is not. Most push reality far down into their souls and pretend everything is fine and this is just a new version of normal.

When Todd Bettan hired Mariah to help out 'on the floor', what he really meant was to bus tables and be hit on by married men. Both of these things shouldn't have surprised her – but for some reason, they kind of did. At the end of the day Mariah liked to give the illusion that she was quite worldly but in fact, she was surprisingly naïve about certain things. Of course Mariah realized that she wasn't about to have a glamorous job at a strip club, but still, she envisioned herself doing something a little more interesting than wiping spilled alcohol off the tables.

But the tips did help. As it turned out, this was an establishment that greatly encouraging tipping. Bouncers were reluctant to allow a customer past the door – even after they paid their cover – unless they first were given a 'customary' tip for their services. Bartenders wanted their share as well as bus girls and if they did their job well, most patrons wouldn't leave their drink unattended for a moment before having it swept away. Of course, you had to be careful when doing so and make it appear as if you sincerely thought they were finished rather than distracted by the entertainment. Mariah had that skill down quickly because she knew that the more drinks bought, the more tips would come her way and considering the customers were expected to have a drink at all times, that could add up fast.

Waitresses were often strippers attempting to mix in the crowd, tantalizing and encouraging intoxicated clients to join them in a VIP room for some personal time. Mariah wasn't completely certain of what that 'personal time' entailed, but her understanding that there was full touching involved and the talented strippers could manipulate their clients, only allowing them to touch them near the end of the song. This often meant that the entertainer would manage to get some men for at least a couple of songs and if the girl was talented, chances are she would encourage repeat visits and referrals.

The clientele were exactly what Todd had suggested. All things considered, it wasn't a dirty bar and most of the men appeared to have money. Not to suggest that meant they had class too. It wasn't a normal night if a bouncer wasn't dragging someone outside for being too 'grabby' with one of the girls. That was something Todd wouldn't tolerate.

The women that came into Hot Spring Water were generally one of two kinds. The first was a genuine party girl, who often thought *they* should be on stage but that was discouraged. The staff would inform these women that they were welcome to audition during off hours or amateur days but not during a regular night. Mariah was told that this customer almost never returned. And the second kind was a woman who genuinely thought strippers were entertaining to watch. Some were lesbians or bisexual but just as many were not. Mariah could understand because there was definitely something engrossing about the performers at Hot Spring Waters. One way or another, female customers rarely caused problems or were kicked out.

After a few weekends of her part-time job, Todd Bettan invited Mariah into his office for a chat. As it turns out, he was getting great reports on her work performance and her professionalism. He thought she was 'one of the family' and was impressed with how smooth she was with customers and he wanted to pick her brain.

"So what do you think?" Todd asked, leaning back in his chair, he observed her with curiosity. "I thought by now you would be begging me to get on that stage." He teased and Mariah smiled back.

"I'm still thinking about it. Things do seem pretty clean here." She agreed with his original summary of the bar. Overall, she was content in her surroundings and not frightened as she had been on the first night. "It seems like the bouncers look after staff."

"Definitely, that's what they are paid to do." He spoke very openly as he drank a bottle of water. "I get it, this is a strip bar and when women take their clothes off for money, there's obviously a certain amount of vulnerability involved so clearly, I have to make sure they're well looked after. That's why I don't let university kids in unless they seem okay. I don't need or want that kind of customer."

"Obviously that works."

"It does." He agreed and moved his chair forward and he leaned on the desk. He wore a similar outfit as the last time they met and she still thought his eyes were kind of a creepy blue, but overall she liked him. "So this is the thing. We're going to teach you the bar next weekend. My sister is coming back from a vacation and I'd like her to train you. She's simply the best! You're gonna love her."

"Sounds great."

A few days later, Mariah would learn that Alison Ruben wasn't really Todd's sister. She found this out when inquiring if her new trainer was married, since the two had different last names. It wouldn't have been difficult to believe that a beautiful bartender might choose to not wear a wedding ring, given where she worked, but as it turned out, the two were merely stepsister and brother. A soft smile curved Alison's lips and she spoke with a French accent when she described it as a 'Brady Bunch situation'.

It wasn't difficult to see why Todd spoke so highly of the young woman, she was certainly very organized and efficient at her job. She quickly described her average night at work, showed Mariah where everything was and went over their most popular drinks. Since it was her first bartending shift, Alison would only allow her trainee to deal with the simple orders. She explained that it'd take awhile to get her familiarized with the different kinds of drinks and wines.

"People drink a lot of wine at a strip bar?" Mariah grinned as the two sat down at a table that first afternoon, just before the bar opened. "I don't remember seeing anyone drinking wine since I started, so I assumed it wasn't popular here."

"Honestly, I mostly sell it by the bottles in the VIP room, but usually it's beer or champagne." She raised her perfectly groomed eyebrows. "My understanding is that it is sometimes... part of the act."

To this, Mariah merely nodded.

"So did Todd talk you into dancing yet?" Alison sipped her drink, tilting her head slightly, with a mischievous grin on her face. "I know he wishes for you to join his harem."

"We've discussed it, but I haven't made a decision." Mariah confessed and suddenly wondered why someone as attractive of Alison wasn't a dancer. Then again, with her stepbrother as the manager, perhaps that would be a little weird. "Have you ever done it before?"

"No." Alison shook her head and quickly looked away. "I do not think it is for me."

It certainly wasn't because she wouldn't fit in with the other girls, Mariah noted. Alison was stunning and in fact, her features looked so perfect that Mariah had to wonder if she had some work done. She wore her hair past her shoulders in gentle blonde waves and her complexion suggested she had just spent an afternoon at the beach. Black liner enhanced the warmth of her large, hazel eyes that carried a trace of mystery.

On that first night, Mariah couldn't help to be a little in awe of how quickly Alison worked, often serving a few customers at a time. It was clear that bartending could be a very stressful job, especially during a very busy night, but Mariah was pretty confident that she could do it but feared becoming overwhelmed. Then again, her training was just starting out.

A friendship quickly formed between the two ladies and by the second week, Alison was driving Mariah home after the work. She reasoned that they both finished at the same time and it wasn't safe for her to be waiting around for a cab alone, after the bar had closed.

"You don't have to do this," Mariah insisted the first time she got in Alison's car. "I don't want you to go out of your way."

"Oh, but it is on my way." Alison grinned and shrugged as if she couldn't understand the big deal. "Seriously, it is not safe to be waiting outside a strip bar in Montreal at this time of night." She made a face and shook her head. "No."

"I'm pretty self-sufficient." Mariah assured her. "But, you're probably right."

Sometimes the girls would head in an all night diner after work for a cup of coffee or a quick bite to eat, often wide-awake during a time when most were sleeping. It was on one such night in late October that Alison once again brought up the topic of dancing.

"So you aren't going to the 'dark' side," Alison giggled as they waited for their food to arrive at the table. "Todd has not convinced you to start stripping?"

"Not yet," Mariah let out a laugh. "Although, who knows, maybe I will someday. Right now, I seem to be doing well on tips."

"You definitely know how to deal with people and put them under your spell." Alison said while wiggling her fingers around with an evil grin on her face.

"I don't know about that."

"You do." Alison assured her just as their waitress arrived with their water, promising the food wouldn't be long.

"Good cause I need the money. I got to get out of my brother's apartment."

"Well, stripping could get you some fast money too, but how come you need to leave his place? Did he ask you to leave?"

Mariah mentioned her brother to Alison before, but hadn't got into the details. "Well, things are cramped in his place and I'm just sleeping on his couch." She watched Alison make a sympathetic face. "But he's going through stuff right now and it's kind of a lot to deal with."

"Oh, sorry to hear that." Alison took a sip of her water as her eyes studied Mariah. "Nothing too serious, I hope."

"No, it is fine." Mariah took a deep breath and felt the need to confess Anton's secret to someone because at that point, she was too exhausted to drag it around anymore. Plus her loyalty was starting to wane.

"My brother, he's umm…he's transgender." She watched Alison's eyes bug out and Mariah automatically worried that it was a mistake to say anything but continued to explain. "I don't normally share such personal information, but I feel like I'm about to explode. I moved to Montreal to spend time with him and I'm starting to think it was a huge mistake. I feel like I'm living with a stranger that hates me."

She hesitated for a moment to evaluate Alison's reaction, which appeared to be serious and yet, understanding.

"I know that he's taking a lot of hormones and that can mess with your emotions, but it's like living with Jekyll and Hyde. I can't seem to say anything right. I'm just hoping that after awhile things will balance out." Mariah paused. "It's very complicated."

"It is." Alison agreed. "And you feel how, about this situation?"

"I'm fine with the procedure. I can't really say I'm surprised." Mariah figured she may as well throw it all on the table. "I found him wearing makeup when I was a kid, I think it was shortly after our parents split up so I kind of knew about it. It never bothered me, but when my mother found out, all hell broke loose and she kicked him out." She noted that Alison looked very compassionate and continued. "So when I moved here, he told me that he was going through with the procedure and I supported him, I really did. I was 100% in his corner."

Alison's hazel eyes widened and she nodded.

"I respect his decision and try to show my support," Mariah continued. "But then he started taking so many hormones and he's getting out of control. In fact, if he heard me calling him a 'he', I would have my head ripped off. I don't do it intentionally it's just hard to make that change after 18 years, you know?"

"I bet." Alison looked up as the waitress approached to drop off their food. After their server left, Mariah wasn't sure what to say, but Alison continued. "So how is he out of control? You mean emotional? Crying a lot?"

"Phew!" Mariah shook her head and rolled her eyes. "I wish! That would be a walk in the park compared to this shit."

"Is he violent?"

"No, but he's just being," Mariah paused, trying to think of the correct word. She recalled an earlier conversation with Anton…ah, Ana where she was swore at for 'being lucky enough to have a period to complain about' and 'pimples not facial hair to deal with'. "A bitch. And I'm not exaggerating when I say that." She continued and repeated the argument they had earlier that day. "I can't seem to ever do or say the right thing anymore, no matter how hard I try. It's almost like he's – I mean, she's mad at me for being born a girl."

"But maybe that's normal." Mariah continued sadly, while digging into her salad. "We used to be very close and even when I first moved here, we were." She shook her head and bit her lip. "Maybe I just don't understand. I haven't been through this before so I have no idea if Anton…I mean, Ana is acting normal."

"I have been through this before and no, I do not think so." Alison's comment surprised Mariah and she stopped chewing for a second before continuing. "Everyone is different and hormones can make anyone crazy, but with this kind of procedure, people tend to be emotional, depressed, anxious, not mean and crazy. That's a whole other thing that has nothing to do with being transgender. I do not think so, at least."

"You've been through this before?" Mariah asked as soon as she swallowed her mouthful of food. "Seriously, you know someone who went through the hormones?"

"The hormones, the surgeries, the whole thing."

"Really?" Mariah was shocked by the luck of having a friend that she could confide in *and* might also give her some insight. "Are you serious?"

"I am very serious." Alison looked down at her plate and finally looked back up at Mariah with a hint of tears in her eyes. "It was my dad."

Chapter fifteen

Many people believe that there's no such thing as coincidences, that everyone enters our life miraculously just when they are needed. Sometimes we don't realize this at the time and sometimes we don't realize it at all.

Most people would've been stunned by Alison's confession but Mariah Nichols wasn't most people. Having already witnessed her entire family ripped apart by divorce, becoming a vampire and then learning her brother was transgender; there was very little that could shock her. Not yet past her teen years, Mariah had seen and experienced things that many middle-aged adults wouldn't have considered in their most bizarre dreams. Some would've thought this to be sad, but others would insist that it allowed Mariah to open her mind and enhance her personal growth at a young age.

Alison confided that she had grown up in a happy family and had no reason to believe that her parent's marriage wasn't strong - that was, until they sat both Alison and her older sister down for a family meeting.

"I thought we were going to talk about our next vacation." Alison sipped her water, her hazel eyes glanced down at the table and eyebrows lifted, as she shook her head. "I was way off the mark. What do they say about living in a fool's paradise?"

Mariah didn't say a word. She just nodded in understanding and decided it was better to remain silent while her friend spoke.

"The shock," Alison stared at her plate as if her mind were a million miles away and suddenly, she snapped back to the present. "Anyway, I certainly was not prepared to learn that my parents were splitting up, so you can imagine how I felt to learn that my father was transgender. It was just too much at one time.

"Do you think it would've been better if he told you the rest later?" Mariah was curious. Her own story was very different, but still, she related.

"You know, I'm not sure." Alison spoke honestly and she stopped to sip her water. "I think I would've preferred to learn the rest later on, after I had time to process the breakup but I just don't know."

"I can sympathize." Mariah cleared her throat and shook her head. "I mean for me, my parents always fought so I wasn't surprised when they broke up and my brother, he was pretty open with me back then too."

"In a way, you were lucky to see reality, so young." Alison shared a small smile and her eyes were full of sadness. "I lived a very sheltered life and had no idea how I was supposed to adapt to all the changes in my family. I got involved in some messy situations and I don't usually admit this to anyone, but I spent some time at a special ward in the hospital because I was very depressed and my behavior grew so severe – but this was much later."

"I'm sorry to hear that," Mariah spoke honestly, while privately considered that she was a much stronger person than her new friend. Her own life had been insane and yet, Mariah was still standing. "But it got better, right?"

Alison's face softened and small lines appeared in the corners of her eyes as a vacant sorrow inhibited her face. "For a bit, yes, they did." Her response was so robotic that Mariah grew concerned about what she was about to say. This story clearly did not end on such a positive note and she found herself frozen in anticipation of what was about to be said.

"He was so happy at first," Alison spoke frankly and seemed to forget the food on her plate and Mariah felt inclined to do the same. Suddenly all the voices around them seemed to no longer exist. "Very happy, in fact, he talked about how free he was, for the first time in his life. In one way I was happy for him, in another, I felt cheated out of a dad. My brain couldn't process all the changes that were taking place."

"I knew it was selfish to feel that way and felt angry with myself for not showing him the proper amount of love and support." Alison confessed, small wrinkles formed on her forehead as she continued. "He was doing great. Went through the surgeries to transform into a whole new person, and even though my mother was heartbroken, she supported him."

"I can imagine." Mariah shook her head.

"Eventually, she moved on with her life and met Todd's dad and our families combined, which was just another change I was not prepared for," Alison recalled. "I think that is why Todd and I grew so close back then. He was a little older and in university at the time, but saw me as his kid sister and took me under his wing. That's why we're so close now."

"You're lucky to have him." Mariah felt a little sense of loneliness when she thought about how Anton used to be that person for her – used to be.

"It was because although I didn't know it at the time, things were about to get much worse." Alison's face grew peaceful, but Mariah could still sense her anxiety from across the table. "My dad was not a young man when he went through with these surgeries, he also was not a healthy man. In fact, the doctors were telling him he would have to watch his blood pressure, take better care of himself because each surgery would be very hard on his body and it was better to prepare himself."

"He followed their advice, but unfortunately, he kind of fell back into his old habits later on and grew ill again." Alison showed no expression. "He died of a massive heart attack two years after the final surgery. I was only 21 at the time."

"Sorry to hear that." Mariah spoke sincerely, unsure of how else to respond. She found herself attempting to calculate Alison's age in her mind, but wasn't sure why that was relevant in that moment.

"It is fine, I have made peace with it." Alison replied. "It has been a few years and a lot of counseling, but time has given me some perspective. I think it is important to be yourself and live, how you wish. That is why it is important that your brother goes through this transformation."

"Having said that," Alison continued. "I don't understand why he is so unpleasant to be around. I know my father had some very emotional moments but I think that was a mixture of a great many things, not just the hormones - fear, relief, guilt –perhaps that is the same with your brother?"

"I don't think so," Mariah said thoughtfully. "I truly believe that he hates me for being a woman. He makes so many remarks about how lucky I am to be born in the correct body. Maybe not though, perhaps I am misreading the situation."

She obviously couldn't tell Alison the truth; that she was a vampire and therefore had immaculate hearing, so had been privy to some of the private phone conversations that Anton had in his bedroom, behind close doors. She could hear him complaining about her, comparing himself to Mariah as if it was her fault that he was going through so much work to become a woman. His words were betrayal in her eyes and Mariah felt sure that living there was a huge mistake.

"He probably holds some resentment and that is not right." Alison suggested before letting out a big yawn. Her eyes watered slightly and she quickly blinked back any sign of tears. "If you're supporting him, then he should be grateful for your love."

"I truly am in his corner," Mariah felt the need to insist in case her story suggested otherwise. "I was 100% in his corner, but I feel that he doesn't care. Like he believes that I am somehow the enemy."

"Just continue to show him love." Alison suggested cautiously. "That's all you can do. Perhaps the hormones are affecting him in a different way than they did with my father. Maybe you can't take anything too personally right now. That would be my advice for you."

Mariah suddenly felt very compassionate toward Anton and some shame for not being understanding. Her brother had been through a lot and perhaps she was simply not as supportive as she could be.

Of course, these feelings swiftly changed upon arriving home. Still on her high from the positive conversation and confessions between her and Alison, she had a wonderful sleep and awoke a few hours later to overhear a phone conversation. Ana - she had to start using this name, Mariah decided - was behind the closed door of the bedroom, but words, once again leaked into the living room, where Mariah slept.

"I don't know," She heard an exaggerated sigh and the blossoming feminine tone of her former brother, now sister. Smiling to herself, Mariah was proud of the fact that she was embracing the change. That was, until she heard more of the conversation.

"I know, right? I mean, I need her here to help pay the bills, but I could tell right away that our relationship changed. We hadn't seen each other in years, so I guess that makes sense, right?" Mariah felt her original enthusiasm began to sag. "And like, she knows how important this is to me, but I don't think she will help. I shouldn't have to ask her for more money. Plus, she never brings her new friend here, almost as if she's ashamed of me."

Mariah felt her heart sank. That wasn't why she hadn't invited Alison to the apartment. If she was ashamed of anyone, it was of herself not him. Biting her lip, she squeezed her eyes shut even tighter, just like she used to when living at home and listening as her mother dragged home some strange man. She wanted to connect with her brother, but was it impossible?

"Yeah, I know." Mariah heard some words muffled, followed by laughter and her heart sank. The conversation ended and Ana walked out of the bedroom, makeup done and wearing a skirt and form fitting T-shirt. Mariah decided to deal with everything head on.

"Good morning." She said and noted signs of surprise on Ana's face.

"You got in late."

"Yes, me and a friend went to get some food after work."

"Guy friend?"

"No, female." Mariah pushed the covers aside before rising and starting to fold them into a neat pile. "Actually, I wanted to talk to you about that."

"You wanted to talk to me about your friend?" Ana appeared almost humored and Mariah wondered if there was even a smidgen of the brother she used to know inside or was it all harvested and replaced. Alison had made an interesting point on their drive home that perhaps Ana was attempting to take segments of what she thought women should act like by watching television programs and selecting an admired trait from some questionable characters. Mariah shook her head no but now, was starting to wonder if her friend was right.

"Well, it's actually an interesting story." Mariah ignored the tinge of coolness in the air, unsure of where it was coming from at all. Why couldn't they just put their cards out on the table? Perhaps her story would help. "I have a trainer at work who is a really cool girl. Um…. we became good friends…"

At the same time Mariah carefully considered her words, Ana snidely quipped, "Oh, and you are a lesbian now? Is that what you wanted to tell me?"

"No, you asshole." Mariah snapped back when she considered how hard she was trying to meet Ana halfway, only to get a snippy attitude.

Jesus fucking Christ. "I was going to say that my friend Alison understands what you are going through, her dad was transgender."

Ana sincerely looked stunned, as Mariah watched all defenses fall to the ground. That quickly changed when she gave a casual shrug and rolled her eyes.

"Alison thought maybe she would meet you and if you had any questions or concerns, she might be able to help or talk about whatever it is you won't talk to me about." Mariah continued in a determined voice, refusing to play this game any longer. "But if you're going to be a jerk, I'm definitely not going to ask my friend to meet you."

"I'm sorry, Mariah." Ana suddenly showed some hint that Anton hadn't completely left yet. "I....I was just teasing. I didn't mean that-

"Look, don't bother." Mariah shook her head. "I'm trying to support you, I really am but I don't... I don't know if you even want my support. I don't know what to say to you anymore cause everything seems to be wrong. It's not like I'm discouraging you from going through with this, but fuck, you can't expect me to put it all together at once. You've had a hell of a lot of time to think about it, much more than I have."

"You're right." Ana said as tears formed in her eyes, then suddenly overflowing to take a quick journey down a face with too much makeup. "You are right, Mariah. You have been supportive of this, but it's just so hard. It's not as easy as I thought it would be."

"Why are you mad at me?" Mariah felt herself calm down. "I don't understand what I am doing wrong here."

"You aren't doing anything wrong, but ever since I started with hormones, all these emotions that I didn't know I had come out and I was so angry. I don't understand it either. Maybe I'm just going crazy."

Thinking about something Alison said. Mariah hesitantly made a suggestion. "Maybe it's because they were there, pushed away. Mom kicked you out of her life, out of her house, out of my life." She shook her head. "She did the same with me, but at least I had you to come to. Who did you have?"

Hoping that she would finally get the answer to a question that had long been in her heart, Mariah searched the eyes that had once been those of her brother and instantly realized that she would never know. "This isn't easy for me either. I feel like my brother is leaving me again, for the second

time. And I know that it wasn't your choice when we were kids. I also know that this is what you have to do now but it doesn't make it easier."

"I know." Ana slowly nodded and wiped a final tear away. "I'm sorry. It's just been me for so long that I didn't have to think about anyone else's feelings. I do love that you're here and you support me, but it's hard to make these changes and I can't even talk to you about some of the stuff going on with me. It's much too personal for me. I appreciate that you mentioned your friend, but I think this is something I have to work out on my own time."

"Okay," Mariah realized that she had to respect this decision. Did she want to know the details of Ana's personal life? Then again, it felt like another wedge was pushed between them. "The offer is on the table if you change your mind."

"Thank you, but I actually know some people who have gone through this already and I can talk to them." Ana picked at her nail polish and avoided eye contact. "And I promise not to bite your head off all the time."

"Okay." Mariah felt very awkward and rather than continue the conversation instead started to make a pot of coffee.

Had this been a Hollywood movie or a predictable sitcom, this would've been the moment when the two shared an affectionate hug and became close again. But this was real life and in real life, you can't express something you don't understand. And you can't understand emotions you never were taught.

Chapter sixteen

Relationships are very complicated. Perhaps because, like everything else, they go through phases and things such as emotions and circumstances often factor in. Sometimes it's the people we thought would always be by our side that go away.

And sometimes it is the people we least expect to impact our lives that sneak up at the most surprising times.

Mariah's relationship with Ana continued to be strained. They were pleasant and friendly to one another, but she started to feel that they were merely roommates, almost like strangers, rather than siblings. It was amazing when she thought of the early days just after moving into the apartment and how the same person who had once been her brother had changed both physically and emotionally, right before her eyes. It was truly unbelievable.

Still planning to move out, Mariah quietly looked for another place and although she checked several, she wasn't having much luck. Alison insisted that it was because the year was coming to a close and few people wanted to move in January. But Mariah continued to be persistent and was optimistic that someday she would find a cozy little place to call her own.

Alison continued to be a close friend and someone who supported Mariah through her many issues with Ana. She insisted that the hormones and many stresses involved with going through the change had often been a black cloud over the original excitement. "It is a huge thing to deal with and even though Ana is being an asshole, you have to be patient, breathe deep and step away. Just allow her to continue this journey and maybe keep a safe distance until you feel the time is right to build your relationship again."

Mariah didn't believe that day would ever come. It filled her heart with sadness, but at the same time, it was a rude awakening about how casual people were when it came to love. It was a bitter pill to swallow and it made her feel like an orphan now that she was no longer in contact with either her parents. It was difficult to not be jaded when you were let down by the people closest to you.

Time moves on. Mariah saw changes in Ana but didn't comment. It truly was outstanding what hormones could do and it made her see that they had a much larger influence on someone's personality than she would've ever thought. When Anton was Ana, she never would've made any of the terrible decisions that Mariah now quietly observed.

On more than one occasion, Ana returned home after a night out with marks on her body. Some looked playful while others looked scary. Bruises and scratches were commonplace, and there was another incident that involved a black eye. Mariah carefully tried to find out how this happened but got no response. She was worried, but had long ago learned when it was time to cut herself off emotionally, that her brother was no longer in existence.

Alison only shook her head after hearing these stories. Admittedly, her own experience had been drastically different and although it was difficult to understand, she remained insistent that Mariah step aside because it didn't seem like her opinion would change a thing.

"Don't rock the boat." Alison would regularly remind Mariah and then they change the subject.

Both had a lot of plans for the future. Now that Alison felt centered and stronger than before, she started to look into college courses and signed up for a couple of day classes for the new year.

"It's a way to get my feet wet because I think I want to return to school full time in the fall." Alison spoke excitedly about the possibility. "It's time to take charge of my life and set some goals."

"I think you'll do fantastic." Mariah praised her with a smile. "You run that bar spectacularly, I'm sure you can do anything."

"Thanks." Alison said with a simple smile.

Mariah on the other hand, didn't have any goals. She was just floating through life and trying to get on her feet in the real world. Her future was a blank slate.

She was fortunate to love both her jobs and have bosses that recognized her confidence and ability in dealing with people. It was quite impressive for such a young woman, just a teenager of 18. Mariah thought herself to be quite mature considering the terrible role models she had while growing up. Miracles do happen, apparently.

Then again, Mariah was always learning. Her powerful senses allowed her to see people in a way others simply could not. For example, as a vampire she didn't just listen to their words or watch their body language; she could see the tiny droplets of sweat on their brow or hear tension in a person's voice, when they were nervous. There were so many subtle things that entered her brain when she looked at a single person that it was as if they were naked and vulnerable, right before her eyes. But it was a secret that only her and the one who turned her would share, on the rare occasion that they spoke. Unless she met another vampire one day, no one would ever know.

As for Teo, the only other person left of her old life, he would still come to see her but not often. She had taken on various lovers since moving to Montreal and they were often more than capable of satisfying her many physical cravings. Being a vampire was a blessing and a curse, all at the same time.

One of these men was a regular at Hot Spring Water and she usually was able to get him after work, when they both were at their highest state of arousal. It certainly didn't bother her that his stimulation was brought on by another woman because often, it had the same effect on Mariah. The strippers at this bar were beautiful and had phenomenal bodies so it was hard to look at them and not feel anything. This combined with the men's reaction toward the entertainment often left her with some pretty intense desires.

She had never intended on mixing business with pleasure, regardless of the attractive and sometimes famous men she encountered in the bar, but there was one exception. They had become intimately acquainted one night after he specifically selected her to be part of a private dance in the VIP room. He threw down a handful of cash and said he wanted to see Mariah perform an act with a stripper named Nina. Money was no problem.

The buxom brunette was one of the club's favorites because she dressed in lacy corsets and wore her hair and makeup like that of a 1940's vixen, rather than that of the average stripper. He regularly paid for private shows with Nina but on that particular night he wanted Mariah involved. Even after his regular girl insisted that she was a bartender not a dancer, he responded by throwing more money on the table. Finally, the stripper approached Mariah and explained the situation.

"You don't have to do anything, just let me take care of it. I know what he likes." Nina said and felt pride in her argument when Mariah said yes, not realizing that perhaps this concept intrigued the bartender as well. Alison raised her eyebrows as the two walked toward the small room, where the attractive man waited. He was probably in his early forties and dressed in a dark suit, with a white shirt that appeared to be hastily unbuttoned at the top, probably after removing a tie. He had salt and pepper hair with a more generous amount of 'salt' in his beard, but his piercing blue eyes were what captivated her.

Nina instructed Mariah to sit down on a chair. When the music came on, she approached the customer across the room and straddled his lap, facing him with her ample breast in his face. Mariah couldn't help but feel her own physical reactions as he began to loosen the tight laces that squeezed Nina's chest into exaggerated cleavage and dive headfirst in between her breasts. Nina continued to wiggle around as the music played in the background, soft moans rising from her throat as her head fell back and Mariah could see each of her nipples pop out from the corset. As the song went on, she continued to dry hump him in such a sexually charged way that Mariah could feel moisture forming between her legs. She had never been with a woman before, but maybe….

The song ended and that was when Nina abruptly stood up and crossed the floor. Mariah was a little nervous, but didn't want to seem like an inexperienced teenager, so carefully hid her fears behind a smile. She heard the man instruct Nina to do the same with Mariah, as she had just done to him. She could see he was very excited as the stripper straddled her legs in the same way and began to ride enthusiastically, while Mariah was surprised to not feel as horny as she watched Nina with the customer.

Her breasts rose and fell with each movement and she breathlessly whispered, "Pretend you are into it. Throw him a bone."

Mariah was curious and reached out and touched her breast. Nina moaned loudly even though she could tell her desire was an act. She was probably thinking about balancing her checkbook or picking up milk after work. "Keep doing it, touch me more." She whispered and continued to grind into her leg while across the room, the client appeared to be jerking off. It was a bizarre way to make a living.

Mariah heard them both gasp when her tongue reached out and slowly licked the end of Nina's nipple. "Take it all in." She encouraged and slid closer to Mariah – and that's when things got a little more personal. Nina's original fake desire had turned Mariah off, but now that she was dry humping Mariah's groin, she suddenly felt her nerves standing on end, begging to climax. Pulling her close, Mariah's mouth eased over Nina's left breast and sucked it. Although the stripper put on a good show, grinding into her passionately, loudly moaning and begging her to suck harder, Mariah felt herself explode in an orgasm as the hard nipple teased her tongue. Nina really hadn't noticed. She was too busy playing a role and now pretending to touch herself while across the room, the customer had done that all along.

He later threw more money on the table and the girls split it in half.

"That's what you gotta do." Nine lit up a cigarette after he left, despite the fact that smoking wasn't allowed in the building. "Just play the role that this is the biggest turn on of your life and the wallet will loosen. It's how you got to play the game."

The experience was very surreal and Mariah noted the smirk on Alison's face as she returned, after shoving a wad of bills in her pocket. It was her most successful night at the bar and later personally, when the same customer approached her with his phone number. He wasn't pushy and obnoxious like most that hit on her at the Hot Spring Waters but he was polite and simply suggested that she 'might' want to give him a call sometime. It turned out to be a good idea.

Her boss continued to encourage Mariah to be a performer and teased that her talents were wasted. With that, she merely shrugged and admitted that she thought about it, but it would be difficult, especially where she also worked in retail and may be recognized by one of her clientele.

"You wouldn't need to work there at all," He reminded her. "Imagine, sleeping in every morning, making a shit load of money every night. Just think about it."

Todd was thankfully not pushy, but he did seem to favor her after learning of the great relationship she had with his stepsister. One day while they were alone, he admitted that Alison had a 'difficult time of it' and was a great person.

"After her dad died, I don't know," He paused for moment and shrugged. "It was just the final straw, I think."

"I know. She told me everything."

"Yeah, well her family completely changed in a few short years." He appeared relaxed in his chair and for once, didn't have an opened bottle of water on his desk. "Her dad went through his surgery, then dies. It was rough and Alison sort of drifted away from her sister and mom. Sometimes you just have to let things go. Live and let live and all that."

"Live and let live." Mariah repeated. "I couldn't have said it better myself."

But as much as you live and let live, sometimes life still could hit you with a wallop. Things were changing very quickly and the new year would prove to be the most difficult one that Mariah would ever have to face.

 Chapter seventeen

The holiday season brings with it a bombardment of commercials, movies and television episodes that suggest that regardless of how challenging your life is for the other 364 days a year, Christmas day brings with it a cascade of miracles. Everyone is so happy. Love always prevails. The misery of fighting for a parking spot at the malls and stress of buying appropriate gifts at the last minute is erased by the magical spirit that envelopes the final outcome. And to a point, there is truth to this belief.

Mariah had never enjoyed the holidays. At least, not since she was a small child and her family was still together. After her father left, everything seemed to fall by the wayside. Her mother would have a glass of vodka and cranberry juice while bleakly observing her kids open their gifts, showing very little enthusiasm for her own. This was particularly disappointing to Mariah who shopped with Anton very carefully to purchase the ideal present. Their mother was passionless and would make snippy remarks about how she was forced to push away her own Russian traditions in order to accommodate her Canadian family. When Mariah asked about Russian celebrations, her mother refused to talk about it and bitterly remarked how it no longer mattered.

In Mariah's mind, it would've been nice to celebrate Christmas with Ana. It would have been nice to bond over the holidays and let go of any misunderstandings or differences created in the past months but that didn't happen.

Ana didn't want a tree and insisted that the apartment was already cramped enough without adding decorations to the mix. She felt they were tacky and a waste of time and money. A week before Christmas, Mariah hesitantly asked if they should exchange gifts.

"It doesn't matter, I'm not going to be here anyway," Ana said, dramatically waving her hand around then pushed a strand of hair over her shoulder. Mariah noted how Ana often did things like wear a scarf to hide the protruding Adam's apple and although she followed a similar path as most women when putting on makeup or doing her hair, it almost seemed as if she only strived for perfection. In fact, she looked as if a professional makeup artist had tackled her face each day, which was astounding to Mariah.

"Why? Where are you going?" Mariah smiled and was surprised to feel relief flow through her body. Perhaps she was only setting herself up when believing that Christmas would somehow change the dynamics of their relationship.

"I'm having my Adam's apple reduced in size and staying with a friend for two weeks." Ana spoke excitedly, her face lighting up as she went on to describe the procedure to a silent Mariah. "It probably won't affect my voice as much as I like, but at least it will be less visible in the future."

"Wow, I didn't even know there was such a procedure."

"Yeah, well, it's going to be one of many times I go under the knife. There are so many things that don't look feminine about me. My nose, my forehead, my chin are all things I need to have fixed and that's just on my face. I still need a breast augmentation and of course, the actual reassignment surgery. It's all so stressful."

"Aren't you scared?" Mariah thought it was an honest question, but apparently Ana had taken it to be more attacking in nature.

"Of course I am scared." She could see Ana's defenses rise as she physically moved away from Mariah. "I'm scared to death, but these are things I have to have done. I want to be 100% woman."

"I'm not suggesting you shouldn't have them done." Mariah calmly insisted, growing frustrated with having to defend herself. "But you've got to realize that most women have some flaws or things we don't like." She pointed at herself. "We don't all have perfect chins or noses or whatever. That's not what makes you a woman."

"What the hell are you talking about?" Ana seemed to grow more frustrated. "I've got the walk, posture and clothing figured out so I think I'm doing pretty good."

"I wasn't suggesting you weren't doing well." Mariah countered and shook her head in frustration. "I just meant that most women don't put that much time and attention to their appearance."

"I don't exactly have a choice, now do I?" Ana snapped and began to fix her scarf as she spoke. "I wasn't lucky enough to be born as a girl so I can't take it all for granted like *you* do. I have to work really hard to even come close to passing myself off as a substandard woman at this point. I go through each day worrying that one of my fake boobs will slip out of my bra or that I wear something too tight and my bulge shows. I don't know if people are looking at me and wondering if I am just some drag queen or are they looking at me thinking I'm attractive. I think about these things all the time. It's easy for you to make judgments. I could only wish to have your problems."

And with that, Ana grabbed her bag and stormed out of the apartment. Mariah was left feeling a sadness overwhelm her, wondering how she could've communicated her thoughts a little better. She wasn't trying to make light of Ana's situation, quite the contrary, Mariah was just trying to suggest that sometimes less was more when it came to fitting in. Most women didn't have the perfectly curved eyebrows, the flawless makeup and immaculately styled hair. Perhaps her attempts of not drawing too much attention to what she was trying to hide, was actually making things worse. It was like covering a bloodstain on the wall by painting the entire apartment: chances are your gesture may alert someone's attention more than if you had simply bleached out the stain.

Alison would later sympathize with her situation, but quickly explained that it was pretty normal that someone in Ana's shoes might over compensate.

"I see both your points on the matter. At the end of the day, you are both right." She insisted as they sat at the bar before it opened, each having a cup of coffee and sandwich. "Ana is scared. Terrified, in fact. It's a long road and right now she feels like a fake on some levels and authenticity in others. At least, that is how it sounds."

"At heart, she's a female, but her body is betraying her and she is fighting against it." Alison patiently explained. "It is like a middle aged woman trying to look like she is 20. She may feel twenty in her heart, but her body may be telling her a different story. And she may overdo it with makeup or surgery in order to feel like her body is on the same page."

"I never looked at it like that." Mariah confessed. "I don't know what to say anymore, I feel like I'm always wrong."

"Yeah, that's a tough one." Alison nodded before taking another bite of her sandwich and chewed slowly, while both remained silent. After washing her food down with some water, she continued. "I think you just need to kind of back off. I don't say that to insinuate that you are doing anything wrong, but it is just a way to keep the peace till you move out."

"I'm going to see a place Monday night, it looks fantastic online, but you never know till you're there. I have another lined up for Wednesday on my lunch break. I just hope that I can get another place before Ana returns in a couple of weeks." Mariah picked up a piece of lettuce that fell from her turkey sandwich and chewed on it. "I feel bad, just bailing on him.. I mean, her, but I can't deal with living there anymore."

"I don't think anyone could blame you for that." Alison grinned. "I might be able to come with you on Monday night if you want a second opinion."

"Absolutely!"

Alison grinned again. "You know Mariah, I think you should stop worrying about this stuff. You're doing the best you can to be supportive and obviously you have an opened mind." She hesitated for a moment and then waved her hands around to indicate the room. "And you work at a strip bar. How much more open minded can you get?"

"That's true." Mariah agreed, a smile curving her lips. "That's very true."

The combination of dealing with Ana's temperament and her two jobs was starting to weigh down on her and she looked forward to the upcoming holidays to have a slight break. Both the shop and the bar were closed for Christmas day. During the time Ana would be gone for her procedure, Mariah would finally have time for herself and looked forward to getting a break from the tension at home.

But everything was changing. Not only was her brother quickly becoming Mariah's sister. Alison was going back to school and had a new boyfriend taking up most of her free time. Teo rarely called anymore and the man she met at the bar that she had an ongoing affair with was also starting to fade out of the picture. Everyone was moving on.

She recently spoke to the man who changed her to learn that he was in the process of moving into the new 'vampires only' building in the heart of Toronto. He insisted that it was a haven for their kind and it made life much easier when surrounded by others who knew their own gifts and challenges, not to mention that the building had been specifically designed for their needs. He talked on and on about soundproof apartments, windows that wouldn't allow any scents from outside to seep through (unless opened of course) and a social area so they could meet other vampires. He seemed really excited about it. Mariah felt a tinge of jealousy.

Ana went off for her surgery and Mariah secretly felt relieved to be alone for a couple of weeks. She wondered if their relationship would change after the surgery? Would Ana feel a little more at ease once this procedure was done? Would Mariah have another apartment and no longer have to worry about living in such close quarters? Would moving improve their relationship?

As it turns out, the story was about to make a sharp change. And with all Mariah's good intentions and the peaceful holiday vibe that was in the air, it didn't matter in the end. Little could have prepared her for what was around the next corner.

January was definitely a time for renewal and change. But it isn't the change you think.

Chapter eighteen

W e are taught that making specific plans and goals are the path to happiness. We chase this notion that down the yellow brick road is the solution to all our problems and then, we can breathe a sigh of relief that all is well with the world. It is amazing that for every time this theory is proven wrong, that people blindly continue to believe it.

The tighter you hold on, the more you lose your grip.

Mariah had survived years of neglectful parenting because she was smart. It was necessary to think ahead, plan your next move and be prepared for the worst. In fact, her brain would be usually so far ahead in the future that she would sometimes fall down stairs, simply because her eyes were three steps ahead of her actual body. It took a few big falls before she made this realization about herself and opted to take elevators when possible.

Alison was more likely to follow her heart over logic. She talked a great deal about intuition and actually gone to seminars regarding the subject, returning with such a burst of energy and delight over the concepts like 'being centered' and 'finding balance' in life. Mariah would listen, smile and nod, but she didn't believe in any of that woo woo nonsense and truly thought people like Alison were taken for a ride when they paid for books or meetings that solicited such ideas. After all, wasn't that how cults started?

More and more, Mariah felt as though her friend was slipping away. Interestingly, now that she got to know some of the strippers at her second job, she began to relate to their world on a much deeper level. They were survivors, just like her. They had stories about why they started to do that kind of work, but at the end of the day, most did it out of financial desperation. Some needed money for virtuous reasons like raising a child or going to college, but others had less socially acceptable excuses. In their world, they did what made sense: show your tits, make some money, it was simple.

Alison refused to get involved in stripping or any backroom entertainment, even though offers had been there. Mariah had few qualms when asked but wasn't ready to completely dedicate herself to being a stripper. She felt it was acceptable to dabble in almost anything as long as it wasn't how you were defined over all. A little coke once in a while was okay, but if you did it everyday, you were labeled a cokehead. By the same logic, you could entertain men in the VIP room on occasion and it didn't make you a stripper, but if you did all the time, you'd gain that title. Besides, it made her less accessible and therefore more valuable when she did accommodate men's requests.

On the home front, Mariah wasn't happy living with Ana so searched for another apartment. One advantage of not being tied up with friends and family during the holiday season is that she had time to check out new apartment listings as soon as they were posted.

Mariah discovered a small, yet cozy apartment that wasn't far from her day job. It was located in a nice building in the downtown area so she would be central and most of all, alone. Not that she didn't love Ana but it was becoming too much to live in the same cramped apartment with her sibling. Regardless of how hard she tried to recreate their bond or understand the change Ana had taken in order to become a woman, it was time to move on. Having paid half for everything since moving in the previous July, it gave Ana a bit of a financial boost and allowed Mariah to squirrel away money for the future.

Fortune seems to come all at once, when Mariah received a message from her father telling her of a savings account he had started just her parent's divorce. Apparently he put money aside from each paycheck and although he admitted it wasn't a huge sum, he felt that would help her out if she decided to go to university in the future. She was also surprised to learn that he made several unsuccessful attempts to connect with his Anton over the years. For this reason, he decided to only invest in his daughter.

Mariah was originally ecstatic. This would mean she'd have the resources to purchase some furniture for her new place. She immediately jumped online and searched various sites, excited about the beautiful things she could buy to make her place look amazing. But then suddenly, she stopped.

Maybe it would be better to put some away for a rainy day, she decided, just in case of an emergency.

Then she thought about Ana. Her father did say that his oldest child hadn't met him halfway with any attempts to reconcile. Hadn't Ana told her the complete opposite? Who was lying here? Feeling slightly disloyal, she decided that maybe some of the money would be helpful to put toward Ana's dream to cross over from the masculine to feminine world. Was she being selfish? Should she share some of the money her father had stored away?

Something told her that helping Ana was the right thing to do, so she would. At least, that was the original plan.

When Ana returned home after the two weeks, Mariah expected a more chipper roommate, having had one procedure crossed off the list and finally seeing some real progress made in her pursuit. She assumed wrong.

Ana appeared groggy and although she was freshly made up, a beautiful pink scarf covered the proof that the surgery had taken place. Mariah attempted to be cheery and gave a half-hearted smile, covering the regretful that her much loved alone time was ending.

"How are you? I was hoping you would check in. I noticed your cell was-

"I don't want to talk about it." Ana snapped and headed right for her room with her one bag in hand; she slammed the door behind her.

Mariah had to go to work and didn't see her again until late Sunday afternoon. She arrived home to find Ana on the couch, curled up in a blanket, watching television. Unsure of how to approach, she once again acted cheery (but not *too* cheery) and sat on the arm. "How are you feeling?"

"Like I was just run over by a truck." Ana didn't remove her eyes from the television.

"Really, I thought recovery was only a couple of weeks? Did the doctor give you extra medication or-?

"I don't feel like I was hit by a truck because of the recovery." Ana turned with a cold glare and Mariah noted that regardless of her frazzled exterior, she still had on her makeup, with her sleek black hair pulled back in a bun. "I feel like I was hit by a truck because I went under the knife and you can still see my Adam's apple plus now, I also have a scar."

"Well, won't that heal?" Mariah rushed for an answer, making some attempt to calm the waters. "And you probably still have swelling, I'm sure that as time goes by, you will start to see-

"No, you don't get it, do you?" Ana thought nothing of cutting off Mariah and seemed insistent that her idea was ludicrous. Muting the television, she pushed the blanket aside to show that she was wearing some of her old 'Anton' clothes, a ratty sweatshirt and a baggy pair of black gym pants. Mariah frowned fearing this indicated that perhaps the dream had made a sudden crash landing. "The doctor said that I should have been okay by now and that this was the best he could do."

Looking as if she was about to burst into tears, Ana's head drooped and Mariah attempted to show comfort but was snubbed. Ana jumped up and physically distanced herself by going into the kitchen.

Frustrated, Mariah sat in silence. What could she say that wouldn't be ripped apart? Her attempts to make Ana feel better were useless. She briefly considered mentioning their father's money, but something stopped her. Perhaps it was the memory of bringing up her own interest in moving out in the past and how Ana insisted she need Mariah there for support. Clearly, any emotional support she offered was rebutted so what else was there? It wasn't inconvenient for Ana to have Mariah there because between her two jobs and social life, she was hardly ever home. She cleaned, paid rent and was stuck sleeping on a cramped couch and constantly walking on eggshells. Who wins in this situation?

In the kitchen, Ana was slamming cupboard doors and banging pots and pans. Fury seemed to escape every pore and her face looked hard, her dark eyes overpowered by animosity, as if the entire world owed her for every wrong she had ever suffered. As if no one else ever was hurt before, either by family or the world in general. And Mariah found her heart beating a little faster as the muscles tightened on the back of her neck, followed by her shoulders and chest. She felt her stomach turn in anxiety, a feeling she hadn't felt since Ana had left two weeks earlier.

She wanted to lash out, but knew better. After all, Mariah needed to live there until the end of the month. Feeling anxious, she knew it was time to tell Ana the news.

"I'm moving out." Mariah was surprisingly calm in that moment. Ana stopped and gave her a cold glare. "I found another place and I'm leaving at the end of January."

"What? Are you fucking kidding me right now?" Ana snapped and reached for her throat as if to protect a sensitive area during a battle. "You're just going to leave me alone?"

"I feel it's time I move on and get my own place." Mariah attempted to sound very business-like while nervously running her finger against the fabric of the couch. "I think you'll be happy to have the place to yourself again."

"Oh great," Ana gave a sarcastic laugh and rolled her eyes to the heavens. "Great, leave me when I need you the most. Just be like everyone else in this fucking family and bail on me when it's no longer convenient."

"That's *not* true." Mariah said, continuing to hold her temper but still managing to muster some strength. "I was here for you and I have been all along."

"So you move right when I am about the change my entire life?"

"What difference?" Mariah objectively tried to reason. "I mean, you're always saying that I don't understand. I think I'm making you more frustrated by being here, so how is that helping you?" Mariah waved her hand in the air to indicate the apartment. "I think you'll find more peace if I am somewhere else. I will still be around, just a phone call away, I-

"Oh yeah, like you are ever around." Ana snapped, shaking her head. "You're either working at that store, after *bailing* on the job I got for you and making *me* look like an idiot and then going to work at some titty bar on the side? I know people who've seen you there by the way and I know you are whoring yourself out, just like the other girls."

Mariah opened her mouth to say something, but was completely stunned. Who was this repulsive person? There were absolutely no signs of Anton having ever lived in the same body that now was full of hostility toward her. Mariah's mind raced back to her childhood and Anton, the brother who loved her so much. Was this the same person who supported and encouraged her throughout childhood? Who gave her a warm hug when she moved in, with tears in his eyes and showing so much love and compassion? It simply didn't make sense.

"First of all," She took a deep breath and rubbed her lips together. "I'm not a whore. In fact, none of the women I work with at the bar are whores. They're dancers who just want to make an honest living. You don't know anything about them and I would think you'd be the last person to be judging anyone."

That was the first sign of hurt in Ana's face and she seemed to drop some of her defenses.

"Second of all, I worked very hard at the job you helped me get and everyone liked me. I just thought it wasn't smart for me to be there, where you were in management. It was a great way to get my foot in the door, but it wasn't exactly a smart move to stay there long term."

"And last of all, I tried to support you. I've done everything in my power to be there for you. I'm sorry that sometimes it is hard for me to wrap my brain around the fact that the guy who I used to see as my gay brother, who liked wearing women's clothes is now my what? Sister? I don't even know what to call you or if I'm even right referring to you as a woman when you are still in transition. This has been your life's goal, for years, but it's new to me and I keep trying, but you're pushing me away."

"I don't know what to do anymore." Mariah said and stood up and faced her brother directly across the room. "But I know moving out is a good start."

"But you need to help me." Tears began to fill Ana's eyes and although Mariah felt bad, she couldn't help but to feel manipulated. Why did it have to be such an emotional roller coaster? "I need you to stay here so that I can save money. Is that what you want me to say?"

Mariah just stared at Ana and didn't reply.

Chapter nineteen

Human nature is kind of funny. As much as we like to believe we know someone, do we ever *really* know anyone at all? Sure, people tend to form a pattern when it comes to habits and thoughts, making others feel confident that they can easily predict their behavior in any given situation; but is that *really* true or is it something we just tell ourselves in order to instill feelings of comfort? When our mind tells us stories, do we listen?

Mariah thought she knew her brother. As a child, he was godlike in her eyes. He represented the two parents that were too wrapped up in their own battles to contribute to her upbringing. Anton taught her how to do basic things like make toast, wash the dishes and how to count money. He hugged her when she cried and made her feel special. He was her whole world.

Their correspondence wasn't consistent after he moved – was kicked out – but Anton did his best to keep in touch and support his sister. He loved her and when Mariah needed a place to stay, welcomed her to his apartment with opened arms. He appeared to miss Mariah and cherished their time together.

It was only after Anton announced his intentions of having sex reassignment surgery and turned into Ana, that Mariah began to have trouble. That's when the beautiful heart that she once knew changed into something that was very unfamiliar to her. Another person erupted and it ironically reminded Mariah of the fables about people turning into vampires, starting off as a normal person and changed to something completely evil and dangerous. If anything, since her own change, she was more sensitive to her environment. She couldn't say the same for her brother turned sister.

But was any of this true? Had Anton really been there for her throughout her childhood? Weren't there huge gaps where she hadn't spoke to him for years at a time? What happened during that time and how did he get on his feet after being kicked out years earlier? Had it not been for Emily Thomas, Mariah would've been on the streets when Polina Nichols kicked her out of the house: literally on the streets.

Sure, when he lived at home, he was very supportive of Mariah but he also relied on her to keep an important secret from their family. Had that been his way to manipulate a desperate child? No, she couldn't believe that, whether or not it were true.

But what about the day she moved to Montreal? Hadn't he met her at the door, smiling, hugging Mariah and happy to see her? Hadn't they shown a deep love and respect for one another that went beyond the level of most sisters and brother relationships? Hadn't it been a magical moment that she had waited many years to live?

Mariah had a sinking feeling that she had just romanticized everything. She needed to believe that the brother, who was her only support system as a child, was an angel on earth and that their relationship was something much more profound than it was in reality.

Mariah attempted to give the image of a cool customer but on the day she moved to Montreal, she had been frightened. She wanted more than anything for her brother to meet her at the airport with a look of anticipation on his face. She had dreamed of him rushing to her, giving one strong, warm embrace and welcoming his baby sister to Montreal. That just didn't happen.

Looking back, she wondered if he had been very welcoming or was her own personal relief for having made the trip, coloring her judgment. Hadn't things changed quite quickly after that original night? Had they really ended up spending much quality time together or had they simply turned to indifferent roommates that ran into one another on the way to the bathroom? Had he shown much interest in how she was surviving in a new city? Was he interested in her jobs? He hadn't even met Alison, even though she had a family member who went through the surgery and understood it quite well?

She had tried to be fair. Mariah knew that he was doing her a favor, not the other way around. Anton could have said 'no' when she asked to stay with him. Then again, her brother had also made several references to the fact that he needed her there as a form of financial support. Was that all it had ever been about in the first place? Judging how their last argument went, it would appear to be so.

Mariah would later watch a famous actor on television, talking about how you 'climbed' into a character and after a change in wardrobe and attitude, you 'became' a whole other person. It caused her to wonder if Anton was the same way. When he changed into women's clothing, put on makeup and 'became' Ana, were all traces of Anton gone? Had they mysteriously disappeared overnight, almost as if he had never existed? Weren't they part of the same soul? It was almost as if Anton loved her, but Ana hated her. Did that make any sense?

Regardless, it was too much and Mariah had to leave. Even a woman like herself, that hadn't been much for listening to an 'inner voice' that Alison spoke of, knew it was time to go.

Mariah thought their argument was over on that particular afternoon. In fact, she didn't see it as an argument, but a discussion, simply stating her intentions to move. Mariah figured that as long as she remained calm, that Ana would eventually calm down as well. That didn't happen.

Turning away, deciding to throw some cold water on her face and maybe go for a walk, Mariah was surprised to feel fear curling up her spine when the rushed sound came from behind. Ana had flown across the room and with one swift motion, shoved Mariah.

Stunned, Mariah grabbed for the couch on the way down and felt pain shoot through her arm, quickly pulling herself up. Instinctively, she moved away from Ana and her brain raced to monitor the situation. Most of her stuff was still packed and sitting in the corner, if she had to escape quickly, it was doable.

"You were always an ungrateful bitch." Ana ranted angrily, as tears formed in her eyes. It was clear that she was not the only person who had necessarily caused pain for Ana but at the same time, she sure as hell wasn't going to put up with this abuse. Mariah only half listened to the cruel rant that followed, wondering if she could stay with Alison until her apartment was ready. Even if things calmed down, something told her it was time to get out – and fast!

Ana seemed to grow exhausted by the argument and with no more words grabbed her coat and rushed out the door. Mariah wasted no time in calling Alison to ask if she could stay with her, simultaneously rushing through the apartment and grabbing her stuff. Alison was very concerned when she heard the abrupt, summed up version of the incident with Ana, especially when Mariah told her about being shoved to the floor.

"Mariah, you get out of there now." Alison insisted. "I don't have a good feeling about any of this and I don't want to scare you or to put Ana down because I know it is a family-

"You know what," Mariah felt the words stick in her throat and wasn't sure how to finish that sentence. "I know. I mean, I got my stuff together and I…" She felt emotions come on like a tidal wave and her body slowly collapsed on the floor. Her tears were crippling, her entire body weak and exhausted.

"Are you okay? Mariah?" Alison sounded alarmed and panic sprung from her voice. "Is Ana back? What's going on?"

Mariah took a deep breath and wiped away the tears with the back of her sleeve. Her entire body suddenly felt weak. "No, she's not. I'm just, I mean, I got everything together. Can you come get me?"

"Of course." Alison replied. "Go downstairs. Get out of the apartment. I just don't feel like you should be there right now."

Mariah nodded and realized that Alison was relying on a vocal response. "I mean, yes, I understand."

She had mixed feelings as she walked out of the apartment that day. Leaving only her set of keys, Mariah had briefly considered writing a note to say a million different things but something stopped her. Emotionally frozen, her mind was in neutral and felt weak. Instead, her eyes wandered through the room and she wondered if it was really her brother she was leaving. Wasn't he already gone? Hadn't Ana made sure of that already?

And if there was one thing Mariah was certain of it was that she owed Ana nothing. She hesitantly made the decision to leave a note with her temporary address.

Alison didn't take long to arrive and quickly jumped out of the car to help Mariah with her suitcases, only stopped to hug her friend. It was a cold January afternoon and neither took very long to toss the bags in the trunk and climb in the car. Before heading back on the road, Alison turned to Mariah and studied her face.

"Are you okay?"

"Yes." Mariah assured her and slowly began to nod. "I'm okay."

"Did Ana hurt you?"

"No, I caught the couch, so I'm fine."

"But the fact that she would even do that...."

"I know." Mariah nodded and managed a small smile as she looked into Alison's eyes. Knowing how haggard she probably looked at that moment, she merely added, "I'm okay. I'm just so shocked. I think I probably didn't want to face the truth."

"My dad had the surgery too, Mariah. I know the hormones can make you a little crazy and I know you kind of become this whole new person." Alison pursed her lips. "But not that kind of person. There's some other stuff going on with Ana and that's what I always thought. But you can't help someone who might possibly hurt you. You are welcome to stay with me until your new place is ready. I don't mind."

"I don't want to be in the way, I can-

"You won't be." Alison insisted and put the car back into drive. "Everything's going to be fine."

Mariah had a sinking feeling, but agreed with a silent nod. Of course, everything would be fine. She would stay with Alison, eventually move into her new place and someday when Mariah felt it was the right time, she would contact Ana again and try to resolve their differences. Deep down, she had to believe that a wonderful person was still inside and just had too many emotional issues spring up with the hormones, perhaps they just needed space from one another. Maybe someday, they would meet again.

But Ana had a lot more issues than Mariah knew about or could've ever understood. After being kicked out of the family home, Anton went through some very dark periods that profoundly affected him and like his sister; he denied it and shoved those feelings down. So far down that he felt confident that they were out of sight and out of mind.

But nothing goes away. It's there even when you can't see it and if you don't eventually pick it up and throw it out, it'll sit and collect dust until you can no longer ignore it.

Hormones are powerful, especially when you are taking strong dosages in order to rush through to the next phase. In essence, you are tricking your body into something it wouldn't naturally do at all. Some people just cope better than others. Ana did not cope well.

The news would come to Mariah late that night. Alison gently woke her from a deep sleep and it took her a minute to remember where she was and why. Had her own mother been so nurturing, Mariah instantly thought, perhaps she would have become a different kind of woman. Who would she be now? These thoughts flew through her mind until she was suddenly wide awake, after Alison sat beside her on the bed and told her that someone was outside to see her.

"If it is Ana, I can't deal with it."

She could tell something was wrong by the expression on Alison's face. Defeated, she was clearly reaching deep inside herself to say the right words. "It's the police."

Mariah already knew what was next, but she fought her tears and mechanically got out of bed. She couldn't remember walking to the door. She couldn't remember the words that the police officer said to her or that Alison had one arm around her waist, supporting Mariah's body. She couldn't remember anything except for one fact. Anton Nichols was dead. And so was Ana.

Chapter twenty

Broken people shouldn't live with other broken people. It's just a recipe for disaster. Left to their own devices, a broken person might slowly stumble toward some answers, knowing that there is work to be done. It may take a while and that person might fall many times, but its progress. However if you throw another damaged person into the mix, the result can be disastrous.

In theory, it would make sense that the opposite be true. Idealistically, two damaged people would support, help and encourage one another. Kind of like a group theory session, they could learn about themselves from one another. But that is somewhat naïve.

Sometimes our worst enemy is in the mirror. And sometimes, our worst enemy is mirrored in someone else's eyes. It's one thing to listen to another person's problems when they don't quite resemble your own. It is quite another when you *have* had the almost identical experience.

Mariah and her brother had a lot in common. They were both kicked out of their family home. They both tolerated an intolerant mother. They both had an absent father. They both couldn't love. And looking at one another each day was like looking in a mirror and sometimes, that is just too much to take.

No one knew why Anton Nichols jumped out of a window. Mariah went over it a million times in her mind. Was it the hormones that pushed him too far? Was it the childhood that they both suffered? Were there other things she didn't know about? It had even crossed her mind that some terrible person with hate in their heart had accidentally discovered a transgender in his bedroom and pushed that person from a window. Was that so hard to believe? How many times had Ana arrived home with a black eye or bruising? Mariah shivered at the thought.

Regardless of the situation, the result was almost unbearable.

But she got through it. Life had already given Mariah challenges to face and she knew there was little else she could do but to take it head on. Fortunately, Alison was there for her and insisted that she had a place to stay until her new apartment was ready. She also offered to help with the funeral arrangements, but Mariah was relieved to report that her father had already taken the responsibility. It would've been much more than the 18 year old could bear. She was strong, but not that strong.

Mariah was frozen in time, unable to eat or sleep. Her mind raced through the last conversation with her brother. Why was he angry with her? Was there something she could've said or done that day that would've made a difference? Had it been her fault that Anton jumped?

The mind is a powerful thing and it can torment you if you let it. Mariah couldn't stop visualizing her brother in those last few minutes, the last few seconds, making the final decision to jump and end his life. What was he thinking? What had been the final straw? Should she have stayed in that tiny, cramped apartment rather than finding her own place? Had her presence been more important to him than she realized? Had her decision to leave seem like a form of rejection?

She didn't talk to anyone about what was going on in her mind. She didn't share with Alison that it was her fault that her brother was dead. It was politically correct for people to not blame a family member, so Alison would feel obligated to rattle on about how it was no one's fault and that Mariah was just upset. Perhaps she would even believe this story, but Mariah wouldn't. She recognized her contribution in the situation. But she would never share this with anyone.

On the day of the funeral, Mariah didn't hear a word that was said during the proceeding. Alison sat one side of her, Frank Nichols on the other. His new family had stayed at home, fearing it would create an unneeded awkwardness.

The words were empty. Mariah's request to have Anton known by his female name was ignored. Her father wasn't comfortable with the idea and the man who helped arrange the funeral suggested it wasn't appropriate since Anton had not legally changed his name. Mariah hadn't the strength to argue.

She thought their mother hadn't shown up until catching Frank Nichols turn around, sending a cold stare to the back of the room. Mariah turned to see her mother sitting close to the door. Was it to make a quick getaway, to dash out before anyone noticed that she was associated with this transgender young man that had embarrassed her so much? Mariah was angry to see her there, but at the same time, she would've been equally as annoyed had she not bothered to show at all.

It was when she stepped out of the church on that cold, January day that Mariah decided to leave Montreal. She would never see the city the same way now that her brother was gone. He was the reason Mariah had moved there in the first place and although she had made a life for herself there as well, it suddenly felt very frail as if it were about to be evaporated into the clouds above. It was time she moved on and started off fresh somewhere new.

It was later that night that Mariah confessed her decision to Alison, leaving her stunned. The two were sharing a bottle of wine and having a quiet conversation about the day when she had suddenly tossed in her piece of news as if it were the most natural part of their conversation. Death. Funerals. Family. Moving.

"Mariah, you can't move. Your brother just died." Alison spoke softly, her fingers gently touching her friend's arm, almost as if to make sure that it was the 'real' Mariah and not an imposter.

"I know it won't be right away." She spoke evenly, watching the relief temporarily cross Alison's face. "But after I clean out my brother's apartment and get that stuff sorted out, I think it would be a good time to go."

"But you're still in shock." Alison attempted to reason with her as she slowly shook her head. "It's too soon to make a big decision. You need to take some time to sort it out."

"I don't think I will ever sort it out." Mariah spoke honestly. "I think the best thing is just going somewhere new. Somewhere that doesn't remind me of my brother. I'm actually thinking about Vancouver."

"But that's so far away." Alison's voice was low, her eyes full of disappointment. "Are you sure you want to do this?"

"Yes."

"Can you at least do me a small favor?" Alison spoke carefully. "Can you just sleep on it? See how you feel tomorrow and we'll talk about it some more?"

Exhausted by the day, Mariah wearily agreed but her mind was already made up. If anything, she felt more convinced the next day.

When Alison went out that afternoon, Mariah decided to contact the one who changed her in order to learn more information on the apartment buildings only available to vampires. Mariah didn't share the news about her brother and was relieved to not discuss death, for the first time in days. It felt better to talk about the future rather than the misery of her present circumstances.

"I don't know if there is anything available in the Toronto one," He had regret in his voice and knew it was sincere. "I can ask about Vancouver and Calgary, if you wish."

"Yes, I was thinking Vancouver, so that would be perfect."

"You're looking into moving?"

"As soon as possible."

"Vancouver is far away." He replied. "Are you sure you want to do that?"

"Yes." She insisted. "In fact, if there is anything free, please let me know who I can contact for more information."

By the time Alison arrived home with coffee with Todd in tow, Mariah had already made the arrangements with her new landlord. She was moving in on February 1st.

Alison and Todd exchanged looks.

"Are you sure about this Mariah?" Alison sat the tray of coffee down on a nearby table and removed her coat. Concern filled her face and Todd stood back with thoughtful eyes. "You don't have to decide that quickly and you did put a damage deposit down on a new place here, right?"

"I don't know, I guess I'll have to talk to the landlord tomorrow." Mariah shrugged, admitting she hadn't even thought that far ahead. It had been so easy to deal with Anton's landlord after his death that she assumed it would be as simple with her new place.

"Look, if you need me to, I can check in with this guy." Todd stepped forward and reached down for his coffee, never ending eye contact with Mariah for even a second. "I don't want to see you go, especially at the bar, but at the same time, I totally get where you are coming from. If you need me to sit down with this landlord and explain the circumstances, I'd be happy to do so."

Alison looked as though someone had slapped her in the face. "I don't think this is a good idea. I mean, not this soon."

"I know," Mariah said and shook her head. "I thought about that too, but I just don't feel like this is where I belong anymore. I won't be able to walk down Anton's street again and not think of him. It's too much for me right now. I think I need a fresh start. It'll be better for me."

The three sat down and sipped their coffee, discussing the matter further until both Todd and Alison couldn't argue that Mariah had thought of everything. Maybe she was right, it was time to move on.

The next day, Mariah insisted that she would be okay to clean Anton's apartment. Her father had offered to stay around and help or to hire someone to do it, but Mariah said she wanted to take care of it. He reluctantly agreed before returning to Ontario.

Mariah spent the next few days doing a little at a time. First she got rid of the furniture and dishes, having a local charity come pick them up. She then cleaned through Anton's personal items, which proved to be very difficult. It was while doing so that she found a large supply of female hormones and wondered if he had been taking too many? Had that affected Anton's moods, causing him to be so emotional? She also found some other pills with no labels and although a part of her wanted to know what they were, another did not. She threw them out.

She made some more donations to various places and threw other stuff out until there was nothing left. Mariah only saved a few photos. Her mother had not reached out and Frank Nichols insisted it was okay to do as she wished with any items in the apartment; he didn't want anything more than photographs of his son.

She went to the apartment one last time to make sure everything was fine. It was pristine, clean and the rooms smelled fresh and lovely, but the many painful memories filled the atmosphere in a way that Mariah never could've anticipated. She knew that it would be normal to shed a tear upon leaving that morning but instead, she remained stoic.

It was almost like this apartment was full of lies. The many lies Mariah had told herself upon moving in. She had arrived the previous summer in hopes of recreating a strong relationship with a brother that hadn't been in her life for years. Instead, she found a stranger who never lets her in.

Mariah spent her last evening in Montreal with Alison. Sharing a bottle of wine, they talked about their dreams for the future rather than focus on the dark days of the past. Alison remained unconvinced that her friend was ready to make such a drastic decision to move on but made it clear that her support was always behind Mariah, regardless of her decision. With a solemn, if not sad smile, she left her friend with one final piece of advice.

"Just remember that the world is full of sheep, but sometimes, there's a wolf in the mix." Alison offered the words, allowing a trickle of concern to sneak in her voice.

Mariah felt a smile attempt to embrace her lips, but it never quite made it. "Don't worry about me," Her eyes jumped away from Alison's face and to the other side of the room and she silently added.

I will be the wolf.

Chapter twenty-one

S ometimes we deny what we're not ready to face. It's a natural reaction and it's anything but healthy; but we do it, just the same.

Mariah felt she had handled everything in Montreal with maturity and strength. She managed to get through the funeral, tie up the loose ends and neatly package up her life and move to another city. In fact, it was during a layover at the Toronto Pearson airport that she decided that the topic of Ana would never be brought up again. Mariah would not tell anyone that she had an older brother, who would later make the brave decision to start the transformation to become a woman. It wasn't that she was ashamed about the situation, but that she felt it was better to keep the past behind her. It was easier not to talk about her family at all.

Vancouver would be a new beginning. She had fit into Montreal with ease so she assumed this move would have the same result. It was the opportunity to become a whole new person, whomever she wanted to be: get a great job, date new men and meet different people. Mariah enthusiastically believed that she had the power to design a whole new life and it was going to be wonderful. She would have control this time.

But she was scared. It was a reality that suddenly hit her on the cab ride to her new apartment. The friendly Indian man in the driver's seat attempted to start a conversation and she finally heard herself admit to this stranger that it was her first day in British Columbia. Her former enthusiasm about moving was starting to drain, but it was certainly not because of the cab driver, which went on and on about what a beautiful city it was while pointing north, toward the mountains.

"My family," He interjected himself. "We love it here. But very expensive."

"Yeah?" Mariah felt her nerves creep up, something that was rare for someone who usually kept a cool exterior.

"Oh yes, but it is okay." He nodded. "We are okay. You will be too, soon."

"Can I ask you something?" Mariah suddenly felt very comfortable with this man. "Were you scared when you first came to Vancouver?"

"It was our first time in Canada as well," He remarked and nodded. "Yes, we were scared. Not a lot of English for us and here I am."

Mariah suddenly felt a hint of guilt. This man had immigrated to a whole new country, forget about the province, so did she have the right to be so frightened? At least she was a born Canadian citizen and as such, was aware of laws, various government departments and many other things that she took for granted. Plus, she could speak English. Her heart softened when she considered how hard it must be for someone who had none of those advantages but still managed to make it. Flashes of her mother's face passed through her mind, but she quickly dismissed them.

"A lot of Hollywood here." He grinned, pointing toward the sidewalk. A lady talked into a microphone as a cameraman recorded her. Various people walked by the two, some curiously glanced in their direction but most were not. "Movies, television, all of that here too."

"Wow." Mariah managed while biting her lower lip. She felt her nerves erupt at the idea and she wasn't sure why. It was a bit overwhelming and she just wanted to get to her new place and settle in. Fortunately, they were almost there.

Mariah's apartment was located in a four-story building, located in the downtown area of Vancouver. The cab driver insisted she was in a good location and that it was an ideal spot for a new resident. After helping her inside, Mariah handed him a generous tip before watching him walk away.

A beautiful blonde lady that could've easily passed for a model approached Mariah and said her name.

"Yes," Mariah's voice was strained; a sliver of fear had somehow managed to creep in. "I-I'm her."

"I'm Samantha, we talked on the phone?" Mariah quickly recognized her as the landlord and managed a nervous smile.

"Yes, oh hi." She took a deep breath and reach out to shake hands. "You'll have to excuse me, I'm simply exhausted."

"I bet. That's a long trip plus the time difference." Samantha nodded in understanding. "I'll just quickly show you around and then take you to your new place."

The tour was brief but welcomed. Samantha pointed toward a nearby lounge area, where one older gentleman sat, staring curiously in their direction. Samantha quickly rattled off a few nearby businesses including a drug store and restaurant, and then adding that everything else she could possibly need was probably a short bus ride or walk away.

Grabbing one of Mariah's suitcases, Samantha started toward the nearby elevator. "Let's go upstairs to check out your new place." She continued to smile and Mariah followed her cue, snatching her other suitcase and thinking that her whole world was in two bags.

The apartment was small but it was still perfect. Each room was empty of course, so Mariah would be sleeping on the floor for a couple of nights but she didn't care. She had her own place.

"I wrote down a few places nearby where you might be able to get various things, like dishes or furniture. I guess you can order that stuff online too, if it makes it easier." Samantha handed her a list.

"Thanks," Mariah smiled and nodded. A few minutes later, Samantha told Mariah to call if there were any problems or questions.

Walking around the apartment, Mariah noted that the open concept between the kitchen and living room, with only an island separating the two. The windows were quite big, allowing light to fill up the entire room as the sun peaked through the clouds. The cabbie had warned her that it rained a lot, but after spending years in snow banks, it was kind of a nice change of pace.

The bedroom was a reasonable size with a large, walk-in closet and an adjoining bathroom was also quite small, but it did hold a large, comfortable bathtub and that was the most inviting thing Mariah saw all day. Good thing she packed some towels and soap in her luggage.

Over the next few days, she managed to get a bed delivered and set up, as well as find dishes, bedding and various necessities. Alison emailed her three times on the second day, concerned about Mariah's well being, almost as if in doubt that her friend would be able to withstand the city alone. Although her gesture was with good intentions, Mariah couldn't help but feel it was brought on by a lack of faith in her abilities. Did people expect her to fail?

Her laptop ended up being a God sent. It allowed her to look up various businesses, learn the transit system and connect with the familiarities like friends in Montreal. It also helped her to look for a job, something she had to get as soon as possible. All and all, it was pretty overwhelming and there were many times in the first week that Mariah wondered if moving had been the right decision. But then she thought about the funeral that had changed her entire path and accepted that this was the correct decision. There was simply no way she could've stayed in Montreal.

The first job she got wasn't anything to write home about. Still unfamiliar with the geography of the city, Mariah decided it was better to find something close to home until she became more accustomed to the city. Since she was more familiar with customer service, it made sense to apply at some local clothing stores. A few days after her interview with a chain store that she hated, Mariah had her first job in Vancouver. The staff was immature, the management was terrible, but at least it did rely heavily on commission, something she excelled at: until now. This was something Mariah had done well at in the past, what was different?

Ready to quit one afternoon, tired of making minimum wage, she decided to take notice of how the other girls managed to win customer's over. It was quite interesting. She worked with a Spanish and Asian girl. Both immediately recognized those of their own culture and rushed to help that clientele, often in their first language. Unfortunately, Mariah could only speak English.

She was fired a week and a half after starting.

"But that's not fair," She insisted. "I was always a great salesperson at my previous job. I'm just having a hard time adapting to the way you do things here." She forced a smile.

I worked at boutiques that sold premium quality products not mass-produced crap made in China.

"I just don't think this is the ideal company for you." The Asian lady was insistent. "I think you would be more suited for maybe the discount department store?" The lady spoke kindly but her insinuation was insulting.

Infuriated by the condescending tone and reminding herself that she wanted to be a whole new person since her move, Mariah bit her lip for a second before pulling off her name tag and throwing it on the desk.

"Fuck you, lady!" She jumped up from the chair. "Fuck you and all this substandard shit that you sell here."

The woman's eyes doubled in size as she watched Mariah Nichols walk out of her office, then out of the store. She would never step foot in there again.

Feeling discouraged after a long day, she collapsed in her building's lounge area and momentarily closed her eyes.

"You must be that young miss from upstairs." A British accent interrupted her short rest and Mariah's eyes sprang open to see the same older gentleman who had been watching her on the day she moved in. He appeared to be around her father's age, but upon closer inspection, perhaps slightly younger. He was average height with a husky build and wore a shirt and dress pants, as if he had just arrived home from work – except it was 11 a.m.

"Ah, maybe?" Mariah replied as he sat down across from her and she noted that day's newspaper in his hand.

"Yes, you just moved into the flat upstairs." He proceeded to answer the question meant for her. "My wife Olivia saw you the day you got in. My name is Benjamin Clarkson, by the way."

"Nice to meet you." She attempted to throw some confidence in her voice, something she had been lacking in recent weeks since her move. "I'm Mariah Nichols."

"Nichols. That sounds like a nice English surname." Benjamin grinned. "You know I used to know a Nichols back in Europe, quite a puzzling chap. Oh, but he enjoyed a good pint every night and that's when he got riled up."

"Oh." Mariah was surprised how comfortable this stranger was telling her such a random story. "My mom is Russian but my dad's family has been in Canada for generations."

"So probably no relation?"

"Probably not."

"And your family is from Vancouver?"

"No, Ontario. But I just moved here from Montreal."

"Montreal." Benjamin smiled and looked off into the distance. "Oh the memories I have of Montreal. What a truly spectacular place."

"It is." Mariah agreed. "But I needed a change."

"I see." Benjamin nodded. "Such a beautiful young lady as yourself must be here for acting? An artist of sorts?"

"Ah no," Mariah smiled and looked away briefly, as an attractive young man entered the building and glanced their way as he walked toward the elevator. "Just a new start."

"Do you have a job yet?"

"I did, until I got fired today." Mariah decided to be honest and then made a second decision to tell him the story of her morning.

"Oh, they do make absolute rubbish, don't they?" Benjamin frowned and shook his head. "Terrible. Well, you can certainly do better than that. Let me make some phone calls. I know some people."

"You know people?" A grin spread across Mariah's face. Benjamin's words reminded her of something a mob boss would say.

"I know people. Just let me handle it." Benjamin stood up, holding onto his newspaper as he did so. "We will talk again soon."

And then he was gone.

Chapter twenty-two

Life sometimes gives us a lot of reasons to lose enthusiasm. Circumstances, challenges and fears are reasons why we often give up on our dreams – even if it is just temporarily. We seem to have this notion that results should fall at our feet at the very moment that we expect it and yet, the universe simply doesn't work that way. We have to believe that in the end, everything will be fine. But first, you have to have faith.

Mariah Nichols didn't have much in the way of faith. She had arrived in Vancouver with a burst of excitement and enthusiasm but when things started to fray at the edges, it was quite easy to assume that nothing would work out. Her first job was a disaster and although she wanted to believe that Benjamin Clarkson would help her out, realistically he had no reason to make such efforts. Meanwhile, she wasn't having much luck on her own search. Great references and job experience aside, employers weren't calling and when they did, they didn't hire her.

One day after another disastrous interview with a middle-aged man, Mariah felt defeated. After being chastised for being much too early and walking in on another interview by mistake, it was pretty clear that she had no hope in hell of being hired. It didn't matter how she answered the questions or how positive she was, Mariah was met by pretentiousness that was becoming commonplace in most of her interviews since moving to Vancouver. Had she arrived not dressed properly or wearing too much makeup, Mariah would understand getting a cold reception. If she had arrived unaware of the company's significance in the business world or with unintelligent answers to the most basic questions, lack of job experience or a bad attitude, she could probably wrap her brain around the arrogant disinterest in her all together. However, she made every effort to make a good impression.

After leaving her interview with the overweight man and his very attractive, much younger, female assistant, Mariah was stunned to be waiting at a crosswalk and have the two pass by her as if she weren't there, openly discussing the 'former stripper' they just interviewed and how she wouldn't represent their company well at all. It was in that moment that Mariah realized that she had to take Hot Spring Water off her resume. It never occurred to her that the potential employers would even look into such a place to learn it *was* a strip bar and even so, automatically assume she was more than a bartender.

Lost in thought on the bus ride home, Mariah almost missed her stop. As she walked back to her apartment building, it crossed her mind that perhaps she should look into some of the popular Vancouver strip bars. After all, it wasn't as if she hadn't worked in that kind of place before and although Todd had warned many weren't as 'clean' as his, Mariah was starting to blow through her money and needed a job soon. Moving, buying furniture and clothing for her job hunt had taken a lot that she had set aside.

Deciding to do some research online after lunch, she entered her building and was heading toward the elevator when she heard her name. Turning toward the lounge area, she saw Benjamin wave her over. Smiling, she headed in his direction and watched him put down a newspaper. As usual, he was dressed as if he just left a business meeting with a tailored blue suit. A simple tie clung to his white shirt that had a small, brown stain splattered on it.

Catching her wandering eyes, Benjamin glanced in the same direction. "Imbeciles can't drive in this city. I had to stop on a dime and spilled my Starbucks on the front of my shirt." Looking up with a mischievous grin on his face, he watched as Mariah sat across from him. "And to think I'm the Brit who's used to driving on the opposite side. If anyone should be mixed up driving, would it not be me?"

"Well, you would certainly have more of an excuse, wouldn't you?" Mariah said with a laugh and placed her bag on the floor.

"Do you drive?"

"Yes, but I don't have a car right now." Mariah confessed.

"Then I would say, you don't drive. At least, not at this time." Benjamin sat his paper down. "Did you find yourself a job yet?"

"Not even close. I feel so rejected." Mariah bluntly commented. "I just left another terrible interview."

"Why terrible?"

Mariah dove into the story, explaining how she had insulted the employer by walking in on another interview, unaware that the address she was given belonged to one, lone office rather than a waiting area.

"Well, that is preposterous." Benjamin frowned and she could see a few white hairs in his eyebrows. His pug nose seemed to curl up, along with his lip when he frowned. "Oh, you don't want to work for that kind of an outfit. Clearly, very unprofessional and probably no paycheck waiting for you at the end of it all."

Mariah raised a single eyebrow and nodded. She was impressed with such an observation. "I hadn't thought of that, actually."

"What kind of job was it for?"

"Receptionist."

"Reception? Well, those are a dime a dozen around here." Benjamin waved his arm as if to indicate the room. "I don't think you have a thing to worry about, a young lady like you should have no trouble."

"But I am having trouble." She confessed and calmly went on to explain. "Everyone is super educated and that's fine if it is for a job that requires it, but I don't think I should have to compete with that kind of thing to answer a fucking phone."

"True enough." Benjamin nodded in agreement. "I did hear of something, that's what I wanted to tell you about when I ushered you over. A nice little company, not far away, just started out a few years ago and I believe they sell health drinks or some other kind of bloody new aged crap. I really don't know. The whole lot of Vancouver is into this whole yoga, green juice, crystal healing, woo woo nonsense. Although I shouldn't say that because back in Europe, Olivia and I often went to these retreats that probably would seem pretty strange to some people as well." He hesitated as if about to launch into a story but something stopped him. "You know, I do think you would be ideal for this place. They simply want a salesperson and they tend to look for young, attractive ladies, such as yourself because you're quite slender and healthy looking and you have the image they seem to want to portray."

"Hey, I can do any new aged, woo woo shit, if it helps me get a job." Mariah grinned and reached for her bag. "I can take a resume by right now if-

"Hello, Alexandra?" Benjamin was suddenly on his phone. "I was thinking about our conversation earlier in the day when you mentioned one of your stores are hiring right now. I have a fantastic young lady for you." He hesitated for a moment and made eye contact with Mariah and winked at her. "My niece contacted me this morning that she just moved into town and she would be superb at your establishment downtown. In fact, she is only spitting distance away so it would be perfect for both of you."

After a lengthy phone conversation that went from offering up Benjamin's 'niece' for a job, to the previous night's NHL game and finally, a discussion about a local bar losing its liquor license, he finally said goodbye and hesitated before hitting the 'end' button on his phone.

"Such a blabbermouth, you never get that ghastly woman, off the phone." He abruptly shoved his cell back in his jacket pocket and rolled his eyes. "Nevertheless, I do think I have a job lined up for you. You just have to drop by her woo woo store later today and have a conversation with her."

"An interview?"

"No, people who are competing for a job have interviews young lady, people who are getting a job have conversations." He corrected her while moving to the edge of his seat and gently tapping his newspaper against her knee. "And you have a conversation."

After giving her the details of when and where, he stood up and started to walk away.

"Thank you so much, Benjamin." She called out. He merely turned and gave her a rushed smile before heading toward the elevator. Using her phone, she looked up information about the particular company he told her about. It looked simple enough. Energy Planet Vancouver apparently sold overpriced Vitamins and an array of books, yoga clothing and accessories.

It wasn't her thing, but Mariah would go along with it. She would do her research and be ready.

As it turned out that was a smart move because Energy Planet Vancouver was pretty insistent that its employees be athletic, spiritually open and live a healthy life. The enthusiastic blue-eyed blonde, who practically bounced around the room like the energizer bunny, actually made reference to the company's core value that was splattered throughout the store, like a creepy version of George Orwell's *1984*.

"We believe in clean living, a life full of vitality and excitement. We fully embrace the belief that yoga opens up all five senses, but more importantly, intuition and a connection to the divine." Alexandra continued to ramble on. Although Mariah smiled and reflected the excitement of her new boss, in reality she had only grasped a few key words and suspected that the more she threw them around, the better off she would be in the long run.

Glancing around the room as Alexandra described what she would be selling – which include everything from yoga packages to overpriced items that were apparently 'locally made and of the highest quality' – Mariah noted that the store was a large, bright room full of modern, glass shelving. The store's 'philosophy' and name was written in white calligraphy style letters over a grass green background. Mariah assumed the color choice was attempting to represent them as a 'green' company, in order to be trusted by its customers? Regardless, she played along while Alexandra gave her a tour of the store.

Two other Energy Planet Vancouver 'experts' were on the floor, wearing their trademark yoga pants, fitted tank top and jacket with the store logo. Mariah couldn't help but noticed that one of them showed as much cleavage in her uniform as the strippers at the bar had at any given night. Then again, she did have the full attention of the male customer she was serving, so there was that aspect of things.

Mariah later walked out of the store with booklets, a uniform and a 'trial' pack of vitamins to try, so she could honestly tell customers how much more alive she felt after taking them. It was an absolute bullshit, but she needed a job and would play their game.

Upon arriving home, she once again found Benjamin in the lounge area but he wasn't alone. An attractive man who appeared to be her age was sitting across from him, the two were clearly having an uplifting conversation and she didn't want to interrupt. However, she caught Benjamin's eye and he called her over. The young man with him looked at her curiously, showing no reaction, but merely observing her as she moved closer. He had very appealing amber eyes and slightly shaggy blonde hair that reminded her of a young actor she had watched on television the previous night. He wore jeans and a simple, black T-shirt and expensive running shoes.

"Well, young lady, how did it go with Alexandra's house of weirdness?" Without allowing her time to answer, he nodded toward the items in her hand. "I see she gave you a sample of her overpriced sugar pills and the uniform that has a Wonderbra built right in, I take that as a good sign."

"Yes, I-

"Sugar pills, really?" The young man finally smiled in Mariah's direction briefly, and then returned his attention to Benjamin. "That seems a bit harsh, don't you think?"

"Not at all, I looked up the ingredients after she attempted to push some on me." Benjamin sat back with a stoic expression on his face. "Nothing but sugar, caffeine and some very basic vitamins that you could get for a quarter of the price at any health food store. That's absolute bullshit. The caffeine probably gives people all this energy they rave about and as for the Wonderbra top, well, you've been in the store haven't you? It's tit's galore."

Mariah opened her mouth to say something, but it was a rare occasion when she simply couldn't think of a way to respond. Benjamin was pretty quick and sharp with his remarks, causing her to automatically like him, but at the same time, she couldn't quite top his comments.

"I do agree." Benjamin's friend spoke evenly; his eyes sparkled as he looked in Mariah's direction once again. "They are definitely selling an... image at that store."

"Oh, silly me, Mariah I forgot to introduce you to one of the other tenants in the building." He started to stand up and pointed toward the young man's direction. "This is Landon Owens." Then pointing toward the ceiling, he continued, "I believe he is underneath you. Now, I must run off and see what Olivia is up to."

Mariah felt her cheeks burn at the 'underneath you' comment because although Benjamin portrayed the image of someone that would make a remark innocently, there was an insinuation that was hard to miss. Feeling profoundly embarrassed, she slowly eased into the chair across from Landon. Benjamin disappeared into the elevator.

Looking back into Landon's eyes and feeling all her senses suddenly very alert to every sensation in her body and the scent in the air, it occurred to her that perhaps Benjamin's words were a fair prediction. Maybe Landon would soon be underneath her.

Chapter twenty-three

At the end of the day, you can only be yourself. People sometimes believe that pretending to be someone else is less work than justifying who they really are but they're wrong. Wearing a mask and playing a role can be exhausting.

Mariah Nichols felt slightly superior to her coworkers. It wasn't because her sales were better: although, she managed to do well for being the new girl. It wasn't because she was prettier, thinner or smarter either because both Jody and Marianne matched her in those areas. It was the fact that she was herself everyday.

Marianne, a tall blonde who was slightly fanatic about her yoga and green juice lifestyle, was ironically a very anxious person. It was odd that someone who proactively attempted to be more centered would wander around the store with a 'deer in headlights' expression on her face. Watching her interaction with customers was uncomfortable and awkward, regardless of her product knowledge.

She would often talk to Mariah and carry a combination of fear and reassurance in her eyes, all at the same time. Perhaps the reassurance was for the new girl on the job while the fear was possibly a reflection of everything else in her life. When Mariah attempted to learn about her, she discovered that the 27 year old was also a part-time business student and very active in yoga, often going to weird retreats that to Mariah, sounded like a non-sexual version of an orgy. Considering she insisted that she didn't have time to date, perhaps this was her idea of a replacement.

Jody was the coworker that wasn't shy to show off her cleavage. She walked around Energy Planet Vancouver as if she owned the store and even attempted to hand out orders to her coworkers. That didn't seem to bother Marianne as much as it did Mariah. When she wasn't telling Marianne to get stock in the back (usually sweeping in to take the client and the commission that walked in the door) she was pointing out what Mariah she was doing wrong.

"When that lady signed up for the yoga class, you should've convinced her to purchase some of our yoga wear as well as a mat in order to help your sales." She arrogantly threw the remark at Mariah on her third day. This was after dealing with a customer who had been iffy about joining the yoga class at all let alone purchasing extra stuff. Mariah had mildly mentioned they had other products available for her first session, but could sense that the woman was not interested and let it go. Jody apparently didn't think she made the right decision.

"I told her about our other products and she wasn't interested." Mariah calmly replied and attempted to walk away, but Jody was determined to push the matter a little further.

"You aren't going to get your sales unless you're more aggressive with customers." Jody said with a condescending tone, but still managing to keep her 'Valley girl' voice in check. "You know, like, that's what they expect here. They expect you to push a lot of product on them so don't feel shy to do so."

"I'm not shy."

"Well, like hesitant or whatever." She waved her hand in the air as if to dismiss the entire conversation. "The point is that you won't last long if you aren't more aggressive in your sales tactics."

"You're right." Mariah said gently in order to see Jody's defenses fall down and then she glanced at her coworker's ample cleavage, making sure her line of vision was duly noted. "Maybe I should try a *couple* of your tactics in order to reel people in."

Jody glared at her. Marianne was stocking a shelf nearby, pretending to not listen, but it was pretty obvious that she was, judging by her amplified 'deer in headlights' expression. Mariah ignored both of them and approached a customer that just walked through the door.

Before her shift ended that day, Alexandra called her to the office for a 'quick chat' regarding her progress. Having a bubbly personality, she immediately started with the positive comments. Mariah was doing well with her sales, customers were really 'taking a shine' to her personality and overall, everything seemed to be going well: but there was one little problem.

"There's something Jody mentioned to me earlier today that I wanted to bring up. It's not a big deal, but I would prefer to clear the air." Alexandra's bright smile dimmed for the first time all week while her eyes remained huge, as if she had just snorted coffee grounds on the sly. "Apparently you made a remark that made her...uncomfortable regarding her breasts and although I am sure you were just teasing, it made Jody very awkward and really, it *is* kind of considered sexual harassment."

Mariah couldn't hold back her laughter. "I assure you, I was not sexually harassing Jody." Her heart raced, fearing she was once again going to be fired, but she remained confident and self-assured in appearance, just as her boss remained over the top excited about life, every moment of the day. "I just feel that her cleavage is pretty excessive for a nutritional store. I will be honest, I believe she is using that as a way to grab men's attention."

For the first time ever, she saw the smile completely drop from Alexandra's face. "I don't know what to say, but I don't believe that is her intention. If anything, I think she is actually quite self-conscious about her breast size and I think you should show a little more sensitivity toward her situation."

"Okay." Mariah managed to suppress her laughter and nodded. "I will do that in the future."

"Thank you, Mariah. I can appreciate that. I know you're from Montreal and probably that kind of comment would be acceptable there, but here in Vancouver, we try to be a little more sensitive to this kind of thing."

"Sure."

"And in the future, just try to look the other way."

"Okay."

"And maybe an apology would be nice."

"Aha."

"And she also mentioned something else that troubled her." Alexandra eased into the next topic. "She mentioned that perhaps you weren't interested in taking her training advice to upsell to customers. Now I know it is a bit intimidating when you are new to sales-

"Actually, I've been doing sales since I was 16." Mariah interrupted her, slightly frustrated by her lack of knowledge, even though she had read her resume only a few days earlier. "I understand how sales work."

"Oh yes, I'm sorry." Alexandra began to laugh and tapped herself on the forehead, as if to indicate she had a dumb moment. "Just remember that people come in expecting aggressive salespeople and I know that Jody isn't your boss, but I do rely on her a lot to help out. So if she makes a suggestion, try to take it as a positive piece of advice and not a criticism."

"I will."

"Remember, we're all about team work here at Energy Planet Vancouver. She's just trying to help you out."

"Exactly." Mariah smiled and noted the intense smell of perspiration since the beginning of their conversation. That meant her boss was nervous. It gave her a slight edge to the conversation. She didn't like to hand out these comments any more than Mariah wanted to hear them. "Is that everything?"

"Yes."

"Okay, thank you." Mariah said as she stood up, making sure to make direct eye contact with her boss. "This has been informative."

Walking out of the office, she quickly spotted Jody, as she abruptly turned her head in the other direction, as if to avoid Mariah. Of course, the real kicker was that both her and her cleavage were making friends with Landon Owens, who was there to pick up Mariah. The two had been spending a lot of time together since meeting and had plans for that evening.

The fact that Jody was nitpicking at every little thing irritated Mariah. Her pretentious attitude was frustrating. Her attempts to gain attention by showing off her tits were pathetic. And now the fact that she was leaning over to pick up something directly in front of Landon, giving him a direct view down her top, was perhaps the final straw.

Suddenly, Mariah was a child living at home again and witnessing Polina Nichols trying to catch a man's attention. Wearing skanky little outfits, making inappropriate comments and of course, all the times her mother threw herself at any male that gave her the time of day. From across the room, she could see Landon's eyes widen as Jody quickly rose, making sure everything bounced back into place and giggled like a schoolgirl, gently touching Landon's arm, as if he had somehow saved her from falling on the floor.

Mariah felt her cheeks getting hot and her heart started to race. From nearby, she saw Marianne pretending to work as she watched, with her usual deer in the headlights expression. Landon continued to look amused and hadn't even noticed Mariah in the room.

Taking a deep breath, she crossed the room. Feeling a combination of anger and lust fill her body at the same time, she stopped beside Landon and her coworker, who looked irritated by her presence.

"That's okay, I have this customer." Jody once again said the final word as if it was a question, only further vexing Mariah. "We're fine here, you can go home."

"I'm ah...I'm actually here for Mariah." Landon looked squarely into her eyes with a humored expression on his face. His stare was penetrating and sent a weakness to her knees as a longing inside her made Mariah almost forget about Jody. "We have... plans." His final word carried a hint of seduction.

Her skin suddenly felt extremely sensitive and full of goose bumps. An exhilarating sensation washed over her from head to toe, as Landon's eyes continued to be locked in with her own. She felt her throat become dry as excitement ran through her body.

"Oh." It was Jody's blunt, heavy response that ripped Mariah out of a euphonic state that engulfed her. Feeling her body plummeting back to earth, she suddenly felt her original anger for this buxom coworker resurrect.

"I was just talking to Alexandra." Mariah felt her confidence return and noted that Jody looked taken slightly aback by her sudden comment. "She said that I misunderstood your intention to help me and for that, I do apologize."

Noting that Jody looked slightly ill at ease, Mariah started toward the door, with Landon in tow. But then she stopped, turned slightly and continued. "Oh, and speaking of which," She began in a syrupy sweet voice. "Since Alexandra was stating how you are giving me advice in order to help me out, I would like to do the same thing for you."

Leaning closer to Jody, she spoke in a hushed tone, but well aware that also being a vampire, Landon could hear. "Alexandra told me you were very sensitive about your breast size. You know, I used to work in a ladies wear department, if you ever need someone to help you find a bra that fits properly, I would love to help you." Noting that all the color was draining from Jody's face, she continued to go in for the kill. "In fact, it would probably be in your best interest to do so soon, you know, before gravity catches up."

Giving a sweet smile, she waved good-bye to both her coworkers and turned to leave. Opportunities are always present. You just have to know where to go look.

Chapter twenty-four

Sometimes it's what we hate in others that we also hate in ourselves. If you look at the most irritating quality of your enemy, chances are you carry the same trait. If you think your coworker is a fake, pretending to be something that they aren't, is it possible that you're doing the same thing? Have you spent hours crafting the perfect veneer, hiding your insecurities and fears? What would happen if the beautiful mask were to ever fall to the ground and crash into a million little pieces?

Mariah pushed a lot of things out of her mind. She felt that life was about choosing your thoughts and if you didn't like one, well you just pushed it away. For the most part, her logic was clever, but what she didn't realize is that there is a difference between pushing troublesome thoughts aside, and shoving unresolved pain into hidden corners of your soul. Eventually, they will come back and the longer they're gone and the farther down they're pushed, the more violent their return will be.

Ana Nichols had been dead for months and Mariah had washed her hands of the entire situation. If anyone asked, she was an only child. Her parents were divorced and her relationship with both was strained. Period. She didn't wish to discuss the matter of family any more than that and didn't think it was necessary to think, let alone talk about it.

Alison was the last, real connection Mariah had in Montreal and even they had infrequent contact now. Busy with school and her boyfriend, Mariah just assumed herself to be out of sight and out of mind to her former best friend. It was probably just as well anyway, she decided, perhaps it was better to put everything from those days behind her and move forward.

The few times she had heard from Alison, she voiced concern over Mariah's sudden move and suggested that it may have been too impulsive to leave so quickly, before the dust had a chance to settle. For Mariah, it was the perfect time to get away, before committing to another apartment or anything got much worse. Not that it could. Her brother's death was a sign that the train had gone completely off the track.

Not that she had many friends in Vancouver. She talked to Benjamin on a regular basis and Landon became her lover.

Mariah made sure that the lines in the sand were clear. She didn't want a relationship. They had intense sexual chemistry and that fulfilled the strong urges that came with being a vampire. He brought her body to such intense ecstasy that she sometimes feared it was more than she could handle, but at the same time, it was exactly what she needed.

It was through Landon that made Mariah view her enhanced senses as a blessing rather than a curse. It was he who pointed out the beauty of an early morning sunrise, the intense colors in nature, the birds chirping in the trees. She could taste the smooth, sweet taste of an apple or pear; smell the heavenly scent of a strawberry and a fresh pot of coffee. Blood wasn't just a necessity but a powerful force that lifted her entire being. And then there was the sense of touch.

Her body was in a constant state of arousal. The touch of her clothing against her skin, the sheets on her bed where Mariah slept and the warm flow of water in the shower, where things were sometimes too rousing to her very sensitive skin. There were some specific materials that Mariah could not wear against her erogenous zones because they created unwanted arousal at the most inappropriate times. That was something she learned early on but didn't quite understand.

Landon Owens understood. In fact, when it came to her body, she very quickly started to wonder if he knew everything.

"It's nothing to be embarrassed about," He had assured her after a particularly rapid and fiery sexual encounter that started in her doorway and ended on the couch. Mariah had purchased a beautiful silk bra on sale shortly after Valentines Day and thought nothing of wearing it under her work uniform the next day. It was sexy and she kind of liked the idea of alluring bra under her bland uniform. As it turns out, it wasn't a very good idea.

By the time she got to work, the silky material was rubbing up against her sensitive nipples and sending sensations throughout her body. Although Mariah attempted to put it out of her mind, it seemed to become increasingly difficult as the day went on. In the end she had to place some rough, recycled toilet paper inside her bra in order to remove the sensual appeal of the undergarment.

"It was humiliating." Mariah pulled a blanket over her breasts and enjoyed the serenity that now flowed through her body. Landon merely grinned and ran his hand over her arm, as he sat naked on her couch. His face was flushed and his amber eyes glanced at the blanket that now covered the body he had just ravished. "Thank God I had the sweater over the tank top."

"You can always wear it around me." His words were soft, gentle, and as smooth as the tongue that now was running up her bare arm. Mariah felt her breath grow heavy as he pushed his hand underneath the blanket and between her thighs. "I'll show you what to do the next time you feel that way at work."

His tongue trailed to her pink nipples that were quickly getting hard, causing Mariah to moan very loudly, enjoying the finger work that Landon was orchestrating underneath the blanket. Their playfulness eventually ended and it was only as Landon was about to leave that same evening that he concluded his thought.

"Don't stress about it. A lot of women who aren't vampires have the same problem with certain fabrics." He gave her a quick kiss before gathering his clothes and putting them on. A Marketing student at the local college, he usually wore jeans, shirts and hoodies but on that particular day, Landon was dressed in a shirt and tie. "Actually, I've known a few women that weren't vampires that had the same issue."

"I bet you know a lot of women," Mariah replied in a seductive voice as she put her clothes back on – minus the bra. She would keep that for special occasions. "You definitely have the skill to back it up."

Landon grinned and didn't reply. "You know I'm no virgin, but I still bring something to the table."

"Well, you obviously aren't a virgin." Mariah finished dressing and was pulling her long hair back into a bun. "You're too skilled and I don't think the intrigue of a virgin is the same to woman."

"Well, not normally." Landon finished dressing and sat on the couch, while giving her an inquisitive look. Tilting his head slightly, his eyes seemed to shift from side to side and finally landed on her face. "So, you don't know the whole virgin thing, do you?"

"I know vampires prefer virgins, I was told that. But I think all men do, right?" She grinned, straightening up her clothing. "I don't see the big deal."

"No, I mean, the virgin thing and why they are more appealing to vampires." Landon slowly dove into the subject, almost as if he wasn't sure if he should tell her anything more. He looked away and down at his feet before continuing. "Vampires like virgins because of how they taste when you bite them." He seemed to subconsciously pull his shirt to the side in order to hide the bite mark just below the back of his neck.

"Well, it's not just that they taste better its that they give you more a…" He seemed to be searching for the words carefully and allowed himself to fall back on her couch, his eyes peering up at the ceiling. "They have a warmer flavor, they energize you more… it's almost like the crème de la crème of blood. There is no better and it's like a drug, almost. I guess for lack of better comparison."

"Really?" Mariah was intrigued. She had been told there was a difference, but she hadn't realized how significant it was to her kind. "And where do you find these virgins you speak of?"

A grin crossed his face and his eyes studied her face. "You have to be careful cause a lot of us were formed by overly enthused vampires. The experience is such a high that it's very easy to get lost in it."

"Really?"

"Yeah, I can already tell I shouldn't have told you about this." Landon's comment was full of skepticism even though his face remained calm. Picking up his tie from the side of the couch, he hung it loosely around his neck. He patted his hair back into place and continued to quietly watch her before continuing. "It's important that you don't change anyone Mariah, I hope you understand that."

"I do." She assured him. "I promise."

"You'll know a virgin when you meet one. In fact, you probably have met many in your day and just didn't know. They have a very unusual scent, but it's almost intoxicating. It captivates you, but then again, you may have thought that to be something else at the time."

"I think I have smelled them before, but I'm not sure."

"We will go out sometime and I will help you distinguish the smell. It'll be familiar to you, even though that may be hard to understand right now." He didn't go into greater details and Mariah began to see that it was probably impossible without an example. "But as soon as you bite one, you will know. It's a magnificent experience to try at least once, but I also don't encourage it on a regular basis. There are some vampires that prey on virgins and it's purely for their own selfish reasons. I hope you don't become that kind of person."

"You don't seem to have much hope for me." Mariah felt self-conscious making the statement. Although they were not a couple, she still worried about what Landon thought of her. He was someone she deeply respected. "I'm not an animal with no soul."

He merely smiled and she felt her heart sink by his reaction. She quickly pushed these feelings away and replaced them with a question that was floating over the entire conversation.

"Is that how you changed, Landon?" She gently asked, leaning against the couch while his eyes continued to watch her. "Were you a virgin?"

"Yes." He nodded and briefly looked away, only for his eyes to return to her face. "I was too young. Much too young and I shouldn't have been bitten. Vampires are forbidden to bite anyone who is going through puberty. Nineteen is usually a reasonable and expected age of consent, but not before that time."

"It happened to me just before my 18th birthday, so it wasn't like I was super young. I'm sorry to hear your story, though." Mariah attempted to respond how she thought he might want her to, unsure of what the normal reaction to this situation.

Landon began to laugh and shook his head. "You aren't sorry, Mariah. It's not necessary you say you that to humor me. We aren't a couple and we don't have a relationship, so you aren't required to comfort me." He hesitated and noted her reaction before continuing, "We get together to relieve some sexual urges because we get one another and have chemistry.

I'm not saying you are a heartless bitch, but," He stopped for a moment. "Actually, you are kind of a heartless bitch. But that's okay. I don't care."

"You think that of me?" She felt shocked by his blatant honesty. "I can't believe you would say that."

"I'm saying it because it's true." Landon stood up. His eyes were locked to her face, but showed no judgment. There was a calmness to him that suggested that he had no emotions toward her one way or the next. "I've seen how you talk to people when we're out. You can be rude, condescending and obnoxious. I heard how you spoke to your coworker at the store recently and you just started there. You never talk about friends or family and pretty much told me your parents are dead to you. How am I supposed to view you?"

She didn't reply.

"I didn't say I thought less of you. I think you're a cool girl. I think it's hot that you're aggressive. In fact, it turns me on." He shrugged and started toward the door. "But we don't want a relationship. We have great sex. We help fulfill something in each other and let's face it, we are vampires and because we have a very high sense of arousal, we live in the same building, it's a good match. Unless you want to start trolling the bars and the lobby for someone else, it's also very convenient."

"We know what each other wants." He paused for a moment. "And there's nothing wrong with that, but let's not pretend that we are something more than we are and feel the need to talk about feelings or make an emotional connection."

He smiled, took a couple steps back and gave Mariah a quick kiss on the forehead before leaving the apartment.

Chapter twenty-five

Words are very powerful. They can send warmth through your heart and can change your entire perception in a single moment, transcending the listener into a euphoric state that lifts them to a higher level of consciousness. It can be quite beautiful.

But on the less pleasant side, words can hurt. They can slash you so fast that you are left feeling the cool air as it strikes an opened wound, only seconds before the initial realization that anything has happened at all. Most people fall silent in those seconds, stunned and unable to get their bearings, left without being able to say a word.

Landon had called Mariah a heartless bitch. He hadn't done so in a state of anger meant to be bitter or hurtful but merely a fact. In his mind, nothing could hurt her and she felt no offense to the remark. She was an emotionless woman who sat comfortably behind a series of thick walls, each stronger than the last. In fact, the only moments that she ever showed any form of vulnerability were those very few seconds when Mariah slipped from the world of pleasure, into the realm of climax. It was only then that Landon was able to witness any evidence of a soul that was connected to a sensual and human being rather than simply a body that looked to have her physical needs met. But he knew that it didn't matter. He could fuck her brains out and she still would not have a strong emotional attachment to him. It just wasn't her nature.

In a way, he envied her disconnect to the world. She sailed into work everyday and played the game; she could be nice to customers while working on the insecurities of her coworkers. She didn't appear to care what anyone else in their apartment building thought of her and for that reason, most seemed to like Mariah. Perhaps, Landon considered, he should follow in her footsteps.

If only it were that easy.

He was in college and therefore, busy. That's why his arrangement with Mariah was ideal. It was convenient and gave him the balance he needed. He just had to remind himself that their time together was meaningless and therefore, entered her apartment with a goal in mind.

Weeks became months and months added up quickly. Soon his first year of college was complete and he found himself working at both a grocery store and restaurant. He hated both jobs, but tried to make the best of it. He barely saw Mariah during the summer because she spent her spare time in hot, sticky bars and he assumed, had many anonymous affairs.

It was only a few weeks into his second year of college when Mariah made a sudden reappearance in his life. She showed up at his door on a Friday night, wearing her uniform from the job Benjamin helped her get months earlier.

"Hey," He moved aside and noticed she was carrying a bottle of wine as she walked through the doorway. "Wow, you're seriously still working there?"

"Yes, I am." Her chocolate brown eyes glanced seductively over her shoulder and held out the bottle, while pointing toward the kitchen with her other hand. "I thought you might want some wine, can I pour you a glass?"

"Sure." Landon replied with some hesitation. It was a long time since they spent any time together. He closed the door and stalled between the couch and kitchen, unsure of what to do. Books and sheets were strewed all over the couch and his laptop sitting on the floor. He decided to turn it off, grab his schoolwork and move it to the next room. "I'm surprised to see you here. Where have you been all summer?"

As he sat everything on his dresser, Landon hesitated for a moment to look in the mirror. Mariah could be heard rattling around in the kitchen. Taking a deep breath, he returned to the living room. Mariah had two glasses sitting on the tattered coffee table that he found on a sidewalk and dragged home two weeks earlier. She continued to talk.

"... so I decided to stay for now and just see how it goes." She stopped and gave him a small smile while sipping her wine. Sitting on the other side of her, Landon merely nodded. "How about you? Did you have a fun summer?"

"Fun?" He gave a short laugh and ran his fingers through his hair. "Yeah, working two jobs was the most fun I could ask for."

"That's tough. I've done it too." She quietly commented and took a big gulp of wine. He hadn't touched his at all. She was engaged in the conversation, but at the same time, appeared preoccupied. Nervous? Nah.

"You do what you got to do." Landon replied in his usual relaxed manner and reached for his glass. He wasn't sure what to make of this approach, but decided to go along for the ride. It didn't matter, he was pretty certain of how their night would end. "I know that I'll be busy between now and when I graduate."

"And then? Plans?" Mariah continued to show some interest in their conversation, which was weird. She rarely asked about his... well, his anything. "Marketing is pretty impressive."

Landon shrugged. "I'm actually thinking of going to Europe for awhile... and yeah..." He felt awkward having this conversation and wasn't sure why. He didn't bother to give his usual explanation of wanting to explore life in another continent, the one he told classmates and friends. It felt unnecessary.

"Europe, wow!" Mariah finished off her first glass of wine and poured a second, more generous one. "Did I ever tell you that my mother is from Russia?"

Her question was awkward and she quickly followed it up with, "Northwestern, I think." She stuttered through her words and he was surprised to see Mariah in a self-conscious moment.

"Russia is supposed to be a beautiful country." Landon spoke evenly while watching Mariah carefully, as she stared down at her glass. "You *do* kind of have that Russian look."

"Oh well!" She looked up and rolled her eyes. "I don't like to think I look like my mother. I don't want to have anything in common with that woman."

"Oh yes, that's right. You have no emotional connection to your family, I keep forgetting." His words were meant to tease her and merely quoting what Mariah had abruptly told him in the past but this time, he could see something was different. Rather than show anger, she fell silent and abruptly took a quick swig from her glass. There was an awkward silence that was making the night suddenly feel weird and Landon wasn't sure what to say.

"My father almost died."

"What?" Landon was thrown by her words, the tenderness in her voice and suddenly felt a flash of heat overwhelm his body. "Your father almost died?"

"Yes." Mariah looked up and blinked back a tear that almost escaped her eye. She took in a deep breath. "Last night. He's had a heart attack."

Landon opened his mouth and froze. They never shared a tender moment and he wasn't sure if it felt normal to do so now, but he also felt compassion attempting to break through a dam in order to comfort her. "I'm sorry, Mariah. I didn't mean to make the joke about your family."

"It's fine." She finished her glass of wine and poured another one. "We weren't close, but it was still a shock when my step-mom emailed me."

"Again, I'm sorry," Landon heard his voice turn gentle, caring and he feared that he was either not showing enough comfort or too much. With Mariah, it was difficult to know where you stood and you sort of had to feel your way through a situation. However, he had never seen her this way before and didn't feel right not addressing it further.

"Are you okay?" His hand reached out and gently touched her shoulder. "Is there anything I can do?"

"No." She quickly shook her head and sat back with her wine, as if this conversation was about to end. "I'm fine. I just wanted you to know."

The rest of the night was surreal and although she briefly discussed her father's touch with death, Mariah hadn't gone into much detail about her relationship with her dad. He just let her talk and contributed a few words, but mainly listened. At one point, Landon suggested that perhaps she should slow down on the wine but his words were ignored.

Unlike any night they had spent together in the past, they didn't hook up. She left early.

After she was gone, Landon considered that maybe their relationship had changed. He saw a compassionate side of her that night and it confirmed that she chose to put an act on when they were usually together.

Was it fear? Was she scared to get close to anyone? Were things different now? Did he want things to be different now?

As it turned out, his thoughts and concerns were for nothing. The next time she dropped by, it was as if this conversation had never taken place. When Landon attempted to ask about her father's health update, she merely shrugged it off as if it wasn't a big deal, commenting how she had to change her email in order to get her 'crazy stepmother' off her ass. Rather than have a conversation and learn more about her, Mariah simply stated, "I'm not in a talking mood."

It was the last time he attempted to allow their affair to turn into something meaningful. Mariah never again revisited her emotional side with him. Things went back to the way they had been and he decided that it was perhaps for the best.

They met pretty regularly and many people in the building just assumed they were a couple: but they weren't. It was easier to let others believe as they wished rather than explain that they were, in fact, having a relationship that had not surpassed a physical level.

Benjamin was the only person who knew the truth. Regardless of his antics, the older Brit was very much a close friend to Landon and had warned him not to take Mariah too seriously.

"The lady is a man-eater and as long as you accept that this will never go any further than the bedroom, you'll be fine." He warned one afternoon after Landon expressed concern that perhaps he was somehow doing the wrong thing. "Just as long as you have no further expectations, I see no harm in it."

Landon agreed and decided that it didn't matter. In a few months, he would be finished with college and headed to Europe. Whether or not he'd return to Vancouver was still up for debate. Maybe it was for the best if he did not.

He had anticipated that perhaps Mariah would have some kind of an emotional reaction to him leaving when the time came, but he couldn't help but feel a tinge of disappointment when she appeared apathetic.

"You should go," She encouraged and for a moment, he actually thought she was going to add something meaningful at the end of her thought. Instead, Mariah showed no emotion. "There's nothing for you here."

Had he expected anything more?

Chapter twenty-six

Everything is built on a foundation. A plant is the result of a seed. Creativity grows out of an idea. Hope springs from faith. And for many people, a job or a loved one is what holds their world together while in others it's a dream that guides in the future. Removing that foundation can throw everything out of sync.

When Landon first told Mariah that he was leaving the country indefinitely, she didn't believe him. In fact, she made the assumption that he was simply all talk and perhaps he was attempting to impress her by speaking of his big plans in the future. But she underestimated Landon Owens. Had she spent more time getting to know him outside of the bedroom, chances are Mariah would've figured out that he always did exactly what he said he would do. This time was no exception.

Up until that point, everything had been going smoothly. There hadn't been any major bumps in the road for Mariah. It wasn't that her life was fantastic and exciting – far from it – but it was consistent. She was definitely in her comfort zone since moving to Vancouver, almost two years earlier. Now at the age of 21, she had a full-time job that bored her, lived in a cramped, little apartment that didn't inspire her to even decorate and had a few drinking buddies that she hit the clubs with on occasion. And when she didn't do any of those things and the urge hit, she would visit Landon.

It wasn't that she had necessarily taken him for granted during their time together. She had been very clear on the boundaries within their relationship and in her mind, it was a perfect fit for both of them. Landon was busy, had little time to socialize and clearly found pleasure in her company. He was obviously very attracted to her and had ravished her body on a pretty regular basis, but he knew where things stood with them. It wasn't meant to be more than a physical, fun relationship that suited them both at this phase in their lives. After all, wasn't that what most men wanted? Sex with no strings attached?

Mariah sometimes worried that she was incapable of caring for a man. It even crossed her mind that perhaps she was a lesbian because she had no desire to build an emotional relationship with any of the men that she slept with but after a drunken make out session with another girl one night, it became pretty clear that she wasn't gay either. She desired men: she just didn't want a commitment.

One man she had a fling with pointed out that this didn't indicate anything was wrong with her, it simply meant that she was a progressive thinker who knew what she wanted. He suggested that she questioned her own judgment because of the restricted ideas about what women should want rather than what they actually do. Society, he claimed, sent a strong message that women were supposed to want to fall in love, get married, have babies and anything outside those objectives were questioned. That gave Mariah some peace of mind. At least there was nothing wrong with her.

Then again, would it be so shocking if she were screwed up? She grew up in an atypical home. Although Mariah was now hearing stories that made her realize that she was not the only one with this experience, she still believed that her childhood was stranger than most. Not that she shared the details of her transgender brother, mail order bride mother or the fact that as a teenage woman, she became a mortal vampire. The latter was a fact that she only shared with people in her building because they shared this status. It was odd that all the things that made her life's story different from most that this was the one thing that she had in common with people in her life.

Of course, there was one theme in her life and that was that people always left. So, in a way, it wasn't surprising that the one person she had some kind of connection to in Vancouver would move away. That's what people do, right? In a way, it made her relieved that she never had a real relationship with him because where would that leave her now? She would be one of those heartbroken women that she saw crying on television (the ones she rolled her eyes at for being weak) and really, who needed that headache?

Slightly pretentious, Mariah gave herself credit for making the right decision and thought it would be as simple as that; she would move on. Maybe there was another man who would move into the building and become her new 'Landon'. It was possible, right?

But things didn't work out quite as she hoped and although she denied it, Mariah's world began to come apart. Despite the fact that she didn't want to recognize that Landon had been the foundation for any consistency in her life, he truly was and his departure created an unwelcome change of pace that threw her out of the comfort zone. Plus the fact that he hadn't bothered to keep in contact with her was slightly unnerving. He refused to join the Facebook world and so only could be found through email. However, he apparently was too busy with his new life and hanging out with Eurotrash to reply to her emails.

This assumption made her angry. It wasn't a sudden thing, but a slow growing bitterness that greatly affected her attitude both at work and socially. Although she had long been viewed as having a very professional attitude, both in and out of work, the facade she had created as a teenager who wanted to stand out from the crowd, was no longer working for her. Now it caused her to blend in with everyone else and no longer felt right and Mariah found that ripping it away was a very liberating move. Not that she would be a total idiot either, but she wouldn't be as inclined to be one of the sheep that she meekly followed along and played the game.

It started with her becoming more vocal. When Mariah had an opinion at work, she shared it with her boss and coworkers. This didn't make her popular and Mariah could see the look of bewilderment in their eyes. If anything, this only irritated her more and often caused her to make even more comments that were deemed unpleasant. At one point, she was taken aside by Alexandra and asked if anything was wrong.

"What do you mean?" Mariah felt her defenses rise like a smoke that was filling up the entire room around them. They were, of course, in the manager's office with the door closed. "I just wanted to express my view in our early morning meeting. I think that these new vitamins for weight loss are a complete hoax. If we want to lie to the customers and tell them otherwise, that's fine, but can we at least are honest with us."

"Mariah, I don't understand why you assume they are a hoax. Are you suggesting that this company would lie to their customers?" Alexandra tilted her head and almost looked intrigued by Mariah's ideas. "I do understand why you might be suspicious if this was a competitor making such claims, but I'm curious as to why you would assume that this particular store would deceive people?"

"I don't know if deceive is the word I would use," Mariah wrinkled her nose; her eyes cast a look in the upper, left hand corner of the room. "I just think it's misleading to make it sound as if people can eat whatever they want and just pop a pill and not gain weight. That doesn't even make sense and in fact, if it were true, wouldn't it suggest that maybe there was something perhaps, unhealthy about the pill for it to have such a drastic effect?"

"I do understand your concern, Mariah." Alexandra said, her posture suddenly became more erect. "And you know, I appreciate that you care about our customers enough to bring up this issue. And you are right, if we were suggesting such a thing, it would be suspicious, right?" She waited for Mariah to nod before continuing. "What we are saying is that it could be *part* of their healthy lifestyle. So, exercise is important, of course and eating right, but this pill will enhance the entire lifestyle choice and help move things along a little faster. We aren't trying to give the perception that it's the miracle pill, but simply part of a system that works."

"But wouldn't just eating right and exercise work?" Mariah injected. "Without the pill?"

"I suppose, to a certain degree that is true," Alexandra folded her hands together and calmly went on to explain to Mariah. "I just feel that this pill helps to give the metabolism a boost, especially for people who are having trouble losing weight for whatever reason. You're still quite young and slender so it might not be something you completely understand, but sometimes women who are older or say have had children, may find it a challenge to get off those extra pounds. These pills just help things and if a customer inquires about them, you simply make sure that you don't say they will work on their own, but as part of their routine, that includes exercise and eating right."

"Okay." Mariah smiled and agreed. She still felt the pills, like many in their shop, were a crock of shit, but was growing tired of this conversation and wanted to get out on the floor again and finish rearranging a shelf she had started earlier that day. "I understand."

"That's fantastic." Alexandra enthusiastically replied. "I'm happy to hear that. Now, I wanted to talk to you about something else. We're opening a new store in Burnaby, as you know and I guess Marianne has decided to relocate since it will be closer to home. So if anyone comes in looking for a job and you get a good feeling about them, would you let me know?"

Slightly disappointed that the coworker that Mariah found tolerable was leaving, she was sincere when expressing her regret over this upcoming change. Why couldn't Jody leave? Although the two managed to work together, they were hardly friends and regardless of what Landon suggested, it certainly wasn't because they were a lot alike. He insisted that this was the real reason they hated one another but Mariah was quite certain that one of the few things her and Jody would agree on, was the fact that they couldn't be more different.

Things had been pretty consistent since her move to Vancouver and suddenly her horizons were changing in ways that made her uncomfortable. First Landon left in September, now Marianne was about to go to a new store in late November. The year was coming to a disappointing close. Then again, was it?

With every door closed, there is said to be a window open in its place. Perhaps Marianne was leaving, but it highlighted an opportunity for someone else to fill her position and it was Mariah's mission to find someone cool.

As it turns out, this didn't take long.

He was a fitness instructor named Paul that she hooked up with after the bar one night. He was tall, muscular build and had a healthy glow to his face, making him a candidate that would stand out to Alexandra. After all, she talked about how their line of vitamins made people 'glow' and he was already trained in a corresponding line of work, so it would be perfect. His only concern was that Energy Planet Vancouver's main focus tended to be yoga, something he was not trained in.

"Fake it." Mariah brushed off his concerns while they discussed it one night on the phone. She had managed to convince Alexandra to give him an interview and wanted to let him know the news. She let out a short, mirthless laugh. "Do you seriously think I take yoga three times a week, like I tell them?"

"Well, you did seem very flexible on the night we were together." Paul teased in his deep, husky voice. He was so incredibly sexy. She recalled his long, lean body in her bed, his penetrating blue eyes and the tattoos across his chest. "So that's something."

"Yes, it is," Mariah smiled, convinced that she would enjoy working with Paul. In fact, she may be able to be less frustrated with her nemesis Jody, with this guy around. Maybe that was the problem with her workplace, she decided, too much estrogen and no men.

"Thanks in advance because I need another part time job and if Alexandra asks how we know one another?"

"We take a yoga class together."

They both laughed and hung up.

He was hired, but wasn't scheduled to start till after Marianne left, something that was surprising to even Jody, who insisted that Christmas was coming up so they needed the extra help. Training in December would be difficult.

"Then again," Jody stood beside Mariah while yanking up her bra strap, "If he already studied fitness and nutrition, plus works at a gym, I guess he probably knows as much as we do."

"Probably more." Mariah snickered to herself. She barely knew a thing and had merely adopted things she heard both Jody and Marianne say to customers, as opposed to studying the books she was given upon starting the job, almost two years earlier.

"Yes, he would study things in more depth."

"Plus, how many people will be doing their Christmas shopping here?" Mariah spoke honestly. "Other than buying yoga packages, it's not like they will be buying vitamins for their friends and family for stocking stuffers."

"You'd be surprised." Jody insisted. "I would be quite happy with anything from our store for a Christmas gift."

"Oh yeah, I would take a yoga mat over a bottle of perfume any day." Mariah quipped and she noted that Jody almost appeared to be grinning. Maybe she was only playing the game too, Mariah decided.

Chapter twenty-seven

Fear is a sneaky emotion. It eases into our hearts and slithers its way into our thoughts, convincing us that we are in danger if we go out of our comfort zone, if we dare to step across the line of familiarity. It wears a mask that deceives us into believing that we're psychics that can predict the future: and it's a future where everything goes wrong, we always miss the bus and our loved ones die a brutal death.

Well, maybe sometimes…

Most of the time, however, fears simply seeps into our consciousness and small, minor insecurities trickle into our thoughts until one day we wake up and find that they have collapsed and forced us to make the move, we originally were scared to do in the first place.

Mariah knew it was time to leave Energy Planet Vancouver. Everything was becoming too routine, too predictable and the company's 'team building activities' were starting to feel redundant. Was it realistic to make your staff more enthused about your brand, by forcing them to play childish games in order to build morale? Besides their 'team' only consisted of three people, soon to be four. Of course, Mariah's friend Paul was hired, but so far, hadn't been given a start date. It was kind of senseless, but when Mariah attempted to point this out to Alexandra, even repeating Jody's point on the holidays coming up, it seemed to fall on deaf ears.

"Common sense just isn't so common anymore, did you not know that?" Benjamin observed after hearing Mariah's complaints on the subject. The two were sitting in the lounge on a rainy, Saturday afternoon, each drinking a cup of coffee that she had run across the street to get to them. They were doing this a great deal lately, especially since Landon left for Europe. Mariah hadn't heard from him as of yet and was a little disappointed when Benjamin reported the opposite. She didn't confess her sadness.

Glancing toward the nearby window, Mariah didn't reply at first. Her thoughts, a million miles away until suddenly shaking her head, as if it were an Etch a Sketch that would go back to a blank page of thoughts.

"I suppose," She finally returned to their conversation and took a sip of her coffee. It was so delicious and fresh, something she had a new appreciation for since gaining her vampire senses. She hadn't noticed things like bitter or cheap coffee in the past but now was able to see the distinction. In some ways it set her up for a letdown, while in others, it was like a perfection detector. "I just feel like Energy Planet has some fucked up ideas."

"Do tell." Benjamin tilted his head. He appeared relaxed and calm, as always, curious about her every word.

"Well, first of all we are pushing vitamins and crap that people don't need."

"Yes, well, I do believe that is the nature of the beast, is it not?" He raised his eyebrows; a humored smile perched on his lips. "Retail wouldn't exist if it were not for pushing products we simply don't need."

"True," Mariah said. "You do have a point there, Benjamin. But it's not just that, the entire atmosphere is just fucking weird."

"Says the girl who used to work in a strip bar." He quipped under his breath, knowing that Mariah could easily hear him. For that, he received a devil's glare and a sanctimonious grin.

"I'll have you know that I learned a great deal about the real world while working at that strip bar," Mariah spoke slowly, enunciating each of her words carefully as if to make sure she got her point across. "It's the one industry that I guarantee that people show their true colors. There's no ridiculous team building activities like singing songs, while dancing around like a moron before the place opens up every day. We don't volunteer – sorry," Mariah hesitated and put her hand up and swiped it through the air as if to indicate the words were floating above her head.

"Volunten-TOLD to 'do great things for our community' like cleaning up fucking dog shit in the park."

Benjamin remained stoic, nodding his head in understanding. The urge to laugh looked like it was teasing his lips, but he successfully fought it off. "Well, I dare say that watching some little trollop with a metal stake in hand, stumbling through the park in her stilettos would be highly entertaining, and I'm a little confused about why Alexandra has you running around cleaning up shit in the park. And furthermore," He leaned forward with a disturbed look on his face. "Are you sure it's dog shit? Downtown Eastside? One just never knows."

Settling back in his chair, he suppressed a grin and took another drink of his coffee. Mariah let out a short laugh and nodded.

"You got me there, Benjamin. I'd prefer not to think about it."

"So when is this little collecting activity to take place and will you be wearing your lovely uniforms and name tags on that particular day?"

"Probably. We're only doing it to create a positive image about our company." Mariah attempted to analyze the situation from a cynical point of view. "And it's company wide, so it's people from all our stores."

"I'm surprised considering your store is usually open. Wouldn't that be a bit discouraging for customers who are dying to get in and learn about the latest yoga retreat?" Benjamin commented thoughtfully. "I would think that *someone* has to mind the store?"

"No, well, apparently we have put signs up for days in advance, posting it all over social media and having an ad in the paper telling the world of the good deed we are doing and thanking them in advance for their patience, and encouraging them to shop online for that day only or get in on one of our customer appreciation specials when we reopen the next day." Mariah pushed a piece of flaxen hair behind her ear pursed her lips as she gave a condescending nod. "But it's just for the good of the community. Nothing more than that. We simply feel that it is more important than sales."

"Oh, I see," Benjamin showed no reaction, but gave a simple nod. "Well, I'm happy that your company is so concerned about the community that supports them. I'm sure they are counting on others to feel the same way."

"It's not just that Benjamin, it's everything." Mariah sighed, her finger rolling over the lid of her coffee cup. "I just feel like I'm being brainwashed to believe that this shit they sell works, when I've done research online and it actually doesn't. Not that I ever thought there was a magic pill for weight loss or to improve your memory. I'm not saying that all natural stuff is bullshit, but it seems like the stuff we sell is just overpriced copies of products you can get at any health food store, for less money. I just feel very uncomfortable with the whole idea."

"And you're bored, maybe?" Benjamin raised his eyebrows. "Perhaps you need a change? Maybe even a promotion."

"I don't know if I want to be promoted in this company." Mariah bluntly replied. "The problem is that I don't know where I would like to be at all."

"Well, I do believe that is a common dilemma of you twentysomethings? Not that this is anything new," Benjamin said while making a face. "I mean, look at Landon. He didn't know what he wanted to do, where he wanted to work or even where he prefers to live. So he went and buggered off on us, went to Europe to raise some hell and see where it finds him."

Mariah wasn't sure what to say. She didn't want to admit that he hadn't contacted her since leaving, even though Benjamin had already made it obvious that Landon had communicated with him several times. She simply nodded and said, "Yes."

"Maybe you should do the same, take off and discover new lands?"

"No thanks, at least, not right now." Mariah finished her coffee and sat the cup down on a nearby table. "I've already moved enough for awhile. It's stressful and expensive. As it is, I barely cover my bills."

"Well, I would say you should branch out and see what is out there." He suggested. "Eventually you will find your path."

"True."

"And eventually, Landon will find his too." Benjamin appeared to be needling at her and she wasn't fond of it. She ignored this remark and made an excuse to leave. Chances were good, she could only avoid talking about Landon for so long, especially when Benjamin circled the topic on more than one occasion. What more could she say? He left. He was really gone. They were over. Hadn't she claimed to not get tied down with feelings?

She did miss him though. It was true, you don't know what you got till it's gone. It wasn't that she was in love with him or any of that nonsense; it was more a thing where she missed his company. And not just the company between the sheets, but his presence, his calm, soothing voice and knowing he would be around if she ever needed anything. Had she taken this for granted? It would appear that he hadn't felt the same way, since he hadn't reached out to her in weeks. Maybe it was for the better.

Moving forward, she focused on trying to find a new job, but alas, nothing grabbed her attention. She made some half-hearted attempts to get employment at a local radio station that sounded fun, but they didn't even acknowledge her resume. She looked into other companies that sounded interesting, but the only one that replied was another clothing store, but it was only offering a part-time position (regardless of what it said in the ad) and wasn't interested in paying more than minimum wage. Mariah was barely squeaking by as it was and she was making reasonable money.

Of course, her boredom caused her to stop looking all together and once Paul started to work at Energy Planet Vancouver, she felt as though she had a partner in crime and started to enjoy her work again.

Again? Had she ever really enjoyed it?

The holiday season came and went, followed by the spring and her 22nd birthday. It wasn't very eventful and ended up drinking a lot of wine with Paul before they had some lame sex. He attempted to make up for his lackluster performance in other ways, but by then, Mariah was starting to feel very lightheaded from the wine and the next morning, she simply wasn't in the mood. Partially cause she felt a little ill, but mostly because recollections of the previous night turned her off.

Work was slightly awkward after that, but Paul continually insisted that he would 'make it up to her' but she brushed it off and insisted that it was probably best that they don't date while at the same employer. She claimed to be looking for another job and they could pick things up after she found one. He acknowledged that it made sense.

Much to her surprise, Jody questioned her about Paul one day. Assuming that her coworker was trying to pick him up, Mariah jumped into the conversation with both feet and thought that such a situation may actually help to get him off his interest in dating her. Unfortunately, this wasn't the case.

"I don't trust him." Jody stunned Mariah with her comment. The two were working alone on a quiet Tuesday afternoon, cleaning and restocking shelves. "I know he's a friend of yours so I shouldn't be saying anything, but I think he stole some of my sales the other day."

"What?" Mariah halted what she was doing and faced Jody. "Why would you say that?"

"I was helping two customers for a long time and I noticed he was kind of bombing with everyone. Anyway, I couldn't ring in one particular lady when she was ready to leave so he offered to do it for me. I thought I could trust him to put the sale under my number, but I don't think he did," She spoke earnestly and Mariah could automatically tell that she wasn't lying. "I checked with Alexandra and she said that I didn't get a sale for around that time."

"What?" Mariah shook her head and began to rack her brain. Hadn't her sales been kind of low for that season? Hadn't she usually done well in the spring when customers were attempting to lose weight and get healthy for the summer months? "I hope you're wrong."

"I hope I'm wrong too." Jody admitted. "But I don't think I am. Just please don't tell him, but keep an eye out. You know, just in case he is doing something shady"

Mariah didn't like the sounds of this at all. If there was one thing she hated, it was the thought of anyone taking away from her well-deserved cash. She worked hard and struggled with her finances.

Although Jody also told her that Alexandra was watching things around the shop very carefully, Mariah doubted that she would be able to prove he was stealing sales even if she wanted to do such a thing. It got pretty busy sometimes and it was simply too difficult to watch both her coworkers and help customers, not to mention making sure that their products weren't stolen.

She finally gave into Paul's advances and allowed him to take her on another date on a long weekend where she had no other plans. He promised to cook her dinner and show her a wonderful time and although she was still weary of him, she reluctantly agreed, figuring that it was easier to just let her suspicions go. Life was too short for that.

Unfortunately, they had a wonderful night. The food was excellent and prepared with care. The wine, bottle after bottle, was delightful and later that night, he rocked her world – repeatedly, until she was completely exhausted.

So why was this unfortunate? It ended up causing a lot of trouble.

Chapter twenty-eight

People often see boredom as a harmless state, possibly a trademark of the lazy that simply have no interest in doing anything. In fact, boredom sometimes indicates that we have fallen into a rut and even a depressive state that doesn't encourage change. The unfortunate side is that people see this as a harmless, normal, reaction to life and merely a comfort zone that is inevitable. But is it?

Mariah Nichols could only dust so many shelves before wondering what the hell she was doing in Energy Planet Vancouver. The store was a joke. She wasn't selling products, but an image to a bunch of ego driven clientele. Customers would come in and purchase their overpriced yoga mats in 'soothing blue' or 'love forever pink' as if the price they paid was somehow indicating a stronger dedication to spirituality.

Spring rolled into summer and her job grew more tiring. Most customers flocked to the store in the winter, in hopes that the right combination of supplements would somehow give them a bikini-ready body by the summer. June and July were known to be the boring months when everyone was too busy either vacationing or spending time outdoors, rather than stopping by Energy Planet Vancouver. In fact, it almost seemed that their only customers were people wandering in to see if they sold fruit smoothies (why weren't they doing this?) or looking to replenish the vitamins they were already taking.

Marianne had long ago relocated to another store and was now the manager. Meanwhile, Jody continued to act as though she was the boss at their store, something Mariah had grown used to and continued to ignore. Still the two women worked in harmony and their sales tended to be neck and neck. Any mention of Paul possibly stealing their sales was somehow forgotten over the months, after he helped Jody get a discounted rate at the gym he worked at four days a week.

Mariah sensed that Jody may have a crush on Paul and having grown tired of their fling, attempted to encourage the buxom brunette to pursue the newest employee, but she seemed reluctant.

"I thought you and Paul had something going on?" Jody questioned suspiciously when the topic was first brought up. "He said something about the two of you dating, at one time."

Fucking idiot. I told him not to say anything about that at work.

"Yes, we did have a couple of dates at one time," Mariah attempted to brush the whole thing aside as if they merely went out for a glass of wine and fine dining, as opposed to having lackluster sex. She had attempted to make him her new Landon, but unfortunately, he didn't come close. In the future, it would make more sense to just stick with other vampires if she wanted to recreate that experience again. "He just wasn't for me. He was sweet, very polite and kind, but I just saw him more like a... brother. You know, I just wasn't very attracted to him."

... Well, at least, not anymore.

Jody briefly played around with the idea, but didn't feel she should date a coworker, regardless of how much Mariah attempted to play up his athletic physique or his rich, blue eyes. She even hinted to Paul that she thought Jody had a crush on him, hoping to get his motor running but it didn't appear to be working. Mariah figured that since she was showing him less attention lately, that he would be intrigued by the attractive, busty brunette – at least, it appeared that everyone else was, so why not? Plus, it would get him off her track, making work less awkward.

Not that they had many shift together anymore. Paul worked most evenings, while Mariah was in during the day. If they worked a few hours together a week, it was rare and that suited her just fine. She felt that he was clingy and trying much too hard to get her attention. He usually managed to do just that for a short amount of time before she grew bored again. She was actually starting to wonder if he was physically exerting himself at the gym because his performance in the bedroom was often lacking.

But he continued to try to impress Mariah and sometimes, she gave in and they spent some time together. It wasn't until around mid-June that he found a way to captivate her to a much larger degree.

Perhaps it was in part because her day job bored her so much; maybe it was just a 'dry' summer for Mariah but when Paul started to show her affection in public, things took a stimulating turn. And it started out innocently, but picked up very quickly.

He thought it would be romantic to have a picnic in one of the city's less busy parks. Mariah thought the idea was lame, but quickly felt guilty for not appreciating the gesture and went along with it. They shared a fruit and cheese platter, talked about work and drank some carefully hidden wine. It was a very simple afternoon that seemed harmless enough, but in retrospect, Mariah considered that perhaps the combination of the hot temperatures and wine possibly created such a rousing atmosphere. Then again, maybe it was the gentle breezes that softly rustled the light material of her sundress, over her thighs and discovered dewy skin that lie beneath. Maybe it was the warm sunlight, as it caressed her shoulders, down her body and into the ample cleavage between her breasts. Perhaps it was Paul sitting so close to her, his words smooth as honey and she could feel his breath sending hot waves down her neck and into her libido.

His hand touched her arm and softly ran up and down, barely grazing the sensitive skin inside her arm, but managing to alert her senses. From behind her Ray-Ban sunglasses, her eyes glanced around to happily notice people were nowhere near and possibly not even paying attention to their presence. His hand continued to move, this time to her thigh, showing no signs of shyness as his fingers massaged her legs, people still completely unaware, all involved in their own activities and Mariah felt herself squirm slightly as his hand continued to move over the material of her dress and sink into the valley between her legs. She showed no reaction in her face – at least, not from what the world could see – but her hips did move up and down, ever so slightly and her thighs squeezed together in pleasure. It didn't take long before his fingers slowly brought her to those sweet sensations that her body begged for on a regular basis.

That's how it got started.

Every day afterward, the two attempted to find public places to get intimate. The possibility of being caught have only increased the intensity of each encounter, causing Mariah to have a much more intense reaction each time. They did it everywhere – parks, public bathrooms, in the water at the beach, in his car, at the gym, one time they even managed on an empty SkyTrain – each time, it was a little more exciting. Mariah assumed that part of the reason it turned her on so much was due to the mad race between orgasm and being caught.

Unfortunately, with each risk, the greater the next one had to be in order to continue with the original 'high' and excitement of the first time around. In fact, it was the only time she could tolerate any kind of physical contact with Paul. After all, she was already living a very lackluster life; she didn't need a monotonous boyfriend on the side.

It was because Jody went on vacation just before the July 1st weekend and that Alexandra had the day off that Mariah and Paul were even put in the position of working alone together, in the first place. Neither had thought anything about it and both took their job seriously enough to not do anything to put it in jeopardy.

Well kind of, anyway…

The July 1st holiday wasn't busy at Energy Planet Vancouver and the workday was going slowly. After doing everything on Alexandra's list before the day was halfway over, Paul went searching in a drawer near the cash to see if there was any tape, in order to fix a sign that Mariah had accidentally knocked down earlier that day.

"Why do we keep these samples in here?" He held up a handful of individually wrapped pills that could've been mistaken for condoms from the other side of the room. Fortunately, the pair was in the store alone.

"Did you even look to see what they were?" Mariah felt a smile erupt on her face. "They are the herbal equivalent of Viagra. I don't know about you, but I don't particularly feel comfortable asking our customers if they want a free sample of boner pills."

Paul laughed as he studied the packaging and nodded at the same time. "Okay, you got me there." He shook his head. "But I'm assuming we have them in case someone wants to know if they work? Not that I can see anyone actually asking."

"We have them on the shelf." Mariah pointed over her left shoulder and slowly made her way to the cash register. "People could ask. I mean, they just ask about everything else around here."

"I never have anyone ask me weird questions." Paul made a face and removed one of the packets from the elastic band that the collection was gathered in. "And I somehow can't see someone asking us if these things actually work. I mean, really? And what would we say if they did?"

"You're in luck? We happen to have some free samples you can take home and try." Mariah quipped and began to laugh.

"Yes," Paul went on with the joke. "And please, please take them home before trying them.."

His words drifted off and Mariah's mind started to wander. They were in the store alone. No customers had been by in over an hour. The beautiful sunny weather and various celebrations around town were much more appealing than overpriced supplements and yoga packages. There was nothing more to do...

Their eyes met and Paul's face grew serious. Waving the foiled wrapped around, he titled his head slightly and looked into her eyes. "Do you think this shit actually works?"

"I don't know." Mariah admitted and let out a quick laugh. "I just assumed nothing in here works."

"What? You've worked here for..." His voice drifted off and he shook his head. "Never mind. But I can see how you would be skeptical of this one." He held up the package. "But you know, since we do work here, it is only right that we try the product to make sure it does do what it says it will."

"You seriously are going to take that pill?" Mariah inquired as he began to rip open the package. "You could have an erection for days or a heart attack. You really don't know what's in there."

Paul shrugged with no concern in his eyes. Grabbing his bottle of water, he tossed the little, blue pill in his mouth and followed it with a gulp of water. "I guess we will find out."

"We're at work." Mariah said and immediately felt like an idiot. Was *she* really in the position to suddenly be a prude?

"Never stopped you anywhere else." Paul shook his head and leaned against the counter. "So what? We aren't busy, nothing is going on here and chances are, it is a sugar pill of some kind." He shrugged. "I don't see the big deal."

Mariah considered his words. She *was* pretty bored, so what could it hurt? Chances were good, the pill was nothing to be worried about anyway and probably just would cause Paul's heart to race, if anything. She grabbed one of the packets and read the ingredients. She didn't recognize anything.

"I don't think it'll do a thing." She said skeptically and sauntered off.

She was very wrong.

Fifteen minutes later, the doors were abruptly locked and the two were having sex on top of a box of clothes in the stock room. Mariah's original dismissal of the product was proven wrong and Paul's usual lackluster performance was enhanced to what she considered to be, a Landon Owens' level of satisfaction. The only thought that ran through her head in the next 30 minutes was how she would have to grab a few more samples on their way out that day.

Unfortunately, the idea completely escaped her as she left the store later, after they 'officially' closed, but both commenting how they would just grab the samples the next day, during their shift.

That didn't happen.

Mariah was quickly ushered into Alexandra's office the next morning and promptly fired. At first, she thought it was because they had the door locked for an extended period of time, assuming someone complained and as she quickly gathered an excuse to use for doing such a thing, that is when the truth came out. Alexandra knew they had sex in the stockroom.

Mariah was stunned. Completely lost for words, she instead remained silent and considered if there was any possible way to get out of this mess. There wasn't one.

"I can't believe you would do such a thing!" Alexandra shook her head. "I thought so highly of you as an employee, you were doing so well and I thought I could trust you, but this..." She turned her laptop around to show Mariah a gritty black and white image of Paul fucking her on a box of Energy Planet Vancouver yoga mats. Mariah thought it was the 'Soothing blue' item.

"I..I don't know what to say." Mariah spoke honestly. "Paul decided to try some of the erectile dysfunction pills for fun and..." There was simply no good way to end that sentence when dealing with your boss. She was caught with her hands in the cookie jar and there was no denying it.

In the end it didn't matter, though. This was a theme that would follow her through the next 5 years of her life. No job, man or friendship would be consistent. Mariah Nichols was about to burn a lot of bridges and it hadn't occurred to her that her actions might matter one day. It hadn't even crossed her mind.

Chapter twenty-nine

T ime affects everyone differently. Some people mellow over the years, taking in all life's harsh lessons, choosing to use them on a path of personal growth. Others get trapped in time, neither progressing nor regressing, but stuck on repeat, like a song that never ends. Others still choose a lonely path of bitterness and resentment, preferring to see the negative and unpleasant sides of life.

To a degree, Mariah Nichols did all of these things.

Where she mellowed out over the next 5 years and lost some of her original intensity, there was still an anger that sizzled beneath the surface, a slight glow inside her chocolate brown eyes. She grew more confident in herself, no longer the unsure, teenage woman that had sought her older brother's approval; in fact, in her mind, those days were long past and buried. Like a warrior, she focused forward and never allowed herself the luxury of thinking about the past.

If she gave herself the opportunity, Mariah would've considered that her life was actually quite dull. Her goals were reachable, usually involving the latest sexual conquest or winning over the human resource department at yet another job, where she would eventually find herself fired or quitting under dramatic circumstances. Life was about living in the moment and not feeling entrapped by other people's expectations. She would not marry. She would never have children. She would not feel obligated to become another one of society's sheep, never questioning life or why it was necessary to be confined by ridiculous rules in order to 'fit in' and be accepted.

And this is where she got in trouble. Mariah felt a constant need to express herself and not being allowed to do so whenever she felt, was an unjust reaction from a society that feared the truth. They didn't want to hear what she had to say because they were afraid and their fears were crippling her into silence. It angered her and rather than succumb to an acceptable level of silence, she instead would impulsively rebel and as Benjamin often referred to as Mariah 'showing her fangs'.

"I think that's a bit of an exaggeration." Mariah countered on one such occasion, days after being fired from another receptionist position at a downtown office that was probably a bit too conservative for her in the first place. It was late on a dreary Friday afternoon, a particularly chilly June day and she had spent the latter part of the afternoon trying to find an office where her latest interview was to take place. Showing up late and cordially attempting to explain to a young Chinese lady that their office was a bit difficult to locate, she was met by a stern and unkind reaction. That set an unpleasant scene in motion.

"Oh really, so do tell more about this interview today." Benjamin spoke evenly, giving her his full attention with a stoic expression. "Do you think you got the job?"

Mariah bit back her frustration, completely aware that he was baiting her. She refused to let him know that she had any responsibility in this latest fiasco, but in truth, Mariah had been late heading out and although she had got lost while attempting to find the sketchy little office in the Chinatown area, it wasn't as if she would ever consider this particular job. She felt it was the home of a shady operation and had she even been desperate, chances were good that the stern Chinese lady wouldn't have considered the possibility for a second. Her narrow eyes had searched Mariah's face as if she were staring at the devil, her bluntly cut bangs only managed to put more emphasize on her flat nose and oily, uneven complexion. Hardly an attractive woman, she didn't say a word, Mariah attempted to explain her reason for being late.

When the expressionless woman finally did say something, it was curt and to the point. "You will not do." She immediately turned and started to walk away. However, Mariah was someone who considered this to be disrespectful and wasn't about to be dismissed so easily.

"Hey, wait the fuck up," Mariah had pointedly commented. The woman who had been so cold only moments before, was quick to swing around, her eyes expanding in size while fear seemed to flow through them. Her lips parted and she suddenly flourished into a moderately attractive lady in front of Mariah's eyes. "I was five minutes late and you had zero idea of my credentials and you automatically dismiss me like I'm a child. That might work with some people, but that sure as hell not working with me."

The lady appeared defenseless when faced with Mariah. She hovered over the delicate Asian woman, who wore a long, unflattering skirt that buttoned down the front and a thin, white mock turtleneck that covered her thin figure.

"I.. I do beg your pardon." The Chinese lady spoke slowly, then as if in fear that she would not be understood, she spoke slightly faster. "I do not understand." She suddenly turned in a frail young woman, barely able to communicate in English. Mariah considered that her English seemed quite sufficient only moments before and had only fallen in the last few minutes.

"You don't understand?" Mariah spoke in a slow, patronizing voice and slowly inched closer to the lady, who continued to appear afraid. "Well, let me spell it out to you. I don't want your fucking job. I don't want to work in some shady, dirty little office that probably has a bunch of illegal immigrants hiding upstairs, making fake licenses and Gucci bags, nor do I want to answer the phones for some rub n' tug while a bunch of under aged whores jerk off older men. No, I do not want your job and I do not want to work for you."

"However," Mariah continued and moved closer to the fearful woman who seemed to ease away from the angry woman that confronted her. "You are not going to dismiss me at the door, just because I don't look the way you thought I would or because I was five fucking minutes late. You are not going to show disrespect toward me for no valid reason other than your own narrow-minded views or assumptions. You may pull that crap on other people, but you aren't doing it to me."

Noting the stunned silence in the Chinese lady's face, Mariah gave her one final glare before turning on her heels and heading for the door. Now, as she sat across from Benjamin, she recalled her reaction to the situation with some satisfaction.

"It wasn't for me." Mariah spoke honestly, with no signs of frustration or anger in her voice. "It wasn't a good spot."

"What do you mean? Where was this spot, exactly?" Benjamin stuck his lips out in a duck expression and Mariah made a point of avoiding his eyes.

"It was in the downtown area, actually." She took in a deep breath before continuing. "It was in the Chinatown and to be honest, I thought it kind of smelled of illegal activity."

"Hmm, well, there is a lot of that around these parts," Benjamin gave her comments some consideration and seemed to back down from his original taunting. "Yes, I do believe that if you saw it as a shady area, you were perhaps right to not get involved in such an operation. I certainly don't want to see you in the news some evening after multiple arrests are made or anything of the like. Mind you, with your vampire senses, you would most likely be alerted to any shady activities before it ever came to that anyway."

"Hopefully." Mariah didn't feel compelled to get into any more detail. Since getting fired from her latest job, she felt completely drained and uninterested in looking for work, so she started to apply to everything she could locate on Craigslist and figured that eventually, something would work out for her. She ended up finding more dead ends than potential employers. "Maybe it is time I move on again."

Hearing herself say the words that had often crossed her mind felt much differently than when they were merely floating through her head. There was something more permanent about them now and she hoped it was something she wouldn't regret confessing. "I've considered that I've unfortunately burned a few bridges since moving to Vancouver and now, I'm not so certain that there's a lot here for me."

"Do you think?" Benjamin once again made his duck lips expression and nodded his head. "You've been here for a few years, have you not? Maybe a fresh, new start in another town would be to your benefit?"

"Perhaps." Mariah began to nod as her mind made a rare visit to the past and she saw the faces that were part of her life in recent years. Some she recalled fondly while others; she could barely remember their names. A grin of satisfaction captured her lips.

"I do believe that a fresh start in a new city would give you a much greater chance for employment, perhaps do some research where the greatest vacancies now sit and maybe it would give you a chance to restart your personal life, wouldn't that be exciting?"

"It would." Mariah was finding herself intrigued with the idea and continued to nod. After all, she was now 27 and well, she couldn't waste her best years in Vancouver. Not that it had been a terrible place, but it was quickly becoming a series of 'been there, done that' and she found it to be boring and a bit depressing.

"And I suppose, you could become whomever you pleased. Tell people the stories that best suit you, without any repercussions. No one would be the wiser of your past affairs or jobs you were let go from, it would be a fresh new start with no mistakes made or regrets created." He paused for a moment. "In fact, I'm a little jealous."

"Of me?" Mariah grinned with a sense of satisfaction. "Why would you ever be jealous of me?"

"Oh, I don't know." Benjamin mimicked her body language. "I guess because I have lived in Vancouver over ten years now and Olivia really enjoys the climate here, so we decided to stick around. But in my younger days, I was all over the world, searching for excitements with stars in my eyes. Sometimes I miss those days."

"You can still travel around with stars in your eyes," Mariah gently reminded him. "Just because you are older doesn't mean you have to stop dreaming."

His reaction was nothing more than a smile and that is when Mariah felt her heart sink. This was clearly a message he wanted to reflect back to her.

"Indeed." He nodded his head in slow motion. "Indeed, one should never stop dreaming."

Suddenly feeling ill, Mariah lost some of her confidence and felt uncomfortable with the questions that overwhelming her consciousness. It was something she had, as a rule, not allowed to happen and usually cut them off at the first sign but something was different this time. It was as if she had no control over the bombardment of voices that were filling her heart.

What are you really doing with your life? What would Anton say if he were here? How come you refuse to think about your brother? Why have you cut off all ties with everyone in Montreal? Why do you lie, say you have no family?

Why do you never allow anyone to get close? Why do you say such vicious thing? That lady today, she was frightened of you, why did you enjoy it?

Closing her eyes tightly, as if to shut them all out, she felt her heart race and her throat grew dry. Attempting to hide her physical reaction from Benjamin, she swallowed back and regained her composure. Shaking her head quickly, she met with his eyes, which were full of concern.

"I didn't mean to upset you." Benjamin commented, tilting his head slightly.

"No, that's fine," Mariah insisted and threw on a fake smile. "I just had a bit of a headache, probably just after a long day."

"You must watch these headaches, you know. Sometimes they are indicating something much more serious." Benjamin remarked as he moved toward the edge of his chair, as if to stand up. "One's body tells the truth, even when we are not ready to face it."

Mariah fought off feelings of illness and wasted no time rising from her chair, deciding that it was time to return to her apartment. She suddenly wanted nothing more than to be alone and find a way to distract herself from the thoughts that were invading her mind.

Benjamin chatted about a farmer's market he was planning to attend the following morning, as the two entered the elevator and hit their corresponding floors. And while she attempted to focus on his words rather than the never ending stream of questions that were taking over her mind, she found herself struggling just to keep her stomach settled, as it began to churn with each passing second. Why was she feeling this way now? What in the hell was going on? Taking a deep breath, she noted that Benjamin was staring at her and she raised her eyebrows.

"I would've thought you'd have more of a reaction to my news than that." He showed no judgment as the elevator stopped and the doors slid open. "I would hope you'd show at least a little excitement when he gets back, else it may be a tad depressing for him."

"For who? What?" Mariah felt as though she were lost in a fog. Had she been so preoccupied that she missed a portion of their conversation?

"Landon, of course." Benjamin once again made his duck face and raised his eyebrows. "I'd think the fact that he is moving back after all these years would be more of an interest to you, but perhaps not."

That's when Mariah fainted.

Chapter thirty

Few downhill spirals happen over night. They usually are a result of a collection of tiny heartbreaks and disappointments chipping away at one's soul, often long after a painful event has taken place and the belief is that it is no longer relevant. But is that how things work? Does out of sight necessarily mean out of mind?

The first chip in Mariah's world was certainly noticeable, but like many other things before it, simply swept under the rug in hopes it would go away forever. That's how life worked, right? You dealt with what was in front of you, even if it were merely to push it aside and move on to the next day, the next challenge, the next concern and hoped for the best. Life was just a series of events that really, Mariah assumed, meant nothing. Her brother's death, her parent's neglectful behaviors, relationships; none of it had any meaning. People made the mistake of putting too much importance in everyday experiences and that's where they found themselves in trouble.

And so, when she found herself blacking out for no reason, she also assumed it to mean nothing. Just as Benjamin suggested, after helping Mariah back to her apartment, it was merely a lack of blood in recent weeks that inspired such a condition. After all, she made the same mistaken many times before, often neglecting her natural instinct to keep vials of blood on hand and drinking them on a regular basis. In Mariah's mind, blood was something you got from a sexual encounter and any other way, well, it was just kind of strange to her senses. Even after many years of being a vampire, she hadn't *fully* accepted it in the same way that others had and honestly, she didn't want to either.

To this, Benjamin would merely shake his head.

"Young Miss, you don't just decide that you are above the rest of us and only pick and choose the when and how you acquire the blood. It just simply does not work that way." His eyes narrowed into little, gray slits as he scolded her, after pouring a vial of blood from his personal collection down her throat after she passed out. "You must understand that the rules apply to you, just as they do for others."

Mariah nodded and decided not to tell him that although the blood had given her a bit of a boost, it simply wasn't taking her out of the slump that caused her to pass out in the first place. She felt dreadful in a way that she could neither pin point nor describe. It was as if someone had set fire to the blood inside her veins while simultaneously draining her of all physical strength, causing her arms and legs to feel heavy, as if they were about to sink through the floor. A pain shot through her eyes, making her want to close them, but finding no relief when she did and her throat was dry, even as drops of blood sat on the back of her tongue. She didn't want to sleep, but yet, she didn't want to be awake either.

It wasn't until after he left that she felt water running from the corner of her right eye, She hadn't shed a tear in years, so the feeling should've been foreign to her but instead Mariah felt oddly embarrassed as if someone other than herself had witnessed it. She quickly wiped away the stray droplet of water and shook her head abruptly, as if it were the spin cycle on a washing machine, attempting to eliminate every last bit of moisture, as if it were completely vile and a weakness that she wouldn't accept. She went into her bedroom.

Feeling numb, she lay on top of the covers and was powerless over her thoughts, which crept through her childhood, allowing flashes of both luminous and painful moments to appear on the projector in her mind. For some reason, a song that she associated with family troubles was the soundtrack that forced her through this dark and excruciating world that she hoped to never travel through again. She felt bolts of electricity run up and down her arms and she almost cried out from the pain, unsure of why she was experiencing a physical reaction to the flashes of her parents, brother and even her former childhood home. Was she going out of her mind?

She finally fell into a restless sleep, infused with dreams of a violent and unpleasant nature, she awoke the next morning to the sound of a ringing phone. Reaching for it, she noted that the time was just after 9, definitely a late sleep for her. The call was regarding a job she had applied for and she noticed that her voice sounded like that of a much younger girl, when she replied that she would be available for an interview later that same day. Had she slipped back in time and inhabited the body of a 17-year-old woman once again?

Ironically, when she looked in the mirror, Mariah saw the tired, dim face of a much older woman. Her frown seemed to pull down her entire face and cause it to look tired and even more so, completely unattractive. What was happening to her? Only the day before, she saw the reflection of a confident, young woman and now it was as if years had passed by in only one night.

She was compliant in the interview. It was for another boring job, one that she cared even less about than the last one and would probably get fired from, in the weeks to come. But oddly, Mariah no longer cared about such things. In many ways, she was just going through the motions in her working life and although she was not ready to admit it yet, in her personal life as well. She was no longer the passionate, strong woman she had been at 20 and Mariah couldn't understand why? Hadn't experiences caused her to improve over the years, rather than the other way around?

After what she considered to be a successful interview, Mariah did something she had been doing more and more of lately: stumbling into a bar and getting a vodka martini. The bartender knew her by name and while he usually ignored her sexual advances (except for that one time in a supply closet, when the bar wasn't very busy) he was almost certain to point her in the direction of someone who would find her impulsive actions to be quite attractive.

Sexual desire was merely another fire to be put out and she rarely felt that hooking up with men to be a challenge. Married men, single men, bisexual men, men from different countries and cultures, it didn't matter to Mariah because at the end of the day, they were pretty much all the same. Some were more sensitive and gentle, while others were rough and had the moves that didn't require a great deal of time and patience, but almost all were faceless in her mind.

There had been one accident, once. Although she had been very careful over the years, something must've gone very wrong because she found herself pregnant in the most unpleasant of ways. She woke up one morning and could feel something growing inside of her. She attempted to explain it to a few people who weren't vampires and they gave her the strangest looks, suggesting she had everything from tapeworms to a stomach virus. But as the weeks moved along and it accompanied other noticeable symptoms like increased sensitivity in her nipples and stronger urges to vomit when passing a garbage can or certain restaurants, she knew something was up. A pregnancy test revealed that it was time to visit a doctor in a women's clinic, who confirmed her biggest fear.

Feeling stunned by the news, she heard herself making a comment that didn't go over well with the young woman who gave her the news.

"My pregnancy test apparently had too many lines," She commented airily, as if she had just received news that her car needed a new set of tires, rather than the potential to have a baby. "They should make those things with a stick figure hanging themselves to show you are pregnant and another one rises a glass to cheer, if you aren't." She quipped, but Mariah was the only person in the room who saw the humor in her comment.

Without a second thought, she made an appointment for an abortion. Called the clinic, set the soonest time and date, booked the days off work and simply said she needed 'day surgery' on the day before the procedure.

It hadn't occurred to her that maybe someone should've gone with her that day. Not that she necessarily had a friend to ask. Mariah refused to let herself be scared, but got up and prepared for the appointment, as if it were merely just another day in the office. She put on her makeup, wearing a comfortable pink cotton T-shirt and pair of pants she still had from her days with Energy Planet Vancouver and headed out the door. She decided to take the Sky Train rather than her car and hid her eyes behind her Ray-Ban sunglasses, with no interest in even looking at anyone around her.

It hadn't occurred to her that protesters would be waiting outside the clinic and it didn't occur to them, that unlike many women that went for an abortion, this young woman feared nothing and certainly had no conscience about what she was about to do. An old man approached her, shaking his head and with compassionate he bluntly said, "Young lady, you don't want to do this and you *will* regret it."

"Fuck off, old man," The words sputtered out of her without even a second thought, as she forged ahead. She managed to avoid most who were enclosing her with each step, some waving posters while others attempting to show her pictures of the fetus that sat in her stomach, which she felt was a seed of control, that she wanted to relieve herself of, as soon as possible. One woman was reading something out a book that Mariah quickly realized was a Bible and she merely shook her head in disgust. She muttered a quick, "What the fuck is wrong with you people?"

Just as she was about to enter the office, a woman appeared in front of her and Mariah felt as though she had been slapped across the face. Her blood ran cold as she looked into the eyes of a woman that she had thought – if even for a split second – was her mother. Of course, it was not, but another woman, who appeared to be Russian and approximately the same age. The two women stared at one another for a long moment before she began to speak, breaking Mariah from her spell. "You must not do this. It is very wrong. You were brought up better than that. You should know better. Do not embarrass your family."

Mariah felt her heart race and for the first time she felt anxiety crawl through her body, clutching onto her heart and each breath suddenly became shallow. For a split second, she entertained the thought of turning and going back home. But then something else forced a stream of wrath through her body, forcing her eyes to open a little wider and heart to race, her body full of adrenaline.

Giving one quick push, she shoved the lady who stumbled, almost falling to the ground. The look of rejection and shock in her face pulled Mariah back to the day that her own mother hit her so hard, pushing her against the wall and threatened to kick her out of the house. The memory had never been as vivid as it was in that moment and suddenly, Mariah felt her calm exterior drain away as she ran toward the clinic door and into the safety of the quiet waiting room.

Glancing toward the receptionist, a young woman of no more than 23, she gave Mariah a hesitant, yet encouraging smile. Her legs felt like lead as she crossed the floor and in the same childlike voice she had the morning of her recent job interview, Mariah quietly recited the time of her appointment as well as her name.

For some reason that memory was twisting through the crevices of her mind on that particular afternoon, as she nursed a drink in a secluded corner and ignored the blaring television on the opposite side of the room. Although that establishment was busy during the evening and lunch hours, it was anything but on that day. She didn't even remember drinking her Vodka martini, but merely discovered the empty glass on the table, followed by two more and finally, she headed out the door, after giving a quick wave to the bartender who held a skeptical look on his face.

"Are you driving Mariah?"

She found herself giggling as he said her name because for the life of her, Mariah didn't know who he was, even though the two had spoken many times and had fast, furious sex on one occasion. He was another nameless, faceless man that didn't matter. They all were.

"No sir," She saluted before heading out the door and suddenly finding the outside world to meet her at a ferocious speed, while she felt as though her body was moving quite slowly. It was strange and yet after a few steps, she seemed to adapt to the strangeness of it and find her way home.

Discovering that the little food that didn't repulse her was actually becoming a bore, Mariah found herself quickly replacing her meals with a glass of vodka or wine – sometimes two - and when she wondered out loud why liquor didn't insult her sense like most food did, she was told by another vampire that it was because she generally chose liquors that didn't involve any kind of sugary mix and therefore was tolerable and also, alcohol did dull her senses; vampire or not a vampire, that was a pretty universal thing.

Soon, the intolerable emotions and sporadic memories would disappear with a couple drinks and eventually, Mariah discovered that sometimes it was best to wet the ground rather than put out a fire later. It just made sense to start with a few drinks earlier in the day in order to slowly ease into the evening: didn't it?

For the most part, her drinking went unnoticed. She could function quite well, if anything, it made her more alert to what was going on around her in order to appear normal and stone sober. It was assumed that perhaps she was a nervous individual and sometimes-made mistakes because of her own uneasiness, rather than too many glasses of wine over lunch. And realistically, who cared? It wasn't as if no one else in the city of Vancouver had a few drinks over lunch, right?

At home, she was careful to not allow liquor bottles to lie around and over lunch, she tended to avoid coworkers in order to hide her little secret. Liquor was obviously not a problem for her as it had been for her mother because she was usually calm and collected, rather than a ranting lunatic that Polina Nichols had proven herself to be, time and time again. There simply was no comparison.

Until one day, later that same fall, someone brought her back to reality and she didn't like it at all.

Chapter thirty-one

Time changes people and it's often in ways that we don't expect. It could be something as simple as a new attitude or an altered perception of the world around them. Sometimes, we can see it in their eyes and through the many lines on their faces, but often, it isn't as easy as that and isn't apparent right away.

Physical changes are the most misleading of all because we tend to make certain assumptions about what those changes mean. If he is overweight, does it also mean he is lazy? If she is unnaturally thin, does that mean she has an eating disorder? If someone looks disheveled, does it mean they have no regard for their appearance? So many things can be greatly misunderstood and with no real evidence, just basic assumptions.

Most people didn't notice the changes in Mariah Nichols. Her tongue was as sharp as ever and her appearance never fell short of perfection. She flaunted her curves and sexuality almost as much as she expressed her opinions on many things, most of which were probably none of her business. She was hardly the cute and cuddly sort of girl that made men feel safe.

Then again, this suited Mariah just fine. She knew where she fit in the world and had no interest in being that 'relationship' type of girl and in truth, she wouldn't know how to be one if she were to change her position. It simply was a prospect that she thought was as intimidating as irrelevant. The last thing she needed in her life was to be tied to another human being. The last person she felt such devote loyalty to was her brother and that hadn't turned out well at all. Her family was just more proof in the pudding as far as love and connection was concerned and she had no desire to put herself into such a vulnerable world.

It was often in the still of the night, long after a bottle of wine had worn off and before the light of day brought new hope, that Mariah would consider that perhaps there was something very wrong with her. Was it normal to feel that the intoxication she felt from a drink didn't compare to that of a lover's blood, the heat that it sent through her own body as it touched the tip of her tongue? There was something about consuming someone's vulnerability that was more of an aphrodisiac to her than the blood itself. It simply was not what she had once experienced, but something new, that she had recently felt that combined with her drunkenness, was a way of reaching far down into her own soul.

It was the only time she liked to be surrounded by the defenseless and although she was quick to recognize that she was the most powerful person in these situations, another part of her felt like she was drenched in vulnerability by mere association. And it was that part of it that made her uneasy.

Mariah felt liquor eased the tension of life. At the time she simply saw it as a cushion and by no stretch of the imagination, a problem. After all, everyone drank. The bars were full from breakfast to well after midnight and people allowed wine to flow in everything from garden parties to work functions. It was acceptable and no one thought anything of her constant purchase of alcohol. She was well put together and never slurred her speech, missed work or smelled like booze, so clearly she didn't have a problem.

It wasn't like she was her mother. She didn't duck into a dark corner and pour glasses of vodka and orange juice down her throat, bitterly glaring across an empty, silent room. She merely had a few glasses of wine to unwind or while getting ready for an evening out – didn't everyone do the same thing? Life was stressful and people needed a little something to keep their motor running, did they not?

There were times she drank a little more than intended, but she rarely allowed it to get out of hand. A recent Facebook photo of her former lover, Teo and an equally beautiful young woman, with caramel skin, sent a jolt to Mariah's heart. The two recently married and even someone as cynical as Mariah had to admit that the love that flowed between them in each

MIMA

snapshot was unmistakable. A sharp twinge of jealously followed by a second bottle of wine, helped to ease the feeling she wasn't ready to admit but only drive the knife in a little further by looking up other former flings and finally, an old friend from Montreal. Alison was now married to a man that Mariah didn't recognize and had three small children.

The final person she would look up was Landon Owens, but her Google search turned up nothing. She knew he planned to return to Vancouver, but no one seemed to know when or why. Perhaps it was just time to come back with some dazzling woman on his arm, someone else who would find love in a way that Mariah couldn't relate to or appreciate. In a way it kind of frustrated her because she wasn't capable of understanding that feeling of devotion and joy. In fact, her life was anything but joyful, but for some reason, she assumed that it was normal to be discontent and bitterly waiting for the next 'thing' that would bring a few, fleeting minutes of happiness.

The days slid by and gathered in a week, which also collected to become a month. Sometimes Mariah was completely unaware of what was going on either around her or right in front of her eyes. Work is work. She got through it, had a few drinks on her lunch and faced the afternoon. The commute was frustrating and for that, she had another drink immediately after arriving home. Some nights she had a date while others, she stayed in and had a few drinks while watching televisions or reading a Chuck Palahniuk novel.

She rarely slept well. Now, as an adult, she still followed her childhood ritual of listening to Metallica when attempting to fall to sleep. Almost twenty years later and she still found safety in their music.

But that was the thing about forming habits. They become such an integral part of life that we sometimes absently follow them without giving it a second thought. It's almost as if the habit controls us rather than the other way around. It's automatic and about association more than need.

A lackluster summer was followed by a less than endearing fall, which included looking for another job (although unlike most times, this one she was laid off rather than 'let go') and going through a particularly long dry spell, as if every male in Vancouver was suddenly much too busy with other things like relationships, school and careers. It was a strange phase and although Mariah didn't give it a great deal of thought, had she bothered it probably wouldn't matter anyway. She tended to not analyze such details. It only made her think a little too much about things she had no control over.

Late autumn was a time she hated. To cheer herself up, she recently purchased a thick, wool scarf that had caught her eye one weekend, after she staggered into a craft shop with a strong Starbucks and even stronger Ray-Bans. She found something comforting about the dark gray handcrafted item. It was almost as if the color immediately soothed her and although it was slightly scratchy to touch, she found herself gently caressing it and making an impromptu decision to take it to the cash. This would somehow help her get through the next few dark weeks.

The dismal period when fall quickly raced to winter was full of memories that she held so close to the heart that even she was no longer able to distinguish them. Her father left in the late fall. She was merely a child so wasn't sure of the time frame, but it was before Santa and after trick or treating. She remembered running down the streets, her brother wandering behind, talking to a male friend that she now realized was possibly a secret crush. They were casually wandering along, both slightly self-conscious and awkward, as Anton carried the broomstick that went with her witch costume; an object she almost immediately discarded. Her father left shortly after that night.

A sudden pang ripped through Mariah's heart and her mind was back in the present moment, as she stopped on the busy sidewalk. She felt claustrophobic as strangers pushed past her, mostly staring at a smartphone and barely aware she was there at all. Certain that she was about to have a heart attack, Mariah attempted to take long, calm breaths while her brain raced, wondering if she would die right there, on a Vancouver street, alone and with no contacts in her purse and insignificant ones in her phone? If anything Benjamin was the only real friend she had and would he care if she died?

Feeling the clenching in her chest finally end, she began to walk as if nothing were wrong, her legs slightly wobbly as she continued toward a nearby wine store. A single tear escaped the corner of her eye and slid down her face and Mariah blinked rapidly to prevent another from following. This wasn't the first time she cried in recent months and in fact, it was the tears that scared her as much as the chest pains; they always went away, but the tears often made an unexpected return, often accompanied by a memory she preferred to forget.

Continuing along, she eventually stepped into the same wine store that she frequented. So much so, that the cashier knew her almost as well as anyone else in Mariah's life; not that they had extended conversations about her life, but because she knew her preferences in alcohol and introduced her to sale items or limited edition brands that were new to the store. It was oddly like a friendship in Mariah's world while at the same time, she recognized that the lady probably saw her as nothing more than a customer.

She thought about friendship a lot now. Maybe it would be nice to have someone to shop or have lunch with, but how did one make a friend as an adult? Knowing her terrible track record at jobs, it seemed like a bad idea to attempt making friends with a coworker and she had no interest in joining a gym - or whatever else women did to meet people.

Glancing at the liquor store lady, just slightly older than herself, with a pale complexion and dark brown hair, a smooth white blouse and black pants, it seemed highly unlikely that they would become friends. There were so many secrets to being a vampire that one had to choose carefully. But she did seem nice though.

Turning away, Mariah felt another, although less intense pain in her chest, when she was suddenly face to face with Jody, her former coworker from Energy Planet Vancouver. Much to her surprise, she did not receive any cocky attitude or arrogance in the meeting, but quite the opposite.

"Mariah?" Her eyes lit up and her lips formed into a smile. "Oh my God! It must be, what? How many years since I saw you last?"

"I-uh-"

"I mean, I quit that place probably 3 or 4 years ago and you left long before me," Jody, her one-time enemy did something that shocked her more than anything had in a long time; she hugged Mariah. Feeling her warm embrace almost brought another tear to Mariah's eye when she realized that this was someone who was sincerely happy to see her, perhaps even cared. Her throat was too dry to talk, so she was relieved when Jody continued. "Wow, you look fantastic. It's like you haven't aged at all."

"I- thank you," Mariah spoke sheepishly while continuing to stare at her former coworker. It was hard to believe how much she hated this woman, but now it was completely different. Had time changed everything? "You look great too."

"Well, you know, as great as I can these days," Jody gleamed while patting her belly and for the first time, Mariah recognized that she carried a tiny bump just below her heavy breasts.

"Oh my God, you're pregnant?" Mariah was surprised to find a smile overtook her face, but a lump in her throat quickly followed it, when suddenly she thought about her own, aborted baby; A child that meant absolutely nothing to her but somehow, something changed in that moment. Has she made the right decision? What if-

"Yes, I met my current boyfriend last year and well, things happened fast," She signaled toward her stomach and her eyes were filled with a gentleness that was never there before and it softened Mariah's approach. "But you probably know what I mean, you always had men flocking to you when we worked together. I was so jealous of you." She giggled with the impromptu confession. "But, oh well, that goes with the territory when you are young and immature."

"Yes, about that," Mariah felt herself blush and her heart fluttering so erratically that she wouldn't have been surprised if it had lifted out of her chest and flew away. "I'm..I'm really sorry, Jody. I was terrible to you so many times and-

"Oh please," Jody waved at her with such ease that it was clear that this was not a significant matter. "That was so long ago and so irrelevant. Like I said, we were kids and insecure and crazy. Just, forget it Mariah, I know I did."

The words were minor, but their effect was profound. They opened a gate that caused relief, but unfortunately, it was also a gate that was hard to close.

Chapter thirty-two

S ilence can be a frightening thing. To some it is a welcomed treat that permits them to bathe in the tranquility, allowing the soothing nature of internal peace to flow through their bodies. Other people find silence an invitation for the ghosts of the past return to haunt the present, reminding them that there is some unfinished business that they should be attending to – but they rarely do, which only multiplies it instead.

A conversation with a former coworker had shaken Mariah's world much more than she would've expected. Although it was brief and normal chitchat, there was a power behind those words that continued to haunt her throughout the upcoming days. There was also a serenity that surrounded Jody that was a harsh reminder of how the opposite was the reality of Mariah's existence.

Christmas and all the fa la la la la madness kind of crept up on her that year and although it usually passed with ease, this time it seemed to stumble and lodge into her life in the same way a dry piece of food would catch in her throat. It was maddening that she was unable to avoid it because of its constant bombardment of television, the shopping malls and even her workplace when she was asked if she wanted to be part of a gift exchange program.

"No, it's not my thing." Mariah smiled brightly before abruptly turning away from her coworker. Then she looked back to see the middle-aged mother of two, with plain hair and little to no makeup on her pale face, giving her the same look that she perhaps used to manipulate her children. Rather than saying anything further, Mariah jumped in and found she was suddenly locked in a staring contest of sorts, as both remained silent.

"You know, it doesn't have to be an expensive gift at and it's lots of fun. We do this *every* year and then on the last day at the office, we exchange them." The petit coworker continued to press the matter, a subtle smile slowly curved her lips but just as quickly, it would disappear and Mariah grew irritated. "It's so much fun and we just have a blast. It's just a terrific way to end things before the holidays and…"

Her words continued to drone on and Mariah bit her bottom lip, wondering when she would be allowed to get a word in edgewise, reminding this boring, little woman that she simply didn't wish to join the others. Was that so hard to understand? It wasn't like she had been a long time employee who had formed a relationship with her coworkers. She kept things professional and simple. And yet, here she was, listening to a long-winded story about the previous years Christmas gift exchanges, that was apparently supposed to woo her into their tradition but in fact, it was having the opposite effect

She would later recap the story to an intrigued Benjamin in the apartment building lobby, as both held a cup of coffee she had picked up on her way home. Neither were interested in Christmas or the activities associated with it and therefore, he would understand her frustration. Benjamin sipped at his coffee, made funny faces (including his 'duck' face – what was with that anyway?) and occasionally, a grin would cross his lips.

"So basically this daft cow wasn't about to listen to your clear indication that you weren't interested in their silly little Christmas games and rather than bugger off like you wanted her to, she talked your bloody ear off?" Benjamin sat further back in his chair as if carefully searching for his ass groove; he slowly shook his head and pointed toward a small, elegant Christmas tree that sat on a tabletop across the room. "It does not surprise me, Mariah. In fact, I've encountered such situations in the past and found it to be absolutely dreadful."

"She wasn't willing to just accept my 'no, thank you' but was incredibly persistent on the matter." Mariah took another swig of her coffee and started to visualize the bottle of wine that sat in her bag. She couldn't wait to open it and settle in for the evening, cutting out everything that's involved in the holidays.

"Well, you do know that it has nothing to do with celebrating Christmas," Benjamin interjected and swept his hand back and forth dramatically, not breaking eye contact with Mariah for even a second. "It's just a bunch of bible thumpers who feel that your lack of interest in participating in such festivities also means that you aren't Christian, which is probably the center of their concern."

Considering his words, Mariah nodded when she realized that he made a lot of sense. Hadn't she overheard the plain lady (whatever her name was) talking about almost being late for church the previous Sunday morning, as if that one single event would possibly throw off her week?

"I too have dealt with such things in various work and social functions, and it surprises me how bold people can be and how they assume you should have the same values and beliefs as they do. It is almost criminal with some people to not have a strong sense of faith and specifically Christian values." He seemed to ponder his own comments for a moment before continuing. "I was once at an event that was for charity and it also had a slight political factor involved. Now, you wouldn't believe it, but they actually said a prayer before the meal."

Mariah raised her eyebrows.

"I thought it was highly inappropriate, but when I went on to mention it to someone, I quickly realized that I had in fact made a serious social faux pas." Benjamin tilted his head and fell silent for a moment. "Yes, I would say that the event that took place at your work earlier today was more about testing the new girl's faith, more so than her team spirit. So, what did you end up saying? Do you cave in?"

"No, of course not." Mariah quickly answered, shaking her head. "Not at all."

"And for that I say, good for you."

"I just want it to be over." Mariah grimaced and she glanced toward the lobby, her eyes suddenly caught as the door started to open. "The Christmas music on the radio, the television shows the-

Her words suddenly halted and a silence lunged into the room, as if it were a swooping bird that boldly dove into a window with no regards to anyone else. A thousand eyeballs could've fallen from the sky and had less of an effect on her as his face but she remained stoic.

"Oh yes," Benjamin cut into her trance and brought her back down to earth. "In our conversation regarding your unusual day at work, I forgot to mention that Landon was moving back into the building today. Unfortunately, his apartment was not available yet, but the good news is, that I was happy to welcome to our spare room for the time being and…"

His words seem to float away and for a moment, Mariah was in another time and place, returning to the woman she used to be, long before the layers of glass carefully surrounded her heart and made her the cold individual she would become. Not to suggest she was ever a soft touch, even back in her late teens and early 20s, but she certainly had layered many shields to protect her since those days and it wasn't until that moment, that she realized just how many.

"… So you see that it was just the plan, that worked out perfectly for all of us," Benjamin continued as if he hadn't noticed her lack of attention for a few seconds, but it was unlikely that he missed this information at all.

She noted that Benjamin was rising from his chair and she did the same. Throwing his empty coffee cup into a garbage can, she followed his lead and watched the remaining liquid splash inside the garbage can. It somehow was lost on her that she still had some coffee left to drink. Shaking her head, suddenly feeling self-conscious, she was relieved to see that he hadn't noticed, too busy showing all his attention to Landon. As he walked toward the former resident, speaking with absolute glee in his voice, the scene could've been a father welcoming his son for Christmas holidays. Benjamin quickly reached for one of the two large suitcases that Landon pulled behind him and insisted that he help him to the elevator.

The two were so involved in their conversation that it was clear she was merely an afterthought, if any thought at all and Mariah silently stood back and awkwardly hoped that no one else noticed her discomfort. It appeared that neither Benjamin nor Landon was even aware that she was nearby and so Mariah pretended to be looking for something in her bag as the two slipped into the elevator.

The door closed just as Mariah looked up again and she felt a sinking feeling of disappointment. Other than a quick moment of eye contact, Landon had neither acknowledged nor even cared that she was there. She was merely a part of a familiar backdrop in the room, nothing more or less. Feeling disappointed and a little depressed, she finally took the stairs and headed to her apartment. There, she would slip into some comfortable clothes, open her bottle of wine and forget about the rest of the world.

It didn't work out quite that way.

Upon returning to her apartment, she found a message on her phone that had apparently been left by Landon earlier in the day, suggesting that they get together later that week, depending on her schedule. Feeling an ounce of excitement, she quickly reminded herself that he barely glanced in her direction when arriving earlier and couldn't help but feel that this was a shot of rejection.

Shaking her head, she changed into shorts and a T-shirt, turning up the heat in order to feel comfortable without putting on layers of clothing. She swiftly opened her bottle of wine and wasted no time downing a large glass, followed by another. By the time she heard the knock at the door, Mariah was staring at the last few drops in the bottle and wondering how it had all disappeared so fast, her brain slightly fuzzy and incapable of putting a clear thought together.

Already knowing who was on the other side, she made her way to the door and swung it open.

He hadn't changed very much. With the same dark eyes and mocking expression, Landon didn't say hello, but forced an insincere smile on his lips and waited, as if it were her place to say something rather than the other way around. He wore a designer shirt and a pair of jeans, a slight upgrade from his college days. Feeling awkward, she finally spoke.

"Landon? I had no idea you were coming back so soon." She moved aside and allowed him to enter the room. "I know Benjamin mentioned-

"I bet he did." Landon answered abruptly; a strong confidence enriched his voice in a way that it hadn't only a few years earlier and his walk was that of someone who was fearless and stronger, rather than the boy next door, who sought approval. It was surreal that he was back, let alone in her living room.

"I didn't... I mean, it was a while ago, but I wasn't sure," Mariah felt her lips clasp shut and she gently closed the door behind him. She noted that he was heading toward the couch where he made himself right at home, sitting on what was sort of known to be her 'spot' on the furniture, but she remained silent.

"I had an opportunity to leave my job a couple of weeks early and here I am." Landon gestured his hand to indicate her room. "Back in town again, I guess you would say."

"That's great." Mariah quickly replied before sitting beside him and licking her lips.

"I suppose you're wondering why I'm here right now." He offered and casually sat further back on the couch, his eyes dancing around, with a hint of anger hidden deep inside. She hadn't missed it and scanned her brain to see where that would be coming from at all. What had she done to offend him? Their relationship was casual and never serious.

Shrugging, she decided to say nothing.

"I wanted to see how you were doing after all these years." He stalled, his eyes showing no judgment but was full of curiosity. "I hear you have some job related issues, no solid connections in your life and from what I see right now, drinking is probably your new favorite pastime. Am I right about that?"

Having her life cut down to a few short, unpleasant sentences didn't settle well with Mariah and she felt anger creep up and enter her voice. "What do you care what kind of life I have had since you were gone? It is not like you kept in touch." She hastily reminded him. "I live my life on my terms, just as I always have."

"One bottle of wine at a time?"

"What the hell are you trying to suggest, Landon? We aren't all squeaky clean like you." She snapped and suddenly wished he would leave. She wasn't in the mood for an interrogation.

"I'm not suggesting anything, actually." Landon insisted, continuing to watch her. "I just find it interesting that someone who wants to be in control of everything has picked a habit that actually gives her absolutely no control."

And with that, he rose from the couch and left her apartment.

Chapter thirty-three

I t's important to be cautious of what you believe. Whether it's a story about a celebrity, the lady down the street or the person in the mirror, you can't always believe what you hear. Then again, there are other times when maybe you should.

Mariah was stunned by Landon's blatant remarks. For someone who had no issue telling it how it was - regardless of how sharp the words - she certainly didn't appreciate being on the receiving end. He left her on the same shaky ground that recently became a more prevalent part of her life. As much as she wanted to deny it, his words hurt and they taunted in both her waking and sleeping hours.

What did I ever do to him?

After that night, he avoided her for weeks. In fact, it was rare that the two came face to face and when they did, his reaction was respectful and friendly. He always nodded, gave a half-hearted smile and said hello, as his dark, cold eyes continued to stare through her as if she were nothing to him – but then again, if she were nothing to him, then why did any of this matter?

In a fury, she finally decided that this was his fucking problem and she was having nothing to do with it. If they were to walk side by side as strangers, so be it. That's how life is. File it away and move on.

But his words haunted her. Did she drink too much? Mariah became cautious about the amount of liquor she bought at a time, where she stored it and made more of an effort to drink when she was out. It wasn't that she was attempting to prove anything to him, but at the same time, it wasn't that she was not either.

Mariah knew her life was off track, but wasn't sure how else to live. Growing up in an unstable family, she learned that surviving was an accomplishment. She was the warrior who forged ahead, weapon in hand, hoping to fight off any threat that faced her in the future. There wasn't time to consider long term plans when you were living for today.

But weren't people supposed to live in the moment? It seemed ridiculous to create a career path, knowing that most went astray from their original objectives. Wouldn't it make more sense to just see what happened in life? Mariah had set goals in the past and they went belly up within months. Her plans to live and work in Montreal, bond with Anton and start a wonderful and exciting life had crashed and burned in less than a year. It'd been what she lived for during the course of her childhood and was what she thought about during those awkward months at Emily's house. A part of her knew that she should dream again, but something inside of her simply wouldn't allow it to happen.

But she did wish to have a friend.

Mariah had been fighting off the need for a companion to spend time with for many months. She'd never thought the day would come when a string of lovers wouldn't be enough to make her happy, that her friendship and long conversations with Benjamin wouldn't be enough to make her content. There was something unsettling about having a relationship with another woman and yet, all around her were herds of women together every day; having lunch, shopping, talking and laughing, as if nothing mattered.

A part of Mariah longed for a friendship, but feared it at the same time. She didn't feel very comfortable being vulnerable with another human being and the truth was that this was rarely required with men. The empty affairs that Mariah conducted had very clear boundary lines that didn't allow anything to penetrate further than the superficial conversations and compliments. Her relationship with Benjamin was mainly light conversation and an exchange of ideas, but neither talked about anything of substance in their own lives. She wasn't sure if that was because Benjamin also had the same limits to his social life or if he simply had sensed her own.

The truth was that Mariah didn't trust most women. It was a natural instinct brought on after a difficult relationship with her mother and unfairly reflected onto those around her. She saw Polina Nichols, close mindedness in Emily Thomas and her desperate need for male attention in former coworker Jody, from Energy Planet Vancouver. In fact, most of the women she met throughout her life's journey shared some of the infuriating traits of her mother.

Then something changed. She now longed for someone to have a coffee with on Saturday afternoon or dish dirt with, over a glass of wine.

It was much more difficult than she anticipated. It appeared that women were very particular about the people they chose to hang out with, for example, she noted that many coworkers preferred to keep their work relationship separate from their personal lives, while even more women appeared to already have 'their people' and weren't looking for new friends. She made coffee dates that fell through and she began to wonder if perhaps it was better to keep the door of friendship closed indefinitely. Mariah felt the sting of rejections that was much more intense than had she approached a male of interest, only to be shot down. It felt much more personal for some reason, almost as if she wasn't good enough to be part of anyone's inner circle.

Realigning her focus, she decided that it was better to not think about her failure in the friend department, but instead continue her pursuit of attractive men. After all, casual affairs didn't hurt her and never left her feeling excluded.

It was months later, shortly after her 29th birthday that this old wish would resurface. As she walked into her building on the arm of a man she was having an ongoing affair with, Mariah spotted her: A lovely young lady who she recognized as a vampire, alone in the lounge area. She looked very small and delicate, sitting on one side of the chair, as if not wanting to indulge herself by taking up too much room. She had dark hair, pulled back into a ponytail and she nervously picked at her nails, avoiding Mariah's eyes. She didn't recognize her as a tenant, but then again, people moved in and out of the Vancouver building all the time.

She didn't see that same young woman again for weeks.

Then, during the humid month of July - when it was almost more of a luxury to stay inside and enjoy the building's air conditioning - Mariah spotted her again. She was walking out the main entrance with the self-obsessed blond guy from the second floor; the one who was known to charm every other woman with a boyish smile, something that didn't work with Mariah. Was she his girlfriend or simply another vampire that he had managed to seduce? She felt her intrigue drain, making the assumption that this girl was just another single digit IQ princess that followed moronic guys, trying to make them fall in love. Good grief.

But it was after she spotted the same lady sitting with Landon at a nearby coffee shop, that Mariah was certain that the two would never be friends.

She was wrong.

Her curiosity was peaked when Benjamin brought up her name.

"Have you met the latest resident of the building?" He asked during their usual, Saturday morning coffee in the lounge. His eyes wandered toward the elevator as the same brunette walked out with Landon, who appeared to be acting casual, even though Mariah sensed that something was odd about this situation. "She was in and out for a little bit, but I guess she is officially living here now."

"With him?" Mariah spoke before she thought, her eyes glancing in the twosome's general direction as they exited the building. Attempting to play it cool, she shrugged. "I have no idea who she is. I think I may have seen her around. Why? Do you know of her?"

"I met her briefly the other day, when she was with Landon but she doesn't live with him," Benjamin pursed his lips as if deep in thought. His eyes narrowed and he seemed to almost be staring into space as he tapped his finger on the arm of the chair. "I believe her name was Ava, if I'm not mistaken and she seems quite friendly. I'm not sure how she and Landon met, but it's interesting since I've also seen her about with the pretty boy upstairs not long ago."

"Bryan?" Mariah cautiously played along and watched Benjamin nod.

"Yes, that would be him. Quite a stretch to go from him to Landon, I would say." He tilted his head slightly, as if he was attempting to read her mind and remained silent, indicating it was her turn to speak.

"I don't know." Mariah admitted. "I don't know the girl and I make it a point to not know Bryan."

"Yes, well that does seem like a smart choice from what I know." Benjamin grinned and raised his eyebrows. "Not the sharpest tool in the shed, as they say, but it's neither here nor there to me, I just thought that this Ava woman may make a nice little friend for you."

It was moments like this that threw Mariah off guard. It was as if he somehow knew about her longing for a friend and was providing Mariah with the answer she might need. She shrugged and looked away.

"I don't know. We probably wouldn't be friends or anything." Mariah smoothed out the material that made up her skirt, as if primping suddenly took priority to everything else. "I doubt we'd have a thing in common."

Suddenly aware of what Benjamin was most likely thinking, she glanced up and gave his gleeful eyes a dirty look. "You know what I mean." Her comment was abrupt. "And don't look at me like that."

With innocent eyes, Benjamin shrugged his shoulders and shook his head. "Like what? I merely suggested the two of you might have a thing or two in common. Is that really so bad?"

Mariah decided to not answer, but instead, consider his reply. Was he purposely attempting to peak her curiosity. She hid her feelings well and changed the topic.

But the two would meet, a few days later. And Mariah and Ava would become fast friends, proving that her first instinct had been correct all along

 Chapter thirty-four

Without realizing it, we often choose in a friend, the traits we wish for ourselves. So that means that the shy, awkward child will seek out a friendship with the loudest kid on the playground. Often it is our subconscious leading us in the direction that will expand our personality and discover new dimensions that we never knew existed.

Mariah certainly found her opposite in Ava Lilith. While the two were vampires, they didn't have much else in common. At least, it didn't seem like they did at first, but after further exploration, it became abundantly clear that once you remove a few layers, that we all have more in common than we originally thought.

As it turns out, both Mariah and Ava came from dysfunctional backgrounds. Mariah, who often professed that she had no family, felt a tinge of guilt upon learning that Ava's parents died in a plane crash. For the first time in ages, Mariah found herself telling someone the truth; well, sort of, leaving out the part about her brother. It was a much too complicated story to get into at this point and well, maybe later?

"So, your parents don't keep in contact with you?" Ava showed no judgment from the across the table, where she nibbled on a Caesar salad and sipped on a glass of water. The two were having dinner in a restaurant that was part of a popular chain, on a quiet Thursday night. One of the advantages of living in the same building is that they could make impromptu plans at the last minute, something that had been pretty regular since meeting in the apartment lounge a few weeks earlier.

Mariah had decided to make an effort. She was too curious about Ava to not at least have a conversation to see what she thought. Sitting alone, the brunette welcomed the company and unlike what Mariah expected, she was easily approachable and friendly. Mariah made small talk; how did she like the building? When did she move in? How did she know Landon? Where did she work?

Ava smiled and showed no hesitation when answering each question; she just moved in earlier that month, she had been Bryan's girlfriend but apparently things ended on an unpleasant note and had only recently met Landon. She stated that they 'weren't really' a couple and Ava was in the process of finding a new job, but had been working at bar.

The two developed a friendship that day and had been in pretty regular contact ever since.

"Not in years," Mariah answered Ava's question and was relieved when she didn't follow it with anything further because it wasn't a topic she wanted to get into. "I'm sorry to hear about your parents, that must've been devastating."

"It was," Ava's voice was soft and gentle, her eyes downcast. There was a sense of shyness that occasionally covered the 24 year old like a thick veil and Mariah found it to be one of her more endearing qualities; unpretentious and calm, there was a sense of safety that she felt in her new friend's presence. She wondered if it was these same traits that attracted Landon. "But time moves forward and you are forced to just accept it."

"Where did you go when they died?" Mariah sincerely was curious and intrigued by Ava's story. It was kind of refreshing to know that she wasn't the only one with a messed up family history and who was forced to grow up way too fast. It wasn't that you necessarily found joy in the fact that someone else had experienced the same thing, but there was comfort in knowing that you weren't alone. "Did you have other family?"

"Yeah, my grandmother," Ava spoke bitterly, for the first time since they met and for a moment, it kind of threw the conversation off course. It was an unexpected reaction and rather than to ask, Mariah chose to fall silent. Ava continued to play around with her food before looking up from her plate. Her caramel eyes explored her friend's face. "Not that she wanted me around."

Oh. That was something Mariah knew all too well and laughed in spite of herself while nodding her head. A sense of relief flowed through her body and she shared a comforting smile with Ava. "Trust me, I know that feeling. You certainly aren't alone. Imagine having a mother like that." *Then a brother,* she silently added.

"Wow, really?" Ava tilted her head, her voice was soft and while her cheeks flushed. "I'm sorry to hear that, but I can definitely relate. It's hard when you feel like you're in the way or like you have no right to be somewhere." She seemed to hesitate for a moment. "It's almost like… it's almost like you should be apologizing for something that isn't your fault."

"Like being born?" Mariah grunted cynically, knocking back the rest of her wine, the bitter taste stimulating her tongue and created a burning sensation down her throat. She shook her head and pursed her lips in the form of a fake smile. She glanced across the table and was enjoying Ava's reaction, a soft laugh that lit up her face with glee. "Yes, believe me, I know all about it."

Signaling to the waiter that she wanted another glass of wine, Mariah felt warmth flow through her body and was surprised by how much she was enjoying her time with Ava. It hadn't occurred to her that having a female friend could be fun because so many women she encountered seemed to thrive on gossip, complaining and talking about silly things. Ava wasn't like that and in fact, she was actually a pleasant distraction from everyday life and the problems it entailed. Lately, this included her most recent job. On instinct, Mariah decided to bring it up.

"Anyway, let's not talk about family stuff, it's depressing and its history? Is it not?" Mariah smiled sincerely at the waiter who approached and quickly replaced her empty glass of wine with another. Thanking him just before he rushed away, she returned her attention to Ava. "How is the job hunt going?"

"It's going, I guess." Ava replied while taking a sip of her water. "I mean, I go to interviews and everything seems fine, but then no one calls back."

"Sometimes it takes a while though." Mariah reminded her. "Don't be too hard on yourself. Do you have any savings to help you out, when the bar doesn't give you enough hours?"

"Yeah, my parents left me some money when they died." Ava spoke softly and let out a small laugh. "So much for us shifting gears and not talking about our families anymore."

"It's fine, it's not the main area of discussion." Mariah joined her in laughing and took another sip of her wine. She liked how her new friend didn't appear to notice or think anything about the amount she drank. Not that it was such a big deal. "So they left you some money? Well that's good, right? It makes it a bit less stressful, right?"

"Yes, well, sort of. Sometimes, I'm scared I won't find anything."

"You're looking for reception work? Nah, there's tons of that here." Mariah assured her. "I mean, look at me, I've been fired and quit more jobs than you can imagine and I still manage to find work. You will too, soon."

Ava looked as though she wanted to say something but didn't. It made Mariah slightly paranoid, but rather than get into detail about her previous jobs, she decided to switch topics again.

"So are you still spending a lot of time with Landon?" Mariah asked casually.

"Yes, in fact, he's been a huge help to me since turning," Ava referred to her relatively new status of becoming a vampire. Mariah was aware that he was helping her adapt, but was a little confused why, after all she certainly didn't have someone help her along for six months after her own change. "After Bryan left, I was so scared and had no idea what was going on or what was normal."

"It was wrong of him to not tell you anything," Mariah shook her head and although it hadn't been a problem in her own life, she recognized that Ava was hardly playing the damsel in distress regarding this matter. She had heard stories from others on how adaption was difficult for the first few months. "Then to just leave you? Seriously, I didn't know the guy, but that's a pretty asshole thing to do."

"It was. I was angry at first and I guess a part of me still is," Ava admitted and sighed. "But Landon has been amazing and I'm lucky to have him around to answer my questions and not make me feel like a freak."

"You wouldn't believe it," Ava quickly continued. "But I didn't even know that I was living in a building full of vampires at first. I was staying in Bryan's apartment when he left to do that film and I stupidly thought that we would be in contact after he left. I just felt so alone." She referred to the fact that the man who changed her was an actor who often was out of town for work.

"What a cowardly thing for him to do." Mariah threw in while finishing another glass of wine. "And to think you were surrounded by us, all that time?" Her lips slid into a grin. "Well, if anyone can help you, it is Landon. I do believe he has been a vampire for a very long time."

"That's what he says," Ava said and reached out for a napkin. "But he doesn't talk about it in detail. He won't say how it happened or why he hates it so much."

"He hates it?"

"Yeah, he's been going to great lengths to find out how to just be a regular mortal." Ava was wide eyed as she spoke, as if to get her point across more intensely. "When he was in Europe, I think he was looking for people who might be able to help but it didn't seem to work. I think he learned a lot just not what he was hoping for and well, he's still one of us."

Mariah felt her mind race and suddenly it made sense why he had been so desperate to go to Europe. Benjamin made reference to the vampires that lived in European countries, including the immortals that supposedly existed, although Mariah was starting to think they were just a myth.

"I guess some things just aren't meant to be." Mariah replied and the two fell silent.

Mariah restrained herself from asking Landon about his search for answers in Europe, when they ran into each other by the elevator the next day. However, she probably didn't start the conversation on the best note either.

"So I met your new little girlfriend." She narrowed her eyes and forced a fake smile on her red lips, attempting to show no judgment but knowing that her half-hearted attempt was unsuccessful. "She's a lovely girl."

"What is with that exactly?" Landon held back no hostility as the two entered the elevator and hit the appropriate buttons. His eyes shot through her like a bolt of lightening and that was when Mariah knew she had hit a nerve. "Why are you suddenly interested in making friends? That's a new concept for you. I thought you were only about seducing, unless that is the case with Ava?"

"Not at all." Mariah brushed off his hostility and innocently shrugged. She felt her skin grow hot, sensitive and aroused by his presence in such a small space. At that moment, she would've been happy to bring him back to her apartment and make up for lost time but decided to hold back instead. "I happen to think that she's a nice person and maybe it's about time that I made some friends. We just have fun together."

Landon grunted and continued to glare at her.

"What?" Mariah snapped defensively. "Are you annoyed that I am hanging around your pet project? Am I taking time away from you 'mentoring' her or whatever the fuck you're doing?"

"I'm trying to help her." Landon insisted defensively. "Not everybody has an agenda like you, Mariah."

"I don't have an agenda this time." She was candid as the elevator stopped on her floor. "I just like the girl. Maybe you are making accusations based on yourself. What are you getting out of it? Obviously a little more than the satisfaction of helping others."

"Mariah, you don't know the first thing about me." He spoke in a somewhat subdued voice, not at all what she would've expected. "You never did. It was always about you and you only, but sometimes people's intentions are honest. And I know yours rarely are, so maybe you could just leave Ava alone."

She hesitated getting out of the elevator and stopped the door just as it was about to shut. "What is that supposed to mean? And who the hell are you to say who I should or shouldn't be friends with? Maybe you aren't the only person who sincerely likes this girl. Maybe you aren't the only one who needs people in their lives."

She hadn't meant to show vulnerability in her voice, but it somehow had escaped with her last words, surprising both her and Landon. She didn't say another word, but quickly rushed away.

Chapter thirty-five

There's magic inside of music. It's not something that everybody will recognize, but for those who do, it sends an alluring light that flows through every sense and eventually, making its way to the deepest part of the spirit. Most people don't understand the impact it has or how it can grasp a specific moment in time and never let go, but they do see the results when a song makes them cry or brings an impromptu smile to their face.

Mariah Nichols wasn't a spiritual person. She didn't believe in God or religion, nor did she believe in karma or the concept of having faith. In fact, she was pretty certain that churches were meeting places for the weak and that nothing happened after death: no heaven, no hell, no reincarnation, just a lifeless body rotting into the earth. It was logical to her and Mariah refused to pay attention to anything that didn't make sense.

She did realize that such beliefs were usually best kept under her hat. People tend to look unfavorably at anyone who wasn't part of the status quo and didn't have spiritual beliefs and therefore assumed she was a cruel and terrible person for not believing in something. Mariah was confused and intrigued and at one point, found herself locked in conversations with various people who were insistent that it was appalling that she had no faith. One man even went so far to ask if it was because she was so arrogant to believe herself to be the 'The Divine'.

"What the hell are you talking about?" She shot back and quickly walked away before hearing the answer to her question. Who cares what she did and didn't believe and why did so many people take it so personally? It was just very strange. Then again, she considered that many wars were fought in the name of religion and decided it was better to not incite conflict with strangers over such an irrelevant topic.

But music was different. There was something inside her that attached to music in a way that she was never able to with people. It made her feel safe when she was alone, filling the empty rooms of her childhood home after her entire family disappeared, one by one. It carried her through the misery with her brother and eventually, into a whole new city, where she would start her life over again. There was something very special about a song that it could lift your day or understand your loneliness in a way that felt very safe to Mariah.

Of course, she was no fool. Mariah was aware that most women would find comfort in friendships, rather than a song on the radio. It was supposedly normal to discuss difficulties with a friend, confiding your secrets and hoping that they may have the magic solution that would solve every problem that was enclosed in your heart. Mariah knew better. People wanted to talk about their shit because it made them feel better, but they usually aren't interested in being on the other side of things. In fact, most people were so overwhelmed with their own set of problems that they weren't able to take on someone else's and therefore, it made no sense to bother. That's why she never shared her concerns with Ava, even after their friendship grew over the months. It was better to leave well enough alone.

As much as she wasn't sentimental, Mariah did have an inexplicable connection to music and there were some songs that would haunt her every time they came on the radio or were playing as she walked through the mall. Some reminded her of Anton and their time together: both the good and bad moments, all wrapped up in one. There was also music that took her back to the first few, scary days in Vancouver as she attempted to navigate the city and as much as she hated to remember those vulnerable moments, they never fully went away. And then there were the songs that reminded Mariah of her dad. Specifically, she remembered how he used to repeatedly listen to "Somebody to Love" by Queen, just before he moved out. Was he trying to attract real love in his life, after it was clear his first marriage was going to hell?

Mariah thought it was silly to even consider such a concept. It was ridiculous to think that you had no power over your own faith but yet, people were forever praying, begging God for everything from a slim waistline to good health, as if they had no control in their own lives. In a way, she was slightly embarrassed for them: but only slightly.

It was just after Halloween of that same year that Mariah suddenly found herself out of a job and back on the market, hoping to nab something quickly without too many hours of torturous interviews and wasting her time going through various ads and agencies. Although she never had a great love for any of the work she ended up doing, she often wondered if people simply stayed at jobs because they lacked the willpower to go through this nonsense to find something else. Still, she always got through it and found something new and this time, it was at a clinic. Although the agency insisted that they generally preferred an actual medical receptionist, apparently there was something in her resume that stood out.

"I think it is a collection of all your experiences that grabbed their eye." The middle-aged lady with a terrible haircut – a collection of erratic curls and flat sections on the top of her head – tried to put a positive spin on the fact that Mariah could never hold down a job for a long period of time. Way back when, there had been Energy Planet Vancouver, but since that time, things have been slightly dismal in comparison. The worst part was that she didn't care.

"That's great." Mariah had faked her friendliness and showed the upbeat attitude that these kinds of agencies preferred. That was, after crafting her resume in such a way that her 'short term positions' came across as temp work, rather than her failure to ever get along with management.

"This doctor is new in town and is opening up a practice in the downtown area, sounds very promising." The agency lady (what was her name again? Nancy?) had very warm eyes and a strong, confident voice even though she was quite dumpy in appearance. Not that Mariah cared, her philosophy was simple: get in, get a job and get out as quickly as possible.

"That's great." Mariah continued with a fake smile and wondered why this meeting was taking so long. It was almost as if she was waiting for the other shoe to drop, as she sat on the edge of her seat. "I can't wait to start."

"Perfect. I should have more details for you later today," She spoke apologetically and stood up. Mariah did the same. "I was hoping to have more information in time for our meeting, but this one," she pointed to the file. "He's a hard one to get in touch with."

"Well, you did say he was moving." Mariah offered. "Just give me a call when you get more details."

As soon as the meeting was over Mariah was out the door, on an elevator and out of the building. With a satisfied grin on her face, she felt like a thief in the night as she quickly sent Ava a text, telling her that she was once again employed.

Maybe you will like this job?

Then a second later…

Ha ha

As much as Ava's joke made her smile, she couldn't help but to feel the sting of disappointment. She briefly wondered what it would be like to be passionate about work, but quickly brushed the thought aside.

A few days later, Mariah was on her way to her new position at a medical center. The agency still didn't have many details about the position, other than the time and place to show up. Mariah assumed everything would be covered upon her arrival. She was wrong.

In fact, the entire office was in disarray. For a moment, she thought perhaps she had wandered into the wrong place, until a voice came from behind the desk.

"Are you here about a job?" A man who looked to be in his 40s, with dark curly hair and glasses popped his head out from under the desk. Holding a cord in hand while searching her face, Mariah was taken slightly aback, but quickly recomposed herself before answering.

"Yes, I um… I was supposed to start working here today. At least, I think it's here?" She gave a self-conscious laugh, her eyes scanning the room. A lady was putting up a painting in the waiting room, while two other people were either moving furniture around or opening boxes of office supply. "The agency gave me this address."

"It's here." The tech guy had a gentle voice that was warm and friendly and with his free hand, he pointed toward the hallway close to the reception area. "I was told that if someone came in asking about a job, to point them down the hallways and to ask for Dr. Curtis."

"Okay." Mariah smiled and glanced in the direction he was pointing. Hadn't the agency called him Dr. Wesley? "I'm sure I'll find him. Thank you."

"Very well then," The techie guy gave an awkward bow that was a bit strange but she couldn't help but laugh. Thanking him again as she rushed away.

Boxes of paper were stacked against the wall at the end of the hallway and each of the examination rooms looked slightly organized, with the exception of a few containers scattered on the counters and plastic wrapping a couple pieces of furniture. She rushed on to the end of the hallway and found a small office. The door was open.

She took a deep breath and confidently knocked on the open door before looking in. "Hello?"

"Hey," A handsome man - she assumed was the doctor - slid his chair into her view and for a moment, Mariah felt lost for words. His alluring, green eyes were captivating against his dark complexion. An effortless smile crept across his face and for a moment, she started to question if heaven actually did exist. "You must be a.. Mariah?"

"Yes." She finally composed herself and carefully entered the office. An awkward smile edged on her face and she automatically reached out to shake his hand. "I'm Mariah Nichols and you are, Dr... Curtis?"

"Close, my first name is Curtis. It's Dr. Wesley but that's okay," He took her hand and gave it a strong, yet quick squeeze before letting go and gesturing toward a nearby chair. "Please Mariah, have a seat."

Following his orders, she felt her heart, anxiously race as she glanced around. A box of books on the floor caught her eyes and she noted that the rest of the office appeared to be in pretty reasonable condition, other than a few stray papers on a chair. His desk was immaculate. Her eyes were immediately drawn to a framed picture of an older couple; the woman was white and the man was black.

"That's my parents." He announced proudly, gesturing toward the photo before casually sitting back in his chair. He wore a dark gray shirt and a pair of ripped jeans and had she wandered into the office and saw Curtis Wesley beside the tech guy in the reception area, she would've assumed their roles were reversed. It didn't help that he looked so young. Was he even 30? "They look great, don't they?"

Caught slightly off guard by his remark, Mariah wasn't used to associating with people who spoke highly of their parents. She quickly recovered and regained her composure. "Yes! They look so lovely."

He seemed to struggle with a grin, studying her face, causing Mariah to feel slightly ill at ease. Was this some kind of a joke? Was this really her boss? He looked much too young to be a doctor. She decided to just play it out and not jump to any conclusions.

"So, first of all, I must apologize for the mess." He signaled toward the hallway and rose from his chair, to close the door. "I thought everything would be sorted out by today, but this whole move has been completely chaotic. I'm new to the city, but also, obviously, new to this office so I'm having a little difficulty getting everything organized as quickly and efficiently as I'd like." He began to laugh at himself while shaking his head. Mariah immediately found herself joining in as she watched him return to his chair.

"You're talking to someone who has moved a couple of times, so I completely understand."

"To new cities or apartments?"

"Cities, I'm originally from Ontario, moved to Montreal when I was still a teenager." Mariah paused, suddenly considering just how young she was at the time but regained her footing immediately. "I umm..moved to Vancouver when I was 18 or 19." She found herself pausing again. "So, yes, I know about moving."

"Exactly. Then you totally get where I am coming from, Mariah." His voice was gentle, almost affectionate, his smile, disarming. "So, I thought we would go over a few things this morning, like your schedule, pay rates and also what I expect from you around the office. Once we go over the procedure, I was thinking that this afternoon, maybe I would have you organize the reception area, create a voicemail, whatever you need to do. Does that sound like it could work?"

His smile was eager and enthusiastic and Mariah couldn't help but mirror his reaction. "Of course, that sounds fantastic."

He didn't respond, but continued to smile and nod.

Chapter thirty-six

T hose who live in a regular state of chaos often know nothing about an existence of peace. Whether the conflict is on the outside or the inside, it becomes a distraction that's just a normal part of life. Mariah Nichols was one of those people. She wandered through life, hoping to feel as little as possible. Under the assumption that her coldness toward people was directly connected to being a mortal vampire, she was often disturbed and surprised to meet others who actually countered her original assumption. Ava Lilith was one of those people.

As much as Mariah's new friend insisted that nothing was going on between her and Landon Owens – at least anything beyond the physical and a growing friendship – Mariah knew better. There was a connection between the two that was unmistakable and at times, slightly uncomfortable to watch. It wasn't that she wanted any kind of emotional connection to Landon in the future, but it still was a gentle reminder that her kind was not necessarily immune to human relationships. It was most unsettling.

But as much as Mariah ignored the growing relationship between Landon and Ava, she couldn't disconnect from her own confusing feelings regarding her new boss: Dr Curtis Wesley.

Although the doctor was gentle and easy to work with, in other ways he was extremely difficult. Mariah thrived on having conflicts with most people in her life and her work was no different. There was something stimulating and powerful about being in a bit of a disagreement or power struggle everyday; it was a game of sorts and she strived to be the winner. However, this was not the case with her new boss, who was anything but argumentative. He didn't carry his status as if it made him powerful but quite the opposite. He was so gentle and calm regardless of the situation – whether it was stressful or frustrating – he remained balanced and serene.

"I feel like I'm working with Jesus," Mariah snorted one day after a young woman brought in her erratic, demon child in to fill the entire office with screams followed by the worst case of vomiting that Mariah had ever witnessed. Curtis Wesley didn't skip a beat and went to work cleaning up the mess. Feeling her own stomach turn, Mariah announced that she was going for a 'short walk' and left the temp worker to navigate on her own. These were the times when having stronger senses weren't ideal. Fortunately, it happened at the end of the day and when she returned to relay her earlier thoughts on to her new boss, he merely grinned.

"Really?" His lips expanded from a mere smirk to smile, followed by laughter. His green eyes danced gleefully and he raised his eyebrow in question. "You think Jesus cleaned up a lot of vomit in his day? Is that what you're saying, Mariah?"

"No, I ah…" She let her words trail off, unsure of how to finish that sentence. Feeling her cheeks grow warm, she immediately was resentful of the fact that he was capable of embarrassing her. Men didn't normally have that kind of power over Mariah and she wasn't about to allow this man to either. Boss, handsome, it didn't matter: she had to remain serious and not get caught up in these games of uncertainty. "I just meant you're a saint. I don't think I would be able to handle having someone's kid throwing up all over *my* office without getting furious."

"Now tell me, Mariah, why would you be furious at such a thing?" His words were challenging her, but not in a way that caused her to be defensive. He tilted his head, looking up from the short stool he sat on, as he jotted down some notes on a clipboard. "The child clearly was upset because he was not feeling well and unable to adequately express his feelings and no child enjoys throwing up, so obviously that was beyond his control."

"I..I.." Mariah felt her arms grow heavy and her throat tighten as she attempted to explain her position. "I just…."

"That's okay," He calmly brushed the question aside as if it were no longer relevant. She noted that he used his left hand to write notes. Wasn't he right handed? "I do understand. I was not always so patient myself, but you know, it gets easier as you work with people."

"Really?" Mariah let out a short laugh as she considered that her own experiences had been the complete opposite. She felt her mood lighten and her body no longer felt tense but yet heavy. She was happy their workday was ending. "I kind of find the opposite, actually."

His green eyes darted up to her face, showing no judgment, but fully absorbed in her every word. His long eyelashes batted around innocently and Mariah began to realize why so many women wore long, fake lashes that caused everyone's defenses to collapse. Nodding slowly, he muttered an 'aha' and finished what he was writing and Mariah decided it was best to say nothing.

"I guess it is just a matter of perspective." He rose from the stool and she noted that he was standing very close to her, a little closer than was necessary in that situation, as his eyes searched her face then with a quick eyebrow flash, he turned and went back to his desk. "In order to fully engage with a patient or..actually, most people, you have to understand where they are coming from and rather than judge, sometimes it is better to put yourself in their shoes."

Mariah suddenly felt stupid and looked away.

"We've all been four years old and sick. We've all been in the position where we didn't understand what is going on around us or with us, for that matter." He sat the clipboard on the counter and ran his hand over the back of his neck, as if working out a kink. "It's our job to do the best we can to connect with people and for me, it makes me a better doctor."

Mariah remained silent as he walked toward the exit; she considered how he didn't wear the white coat or stethoscope that everyone associated with a doctor, but instead jeans and a blue shirt. She found herself following him and feeling defenseless in his presence.

"At least, I hope it makes me a better doctor." He flashed her a quick smile and they both left his office.

It was time to leave and the girl who was a temp (Mariah couldn't remember her name and honestly, didn't care) grinned like a moron in the doctor's presence and jumped up from her seat. Mariah disliked her.

"Oh, Dr Wesley, I really enjoyed working with you today." The pale girl with the floppy curls and perfect teeth batted her eyelashes as she reached for her purse, and then walked out from behind the desk. "Will you be looking for another employee because if you are-

"Actually, I think we're good." Curtis was gentle, even with the abruptness of his comment and Mariah was intrigued by how he had done so with such ease. Maybe there was something to learn here. "We have Mariah, of course, and another lady will be starting tomorrow."

Another lady? Mariah wrinkled her nose. Although she welcomed the help, she wasn't sure how she felt about another flirting moron hitting on the doctor. Not that she didn't understand the intrigue; Curtis Wesley was very handsome and approachable, which made Mariah wonder if he had a girlfriend. Not that she really cared Not that she ever cared.

"Oh, well, that's fine." The temp began to ramble and the doctor merely shrugged as he headed toward the door and opened it for both of the ladies. "If we need anyone again, I will have you on my short list and I do thank you for your help here today."

Mariah felt a sudden, strong attraction to the doctor's confidence and hoped to continue their conversation, alone, in the elevator. Instead, she was stuck with the nameless temp in the hallway. The doctor stayed behind for some reason, as they took the elevator to the first floor. They didn't talk.

Outside, the unusually warm December air gently touched her face and she felt as though her entire body was made of rocks. She wasn't tired, but felt very strange. Her usual confident, self that brashly walked through the crowd seemed to be missing in action and replaced by a stranger. A million thoughts ran through her head, from the words Curtis used when speaking of the sick child to her own feelings of discomfort. Her heart was racing and Mariah was certain that for a moment, she felt the blood rushing through her veins. The sun suddenly felt much warmer and her blouse was sticking to her back, then her arms and neck. She almost felt the impulse to remove her coat, despite the cold winter air that embraced her.

Moving toward a nearby bench, she sat down beside an older, Chinese lady who probably weighed 80 pounds on a heavy day, and she couldn't help but to think of Curtis' comment about putting yourself in someone else's shoes. What was it like to be that woman? What was she thinking? What had she experienced? Rather than writing her off as some immigrant who had nothing interesting to say, Mariah briefly wondered if she had any experiences similar to her own? The woman continued to sit there, staring into the distance and didn't appear to notice Mariah watching at her.

Suddenly breaking herself out of the trance, Mariah covered her eyes with one hand and wondered what was wrong with her? Why was she suddenly this different person that was conscious of those around her? Taking a deep breath, she rose and glanced past the Chinese lady and to a nearby bar. She needed a drink.

Wandering inside the dark room, where the main lights were dim, at best and the shiniest objects were the brass colored fixtures behind the bar, a middle aged man with fine, strawberry blond hair showed no expression as he looked at her and gave a quick nod. "Hello."

"Hi." Mariah's voice was small and she felt moisture continue to gather under her bra strap. Perhaps it would've been better to go directly home? Her thoughts were confused and on instinct, she ordered a drink.

"Vodka martini." She heard her mother's voice come out and although it caused no reaction to the bartender, it did make her feel like curling up in the corner and dying. What in the hell was going on? Why was she feeling so strange? She almost cancelled her order, until she noticed the bartender had already gone to work making it. With his head bent down, she saw that his hair was even thinner than she originally thought and his tan much deeper than she would expect from a man who was generally fair completed.

"Did you just go on vacation?" She heard herself ask in a voice that once again wasn't her own.

Looking up, his eyes seemed to soften slightly as he nodded. "Yes, just got back from my honeymoon, actually." His reply was kinder than his brass appearance would suggest. "Australia. It's summertime there now. Wife's family is there."

"Not much of a honeymoon if you were with your in-laws." Mariah couldn't help but to say, relieved to hear fragments of her own voice returning.

"It had its moments." The bartender grinned, exchanging her drink for money and quickly moved on to the next customer, down the bar. It was a short, slender lady who appeared to be wearing a wig. Mariah forced herself to look away, grab her drink and head toward an empty table in the back of the room. She felt her phone vibrating through her bag. It was Ava.

Are we still meeting tonight?

Mariah sat the phone down and looked toward a nearby window. Did she want to meet Ava now? Feeling slightly ill at ease, she decided that perhaps it wouldn't be a good time to do so. After all, she wasn't herself and well, it just didn't seem like a good time to meet up with a friend. People were expecting one person and if you showed up acting kind of weird, then they would bombard you with all kinds of questions – was something wrong? Are you okay now? – questions that Mariah wasn't prepared to answer. She ignored the text.

She continued to feel the blood rapidly coursing through her veins as her usual spark was depleted to nothing. She felt weak as a kitten, which was unusual for someone who thrived on being a tiger. Was she just sick?

Blood! That's it! She decided that it was a lack of blood in her system lately that caused her to feel this way. She hadn't had a casual encounter in days and well that was where she usually got a supply of blood. No wonder she felt so weird and weak.

But then again, when she was low, had she ever really felt this way? Finishing her drink that was bitter on her tongue and lips, Mariah decided to head home and maybe refuel on blood, take a nap and hope for the best.

The bartender gave her a quick nod as she headed toward the door.

"Have a nice evening, young lady."

His words shocked her and Mariah felt her reaction to be much happier than she would've expected. His words carried a strong sense of affection that was both unusual and unsettling to her.

"Ah, thank you." She replied and gave him a sincere smile as she walked out the door and back onto the Vancouver sidewalk during rush hour. She stood while everyone flowed around her, as if she didn't exist. In silence she slowly headed home.

Chapter thirty-seven

There's a beauty and freshness of a new day: a blank slate with no mistakes, no challenges and no problems. It's only when your mind and ego gets involved that things tend to take a turn for the worse, predicting invented problems that may never arise or old situations that are much better left in the past. But for a few brilliant moments when we first wake, we're free from both.

Mariah felt good when she opened her eyes the next morning. There was a gentle calmness in her apartment that welcomed her before the roaring blast of her alarm clock had a chance to kick in. She quickly turned over and flipped the switch, then laid back to enjoy a few moments of peace. It would be a great day.

There was a part of her still nervous about this new job and she wasn't sure why. It was a comfortable environment and her boss was amazing: if anything, shouldn't she have been counting her blessings for finally finding something that resonated with her? Then again, the days would soon get more hectic and as the temp warned, the office would be insane with an increase in patient load: non-stop phone calls, sick and irritable patients attempting to make appointments that simply weren't available, cranky, scared individuals entering the waiting room, occasional tears upon leaving and sick, crying children were to be what was to be expected in the future. But for now, all was calm.

She slowly got out of bed and prepared herself for work. Mariah noticed that she took a little extra time putting on her makeup, choosing an outfit and fixing her hair. The results were positive and although she knew that Dr. Wesley wasn't likely interested in mixing business with pleasure, she also knew that her success rate changing a man's mind was pretty good. Maybe it would take some time, but she would get there.

But would she? Another side of Mariah felt slightly insecure around her new boss. Clearly, she wasn't the only woman who probably hoped to find herself naked, wrapped around this handsome man.

Feeling confident, feeling strong, she made her way to work. Standing a little taller than she had a day earlier, she hit the corresponding elevator button, arrogantly ignoring the other people who climbed into the confining little box with her and felt good about the day ahead. Arriving on her floor, she sauntered out and toward office number 437, which was now labeled Dr. Curtis Wesley and with a smile on her face, swung open the door with a fierceness that she could feel flowing through her veins.

She was quickly met by a set of apple green eyes, which stood out so beautifully against the doctor's caramel skin while his smile was an added extension to his overall attractiveness. Mariah found herself, releasing a small, seductive grin – that was, until she noticed the woman standing beside her new boss.

"Hi, I'm Paulina." The bubbly blonde automatically stuck her hand out to Mariah, who reluctantly reached for it, as if she had another alternative and smile reluctantly crept to her lips. There was a certain irony of having a coworker with the same name as her own mother, but that appeared to be where their similarities took an abrupt end. This woman was slightly shorter than Mariah, standing at approximately 5'2" and unlike her mother's frail appearance, Paulina's voluptuousness seemed to overlap more on the top half, than to be evenly distributed between the breasts and hips. Memories of working with Jody and her need to show cleavage were quickly resurfacing in Mariah's mind; because of her first day at the job, Paulina was certainly not shy.

"I'm Mariah." She offered up with a tight lip and quickly glanced back at the doctor to see his reaction. He was neither overtaken by the attractive women, nor skeptical of Mariah's uncomfortable exchange with their new coworker. In fact, he either hadn't noticed or ignored it.

"Great," Curtis Wesley raised his perfect eyebrows and made eye contact with Mariah, then Paulina briefly, before gesturing toward the hallway that led to his office. "Now that we have another person on board, what I would like is for Mariah to focus on the phones and Paulina, for you to help bring the patients in offices, maybe stick around if there is any kind of exam that requires a second person, and of course, also to help out at the reception when needed. You will cover each other's breaks, that kind of thing, but we all go for lunch at noon." He directed his last comment to Paulina, since Mariah had been already aware.

"You mean, together?" The blonde let out a quick laugh that sounded more like a yelp, then attempted to share a smile with Mariah, whom felt a little stunned by the comment. Hopefully she was joking.

"No, you aren't required to spend lunch with us," Dr. Wesley lets out a small laugh as he gestured toward the hallway again and started to walk in that direction, just as the phone began to ring. He quickly turned, "Mariah, do you want to grab that and I'll give Paulina a quick tour before the patients start to arrive."

Not waiting for an answer, she watched them disappear down the hallway. She could hear them laughing and it made her blood boil slightly. Suddenly, her morning had fallen flat.

Throughout the day - on the rare occasion it wasn't busy - Paulina attempted to get to know Mariah by asking a million questions. Where was she from? Had she always lived in Canada? How did she get this job? Did she like it there? What does she do for fun? Where had she worked before this job? It went on and on and at one point, Mariah considered that perhaps she was also supposed to ask some questions back, but that was inhibited by the fact that she barely had an opportunity to answer the ones sporadically thrown at her, along with the other fact that she simply didn't care.

Overall, the day flew by and before she knew it, the three of them were closing up the office at 5 p.m. Paulina looked pooped but still continued to jabber along. Mariah felt exhausted by her new coworker more than the actual job. Curtis Wesley looked unaffected, alert as he had been first thing that morning, He glanced toward Mariah and she quickly threw on a smile, feeling as though he were inspecting her reaction to everything. The last thing she wanted was for him to think that she was unable to work with this lady.

"Hey, how about we all go have a quick drink at the bar across the street," Paulina glanced at both her coworkers, but Mariah guessed it wasn't her that she preferred to have the drink with, but their boss. Had Curtis said yes, she would've tagged along, but he quickly shook his head 'no'.

"Thanks for the offer, just the same, but I have somewhere I have to be right now," He gently let her down and opened the door. As he waited for his two employees to leave, he followed them with another comment, "Also, I don't drink."

Mariah oddly felt as if it were directed at her and wasn't sure why. It made her slightly paranoid since she regularly had a couple glasses of wine on her lunch break. Did he notice? Could he smell the alcohol on her breath? She was usually good at hiding such things, but perhaps he somehow was aware of her lunchtime habit?

Smiling quickly, she avoided his eyes while Paulina rambled on, apparently unaffected by the rejection.

"That's fine, I just thought I would throw the idea out there. Another time, maybe somewhere other than a bar?"

This time her eyes were directed at Mariah, who had zero interest in spending any time with this woman at work, let alone out of it. In fact, she was quite comfortable with her one and only friend, Ava.

"Yeah, sure," She gave Paulina a fake smile and uncommitted reply. She noted that Curtis wasn't paying attention to the conversation and therefore, she had no reason to continue. The three said a final good night and went their separate ways.

Slightly irked by the day, Mariah headed for a bar close to her own home. She sent off a quick text message to see if Ava would like to join her. She readily agreed.

Ava had been already there and seated when Mariah arrived. Giving her friend a quick wave, Mariah ordered a drink at the bar. While waiting, she briefly considered how she could be having drinks with Paulina right now, rather than Ava. The two were so completely different, that it was almost laughable. Small, with dainty features and docile for the most part, Ava was not one to ramble on with endless questions or dress seductively in the workplace in order to get attention. She couldn't be more different.

"Hey, how is the new job?" Ava asked when Mariah approached the table with a drink in hand. Both chose a glass of red wine and neither appeared to be particularly happy at that moment.

"There's good and bad." Mariah sat down and went on to describe her handsome boss, her irritating coworker and the job itself. Ava listened attentively; nodding occasionally, taking small sips of her wine. Meanwhile, Mariah quickly knocked back her first glass. "I guess no job is perfect."

"Tell me about it." Ava was going through a cycle of job interviews and recently had a second one for one place that she didn't particularly like, but didn't feel she had the option to be fussy at this point. "It's at an accounting office."

"Sounds pretty dry." Mariah commented, catching the eye of the waitress to signal that she would like another glass of wine. "Do you think you could tolerate working there?"

"I guess so," Ava let out a small laugh and her eyes glanced up at an approaching waitress with a glass of wine in her hand. After she placed it on the table and left, Ava continued to speak. "The lady who interviewed me was kind of a bitch, to be honest. Maybe it will be different when I start, if I start. Although, I'm pretty confident that I have the job."

"It's just a job." Mariah reminded her. "Don't put much thought into it."

"I won't." Ava agreed. "But it sounds like you are putting a lot of thought into yours, at least compared to what you normally do. This doctor sure has you intrigued."

"He's very handsome, but I don't think there's going to be anything happening there." Mariah found herself lying and wasn't sure why. Perhaps this was something she simply couldn't share with a friend. "I think it's better to separate the two, especially when you rely on that paycheck. He seems to go by the books too, so you know, whatever... plus, do I really want to see a guy I'm sleeping with everyday? What is it they say about not eating where you shit?"

Mariah noted that Ava almost choked on her drink.

"Well, I guess some people wouldn't mind, but for you, it definitely wouldn't work." Ava let out a girlish giggle and finally finished her first glass of wine. Mariah was well into her second.

"Speaking of which, are you and Landon still having your sorted affair?" Mariah attempted to make a joke, but was kind of curious what was going on with the two. She wasn't sure if it was just a friendship or if Ava was still hitting the sheets with her own, former lover? The thought made her slightly envious since she had never found someone who satisfied her like Landon had, perhaps that had more to do with their comfort level with one another, Mariah considered. Not that she would ever share any of this information with Ava.

"I wouldn't call it 'sorted' exactly, but yeah," Ava slowly nodded her head. "Things are good between us. I think we had a connection. But I'm not sure if the connection is just because he helped me with the transformation to become a vampire or if there is something there. I'm actually wondering that a lot lately."

"Why don't you just go with it and not worry?" Mariah asked and noted the wrinkle form on Ava's forehead, as a frown overtook her face. Pushing a strand of dark hair behind her ear, she shook her head.

"I don't know," Ava confessed. "I want to believe that there is something more between us but maybe it is just sex."

"Is that a bad thing?" Mariah laughed in spite of herself, but quickly noted that Ava seemed much more serious.

"It is if you care about someone." Ava answered shyly. "I'm not so sure he cares about me. There is a distance with him sometimes. I just don't know how to take it."

Mariah shrugged. She didn't understand what Ava was talking about but wanted to be a supportive friend and attempted to assure her that it was probably nothing, just paranoia setting in.

"Don't worry so much," Mariah injected. "It'll give you lines on your face."

Ava laughed and pushed her empty wine glass aside.

"I wish I had your adventurous spirit, Mariah." She gave her a heartfelt smile. "That worry-free attitude that isn't afraid of anything that life throws at you. I wish I could be like you."

Mariah felt laughter bubble from her stomach and it came out sounding louder than she had meant. "Be careful what you wish for, honey." She winked. "You just might get it."

Chapter thirty-eight

L ife's little inconsistencies can be hard to digest. We like to believe we can face change and challenges head on, bravely facing the elements of a situation and hoping for the best, but deep down, most people frown upon that which makes them lose control. We learn from an early age that you need to be prepared, to make lists, be organized and never allow a surprise to sneak up on us, as if it were a frightening and evil thing. But is it really at all?

Mariah rolled with the punches and throughout the first 29 years of her life, change had rarely scared her. In fact, nothing did. She moved provinces twice, with very little concern with what the future held and no mental list of things that could possibly go wrong. She went from job to job, never stopping to wonder if her cluttered resume may set off alarm bells of any kind – or for that matter, even caring. Mariah also didn't care if she dated the same man yesterday as she did tomorrow and whether or not anyone else noticed. If they had, she would say it was none of their business.

But as her 30th year started, something changed for Mariah. All the things that hadn't concerned her for most of her life started to face her in the form of questions. And most of these questions were not something that she was able to digest with the same ease as her younger self. And for every day she was able to run from these concerns that lurked around the corner with a carefree inhibition, the heaviness was growing inside her chest that no longer permitted her to do so. It was kind of like eating chocolate for your entire life with no consequences until one day, you realized that it was causing you to gain weight and that your sugar levels were much too high. When did this happen and why?

She fought with questions daily, but told no one. People were used to the strong, intimidating version of Mariah and didn't know that she had demons within her own mind; demons that were threatening to take over, if she didn't change her ways. Her ego, her pride, they were standing in the way and had no intention of moving on. It was an inner battle that was brewing and although she chose to pretend it didn't exist, she would only be able to escape it for so long before it erupted into her everyday life.

All around her, things were starting to fall apart. First, it was Ava's breakup with Landon, something her friend took much harder than Mariah had expected. It was one of the few times she had comforted someone. As much as she should have felt a sense of empowerment from the whole experience, it actually had the opposite effect on her, instead making her feel more ill at ease with her own life. Mariah did her best to not allow herself to get caught up on these completely, normal, human emotions and instead preferred to see herself as the animal - a 'vampire' - something that the world insisted had no emotions and lived a fearless, selfish life. Watching Ava fraying at the edges was an indication that she, too, could have her own heart broken and it frightened her.

The fact that she was even thinking about heartbreak at all – other than a concept outside of herself, that is – was a bit ludicrous to Mariah. The insanity of it all. She was not someone who fell in love with anyone and it seemed very unlikely that being in her 30s was about to soften up her emotions, much like aging was supposed to weaken the body and mind. She somehow doubted that this was one of the things included in the equation. In a way it infuriated her that these thoughts were even crossing her mind and she automatically resented them.

But there was certainly a reason for this unrest. As the weeks of working for Dr. Curtis Wesley moved forward, Mariah felt an unexpected emotion for him that she rarely felt with other humans: respect. He was an intelligent man, soft-spoken and calm, who rarely showed any signs of frustration or anger. The truth be known, with every pleasant day of working with him, Mariah felt the barriers that she normally wouldn't consider lowering for anyone, beginning to collapse. She trusted him in a way she had never trusted anyone in her life – then again, had anyone ever given her reason to in the past? He was sincere with his word and there was an unmistakable calmness whenever she was in the same room as him, a feeling of gratitude for the moments they shared and for that reason, she loved working for him.

For all the same reasons, she hated working for him. It made her feel as though he held all the control in their relationship and that simply, couldn't have been a good thing. It made her uneasy and it was a strange, unfamiliar feeling that overcame her whenever they had those few, moments alone. She would walk into his office with a concern or problem regarding a patient and walk out feeling completely relaxed, tranquil and as if nothing in the world could hurt her in that moment. It was a burst of freedom that she allowed to carry her through, even if just for a few moments.

And then she would run into Paulina - her nemesis - and everything would collapse back to the ground. It was almost as if she endured her coworker and the slew of miserable patients for the few moments she could share with Dr. Wesley; his beautiful eyes, his serene face and relaxed nature were the antidote to the rest of the world around her.

Working similar schedules and within reasonable proximity of one another, it only made sense that Mariah and Ava would meet for lunch on a regular basis. The two would get together and complain about their jobs and Mariah would sink back a few drinks, enabling her to get through the rest of her workday. As much as she was awestruck by her boss, she also felt tense about her emotions surrounding him and having a drink seemed to help ease her into the afternoon. Ava, on the other hand, just seemed to have a lot of problems.

"She's crazy." Ava used the words that she felt best summed up her boss, an older Chinese lady who appeared to have no respect for her latest employee. Ava, unlike Mariah, wasn't someone who would reveal much in such an environment, but chose instead to digest all disrespect, watering a seed of anger that grew inside her. It didn't seem healthy to Mariah but then again, her way of dealing with things probably wasn't either.

"It sounds that way," Mariah agreed while sipping at her wine. Almost in a daze, she half thought about Ava's complaints along with a mixture of her own unsettled feelings from that morning, when Curtis Wesley briefly touched her arm. Rather than feeling the usual desire that came with the touch of an attractive man, she instead felt a warmth surrounding her spirit and raising her to a level that had never existed before, as if a peacefulness was flowing through her veins, rather than the usual fire that pumped through her heart. "She sounds very…"

"Angry?" Ava's eyes flashed, her own version of the same emotion and she didn't hesitate to take huge gulps of her glass of wine, something she normally didn't do. "She's a condescending bitch who gets off on bullying her employees."

"Well, I'm happy she 'gets off' on something," Mariah couldn't help but to grin and noticed that Ava reluctantly joined in. Gathering herself together once again, she cleared her throat. "It sounds like maybe she needs to get off in more ways than one if she ever has at all. The woman sounds like a miserable lunatic."

"She is!" Ava shook her head dramatically and seemed to swallow back her words then quickly regurgitate them. "Just because I'm 200 years younger than her doesn't mean she has the right to talk to me like I'm stupid, as if I have no experience with life and she is doing me a favor by even giving me a job. She actually told me today that I could 'learn' things from her because she's been in the working world so much longer than me."

"How thoughtful of her," Mariah muttered, sarcasm rang through her voice as she finished a glass of wine. Without batting an eyelash, she gestured to the waiter to get her another one. In one swift move, as he passed the table with a pot of coffee in hand, he grabbed Mariah's glass and headed toward the bar. "Well, I don't think you need to sit back and be treated like a piece of shit either. You're not a terrible employee. You do your job and ask questions when you don't understand. That's just normal. It would be perfectly normal with my boss."

"Your boss sounds like he's actually a human being," Ava commented and glanced up at the waiter dropping off Mariah's fresh glass of wine, nodded after being thanked and put his attention to Ava. "Can I get you something more?"

"You know what?" Ava's face twisted up in frustration. "I think so. I think I would like another glass of wine."

Mariah giggled as the waiter took off toward the bar. "Two glasses of wine, we're really pushing it today, aren't we?" She teased. "The world's not going to fall apart if you indulge in a glass of wine over lunch. Look at me, I've had what? Three or four at the most."

"You're on your fourth." Ava candidly pointed out. "Aren't you worried that your boss will smell the liquor on your breath?"

"I could only wish he would get that close to me." Mariah attempted to make a light-hearted joke, but quickly realized that perhaps it was her inner desires escaping her lips, now that a few drinks had made her feel more relaxed. Maybe it was time to stop drinking; when she finished this glass. "Nah, three or four glasses isn't such a big deal, it's not as if I am performing surgery after lunch."

"True and it sounds like your job can be stressful sometimes." Ava offered as the waiter returned, dropping off her wine. She waited till he left to continue. "What about that girl you work with?"

"Tits and ass?" Mariah swirled her drink around the glass and found herself hesitant to drink more. Noting the humor in Ava's eyes, she felt that the reference to Paulina was worth it, if only to see the look on her friend's face. It was fun making Ava laugh because she appeared to need a distraction from her problems. Unfortunately, sometimes Mariah felt herself adopting Ava's tension and occasionally avoided her for a few days. She often worried that this made her a 'bad' friend, but sometimes, she wasn't able to handle such heavy emotions.

"I can't believe you call your coworker Tits and Ass."

"You would if you saw her." Mariah suddenly didn't feel any reluctance to finishing off her wine. "That's all she is, that's all she is about. We have this little, cramped space we work on together and every time I turn my chair in her direction, I either have a tit or an ass cheek right in my face. I can't believe I have to work in such conditions."

"The girl certainly can't help it if she's proportioned like that, can she?" Ava challenged.

Biting her lip, Mariah briefly considered her comment. "Yes, this is true and I am hardly a waif little thing, but I also don't go to work wearing clothes that allow my boobs to hang out every time I bend over. Nor do I shove everything from my Blackberry to a phone book into my cleavage in a really obvious way. Unlike Tits and Ass, I don't need attention on my rack all day long."

"Maybe she doesn't realize she's doing something…. weird," Ava countered. "Maybe it is normal in her family to dress that way."

"Even at work?"

"Even at work."

"But we work in an office setting not Hooters." Mariah said and swung her hand around. "I mean, look at this place, the girls are dressed in pretty outfits and they are slightly seductive but they aren't pornographic."

Their eyes, both landed on a young, blonde, woman at a nearby table, who appeared friendly and respectful as she wrote down a customer's order. She wore pretty short shorts, but they didn't appear sleazy against her lean, tanned legs and a basic white shirt that was carefully ripped just below the neckline, showing the strap of her bikini top. Her hair was up in a clip, while a daisy was nestled where Mariah guessed a bobby pin was holding back a string of hair from falling in her face.

"See, she looks seductive, but modest at the same time." Mariah offered her opinion while leaning on the table, carefully observing the young woman.

Ava's eyes followed Mariah's and she quickly nodded and looked away, as if she was concerned the woman would see them watching her. "I agree. I would have to see this woman sometime, if I drop by your work."

"Good luck with that," Mariah said. "She's always in the office with the boss, helping out with a patient or whatever.

"Oh." Ava said while taking tiny sips of her wine, as if in fear that she was overindulging on the drink. "So is she more of a medical assistant or something?"

"Or something." Mariah replied and rolled her eyes. "I don't know what she is but let's not talk about her any longer. It's depressing to me."

"Okay."

"So, you haven't talked to Landon lately?" Mariah asked.

"So we are going to a topic that depresses me rather than you?" Ava responded. "I don't know if I like that plan either."

Mariah didn't attempt to suppress a grin. "Hey, look at that hot guy over at the bar, he's kind of cute, isn't he?"

Ava just smiled in response and without saying another word, the two girls rose from their seats and headed toward the cash register. Lunchtime was over.

Chapter thirty-nine

The sun is never appreciated as much as when it makes its first, official appearance in association with summertime. It is almost as if it hadn't existed at all for the many months before, even though it generally peaked through the chill of winter's air, people didn't recognize it until they actually felt the warmth of its delicate rays. That's just the way that human nature is.

People are fickle. What they appreciate today isn't necessarily what they will appreciate tomorrow. It's unfortunate that human nature tends to be so inconsistent, often going on to the next best thing, quickly forgetting exactly what they worshipped to move on to whatever shiny, bright object captures their attention.

Mariah Nichols was one of those people. She spent most of her life going from one thing that would bring her short-term happiness, to the next that would establish the same 'high'. As the years went on however, everything began to fade as if it were merely freshly painted walls under the glare of the sun. She began to wonder if her life would reignite it's passion again and in a way, it was very depressing. Perhaps turning thirty meant entering another stage and it was downhill from there? It was disheartening and just as with anything else that depressed her, Mariah's solution was to avoid it.

In many regards, she hated her job. The patients that entered her office were repulsive, annoying and just never happy with anything she attempted to do to please them. It didn't matter how friendly and professional she was on the phone, how courteous she was in person or how she took care of their file after they left the office, no one ever appreciated the work she did at Dr. Wesley's office. People just took and took until she had nothing left to give, and although Mariah wanted to believe that she didn't care about her job or the people who walked through the door, a part of her sort of did – like the little girl that came in looking pale and sad. She would later leave with a sobbing mother and Mariah would learn that the child had leukemia. Cases like that got to her and she wasn't sure what was worse – the fact that she was getting emotionally involved in a way she hadn't in her life, or that the doctor was able to take everything in stride.

"It's unfortunately the reality of being human. Sometimes we live until we're 95 and die on the dance floor of our great grandchild's wedding and sometimes, we don't make it to preschool because a terrible disease enters our body." He spoke candidly as he moved files around his desk, as if searching for something in the cluttered mess that seemed to increase over the weeks. His original insistence of tidiness simply wasn't working out the way any of them had planned, due to the overlap of patients that were regularly in the office. "I don't like seeing it anymore than you do, Mariah but all we can do is try to help these people and hope for the best."

"But, how do you do it?" Mariah looked in Curtis' eyes, as he patiently listened to her question, after another hectic, overwhelming day. Paulina had left shortly after the final patient, insisting that she had to pick up a family member at the airport, leaving both Curtis and Mariah behind to tie up some loose ends.

Sitting down across from him, she searched his eyes and noticed they showed no emotion. "How do you tell a woman that her daughter is dying? I can't imagine what that must be like. I consider myself to be someone who doesn't normally get emotionally involved with people that I don't know, but it was hard to see."

Mariah recalled the woman in her late 30s, who was in hysterical tears as she left the office with a confused child in tow. Looking into the little girl's eyes as they walked out of the room, a stab in her heart brought her back to her own childhood and the day that her brother was kicked out of the family home. The child demonstrated the same looks of confusion on her face, as if silently begging Mariah to help her, as her mother dramatically pulled her out the door.

"It's unfortunately something you get used to very early on when you're a doctor." His answer was slightly colder than Mariah had expected and she was quite surprised that of the two of them, it was her not him, having the strongest reaction to that afternoon's events. "I know it is hard for you to see now, Mariah but it's something that you learn to accept and feel differently about as time goes on."

"I don't understand."

"It's about perspective." He insisted, leaning on his desk. "Everything is about perspective. In this particular case, I see a little girl through the eyes of science. We caught what was wrong with her and it is not necessarily a death sentence."

"I guess…" Mariah slowly processed his words. "It's just that…"

"Perspective also tells me that I can't do everything for everyone. I can only do my best. If I allow myself to get too emotionally involved in each case, it puts my patients at risk because I may not see something objectively." He finished his thought and reached for a file on the other side of his desk. Opening it up, he studied it for a moment. "This case, with the little girl, it's not as bad as you may have thought. The woman's reaction was strong because she just heard the word 'Leukemia' and probably nothing I said after that point. Lots of people get sick and lots of people get better too. This girl is most likely going to be one of them."

"I see, so she is going to be fine?"

"I'm not God." A grin covered his face and his eyes lit up as he watched her face. "I can't tell you that. I could walk out of here tomorrow and get hit by a bus. No one can tell anyone when he or she will die. It's simply much more complex."

"I know you can't predict if she will live or die." Mariah felt her cheeks burning, knowing that he was partially teasing her, but at the same time, he was trying to get a valid point across. "I get that life is short."

"Too short to be focusing on the negative." Curtis closed the file and pointed toward it. "This file is negative. We can't focus our attention on it, but on what we do next. Of course the initial shock is traumatizing. I totally get that. That's why I asked the mother to return next week for another appointment. She needs time to absorb this news and hopefully, prepares herself to focus on healing rather than the illness itself."

"Does it make a difference?" Mariah's voice sounded childlike as she asked the question. "Shouldn't people also be realistic about their chances?"

"No." Dr. Wesley shook his head. "That's the worst thing you can do. As a matter of fact, I would rather a patient be completely delusional and expecting sunshine and rainbows than stressing about a possible death sentence. Attitude is everything and we create our own reality. If they do die, I would rather it be only after enjoying the remainder of their lives and believing that the best is yet to come."

The best is yet to come....

"But if I thought I was going to die, I would want to know." Mariah observed.

"Would you, really?" Curtis challenged her and his pensive eyes studied her face. "Would you really want to know the when and how?"

Mariah found herself without any words to speak. A small drop of sweat formed on her forehead and her clothes began to stick to her skin. She felt like the entire room had pulled in all the heat from the outside. She had no control in that moment as she stared into his eyes and tried to decide if he was heartless or advanced in his thinking. She felt as though his words were somehow heavier than most he ever spoke to her, but Mariah was unable to muddle through them to find the solution that she was attempting to seek.

They quietly finished their work and she felt like she was ready to collapse when they finally left that office that afternoon. Following her to the office door, his fingertips briefly touched Mariah's arm and she turned to look into his eyes. A 5 o'clock shadow formed on his face, while his naturally crimson lips curved into a slight, yet peaceful smile. "Are you okay, Mariah? You look unusually pale."

"I was just focused on my work." Mariah stuttered, as electrical shocks ran up and down her arms, her heart racing frantically and for a moment, she feared that a panic attack or something worse was looming. But she felt herself slowly calm down, almost as if nothing had occurred and yet, Curtis didn't look away from her eyes. "I guess I'm just tired."

"It's been a long day." Curtis agreed, leaning in close and Mariah felt chills running throughout her spine, her mouth watering as if in anticipation of a kiss – but she was wrong. He was merely leaning forward to turn off the lights, leaving her feeling slightly irritable as he ushered her out the door and into the hallway. Embarrassed, she had to look away out of fear that he had somehow read her mind but knowing that on a more basic level, that wasn't even possible.

"I will see you in the morning then?" He locked the door behind them and Mariah self-consciously played with the zipper on her purse, as if suddenly very involved in finding something in her bag.

"Ah, oh, yes, I will see you in the morning." Mariah said, finally looking up and into his eyes. He gave her a brief, if not sincere smile, before turning and headed in the opposite direction. She watched him walking casually, wearing a shirt and tie today, it was one of the few days he actually looked the part of a doctor rather than a student still in medical school. His laptop bag was pushed casually to the side, his hands slid into both pockets as if he hadn't a care in the world. She finally turned and headed toward the elevator. It appeared he went out the back of the building.

She felt so strange. Her body was heavy, as if she was catching the flu while deep down; Mariah knew it had nothing to do with any physical condition but something else that she couldn't explain. It was something she had decided to not discuss with Ava, it wasn't something she was ready to talk about with anyone yet.

Mariah Nichols was in love. For the first time in her life, she felt helpless, deeply in love with a man who probably would never see her as anything more than his office receptionist, merely the woman who was paid next to nothing to answer the phones and although she was smart, Mariah had no formal education to compete with his own credentials. Even Paulina had a degree in something or another, while Mariah hadn't even stepped foot in college.

Seriously, how did this happen? Was it merely a symptom of age? Fearing that she would get old and be alone forever, was she just falling for the most convenient man in her life? She had struggled with these emotions for weeks and despite her efforts to forget - they continued to lurk up on her and now firmly had a grasp on her every breath. She no longer woke up thinking about her next feeding of blood, about the next man she would bed in order to fulfill her own physical desires but instead, Mariah woke up thinking about him. He was the only man who had ever made her feel safe. The two had many conversations during a few free moments of the day and often even after the office closed. She found herself telling him bits and pieces about her life, things that she would never consider sharing with a coworker or boss under any other circumstances.

And he was curious. Curtis asked about her past. Where was she from? Why did she move to Vancouver? She was vague at first, only talking about how she 'needed a change' or 'got bored easily' but eventually confessed that family issues were the true reason why she left everything behind to move to Vancouver. He had concern in his eyes and questioned if things were okay now and to that, Mariah couldn't lie.

"No, actually they are not."

From across the room, Curtis' green eyes had searched her face in silence and he gently allowed the topic to go, asking nothing more about her relocation. He did attempt to break a few barriers with regards to family and friends, an area she tended to avoid. He inquired about childhood friends, to which she came up empty. She feared that he might have thought something was wrong with her to have so few people in her life and she quickly realized that perhaps that was her, not him, who was considering such a thing.

The words had been on the tip of her tongue so many times, but she simply couldn't tell Ava. Instead, she hid behind abrupt and sarcastic remarks that suggested that things were the same, consistent, and that nothing in Mariah's life had changed the person everyone around her knew. But something big changed and she feared it more than anything. She had opened the door but she wasn't prepared to go inside.

Chapter forty

There are plenty of theories about why we dream. Some believe that dreams are manufactured in our minds as a way to process the day's events, sifting through the many memories and feelings in order to carefully store them away. Other people see dreams as a premonition into the future, warning us of events to come and preparing us for whatever is around the corner. Then there are people like Mariah Nichols, who believe that dreams mean nothing at all.

At least, she hadn't until one dark and dreary night. She had fallen asleep on the couch on a Friday evening, while drinking a bottle of red wine and looking out at the stormy, Vancouver skies. Truth be known, she enjoyed the rainy weather, especially if it evolved into a thunderstorm. There was nothing like watching the lights in a sky, something she attributed to nature's fireworks as they sent a sharp chill through her spine. It was exhilarating.

Drifting into an intoxicated slumber, she slumped over where she sat, undisturbed by the powerful weather outside. Her thoughts floated into dreamland and it was there she was reintroduced to her brother for the first time in years. He was sitting beside her on her childhood bed and reading a story. Glancing down at her hands, Mariah realized that she was once again a little girl, probably no older than five while Anton, oddly enough, was probably the same age as when he died.

He appeared happy, carefree as he read from the page. The story was about a little girl who grew up in the city, after her parents made a long distance move from one place to another. However, many of his words weren't making sense and came out muffled, like an undercurrent that was lost in a much louder noise, sending its vibrations throughout her body and making her slightly nauseous as a result. Anton became harder to understand, as he continued to cheerfully read the book, slowly turning the pages, his animated face was young and healthy. Eventually she felt electrical shocks running through her arms, his voice creating a physical reaction that was only intensifying as he spoke. She wanted to get up from the bed, to run away from him, but Mariah found her legs heavy and she was unable to move. Tears burned behind her lids, she began shaking in fear and frustration and her throat became tight, making her unable to scream.

Suddenly awake on the couch, Mariah felt sweat gathering underneath the clutches of her bra, her heart was exhilarating to an alarming rate. Normally not scared, she found herself immediately jumping up and turning on every light in the apartment in order to release the spooky aspect that she was left with upon waking. It was as if her brother was a ghost, waiting to walk out and scare her at any second and she refused to accept it. Anton was dead and gone for over ten years and there was no way he was coming back. When people died, that was it. There was no returning. There was no heaven and hell. There was no spirit floating around the world. There was just nothing. It was clearly in her head.

Calming down, she realized that the alcohol combined with the terrible storm probably played a role in the situation and that she had foolishly fallen for it. Suddenly feeling silly, Mariah decided that maybe she needed to allow herself to take a relaxing bath, knowing that the warm water on her naked skin sent her into a world of pleasure and would take her away from the dismal thoughts that were floating through her head.

But there are some dreams we can't escape, especially when they return to us in a conscious form. Mariah quickly learned that on the following Monday, when she was once again working late with her boss and he casually brought up a topic she tried to avoid.

"So Mariah, do you have any brothers and sister?" His green eyes sparkled as he searched her face, as if the answer would suddenly pop out through her pores. She felt the same electrical shocks that were running through her arms during the recent dream of Anton suddenly return, her eyes couldn't help but to look away from Curtis. There was simply no way she could lie to him in the same manner as she had with many others before him, insisting that she was an only child and quickly switching the topic.

"Wow, that is quite a switch from asking me what I had for lunch today?" She grinned uncomfortably and finally looked back into his face, unsure of what to say. She felt as if she were backed into a corner and had no escape plan. "How did we get to this question?"

"Oh, no reason," He spoke casually, glancing to the other side of the room and shrugged as if it were no big deal. "I was just making conversation. I remember you mentioned some tension within your family, I was hoping that you at least had a sibling to lean on a bit."

"Um… no." Mariah answered abruptly and instantly realized that her reaction was perhaps a little too harsh, causing her to falter and alerting her boss. Curtis's eyes grew wider, his lips fell open beautifully and concern covered his face.

"I'm so sorry, Mariah. I certainly didn't mean to pry."

Guilt rushed in to replace her momentarily feelings of fear and Mariah felt shame for her words. It never occurred to her before, but suddenly it became clear that by lying about her brother's existence, she was showing disrespect towards his life. Grief filled her heart when Mariah realized that it was her own shame that made her lie, rather than saving her brother's face, as she had once convinced herself. It didn't matter that he was transgender, that he was sometimes horrible to her, that he had committed suicide: all that mattered is that it was her brother that she once loved very much, even though it was easy to cast him away from her mind, pretending he had never existed.

Feeling tears of shame filing her eyes, Mariah suddenly wasn't able to hold back her emotions, as the excruciating pain she felt over her brother's death filled every drop of blood in her body, cascading through her veins at an intense speed, as her own levee suddenly came crashing down. Immediately feeling embarrassed, she jumped from her chair and rushed into a nearby bathroom and quickly closed the door.

What in the hell is going on? Why is it happening to me?

"Mariah?" She could hear Dr. Wesley's soothing voice on the other side of the door, gently reaching out to her without judgment but filled with warmth. "I'm sorry if I upset you. I had no intentions of doing so. Please, forgive me for asking. I shouldn't have invaded your privacy."

Looking into the mirror, Mariah saw that her face was a mess, as her eyes grew redder by the moment and fragments of makeup ran out from the corners of her lids. Her lipstick was smudged and her hair was stuck to her face, as if Mariah were some insane woman who had just escaped the local psych ward. She was beyond humiliated and felt her heart racing in fear, suddenly feeling the most vulnerable she ever had in her life. She never allowed herself to be this way, let alone allow anyone else to see it.

"I'm fine," She attempted to swallow back her tears, as if they were only a momentary outburst and nothing more. Taking a deep breath, her mind raced to think of a logical reason to explain her sudden emotional reaction. "I'm fine, I'm sorry, it won't happen again."

There was hesitation on the other side of the door, as Mariah silently thought of an explanation to cover her behavior. She had a beloved pet die recently? She heard a horrible story of child abuse on the radio that morning? There had to be something that would take attention away from her personal life. That was it. She would just say it was an emotional overreaction that had nothing to do with her brother. Nothing.

"Mariah, I'm not concerned that you are acting unprofessionally in any way," Curtis insisted on the other side of the door, his voice sounding slightly more official and therefore making Mariah even more certain she would lie about what was bothering her. "In fact, I was simply concerned that I was the one acting unprofessionally. I shouldn't have pried about your personal life, and clearly there are some unresolved issues and it was not right of me to bring this up. I really do apologize."

Mariah wiped the stray tears from her face, attempted to fix her makeup and hair, took a deep breath and exited the bathroom. Although she had been brave in the moments before opening the door, this quickly dissolved when face to face with Curtis Wesley. His eyes were filled with sincere concern and sadness that she had no idea, were merely a reflection of what he saw in her face. And although she had a brave front for a moment or two, she felt herself completely dissolve once again.

He reached out for her arm and she quickly pulled herself together. Taking a deep breath, she wondered what was wrong with her? Why was she falling apart like this all of a sudden? It was humiliating. She quickly decided that she would never tell another living soul this story.

"I'm sorry. I'm sorry," Mariah looked away from his face and toward his hand that was barely touching her arm, as if not sure how to react to emotional outburst. How improper he must've thought she was to overreact to a simple question. "I..my..." She attempted to tell him a lie about a pet dying, but quickly realized that she couldn't do it. When Mariah looked into his eyes, she was unable to make up ridiculous stories to explain her behavior. "I have no explanation to..."

"How about we return to my office," Curtis gestured toward the soothingly lit room at the end of the hallway and she found herself walking toward it, almost unconsciously allowing him to lead. Mariah felt a sense of calmness overtake her as they both entered the room.

"I'm sorry." Mariah insisted immediately after she sat down, as he crossed the small office to do the same, grabbing of box of tissues and passing them to her. "This isn't like me."

"I have no doubt about that." Curtis was insistent and serious; his eyes scanned her face once again while he pulled his chair away from the desk and across from Mariah. "I don't see you as an emotional person who is prone to erratic crying, if that is what you think. I see a woman who was fine until I hit a nerve and for that, I sincerely apologize. I didn't mean to pry. I already sensed that your family was a touchy subject and I should've respected those boundaries."

"It's fine." Mariah assured him and let out a loud sigh. Perhaps it would be better to stick with honesty. "I think... I mean, I had a dream about my brother last night and it was kind of disturbing, so maybe that's why I lost it when you brought up the topic. I don't know why. I'm as confused about my reaction as you probably are." She hesitated. "At least, I hope you are?"

"I definitely don't see you as the kind of woman that cries over sappy movies and overreacts to spiders, if that is what you mean?" A smooth grin crossed his face and allowed her to finally relax. "I see you as a very strong woman, Mariah, even in the weeks that we started working together. You're smart and you're observant. You definitely have street smarts and you shoot from the hip. I really like that about you. But you're also human and sometimes as humans, we have our triggers. Apparently your family is one of them."

"They are." Mariah nodded and wondered how much she should share, but found the words flowing from her lips, almost as if she couldn't stop them. "My brother died. It's been a long time, but it was pretty bad."

"Was he sick?" Curtis leaned forward and was giving her his undivided attention, a flash of sympathy crossed his eyes, but the scientist in the background was clearly ready to diagnose and dissect whatever illness she suggested.

"No." She hesitated with the answer, wondering if perhaps he *was* sick, suffering from a mental illness that caused him to jump out of a window. Couldn't anyone lose it and act impulsively? "My brother committed suicide."

"Suicide?" Curtis' eyes opened a little wider and he nodded in understanding. "I can see why that was so upsetting for you and why it continues to be. I had a friend in college," He hesitated and put his hand up as if to surrender. "Not that I am suggesting that a friend is anything like a brother, but he committed suicide and it was pretty traumatic for all of us who were his friends."

"I don't think it is ever pleasant regardless of the relationship." Mariah decided to meet him half way. "My brother," She picked through so many words that could describe him, but none seemed right. He wasn't 'troubled', was he? She didn't want to pick a group of words to associate with the fact that he was transgender, because she didn't want to disrespect that community that her brother was a part of, as if to suggest that any issues he had was automatically connected to him. "My brother was transgender. I think maybe he was taking too many hormones or something because his behavior was sometimes erratic." Her memories floated back to the episode in Anton's living room, when he showed signs of physical abuse toward Mariah. "It's complicated."

Curtis nodded in silence. "I had a patient that was transgender when I was in med school." He pulled his chair back and reached for a sheet of paper at the back of his desk. At first she thought he was dismissing their conversation, until she saw the words on the flyer. It was a seminar on the subject at hand and he passed it to her. "It's very confusing for family members and often, for the people going through it. There is a group listed on the bottom of the page, I mean, if you ever want to talk to them about your brother. If it helps."

"Thanks." Mariah wasn't sure if the medical side of her boss was kind of missing the point until he continued to speak.

"Mariah, chances are that your brother was going through a lot of stuff that you didn't know anything about. He may have been putting on a brave face many times when he was not feeling so brave himself." Curtis watched her reaction before continuing. "I hope this doesn't seem insensitive of me to bring up. I just know about the specific patient I had in medical school that he was hiding a lot to protect his family. I don't want to be so presumptuous to suggest that your brother was doing the same, but sometimes people hold on to their pain and fear... and secrets because they think others don't care or won't want to help and when this is the case, they are alone by choice."

Mariah felt a sense of peace surround her and she found comfort in the silence that followed.

He wasn't talking about her brother. He was talking about her.

Chapter forty-one

A first kiss is deemed sacred by society. Movies display the scene with beautiful music playing in the background, as a gentle breeze blows through the feminine lead's hair and she appears so completely bewitched that one would be left thinking that she had never really 'lived' before that day. It's believed to be a magical rite of passage, one that is supposed to be remembered vividly, lovingly for the rest of her life.

Usually that isn't the case. Hollywood sets us up to believe that certain key moments in our lives are supposed to be wonderful and when reality falls short, some people can't help but to feel ripped off. Those moments that we were led to believe would change our lives, sometimes don't ·change anything or end up feeling awkward, uncomfortable or much less dreamlike than we expected.

First love is supposed to be in high school, possibly college, depending on which movie or television program you're watching and if that isn't the case, perhaps it depends on the magazine you choose to read or if you believe the stories that are posted on a friend's Facebook wall. Branding comes in many forms and some are just a little less contrived than others.

Mariah Nichols laughed at the concept of 'first love'. In high school, she remembered walking past a young woman who was rumored to have been dumped by her boyfriend the previous weekend. Crying, she was isolated from the other students during lunchtime and although Mariah was aware that it was socially acceptable to stop and offer words or wisdom or a hug, she merely trotted by with a feeling of superiority and disinterest.

Throughout her life, Mariah prided herself on not falling into the ridiculous trap called love. She laughed at the matchmaking reality shows, humored by other women who talked about boyfriends, candies and flowers and merely waved off comments about how people were surprised when they learned she was single. Why was that surprising? Cause she wasn't an unattractive cow? Mariah had been around long enough to know that looks certainly had no bearing on whether or not someone married. In fact, she often found the most unattractive people were the first to do so and she assumed it was out of fear of never having another opportunity.

No, Mariah Nichols had refused to believe in the foolishness that other women had fallen for and she truly believed it uncomplicated her life. It wasn't that she had anything against love, but it wasn't that she was dying to be part of that confusing world. Did she want to be one of those women who sat by the phone and prayed for 'him' to call? Giving someone else that much power over your happiness seemed like a recipe for disaster.

But it didn't stop other women from telling her their love woes, as if it were to create an automatic bond between women and they would become best friends. Even Ava didn't talk about her breakup with Landon and well, they were close friends; but Mariah wasn't close with Paulina, her coworker, but it didn't stop her from discussing details of her private life that should've been kept private.

"It's just not the same anymore," Paulina whined as the two sat together behind the reception desk on a Monday morning. Mariah had barely started her large coffee and although she appeared pleasant to her coworker, she certainly wasn't interested in hearing anything that was in this conversation. "We used to be so crazy in love and then one day, he just started acting weird, you know?"

Mariah nodded solemnly. She knew. He was cheating on her. She knew because she was often the other woman in these scenarios. The more Paulina talked, the more she confirmed Mariah's assumption.

"He just would rather go out with the boys more than stay home with me." Paulina sighed loudly, glancing over the day planner quickly, neglecting to grab the files associated with that day's patients but instead continued to ramble on like a wounded soldier. "I was waiting up for him till after 2 a.m. on Saturday night. The guys were playing poker and when he finally got home, he didn't even want to talk to me. He just crawled into bed and ignored me."

Cheating. Without a doubt, cheating. Mariah gave her a satisfied smile, which Paulina seemed to interpret as a sign of comforting.

"We haven't even had sex in weeks," She whispered to Mariah, even though no one else was in the office yet. Pulling her chair closer, she confided in her coworker. "I had on this sexy nightie I spent a lot of money on and he didn't even notice. He just went to sleep."

"Maybe he just… I don't know has a lot going on right now." Mariah attempted to explain the situation away, preferring to not discuss Paulina's sex life. It was clear that she was a woman who used her sexuality to get a man's attention, but at the same time, it evidently wasn't keeping it long term.

"You could be right." She agreed just as Dr. Wesley walked in and flashed a smile at the two young women behind the desk. Mariah felt her heart rate suddenly rose, her face grow warm and had to look away from his face, toward the Starbucks coffee in his hand. He gave a swift 'good morning' and rushed past them and down the hallway toward his office. He was usually running late.

When she looked up again, she noted that Paulina's eyes were following him as he rushed away. "Maybe I'm going to have to start looking elsewhere."

Anger crept up on Mariah's heart and she felt her moment of embarrassment that quickly passed. Her urge to react was strong, but she denied it. This anger grew even stronger when Paulina rose from her chair and made an excuse to go check in on Dr. Wesley, claiming she had something important to talk to him about. By the time Mariah heard his office door gently close, she felt fire flowing through her veins and she wanted nothing more than to rush down the hallway and tell Paulina that just because her boyfriend didn't want to fuck her, didn't mean she had to chase after their boss.

That's when the first patient arrived. An older gentleman who was accompanied by a much younger, Mexican woman entered the room and momentarily looked taken aback by the expression on Mariah's face.

"Are we too early?" The slightly overweight woman with innocent eyes asked and Mariah felt herself calming instantly.

"Oh no, not at all!" She threw in all the enthusiasm she could muster, attempting to listen through the door down the hallway. It was shut very tightly so she could barely make out a murmur and swallowed back her frustration, as the old man loudly gave her both his name and appointment time. She merely smiled and rushed through a quick, "Yes, yes, I see you here! That's fantastic, I will take you to the office."

She jumped from her seat, just as the front door opened and more people arrived. This was supposed to be Paulina's duty while Mariah manned the phones, creating more resentment on her original irritation. However, Mariah hoped that as she led the patient to the office, she would be able to better hear what was going on behind the closed doors.

But that was when a baby in the reception area started to cry and a ringing phone quickly followed and meanwhile, could this old man possibly walk any slower? It briefly crossed Mariah's mind that she could've thrown his 100 lb. body over her shoulder and carried him faster than he was walking but instead forced a smile on her face.

It was just as she started to move the senior into an empty room that an exultant Paulina walked out of Curtis' office. He was behind the desk and appeared to be reading some papers. Paulina attempted a friendly comment, sending a giggle over her shoulder. His eyes looked up, passing her and briefly met with Mariah's.

Her heart racing, she felt her throat tightened as she returned to the desk. More people piled into the room and waited at the reception desk and the phone continued to ring. Paulina seemed unfazed by this situation and just chuckled about how "the doctor is such a cutie."

Mariah was fuming. As she immediately jumped into work, the chipper Paulina was joyfully dealing with the patients that were irritable, as a baby continued to send out blood curdling screams in the seated area. Glancing at the clock, Mariah realized that it was 9:07 on a Monday morning and she was already completely frustrated and wanted to physically hurt her coworker.

By lunchtime, Paulina's perky attitude was getting the best of Mariah and she wasn't sure how she would get through the afternoon. Jealousy was intensifying with each passing moment and it was difficult to keep her cool. The doctor was one of the few people she had allowed to get to know her with a secret fear of rejection, but never allowing herself to over think her true motives. Curtis forced her to discover and face feelings that no one else could have and at times it made her fear, as much as love him.

But what could she do? She certainly couldn't confess her true feelings. Then again, she couldn't have Paulina making the move. What if he was attracted to her? She did have a fierce sexuality that was undeniable, even for Mariah, so why wouldn't he be lured into her web? Would he allow this to happen? Would he do so if he knew how Mariah felt about him? Does he feel the same way?

She hated these feelings. This is something she had managed to avoid for 30 years of her life until now. Mariah felt a combination of shame and regret for becoming one of the women she once had laughed at, no longer able to entertain herself with casual hookups because she was in love. Her every thought was on those beautiful, green eyes, that welcoming smile and the warmth she felt whenever in his presence.

It was such a complicated problem and she found herself drowning her sorrows with a few drinks over lunchtime. Perhaps she had gone a little overboard on the vodka martinis but she had to numb the feelings that were embarking on her very soul and it would be otherwise impossible to deal with the afternoon ahead with Paulina, had she not had something to relax her. With a strong breath mint and a shot of perfume, chances are Dr. Wesley wouldn't notice any difference in his receptionist. She knew for certain that other bosses hadn't noticed in the past and it was unlikely he would either.

But then she got paranoid. After looking in the restaurant mirror before leaving, feeling slightly off balanced after walking across the room, Mariah began to worry that perhaps she wasn't as smart as she originally thought. Perhaps she could pull the wool over Paulina's eyes but probably not the doctor's. She did her best to reapply some makeup, flawlessly put on some lipstick, and then fix her hair. By the time she got back to work, Mariah would be as good as new. She'd just grab a coffee on the way.

But paranoia won over and by the time she returned to the office, Mariah felt like a mess. When Paulina took one look at her and asked if she was okay, it was clear that she was deceiving no one.

"I'm not feeling well." Mariah confessed and forced a smile on her face. "I think I may have eaten something that didn't agree with me, my stomach just feels terrible."

"Will you be okay to work?" She heard a voice coming from the doorway and Mariah automatically felt an instinct to avoid his eyes, but she couldn't. Unlike other times, Curtis didn't appear to be caring or comforting, but stern in appearance. There was no way he could've known, she quickly told herself and yet, something told Mariah that he did.

"Yes, of course." She replied quickly. "I'll be fine."

He gave her a quick once over, said nothing more and walked away.

That's when things began to unravel.

Chapter forty-two

Time goes by so fast. One day we're children, begging for more freedom; and the next, we're an adult and wishing for less responsibility. People never seem to be content with where they are in life and yet, if they only found contentment in the moment, life would run much smoother for us all.

Mariah hadn't noticed the time go by. Wasn't it just yesterday she was a young woman, full of hope and excitement about life, moving to the city of Montreal? There was so much more vitality to the 17 year-old version of herself, a sparkle in her eyes when looking into the dingy bathroom mirror at her brother's place that had long ago faded away. She remembered viewing the world as a huge place where dreams were just around the corner and it was only a matter of time before she found her heart's desire.

What had changed, she wondered. Why did she now have to drag her weary body out of bed each morning, feeling as though she were dragging ten pounds of bricks behind her as she crossed the floor, only to enter a beautifully lit bathroom and see nothing but despair in her eyes. This wasn't how her life was supposed to turn out. Was she the same woman who once was excited to work two menial jobs – one in retail and the other at a strip bar – just excited to be out in the world, earning income? Now she did a job that actually mattered and yet, she couldn't have cared less.

Coffee and blood gave her a lift in the morning, but it was temporary. Mariah wasn't sure why nothing seemed to make her happy any longer; not men, not money, not even alcohol. If someone asked her to map out her ideal future, Mariah wouldn't have a clue what to say. What did she really want? What would truly make her happy? Why was she stuck in this funk?

Months passed since she started to work for Curtis Wesley. It was difficult to believe that it was coming close to a year and yet, despite the fact that she sometimes hated her job, she was still there. All the frustrating patients (not to mention coworker) were worth it just to spend ten minutes alone with the doctor. There was something about being in his presence that brought her a few moments of peace in her day, yet she couldn't explain why. She assumed it was because he remained calm in every situation and was extremely patient with her, something that Mariah had never managed to bring out with anyone else. There was just something in those few moments together that made her feel as though a glimmer of light passed through her soul. If only she knew how to capture and save it.

Every day she rolled into work with her Starbucks in hand; Ray-Bans and a grimace on her face and Mariah wondered how she would possibly get through another day of work. Paulina would ramble on like a moron, the doctor would arrive and his smile would give her a quick lift, then she would get caught up in the frantic pace of the office till noon. She generally had lunch alone, but on some days, she met with Ava. Although it usually gave her a boost, sometimes Mariah simply couldn't exhume the confident, sarcastic version of herself that Ava was used to seeing and therefore decided that it was better to slink into the corner of a bar alone and knock back a few drinks.

The truth was that Ava was suddenly quite obsessed with learning more about the immortal vampires and recently, it seemed to be all she ever talked about during their lunch dates. Although Mariah supported her friend, she had a bad feeling that perhaps she was venturing down a dangerous road; for the little bit she did know about the immortals, suggested that they didn't want people poking around in their business. What if she put herself in danger? It almost appeared as though this fact was irrelevant to Ava and Mariah considered that perhaps the frail friend she met a year earlier, was much stronger than she appeared. Maybe Ava Lilith was stronger than herself, Mariah pondered.

The two would discuss the immortals and Mariah promised to see what she could find out. Truthfully, she had a source, but was doubtful there was much more she could learn about the topic. Although never satisfied with the information she had, it appeared that Ava was discovering new facts all around and was continuing to dig deeper, as if nothing else mattered in life. Then again, she still was one up on Mariah, who didn't feel like anything mattered anymore. Still, the topic grew exhausted and she struggled to change it from time to time in order to get Ava off track.

"How many drinks did you have today?" Ava attempted to make a joke on a warm, October day as the sun peaked through the window and touched Mariah's face. Had all the myths about vampires been true, she briefly considered how she would've sat far into the dark corner, at the back of the room.

Smiling, she stared into the caramel eyes that watched her intently, humored that this woman who was younger by a few years, was acting as though she were a mother hen. Remaining silent, she briefly enjoyed the worried expression on Ava's face and finally shared a smile, as she slowly shook her head. "You needn't worry about me. I'm half Russian, this is how we roll."

"Vodka for lunch?"

"Vodka for lunch." Mariah confirmed in a quiet voice before she took a deep breath, as if to expand her confidence in the moment, like an actress about to take the stage. "In fact, this vodka is what is going to help me from committing a violent crime for the rest of the afternoon."

"Coworker or patients?"

"It's a toss up at this point." Mariah nodded, tilting her head and peering up at Ava. "The patients tend to fluctuate, my coworker? Not so much."

"Is she talking about her sex life again?" Ava made reference to the last conversation the two had about Paulina. "Is that a professional thing to do at work?"

"No," Mariah considered, tilting her head back and forth, as in thought. "But then again, neither is having sex at work and I've done it, so I guess I'm not one to talk."

Ava laughed and much to Mariah's delight, showed no judgment. "Did you ever see this boyfriend that she talks about? Maybe he doesn't actually exist, I once knew this guy who went on and on about his 'girlfriend', turns out she was in his mind."

"Well, I was starting to wonder until he showed up at work one day to give her a set of keys? Maybe for their apartment or something, I guess she forgot them." Mariah spoke calmly, running her fingers over the rim of her glass and glancing out the window. People rushed along the sidewalk and she noted that some used umbrellas, as if they would somehow protect them from the sun that shone through the nearby trees. "But he does exist."

"Is he cute?"

"Cuter than I thought, to be honest." Mariah lifted the glass to her lips and took a sip. A warmth spread down her throat and flowed through her chest and her eyes watered by the strength of the drink, although only briefly. "I mean, not in a dating kind of way, but in an 'I'd fuck him in a McDonald's bathroom kind of way."

Ava burst out laughing. "That's a pretty vivid description of where he fits in the sexual arena."

Mariah nodded and cleared her throat. "Yes, yes it does. Some guys kind of got it going on but not enough to spend an entire evening listening to them. He's just one of those guys."

"So Paulina aims low?"

"No, cause she is currently aiming for our boss and he is phenomenal." Mariah didn't go on about Curtis because to do so, would make it apparent that she was in love with him. "I think her boyfriend is just an easy target, that's the appeal and it is obvious what he likes about her. I don't call her tits and ass for nothing."

Ava snickered and took another drink of her red wine. "Maybe they actually have a lot in common, you never know?"

"He didn't appear to have anything in common with her, from what I saw," Mariah admitted. "He just seemed happy to get away from her, but he was still a step up from what I expected. I figured he would be kind of chubby like her and every time she would talk about their sex life, I was slightly ill because I would picture this fat roly-poly sex going on and it was just... repulsive. It's bad enough that she is probably dragged out and sagged out."

"Roly poly sex?" Ava repeated and threw her head back in laugher. "Did you seriously just say that?"

"Yes!" Mariah felt her lips curve in an unexpected smile. It delighted her to make her friend laugh, for some reason. "Fat sex? I refer it to roly-poly sex because... well, that's what I visualize when I think about it."

"And dragged out, sagged out?" Ava's eyes challenged her, with a smile perched on the edge of her lips, as if ready to turn into laughter at any moment.

"Well, at a certain age, gravity seems to work against a woman and I suspect that Tits and Ass has reached that stage now." Mariah spoke as if it was a matter of fact, as opposed to a slanted and vindictive opinion. "It's her own fault that I'm even thinking about such things. After all, she brought up her sex life to me, not the other way around."

Ava burst out in laughter, slowly rising from her chair. "Mariah, you are such a clever woman. I think your talents are greatly wasted on your job in the doctor's office." Glancing toward the ladies' room, she gave a sincere smile. "I'll be right back."

Mariah merely nodded, proud that she was able to uplift her friend's lunchtime with a few laughs. Of course, they were cheap shots at her coworker, which was perhaps unnecessary, but the words had just flowed from her lips as if it was the most natural thing to say.

The girls parted ways shortly after and Mariah felt light as she returned to the office, slightly buzzed, she decided to grab a small coffee, as if it were to defer any attention to her tipsiness.

However, upon returning to work, Mariah quickly noted that it would be a busy afternoon, as patients were already waiting outside the door before she unlocked it. She discovered Paulina's purse already behind the reception desk and upon glancing down the hallways; Dr. Wesley's office door was closed. She felt a fire released in her heart and it took everything inside of her to not fly down the hallway and rip the door open. It was obvious that the two were having an affair. The hushed voices that she was unable to hear, said it all. If they were discussing a work topic, there would be no need to keep it so low that even her vampire ears weren't able to hear.

As Mariah escorted a young, female patient to an empty office, she saw the door swing open and immediately, her gaze met with Curtis Wesley's sharp, green eyes and she couldn't help but give him a cool glare and look away. When she returned to the reception area, she noted that Paulina was helping the next patient to the other empty office, strutting along, her breasts were practically bouncing out of her low cut top, while her short skirt was so tight that Mariah could hear her the thighs of her pantyhose awkwardly rubbing together. Aware that her vampire ears probably had an advantage that others did not, it still was a little disturbing to her that she was hearing this unflattering noise.

Rushing back just as Mariah sat down to talk to the next patient, an older gentleman, she noted that his eyes were staring in the direction of Paulina and when Mariah turned, she could see his gaze was fixated on the ample cleavage and the one, very apparently erect nipple on her left side, as if it had somehow wiggled out of her bra to make its escape. It was repulsive and Mariah fought the urge to slap the old man in the face, in order to regain his attention.

"As I was asking you," She abruptly pulled his eyes back in her direction. "Do you have your CareCard?"

"Ah, yes, just a second," He reached into his pocket to search and Mariah glanced at her coworker, who appeared to be adjusting herself.

"You might want to do that before you come out of his office." Mariah whispered in a biting tone, noting the stunned expression on Paulina's face, she turned back to her patient and thanked him for the card he was extending toward her, as he continued to stare at Paulina's cleavage.

Chapter forty-three

Vulnerability is one of the most difficult things to face. It's usually so carefully hidden behind layers of fear, distrust and skepticism that sometimes we forget that it exists at all. It would be convenient to never encounter any uncomfortable emotions during a lifetime, but would you really be living?

Church bells awoke Mariah on a dreary Saturday morning in December. Glancing out the window from her comfortable bed, she noted that the clouds were rolling in, possibly indicating rain in the not too distant future. A small grin travelled over her lips, finding humor in the fact that it was probably someone's wedding day and it would be ruined by the weather. She wasn't happy and in that moment and didn't care if anyone else was either.

Rising from bed, she threw on an old pair of yoga pants from her Energy Planet Vancouver days and glancing in the mirror, briefly considered how they fit as well as the day she bought them. Throwing on a tank top and hoodie, she grabbed her running shoes, sunglasses and keys, as she made her way to the door. Run, walk, Mariah wasn't sure what she would accomplish when she got outside, but it was better than sitting around her apartment and dwelling on the misery of her week.

Rushing out the door, she grabbed her iPod as she reached for the doorknob and forced a smile on her lips as she glanced in a nearby mirror, even though Mariah knew she didn't mean it. Her heart was broken and there was no way it was going to be repaired by a run, walk or a pair of pants that made her ass look skinnier than it actually was in reality. Shoving on her sunglasses, she pretended there weren't any tears in her eyes and then she would pretend that she didn't feel as though she were under an ocean of water and unable to rise above the current. She was suffocating with every flash from the previous week and yet, she took a deep breath and told herself - convinced herself - it was over and no use rethinking the many emotional highs and lows, that were like a slap in the face.

She walked away from it. She left the misery outside her doorway, like a ghost that insisted it would never go away, but rather, cast it at her the moment she returned. Maybe the answer was to not return again, she considered as she hit the elevator button and walked inside to find it empty. Suddenly gasping for air, feeling as if the walls were closing in on her, she blinked her eyes and swallowed back the emotions that were threatening to take over.

The doors finally opened and she fiercely rushed out, but was halted by a soft thud against Landon Owens, just as he was about to enter the enclosed space. Quickly ripping off the sunglasses that were thrust against her face, she glared at him and felt her emotions slip away for a moment, as her hoarse voice snapped at him. "Will you watch where you are going? For fuck sakes, Landon-

"Where I'm going?" He defensively snapped back, raising both hands in the air. "Hey, in case you hadn't noticed, I was just standing here waiting for the elevator. You were the one rushing out like a bat out of hell." His voice was calm, smooth and he showed no emotions in his eyes. "But that is where you come from, right? Hell?"

Behind her, the elevator once again closed and Mariah quickly realized that this was not a conversation she wanted to have at that moment. Any other time, she could've risen above Landon's snide remarks and meet them with a few of her own, but today simply wasn't the day.

"I'm not in the mood, Landon." Her voice fell flat and she attempted to move past him but he continued to block her way. "Will you just leave me alone?"

"Wow," Landon raised his eyebrows slightly and gently placed his hand on her shoulder. "So where's the narcissistic sociopath that we all know and love?" He quipped and attempted to sway her toward the lounge area, where Benjamin now sat and watched the two of them, even though he pretended to not notice from behind his newspaper. "Are you not feeling well?"

"I guess you could say that." She shrugged and abruptly pulled her sunglasses back on. Without saying another word, she swung out of his grasp and rushed toward the exit and immediately began to run. By the time she made her way to a nearby park, she felt her original burst of energy disappear and sinking to just below the surface. Mariah suddenly felt as though she would melt and drain right into the earth below her. She wanted nothing more than to die in that moment, as her mind raced through the week that could've been perfect; to the week that was her own personal hell.

It started off hopeful. She felt closer to Curtis Wesley than she had in weeks, if ever. They worked late every night and talked about everything under the sun. He told her about his childhood and how he was often teased and sometimes bullied.

"I'm mixed race," He shrugged while shuffling though some files. "Some people just aren't comfortable with that and some people just don't understand. I wasn't white enough for some and I wasn't black enough for others. I didn't seem to have a place in the world."

Mariah's heart sank as she heard him tell stories of kids being both physically and verbally abusive to him as a child. She could see the pain in his eyes and she knew that he was sharing something very intimate with her, so after a few moments of silence, she did the same.

"I can't personally relate to your story but it kind of reminds me of Anton," She hesitated briefly and stared into his eyes and for just a moment, maybe even just a split second, it felt like the entire world stopped. The connection she felt with him was stronger than anything she had experienced in her life and yet, she felt more at peace than she ever felt possible. It was as if a spell had been cast over her and she never wanted it to leave.

"Anton?" His words startled her slightly and she felt herself breathe for the first time in seconds, perhaps minutes?

"Yes, my brother," She calmly replied, her eyes scanning her fingers and she noted that a chip was out of her nail polish. Her eyes rose to meet his face and her heart rate slowed to a pace of rare, pure comfort. She successfully fought back tears in her eyes, rapidly blinking just in case and bit her bottom lip. "I think I told you once that he was…"

"Transgender?" Dr. Wesley finished her sentence and softly placed the file in his hand on the desk, indicating that she had his full attention. "I guess that he would've known about being between two world."

"Well, yes, I mean, I know it's not the same thing," Mariah quickly felt herself recapture her usual confidence, although she did stutter for a second, trying to get her own bearings. "I don't mean it that way, I just mean-

"No, it is the same thing, Mariah. Slightly different circumstances and actually, probably much more difficult than what I struggled with as a kid." Curtis tilted his head slightly; his strong jawline made him seem more powerful in her eyes, especially mixed with the vulnerability that he disclosed in his face. "People probably didn't accept him in the world he was leaving or the world he was about to enter."

"I can't imagine how that must feel." Mariah confessed while her fingers nervously played with a piece of paper in her hands. "I wish I had been more supportive."

"I'm sure you did the best you could at the time."

There was something in his words that released her. It was as if someone had unclasped a tight harness that had been pulling together her soul for all the years since Anton's death and although she felt slightly emotional at the moment, she wouldn't allow these emotions to rise up and humiliate her, as they had last time this topic came up.

Their conversations were warm throughout the week and only made her feel increasingly safe in his world, wishing to be a larger part of it than merely an employee. It had grown over many months and she felt accepted and his acceptance made her want to become a better person. She would've done anything in the world for him: anything at all. She would defend him, lie for him and love him more than anyone else ever could, but if only he would give her the chance.

But as much as the week started off on a positive note, it would fall short very quickly. Her paranoia and insecurities would rise up like a fountain, ready to shoot up erratically in the air and drench anyone who stood within arm's length of her intense fears. The problem with vulnerability is that it can sometimes push you to act erratically and even though your behavior may logically seem self-defeating and misery laden, a nervous energy or knee jerk reaction causes your fountain to erupt at the worst possible time.

Mariah had done so on a particularly stressful day at the office. The combination of anxiety due to her work, her personal fears of both Dr. Wesley and Paulina's possible relationship and his own distant attitude toward her earlier that same morning, barely acknowledging her in favor of her coworker, she felt herself start to lose control. Was he trying to send her a message? Had he not shared some personal moments with her earlier that week, as well as many weeks before that day? If he didn't care about her, why did he make such an effort to learn about her personal life, her emotions and what mattered to her? Did he do the same with Paulina? Did they get involved? Did they get together and laugh behind her back about what a lovesick puppy she was in his presence? A million illogical thoughts ran through her mind and yet, she couldn't' stop them. They got faster and more out of control until she could hardly function.

"Earth to Mariah." Paulina would tease her while gently placing her soft, warm hands on her coworkers arm, as if they were close friends bonded from the first day. If anything, her overly chipper attitude just encouraged the assumption she had that her boss and co-workers were having an affair. "You're so absent minded lately, it must be love." She added, just before rising from her chair and giving Mariah a quick wink before escorting a patient to the office.

That day Mariah went to the closest bar and drank for her whole lunch. She wasn't drunk when she returned to work, but the alcohol hadn't exactly helped her performance or attitude. She felt herself sinking almost immediately and unlike the other times before it, Mariah didn't have any control. She felt as though she was going to sink to the floor. But somehow, she managed to get through the day and was the first to rush out the door when it was over.

The next morning was when it happened. She had been carrying around these uneasy, unresolved feelings for months and fear was eating up every other emotion, both positive and negative, in her body. Her sleeping consisted of a difficult night of tossing and turning, thoughts racing through her mind while tears plummeted down her cheeks, dripping from her chin. She wanted to die. She hated Curtis. She loved Curtis.

Then next morning, she went to work early and found an empty office. Mariah had hoped that her boss would already be there so she could tell him, finally freeing herself of the small secret that grew and grew over months, until it filled a room and drained her every bit of energy. Feeling nervous, physically ill and like she wanted to crawl out of her own skin, she wasn't sure what to say when he finally did arrive. It was before the office opened and they were alone.

It was all a blur. She asked to speak to him and she felt her heart race as she followed Curtis to his office. She remembered almost melting into the chair across from him and someone confessed her feelings, but she swore it wasn't her. Mariah wasn't in her body that moment, but somewhere in the room, floating about from above, a safe distance and listening to him reject her; it was cold, fast, like a Band-Aid being ripped off. She would recall later how she slunk out of the room, feeling as though her entire body was overtaken by a cold sweat. She was in a protective daze, unable to fully comprehend what had just happened. It just wasn't real. It couldn't be real.

But it was. It was very real.

She loved him.

He didn't love her.

Chapter forty-four

For years people believed that vampires were nothing more than mystical creatures, products of books and movies. No one ever considered that they could be real, mortal or possibly their next-door neighbor, but just nothing more than a fantasy that both frightened and exhilarated their fans. It was assumed they were emotionless, heartless and would kill their prey long before they would ever befriend or love them.

This was the kind of vampire that Mariah wished she had been, even though she knew that they were complete fiction. There were mortal and immortal vampires and both shared the human traits of regular, normal people except for their taste for blood, enhanced senses and of course, the immortals lived forever in secret. But that was pretty much it. They weren't able to escape the discomfort of unpleasant emotions such as humiliation or embarrassment because these were traits that came along with being on earth.

Mariah put on a brave front when she told Ava that she was fired. She even spun a story – mostly lies – insisting that she was angry but simply didn't care. And later, when confronted, she admitted some of the truth to Ava but generally didn't feel safe to tell the whole, true story. She had learned her lesson about being completely open and honest with another human being and it was not a mistake she planned on making again.

Ava was supportive and a wonderful friend and it had been never a matter of distrusting her loyalty, but perhaps it was better that she kept her at arm's length. There was no need of confessing anything about her brother nor did she have to know the entire truth about her transformation or heartbreak with Dr Wesley. There were so many lies told.

The days flew by after she lost her job and with the combination of the holidays and the lack of other available opportunities, Mariah found herself sinking into a massive depression. She would sit in her apartment, drinking bottles of wine and thinking again and again about that horrible morning when she lost her job. The look of disappointment in the Curtis' eyes when he revealed sometimes smelling alcohol on her breath, how he feared that she had some emotional problems that she should look into and that although he did like her, he was currently in love with someone else. Mariah drearily assumed it was Paulina and then would spend countless hours comparing herself to her former coworker, thinking about how she couldn't compete with her physical or inner beauty.

As much as she hated to admit it to herself, Landon was right when he called her a narcissist sociopath. It never occurred to her that he did so in a bitter, teasing manner, but in fact, as a sharp insult that stabbed her in the heart. Was that how other people viewed her as well? Had Curtis viewed her through the same eyes?

A week after she was fired, she was surprised to open her mailbox to find a letter with the return address of Dr. Curtis Wesley office. Assuming it was some kind of formal paperwork, she almost didn't open it but curiosity got the better of her. Ripping it open, she found a record of employment that had her listed as laid off, rather than fired. It took her a moment to realize that he had done so in order to allow her the unemployment benefits that would've been withheld, had she had been terminated with cause.

She found a letter included and was slightly disappointed when she scanned the bottom to find Paulina's name, but found herself reading it with an open heart. It was just a short note to say that Mariah had left her engraved pen set at the office, if she wished to pick it up. Of course, she was referring to a gift Curtis had purchased for both of them during the holidays last year, shortly after the office opened. In order to be politically correct, he hadn't called it a 'Christmas gift' but rather, a 'thank you gift' for their help setting up the office.

The letter went on to say that Paulina would be happy to meet her somewhere, someday if she didn't feel comfortable going near the office.

Mariah sneered thinking that it was actually her that she didn't feel comfortable going near and almost crumpled up the letter and threw it out, but suddenly stopped and sat it on her desk.

After spending too much time drinking, thinking about and hating her life, Mariah finally woke up one morning and decided that it was time to get out of this slump and move on. Although she hated confessing how she felt for Curtis, another part of her felt free for having done so and half wondered if he would one day return to her life, after time moved forward. Maybe it was time to lay off the alcohol and start drinking her normal requirements of blood; something she had been slightly delinquent in doing as of late.

The transition was slow, as if she was a child attempting to take her first steps. She started by cleaning her apartment, getting rid of the many liquor bottles and going to the unemployment office in order to at least get some money through benefits, until finding another job. Getting out of her apartment seemed to be key because when she did so, she felt better. This, along with her continued dose of blood, made her feel as though her sex drive was returning and decided it was time to relight that candle. Who was she saving herself for, anyway? Besides, men had been a source of pleasure and confidence for her, so perhaps that was exactly what she needed to get back on track.

It didn't completely make her forget Curtis, but it did force her to remember herself.

Every day she felt a little bit stronger. And every day she went out looking for a new job, thinking that perhaps it was time to refocus her attention on other things. Perhaps it was time she stop looking for receptionist jobs and consider some other career possibilities. It wasn't like she was a total idiot and Mariah was certainly smart enough to learn how to do anything she wanted. Had she simply fell into a comfort zone and continued to walk down the same path? Maybe it was time to consider going back to school or discovering her passion. What did she really want to do? It was about time she figured it out.

Meanwhile, she assisted Ava in attempting to learn more about the immortal lifestyle. Although she had done some digging in the past, Mariah had only managed to learn very little for her friend and now that she had some time on her hands, she decided to do some more investigating. After all, Ava had been loyally by her side during this whole ordeal and had even forced her way into her apartment during a time that Mariah had stubbornly hidden behind her door, refusing to either come out or talk to anyone. It took a real friend to go that extra mile during such a low point and Mariah wanted to pay her back by finally learning the secrets about this so called 'Rock Star of Vampires' that Ava was obsessively talking about.

Of course, she quickly discovered all the same roadblocks as Ava and along with that, had a couple of threats to back off and leave it alone. Rather than run away from the fear, Mariah stubbornly pushed the door in and forced her way through. After everything she had been through in her life, there was no way that these fucking immortals (or anyone else for that matter) were going to frighten her into backing off. What could they possibly do?

It was an appointment at a temp agency, a place that was supposed to help her locate some work, where Mariah would find her next job. It just happened that they were in dire need of a receptionist because their usual one had quit on a whim. For that reason, she immediately got the job.

"Now, it is only temporary because the girl who recently quit was actually doing a mat leave for another employee," The professional young woman, who was about to become Mariah's new boss, quickly explained to her on the same morning she dropped in with her resume. The two were sitting in Annette Robert's office first thing on Monday morning and apparently, shortly after the temporary agency received the surprising news that they no longer had a receptionist at their location.

"I will have to double check, but I believe her leave is finished in a couple of months, but of course, if you do a great job here, we will help you out on your career path at that point."

"I'm in the best place possible to keep posted on new jobs." Mariah was relieved to finally hear the confidence return in her voice and equally relieved to see a smile cross Annette's lips. She appeared to be a nice lady, possibly slightly older than herself and with short blonde hair, styled nicely in a bob. She had huge brown eyes that were almost freakish in size, while her slender figure was as plain as the outfit she wore over it. Overall, Mariah figured her to be pleasant and felt comfortable working for her.

"Terrific, well, I'll check with your last employer," Annette stood up from her seat and Mariah felt her heart start to pound rapidly. If Ms. Roberts had noticed that her face was flushed or a twinge of nervousness was in her presence, she certainly didn't react to it as she smiled at Mariah and headed toward the door. "I will be right back."

Mariah closed her eyes and felt a cold sweat forming underneath her clothes. She suddenly felt her confidence evaporate out of the room and nothing was left as she sat there, waiting for the other shoe to drop. Curtis Wesley had the power to corrupt her future. What if he told Annette Roberts about her drinking? It wouldn't matter that she had avoided alcohol for the last few weeks or that she had picked herself up since the last job, if he chose to give her a bad reference.

In the end, the worry was for nothing. Although Annette wouldn't share the details, she did provide Mariah with reason to believe that the recommendation was glowing and asked her if she could start the next day.

"I can start *now*," Mariah laughed with relief and nervously played with the button on her blouse sleeve. She had chosen a very modest outfit that morning and looked stunning and professional, something that Mariah wouldn't have thought of herself only a few weeks earlier. "I mean you seem to need someone." She gestured toward the door.

"Although I do appreciate the offer," Annette began to laugh. "It simply wouldn't be fair to throw you into that mess today and I would prefer to go over a few things, just to familiarize you. I will, however, give you some reading material about the company if you wish to step into a free office and read it and of course, I will have some papers for you to sign."

"Of course." Mariah followed her lead when Annette rose from the chair and headed toward the door. Glancing toward the office entrance, she watched as a handsome, young man walked inside and toward the reception area. With a grin on her face, Mariah said, "I think I will like working here."

Chapter forty-five

Restless and crazy energy. Sometimes we find ourselves in a room with someone that drives us completely insane, pushes us to our limits and yet, it is almost as if we can't find the door to leave. Feeling trapped; there is no relief greater than when we finally discover that exit and plunge into the outside world, suddenly feeling gleeful and free.

Other times, we aren't able to escape. Clawing at the walls until our nails are torn off, leaving blood stains on the pristine walls that enclose us. The traumatic part is when we realize that bliss is never any further away than in our own mind.

Memories of her childhood were slipping into Mariah's thoughts and she couldn't understand why. She felt it odd to have a conscience about leaving her family behind when they all had done the same thing to her. First it was her father, trading in his old family for a new and improved one, leaving his children behind with a heartless, disgruntle mother. Her brother was the next to move out and although it was never his choice, he certainly hadn't made great efforts to keep in touch; and then he died.

A series of unpleasant dreams about Anton had reawakened old feelings that Mariah thought had been buried with him. Had she been abrupt to leave Montreal after his death? What if she stayed? What if she had kept in touch with Alison? Her flirtation with social media was highly guarded under privacy settings so Mariah could be certain that past ghosts couldn't find her, even though she often did searches for them. She didn't want to be a part of their life, but yet, she felt that it was within her rights to know about theirs and that often made her feel like a spy, lurking behind the bushes and watching them from afar.

The day would come when curiosity and a trail of nightmares would encourage her to go online and do a thorough search for her parents. She hadn't spoken to either since the funeral, and had hoped to never think about them again, but she felt it was necessary to at least check in and hope that these horrid nightmares about her family would go away.

Polina Nichols was on Facebook. All of her photos demonstrated that she had an active social life, with fake smiles and beautiful clothes covering her frail body, her eyes were empty and soulless. Surrounded by friends, Mariah wondered if any of these people knew that she was a mother.

Of course, there was a man beside her in a few, but when had there ever not been someone who held her hand, even when she didn't deserve an ounce of love. No wonder her father had left, Mariah considered and she suddenly felt her defenses drop when his face flashed in her mind.

She couldn't recall much from her early childhood years, but hadn't Frank Nichols tried to make life better for his children? Even when she was kicked out of Polina's house, he helped her financially – if not in any other way – to make sure she was capable of keeping her head above water. Maybe it was time to forgive and forget, she decided. Maybe it was time to reconnect with the man who had already lost his son. Maybe it was time for him to regain a daughter.

With a gentle, calm smile on her lips and a lightness lifting her heart, she attempted to find him on Facebook but no avail. Of course not, Mariah grinned to herself, why would someone of his generation even have an interest in social media? Not that it was impossible, but it seemed very unlikely in his case.

With a satisfied grin on her lips, feeling more positive about the possibility of talking to her father again and rebuilding their relationship, Mariah decided to do a search on Google. She felt it was time to pack up and go on a trip. Chances are he would show up somewhere, whether it be a retirement party, one of the charity events he used to attend or something else, she was pretty confident of finding him and if not, maybe she would be able to find his phone number and address from years earlier. Everything was online these days, so she felt secure in being successful.

It wasn't what she'd expected. It took a moment of staring at the first link that showed up when she typed in his name to understand what was going on. Shaking her head, the smile fading from her lips and Mariah did another Google search. This time she used her dad's full name and the city where he now lived. Obviously she found the wrong person last time and-

But it wasn't the wrong person. The first listing that showed up in her Google search was in a funeral home. Her father was dead.

Feeling a cold chill crawl up her body, causing her to shake uncontrollably, Mariah couldn't see the words on the screen, as tears temporarily blurred her vision. It just couldn't be true. Her father couldn't be dead! It was impossible. Someone would've told her. Someone would've found her and-

Her body continued to shake. Feeling lost in a fog, she rose from the chair and wandered into the bathroom. She had to have a hot bath, a shower, something, in order to stop the chills that were almost bringing Mariah to her knees. It simply couldn't be true. Her dad couldn't be dead. It has to be a mistake. Maybe it was someone else and she clicked onto the wrong link.

Rushing back to her laptop, she looked again at the link, gasping for air, as frantic tears continued to escape and a painful cry that she hadn't at first recognized as her own, was filling the room. Not her father too! Hadn't she lost enough when Anton died? Clearly this wasn't right. This couldn't be true!!

Lying in the tub a half hour later, Mariah wondered what would happen if she pulled herself underneath, allowing the water to fill her mouth and her nose. Would it finally take her away to a place of peace? She had lost her last chance to regain a relationship with her father and had no interest in doing the same with her mother; therefore her entire family was dead. It was just her and although this changed very little from the last few years of her life, there was a difference in knowing this as a fact, that made her feel like a leaf blowing in the wind. She was now an orphan.

The next few weeks were difficult ones, as she slowly began to go through and dissect the details in her mind. Her father had died several months earlier. It had, according to what she read, happened fast in the form of a massive heart attack. She wondered if he ever thought of her in those last moments. Did he remember the little girl he had with his first wife, the one who had turned her back on him and never looked back? Did he die hating her? Had he ever tried to find Mariah? Did she even have the right to wonder such things?

It was a secret she held close to her heart and Mariah vowed to share it with no one. Ava had often inquired if all was well and would be none the wiser, as the weeks and months rapidly passed and springtime brought with it the beauty throughout the city. The colors of the cherry trees have never been so enriched, so welcoming as they were that spring and Mariah had not experienced life quite the same way after learning of Frank Nichol's passing. It was as if something had broken inside of her and rather than attempt to fix it, she acknowledged it and merely let it go, much in the same way someone would once they stopped caring about the home they lived in and didn't bother to repair damages after a brutal storm.

It was the circle of life. Everyone would die someday and knowing that someone in your family had passed seemed to bring that reality into the light. It wasn't something she had the maturity to realize when Anton died, but she did now. It was very clear.

On top of everything, her job at the temporary agency was slowly coming to an end. Annette promised they would find her more work once her current obligation was complete. Mariah was professional and courteous and they greatly admired her pleasant personality, charming and energetic. There was absolutely no reason to think that she didn't have a bright career ahead of her.

She occasionally thought about Curtis. Was he in a relationship with Paulina? Did he hate her? Did he think she was pathetic? Mariah considered stopping by to visit him, but wasn't sure if her presence would be welcomed. He was more than fair to her when she left, but that didn't mean that he wanted to see her again, even if it were just for a quick hello.

Paulina was on social media and she often had pictures with some children that Mariah gathered were her niece and nephews. Most were with family, some with friends and the boyfriend that had dropped by the office at one time. Sometimes Mariah thought of reconnecting with her, but decided against it. Perhaps it was better to leave the past where it was and move forward.

After learning about her father, Mariah spent a lot of time alone, thinking. She didn't socialize a lot and hoped that Ava and the others in the building didn't start to worry about her again because she wanted some time to herself. Mariah thought about the men she had brief, physical relationships with and wondered if maybe, someday she would want more than a casual fling. She thought about her family and found some peace with the past, but knew there was still a road in front of her that she had to face.

Feeling guilty with all she had hidden from Ava, Mariah continued to dig for information about the immortals. It was her way to make up for all the lies and secrets. Then on the night before her departing interview with the temp agency, Mariah received the call. She learned the identity of the 'Rock Star of Vampires'. Ava would be shocked when she told her.

Chapter forty-six

S ome mornings are distinctively different from the others. There's
a peaceful feeling that overcomes your entire being and although
you aren't sure where it comes from, something tells you that this
is how you should've felt all along. You carry no worries about the day
ahead, but suddenly feel like everything is going to work out just as it
should. Unaffected by those around you, unconcerned about whether the
rain falls from the skies or if it will just be another dismal day, you feel
safe that you're being guided with every step, comforted with each breath
and fulfilling a script that isn't actually your own.

Mariah Nichols felt free when she woke up that morning. Where she
usually harbored a certain amount of hostility, ready at any moment to
come out with both guns blazing, on that particular day she felt a strong
sense of security about her future. Annette Roberts had made it very clear
on several occasions that she adored the young receptionist and appreciated
her professional attitude, quickly adjusting to the new office setting and
outshining the girl who had previously held the same job. There was no
concern about her future. Annette would take care of her, Mariah was
certain of it.

But then, what was this uncomfortable feeling that seemed to grab
hold of her from the moment she walked out the door. Much like the pull
of an elastic band, Mariah felt as thought an invisible object was coaxing
her back to her home. Perhaps it was her sense of loss over finishing a job
that she really hadn't minded or a secret insecurity about the future, one

Her Name is Mariah

that she had stored so far back into her soul that it only managed to grab a moment of her attention.

Annette asked Mariah to meet her before the office was opened at 8 a.m., mainly because she had such a heavy workload for the day and feared that she would fall behind if she waited until later. It wasn't unusual for staff to arrive at work to find the office manager already sitting behind her desk, organizing her schedule and other times, enjoying a cup of coffee and looking out at the mountains that enhanced the Vancouver horizons. She once joked with Mariah that it was the only time in her day where she enjoyed some peace and quiet. Having a photo of two small boys on her desk, it was assumed that her household was full of activity and perhaps something as simple as a Starbucks and a mountain view was enough to help her through the day.

With her own coffee in hand, Mariah arrived at the temporary agency fifteen minutes before her 7:30 appointment and found the door was already unlocked. Grinning to herself, she stepped inside and made her way through the sparingly lit reception area and down the short hallway that lead to her Annette's office. Expecting to find her boss relaxing, taking in the Vancouver skies, she instead found her hunched over a stack of papers on her desk. The welcoming woman she had expected to find was a more serious and showed some surprise when Mariah entered the room.

"Oh, good morning." Annette appeared distracted, quickly shifting her eyes away from Mariah and toward the floor. Uneasiness filled the room and created a dismal silence that was difficult to ignore. Mariah felt hesitant as she sat in the seat across from Annette and secretly feared that the other shoe was about to fall, judging only by her demeanor and not by her flawless appearance, it was clear that something was wrong. "I'm sorry, Mariah, I hadn't noticed the time and was caught up in something. If you will just give me a moment?"

"Sure, did you need me to come back?" Mariah managed to hide her fears that the uncomfortable tension in the room had something to do with her evaluation, instead managing to put her business mask on as a veil of defensiveness surrounded her.

"Oh, no, no, not at all," Annette shook her head and gave a half-hearted smile, making an attempt to regain her composure. She quickly fished a sheet of paper out of the pile and pushed the rest aside. "It's just

273

me, trying to do everything as usual. I've been up since 4 am hoping that I could get some extra stuff done at home, then get here early so that I could catch up on paperwork, but it just seems like I may as well have stayed in bed." A forced, weak laugh escaped her lips and Mariah suddenly sensed that this was a woman who was clearly burning the candle at both ends. Dark circles were evident underneath her eyes, with the right being much more prominent while her skin was especially pale, lacking in any luster, Annette looked as if she were on the verge of either tears or complete exhaustion.

"I sympathize." Mariah's comment was genuine, although she certainly couldn't understand the stress of being a working mother of small children; she could feel the overwhelming emotions that were behind Annette's words. "I mean, I obviously can't relate to having a family and a career, but I can only imagine."

"Trust me, Mariah, having a family is definitely overrated." Annette's words seemed to even surprise her and she immediately looked as if she wanted to backtrack and remove her statement. "I mean, don't get me wrong, I don't regret having children, it's just that… it's not what I thought it would be, you know?" She waited until she saw a compassionate smile cross Mariah's lips. "It can be tough and you're still expected to be everything and more at work, at home, with your friends, with your family. I would never tell you to not have children, but I wouldn't necessarily encourage you either." She let out a short laugh and quickly realized she had found a non-judgmental ear.

"Well, you are preaching to the choir." Mariah's lips curved into a cross between a hesitant and a warm smile, making it clear that she was the ideal audience in this conversation. "I have little interest in having children. I simply don't feel it is a good fit for my lifestyle."

"Well, I can certainly appreciate that." Annette appeared to relax and pulled her chair closer to the desk. "I guess I shouldn't waste any more of your time and dig right into your evaluation."

Just as Mariah expected, her boss gave her a wonderful review and even went so far as to say that her employee needed to expand her career options, suggesting a few different paths she felt Mariah should consider in the future as well as outlining some courses that would enhance her skills. Annette insisted that better things would be ahead in the future.

"Mariah, I just feel that you are a strong candidate for several jobs that require more responsibility and also, I think you should consider what it is that you wish to do in the future. I feel like you have so much potential and I'm actually surprised you have been working receptionist jobs for so many years." Annette tilted her head and studied Mariah's face. "I'd like you to come in tomorrow, if that works for you and maybe do some testing. It'll give us a better idea of your strengths and maybe help us figure out a career path that suits you. Would that be something that would interest you?"

"Yes, definitely." Mariah felt her original defenses drop to the ground and excitement fill her voice. "That would be great. I'd sure appreciate it."

"Terrific!" Annette shared her enthusiasm. "Then, we will set something up for tomorrow and take it from there. Meanwhile, glance through the current positions listed on our website and see if anything grabs your attention. I'll send you an email with the time a little later this morning, if that is okay?"

"Yes, sure, that sounds fantastic." Mariah moved to the edge of her chair, sensing that the meeting was almost over. "I feel like I need a change. My life has sort of fell in a rut lately…." She allowed her words to drift off, not certain of the best way to finish that sentence.

"It happens to all of us from time to time." Annette assured her and started to rise from her chair and Mariah did the same. The two walked toward the doorway, where Annette paused and watched her employee stop in the hallway. "Now it's time to move forward and hopefully advance in your career."

"Thanks again." Mariah offered one last smile before heading toward the exit and then rushed to the nearby elevator. A part of her contemplated an early morning drink at the bar downstairs, feeling that she earned a celebratory shot of vodka but she quickly decided against it. She hadn't had a drink in a few weeks and it wasn't the time to allow this old habit to reestablish itself now.

The springtime air welcomed her as she stepped outside, filling her with a sense of hope that only the optimistic would notice. Annette's words reignited a fire inside of her that Mariah had thought had long been lost, back in her days in Montreal. How things have changed since that time. She didn't even feel like the same person who once lived and worked in the beautiful, eastern city and now, she felt as though she was changing once again into someone that her past self would've scoffed at, even a few months earlier.

Life had a funny way of teaching you the lessons you had to learn. Growing up in an unstable home had taught her to be self-reliant and that inner strength can take you farther in life than anything else. Her brother had taught her about tolerance and acceptance and then his death demonstrated to Mariah that it was necessary to live every moment as it were your last – a creed she had taken in the wrong context for far too long. Working for Dr. Wesley gave her many difficult lessons including how an ego can be a dangerous companion, only coming second to a tainted perception and insecurity. If she had played her hand a little more differently, perhaps she would still be working for Curtis Wesley.

The mere thought that perhaps she was responsible for the end result in that situation, caused sadness to fill her heart. If she hadn't been so erratic back then, would things have turned out differently? Had she sabotaged her own life? Feeling tears fill her eyes, she quickly grabbed and pulled on her Ray-Bans in an attempt to hide her emotions from others. Quickly sitting on a nearby bench, she needed a moment to regain her composure before going home.

Closing her eyes, Mariah heard the faint sound of music in the distance. A smile curved her lips when she recognized the Shania Twain song that Anton had loved so much. How many of her first days in Montreal had she watched him excitedly dance around their apartment, singing off key to a song that talked about feeling like a woman. Mariah would giggle, knowing that her brother was making fun of himself more than anything else. How she had loved seeing him so happy and full of life. How she missed those days!

A smile stubbornly took over her entire face, as the music grew louder, moving closer, she assumed it was in a car. At that moment, Mariah swore she could hear him sing. Tears burned her eyes and she quickly blinked them back, staring into space. She could see him, dancing around, coaxing her to follow him and she rose from the bench to walk in Anton's direction, while a sense of peace flowed through her body. The music continued to get louder and Anton continued to sing off key, brasher than ever before and Mariah smiled through her tears. It was going to be okay. Everything was going to be fine.

And that's when she felt it. A warm, comforting hand on her back as it gently guided her toward the edge of the sidewalk, where she would catch her bus home. A flow of peacefulness filled every limb and warmth surrounded her, as Mariah continued to think of her brother and smile. She somehow pictured him laughing at the crazy moments in her life, as if it wasn't necessary to take them seriously. He was right.

The comforting hand continued to guide her forward and she gave it all her trust. She felt so carefree. Glancing down the street, she saw the bus slowly easing around a curve and in her direction. She would go home now. Everything was going to be okay.

She heard a scream escape her lips as her body was jolted forward into traffic. Mariah could feel herself cry out, attempting to fight against gravity even though she knew it was too late. Her back still felt the warmth of a hand that had so forcefully shoved her, even as she lay on the street.

Everything was going to be okay. She was going home.

Chapter forty-seven

The biggest myth in the world is that we have control of our own lives. The truth is, we never have control at all. It isn't that life is predestined for us or that we are powerless in our decisions, but that a certain mysterious power carries us through the days of our lives. It encourages us to go in a certain direction, like a whisper in our ear, proudly escorting us to the lessons that we must learn and introducing us to the very people that will change our lives forever. It doesn't make sense at the time, but eventually it will come together in blissful harmony and awaken our senses on a level that we never knew was possible.

It is in our death that we finally review the many synchronicities of our life.

Mariah opened her eyes and looked around. People were standing over her with looks of dismay on their faces. She couldn't hear what they were saying, but at the same time, there was so much noise. A loud, ringing blasted through her ears as the group of people moved closer to her, some with a look of tranquility on their faces while others sobbing and speaking another language that she could not understand.

Feeling a flash of embarrassment, Mariah attempted to rise but couldn't move. It was as if her body was frozen to the ground, no feelings could be felt in her limbs and yet she was clearly still alive. As the crowd grew around her, Mariah's discomfort increased and she wanted to tell them all to go away. An older Romanian lady was gently running her hands over Mariah's forehead, speaking to her in a language that she couldn't understand. She could feel fingers grasping to her wrist and another crashed into the center of her chest, while muffled voices moved closer and a heavenly vanilla scent filled her lungs. Soft, black curls briefly cascaded over her lips, as a woman's head floated in front of her eyes. Screaming grew louder while a roaring siren could be heard in the distance and grew closer and some of the crowd backed away slightly, the Romanian woman continued to rub her forehead and speak the unfamiliar language.

A burst of energy flowed through her body, warmth filled her cheeks and Mariah wiggled her toes and quickly realized she was wearing no shoes. Her eyes shot about; quickly assessing the situation and it suddenly occurred to her that she was laying the middle of the street! Her ego filled with humiliation and regardless of the comfort that everyone was showing her; Mariah's first instinct was to get up and walk away.

You guys, I'm fine. I know this looks bad, but I'm totally fine. Please, if you will just move away, I can stand up and show you. I just... can someone help me find my shoes?

Attempting to rise, Mariah quickly made the assumption that it was the people around her that were somehow holding her down. Clearly, she was fine. Clearly, these people were lunatics. Clearly, she could get up and walk away at any moment, if only these strangers would stop holding her down!

This is so embarrassing. Can someone give me my shoes? I can't find my shoes and... my purse; cans someone give me my purse? Just help me up, please, I will find them on my own.

Mariah thought of the beautiful high heel shoes that sat in her closet for years, barely worn. They were an expensive designer brand that she had somehow managed to get at an unbelievably discounted rate and yet, how many times had she worn them? It was very rare. On special occasions, perhaps for a significant date or something that required her to impress others by the elegant, designer shoes.

...and I had to wear them today and now they are probably stolen! No wonder I can't find my shoes, the minute I fell down, some fucking opportunist just ran over and grabbed them, just took them away when no one was looking...

Now full of anger, she was even more determined to rise up and find her shoes but her attempts were unsuccessful. That's when she saw the ambulance pull up beside her.

Oh my God! I'm fine! Why did you call an ambulance? If you would just stop holding me down, I could get up and walk away.

Feeling a mixture of humiliation and humility, Mariah attempted to relay the same information to the EMT, but he wasn't listening. He had such blue eyes that they sparkled in the sunlight and his voice was calm and beautiful, bringing her some sense of peace in a moment when everyone else appeared to be in a panic. Finally, perhaps he would be the one who would hear what she had to say.

Another man and a woman appeared to be telling people to move away, clearly recognizing that the crowd had been holding her down against her will. They quickly went to work, grabbing her arm, opening her blouse, grasping tightly to both sides of her head. The man with the sparkly blue eyes was talking to her and at that moment, he could've been an angel on earth for having recognized that she was fine. Unlike the others, he was soothing and made her smile.

"Okay, young lady, you had a little accident."

Relief filled her body.

Yes! Just a little accident. I fell on the crosswalk, but everyone is going fucking crazy. Will you please help me up?

"We're just going to take you to the hospital and have you checked out."

NO! I don't want to go to a hospital. Can't you see that I'm fine? Oh no, please don't tell me you're like all these other people who won't listen to me. I'm fine! Can you see my shoes? They're really nice, you know. I think someone may have taken them?

"Here's her purse."

Thank you!! Oh, thank God! Can you find my shoes now? They're really nice-

"Her name is Mariah." A soft, feminine voice was speaking to the sparkly blue-eyed man in a hushed tone.

Yes! Mariah Nichols. Please, help me find my shoes.

"Mariah." The blue-eyed man repeated. "That was my grandmother's name."

Yeah. Right. Um…. did you happen to find my shoes with the purse.

"Hold on tight, Mariah." The handsome man gently touched her cheek and she felt a warmth flow through her body that made her feel safe. "Don't be scared."

Feeling her body being lifted, hollowness separated her from the noises that were previously surrounding her body, as it lay on the street. She felt someone holding her hand as a loud siren roared and people continued to talk over her, using words she couldn't make out or understand.

"Hold on, Mariah." She heard the woman's voice calling out and she felt her hand being squeezed and allowed herself to fall silent and squeeze back. A panic filled her chest and she wondered why they were taking her away if she was fine. Would they hold her against her will in a hospital? Attempting to talk, her mouth was dry and a sharp pain poked into her arm. The siren stopped and she felt a rush of lights that only grew brighter, while a frantic rush of activity surrounded her. Feeling her eyes burn, she closed her lids and felt herself escape to a world of warmth and familiarity.

A sense of calm flowed through her body when she awoke in the hospital room. It was bright and beautiful with the most pristine, white walls and a soft light had replaced the harsh ones from earlier that same day. A smile curved her lips and she finally was able to sit up and look around. Beside the bed were her beautiful shoes, the ones she had fretted about since falling on the crosswalk hours earlier. Clearly, the EMTs had brought her here so that the crazy people would stop holding her down because Mariah now moved so fluidly, that it was clear that nothing was wrong with her. She was surprised to not even feel pain in her limbs, and when she evaluated her body, she found no scratches, no scars. She was fine.

Then why was she still here?

An older Iranian man walked in wearing jeans and a shirt, holding a chart in his hand. He acted as if she wasn't there at all and fury flowed through her, but it was quickly followed by grief. There was a deep sadness in the room. He was quite sad. How come she could feel his feelings? Why was he feeling pity for her?

He walked over to the bed and jotted something on her chart before pausing for a long moment.

They said it would get easier, but it has not gotten easier.

She could hear his thoughts? Why was she hearing his thoughts? Mariah laid back down, her heart racing wildly, she felt herself suddenly overwhelmed with anguish that was unlike anything she had felt before in her life. It was a mixture of shock and pain that paralyzed her, sweeping through her body, introducing her to a reality that she could not yet face. She listened to him.

I thought I would be immune to tragedy after the heartache of my childhood. I thought nothing could hurt me in my new life in this country. I was wrong. Tragedy is everywhere. It just has a different face.

Love filled the room; Mariah could feel it surround her like a warm bath, luxurious *and* beautiful, harmonious and soft, welcoming and freeing. All the negativity that had ever filled her soul emptied, causing her to feel light, her body shrinking back to the comforts of a small child, carrying no fears, no regrets, no judgment and suddenly, she felt a freedom that was uplifting and inspiring. She promised herself that it would never be replaced by bitterness or anger again. This feeling was too wonderful to ever blemish with the pettiness that had long held her captive.

So unfortunate to die at such a young age.

Die!! He thought she was dead? Mariah felt her old instincts return, as she jumped up in bed and prepared to let him know that she was very much alive, but it was as if he hadn't noticed a thing, thoughtful musing over her chart, he turned around and walked out of the door.

A sense of panic filled her body and Mariah found herself abruptly jumping out of bed and grabbing her shoes on the floor. Pushing her feet into them, she glanced down at her body and brushed the wrinkles out of her skirt, her eyes darted for her purse, when the door opened again. Her mouth fell open when Curtis Wesley walked in the room.

"Thank God you are here!" Mariah blurted out. "I gotta get out of here. These people think I'm dead." She gestured toward the door and noted that Curtis was wearing a white shirt and a plain, black tie along with a pair of loose jeans. His green eyes were passive, yet full of compassion.

"Please, Curtis," She hesitated, suddenly full of vulnerability, she feared that he would hold negative assumptions about her and refuse to give her the help she so desperately needed. "I promise I'm not the same person I was when I worked for you. Please, just please help me."

Tears sprang from her eyes before she even realized they were there and panic made her breath erratic and uncomfortable. Mariah watched him briefly look away, his eyes glancing at a spark of sunlight on the floor and she felt some relief that she was unable to hear his thoughts, as she had with the previous doctor. Maybe everything was going to be okay.

"Mariah," Curtis lifted his head and hesitantly looked back into her eyes. "I promise you that I have no ill feelings toward you. I have no judgments or anger. I'm not sure what you understand about what just happened to you."

"I don't know," Mariah spoke hurriedly and sat on the edge of her bed. "I remember walking toward the street and I…" she shook her head, suddenly feeling very confused. "Then, I think I tripped or I fell on a crosswalk and all these people were crowding me and not allowing me to get up and I couldn't find my shoes or purse and…. I just want to get up and leave. Then an ambulance appeared and they were bringing me, here… I guess? Now, I'm obviously fine and want to leave, but for some reason that doctor that just came in here. He… he thinks I'm dead."

Mariah found herself giggling at the notion. It sounded so silly when she repeated the story and a hint of embarrassment filled her cheeks. "I'm sorry, I know how ridiculous this must sound."

"No, not at all." Dr. Wesley assured Mariah as he slowly approached her. "Mariah, I know you're scared right now and you don't understand what is going on but I assure you that it's completely normal in this circumstance."

"In what circumstance?" She felt the smile fall from her face. "What are you trying to say?"

"Mariah," Curtis reached out and took her hand and warmth flowed through her, she felt at peace and safe. She felt stronger than ever before and yet, vulnerable. "You *are* dead."

Chapter forty-eight

I t is so simple. The inconsistencies of life are what often throw us off track. We don't understand things and therefore, we assume that they are defective in some way and it makes us nervous. Somewhere along the way, we were fed the myth of happily ever after and the belief that we are here for something more than to love and to learn.

Mariah Nichols felt as though she was floating and Curtis Wesley's words were drifting beside her, as she headed into a place that she did not recognize. It was frightening, but at the same time, she knew that these fears were senseless because she was safe. No harm can ever take away what really matters unless you allow it to and so many did that very thing, giving it power that it never deserved at all.

His words halted her and although she wished them to be a lie, she knew that they were true. As her brain investigated the details, attempting to put it together, the reality slowly started to unfold. The people that surrounded her when she fell wanted to give her comfort until the emergency workers arrived. The EMTs knew Mariah was critical and wanted to make her feel safe. She sat up in her bed, showing no signs of getting hurt – no bruises, cuts or pain because they belonged to the body, not the soul.

"When did it happen?" She whispered, unable to look into the Curtis' eyes but instead down at her legs. A short investigation proved to her that they were flawless, just as they had that morning. Had they been left mangled in her death? Was she even recognizable to those who still lived? "Wouldn't... wouldn't I know?" A hint of denial swept over her even when she knew it no longer mattered. "Isn't there a way that I would know I was dead?"

His eyes full of compassion and understanding, Curtis continued to hold her hand and peaceful silence flowed through her body. He slowly began to nod and after a hypnotic stare that caused her original anxieties to melt away, he finally answered her question.

"It happened on your way to the hospital." Curtis quietly replied. "The EMTs could tell you didn't have much time and did everything they could to comfort you in your final moments. I felt one of them praying for you and I knew it was your time."

She felt more confused with his statement, but serenity caused her to fall silent and listen.

"It's difficult for me to answer that question." Curtis continued. "For no two people is it the same. Death is something that some accept more rapidly than others, depending on their personal faith and beliefs. Some things are the same."

Briefly letting go of her hand, he climbed onto the bed beside her and she felt his voice flowing through her body with such grace and warmth that there was no mistake that he spoke with nothing but unconditional love. "There is always someone waiting, helping to ease the process. That's actually very important."

"But why you?" Mariah felt his words flow from her lips. "I don't understand."

"It was me who reached deep inside your soul. I helped you discover love that you had never thought was in you to give. I was the one who made you question so many things that you wanted to leave buried forever. It was me who made you look beyond the superficial or the physical world because it was the only place you inhibited for the majority of your adult life. It was necessary to bring you away from that place in order to develop your soul."

"When we met, you were a very different person, Mariah." Curtis confirmed with quiet confidence. "When you left my office for the last time, you were broken wide open in a way that forced you to finally discover and meet with all the demons that possessed your heart for so long and finally come face to face to them. It was necessary in your evolution as a human being otherwise, your life would've ended on a less meaningful note."

"Was I... scheduled to die today?" Mariah spoke with a raw innocence that had long left her voice, reminding her momentarily of her childhood before Anton went away.

A grin enveloped Curtis' lips and his eyes shone from a nearby light. "I wouldn't say 'scheduled' necessarily. It's much more complicated than that and it has to do with what you are attracting into your life at any given time. I know it probably doesn't make sense to you right now, but sometimes it is you who decides when your life will end, not some all-powerful force that allows you little or no control. There is something inside of you that tells the universe that you are ready to move on to another journey and when everything is aligned then it happens."

"I don't understand. Why would someone attract their death?" Mariah was confused. "I don't think I attracted mine."

"Yours is a little complicated, I will admit that." Curtis glanced across the room as if he could hear someone on the other side of the door, but his eyes returned to her face. "Sometimes people are in a low place and wish to die, but it won't necessarily happen because your life is so temporary and it is a gift given to you by something outside of yourself. That something outside of yourself has to be in agreement when your time is here. It's not necessarily as simple as you decide you no longer want to live. It's kind of a negotiation process, for lack of better words."

"I don't remember negotiating."

"You never will." Curtis confirmed. "In your case, it was more tragic, so it wasn't as if you were sick in bed for months. It was sudden and in cases such as this, it is usually when you are in profound pain because of an injury, that you will seek relief and it will either be allowed if it is your time and if it is not your time, you will remain in your body and fight your way back."

"That sounds...." Mariah searched for the words, but didn't know how to finish the sentence in a respectful manner.

"Weird?" Curtis smiled and the richness in his eyes enhanced to the most beautiful color she had ever seen in her life. A warm light that washed through her and made her smile back. "It's fine, Mariah. I know it is confusing right now and it is kind of difficult to explain, especially to people who don't consider themselves to be spiritual. The point is that when you feel intense physical pain, it's so overbearing that once you cross over to death, you won't remember it again and honestly, you don't want to."

"I thought I just fell down." Mariah confided. "That's why this all sounds so unbelievable."

"That's what you perceived at that moment because it was rather sudden and you had no time to really process the situation so yes, it would've appeared to you that you simply fell and that you were fine." He waited for her to nod and he mirrored her reaction. "That's completely normal."

Mariah thought for a moment and suddenly felt overwhelmed by emotion. "But why are you here? I know what you said earlier about how you opened my heart. I know that much is true." She felt a warm tear trickle from her eye and slide down her face, falling from her chin to leave a damp stain on her sleeve. "Does that mean you're dead too? Are you an angel, then?"

Curtis response was a smile that filled his entire face, exposing his beautiful, white teeth and revealing small lines around his eyes and lips. A light flowed through the room and quietly evaporated the tears that were waiting behind Mariah's eyes.

"I don't know if you would necessarily call me an angel. Angel is a mortal term that gives the living some comfort. It's a little more complicated and I assure you, I don't fly around with a beautiful set of wings on my back."

Noting the embarrassment that Mariah clearly felt, he was quick to reassure her. "But please don't feel foolish, it's a question that most ask in your situation. The truth is that we are all spirits. Some of us are living and some of us are not. Those who have crossed over will find the spirit that gives them the most comfort during their transition. For you, that is me."

"As for my status," Curtis hesitated and the smile slipped from his lips. "I am no longer alive, however, I wasn't when you met me either."

"I don't understand."

"When you were asking about angels and if you believe in that kind of thing, some would refer to us as 'earth angels'." Curtis paused for a moment as if conflicted by what he was saying. "I use the term lightly because the living sometimes use it completely out of context, but essentially, there are people in the world who you believe to be alive, but they are actually crossed over from the spirit world and their role in your life is to make you open up your heart, to grow on a spiritual level or to heal. They aren't necessarily in your life for a long time, but just long enough to kind of shake things up, for a lack of better words."

"So you, you were in my life for that reason?" Mariah felt herself stutter over the words, her brain attempted to piece it together. "Were you there to help me in some way?"

"I chose to be in your life to help you, yes." Curtis replied while turning more in her direction as he spoke. "At the time, I was hoping to be a close friend who made you step outside of yourself and see life with a more open heart."

"But I fell in love with you." Mariah barely whispered, feeling an anxiety fill her up where peace had previously filled. "I thought you ruined my life."

"I opened up your life. At the time, I certainly see why you feel that I ruined it." Curtis agreed. "It was my intention to hurt you."

Mariah suddenly felt sorrow fill her heart, but it didn't appear to have an effect on Curtis, who boldly stared into her eyes.

"It was necessary to rip off the scar in order for you to look deep inside yourself because there was absolutely no other way you would ever have considered it. Your walls were a mile high; Mariah and you were only hurting yourself. Your brother's death was the final straw and it cut you off from the world. You never allowed yourself to love again."

"Until you." Mariah said and felt salvation overcome her spirit.

"Until me." Curtis nodded slowly; his hand tenderly touched her face. "That is why everything in your life started to slowly crack when you worked for me. Everything was at its breaking point and you began to unravel, but sometimes that is necessary to heal. In the long term, it helped to open yourself up and that was necessary because otherwise, your life was very empty and shallow. You deserved so much more and it was only you holding yourself back."

"It's true." Mariah thought back. "Everything did start to fall apart about that time."

"We learn about ourselves in the reflection of other people's eyes." Curtis confirmed. "It is the people that push our buttons the most that brings the truth to the surface or at least, the questions we have to answer for ourselves."

"So my mother?" Mariah wasn't sure how to finish that question.

"Your mother was one of those people and that's why you avoided her for so many years. You hated what it forced you to face."

"That I'm like her?" Mariah spoke sharply.

"Yes and no." Curtis remained unaffected by her icy tone. "You aren't your mother, Mariah but without meaning to, you did pick up her coping mechanisms."

"What coping mechanisms? My mother never taught me how to cope with anything."

"I didn't say they were positive coping mechanisms." Curtis hesitated briefly. "Drinking was your mother's coping mechanism and it has been often yours as well."

Mariah had brief flashes of a look of dismay on Curtis' face on the days she would return to the office after having a few glasses of wine during lunch. There were times she quickly could see that she was slightly intoxicated and shame filled her, followed by an overwhelming sense of love.

"It's okay, Mariah." He spoke softly. "I didn't show you that to be hurtful in any way, I was simply showing you that sometimes you were in a poorer condition than you may have believed."

Silently nodding, Mariah could see he was right. "Alcohol was one of your escapes while men were another. Sarcasm, hateful comments and avoidance were others." She suddenly saw a flash of Ava frantically searching for her through their apartment building. "You had people who wanted to help you along the way, but you often chose to avoid them, just when they started to make some headway with you. You allowed yourself to open up a bit, then run for the hills because you were so afraid."

Mariah couldn't speak. She knew that everything he said was true.

"But it is time to leave here." She hadn't realized he was holding her hand until he gave it a squeeze and he rose from the bed. "We need to go for a little walk."

Standing, Mariah noted that her beautiful shoes were on her feet and suddenly they didn't mean quite as much as they had earlier that day.

Feeling vulnerable and nervous, she hesitated when he attempted to lead her to the door.

Sensing her fear, he stopped. "It's okay Mariah, everything is going to be fine. I'm not leading you to the gates of hell if that is what you are thinking." A smile crossed his lips. "Although if there were such a place, we'd both probably be there."

A combination of tears and laughter filled Mariah and she slowly walked forward. "Where are we going?"

"We're going to make a few visits and I'm not going to lie," He hesitated at the door before opening it. "Some of these visits will be a little uncomfortable for you, but I think you will finally understand a few things that were holding you back in your journey. You need to understand those who loved you very much and you need to know that your life truly had meaning."

Feeling anxious, yet hopeful, Mariah walked with him through the door and into a place where her mistakes, disappointments and shame were no longer relevant.

Chapter forty-nine

We often don't hear words that we're not ready to accept. Denial isn't a terrible thing it just means that our spirit is not yet ready to receive the information that waits at the door. It's something we cannot allow ourselves to take in and nurture just yet, but instead, leave on the step outside until a more suitable time. Problems only arise when that piece of truth is left out too long; at first it alerts us with a gentle tap, but the longer you ignore it, the louder the sound becomes until it is completely unbearable.

It's at this point when you are faced with two possibilities. Either you bravely answer the door and accept what is on the other side or you find a way to drown out the knocking. Some choose physical distractions whereas others decide to leave the house all together, under the assumption that the truth will not know where to find them. It always does. It knows where to find you, and it will always be there until you acknowledge that it exists.

Mariah spent most of her life in denial about various things – feelings like love and grief, just to name a few. She moved – both physically and emotionally - as far away from problems as possible and when nothing else worked, she had an affair or leaned on a bottle of wine. It worked for a while and then, it did not.

Leaving the hospital room was a way of facing the fact that her life had ended. It felt surreal and she even began to think that perhaps this was nothing more than a dream. Of course! It couldn't actually be true. She fell to sleep or maybe there was an accident and she was in a coma? Hadn't she watched a documentary on such a topic? With a false sense of relief, she felt her steps become lighter as Curtis guided her through the hospital and toward a set of stairs. He didn't say another word until they were outside.

The sun shone down on them and Mariah felt an incredible warmth flow through her body, as if she was recognizing it for the first time. A smile lit up her face as a soft breeze moved through her hair. She turned to see Curtis watching her. Letting go of her hand, he appeared to be searching her eyes and she couldn't stop admiring his beauty as the sunrays flowed over his face, causing his green eyes to sparkle, as a smile curved his lips. People were all around them and yet, there was no one at all.

"I wanted to ask you if you are ready, but it appears you are ready for anything. I can see a peacefulness in your eyes that perhaps didn't exist before today." With some hesitation, he reached out and touched her arms and she saw the smile fade from his lips. With downcast eyes, his fingers slid over her arm and he moved from her for a moment, sending a slight chill through her body and she was scared. What did it mean?

"I know the day that this changed for you." His eyes appeared dark when Curtis looked up again and he seemed hesitant to speak. "You had many ebbs and flows when growing up, but we're so much more adaptable as children, that we can let things go and move on to a new day."

"But then there are those moments," he continued, tilting his head slightly, Curtis stared into her eyes. "When things change permanently and often we don't know it at all. I think I found that moment in your life and think we need to revisit it."

"Revisit it?" Mariah was confused and yet, something told her that she had little choice but to follow his lead. "I don't understand."

Without explaining things further, he took her hand and led her away, but rather than turning the corner of a familiar Vancouver street, they instead were walking through her childhood neighborhood. Astounded, her eyes quickly scanned the houses, the cars, the families that surrounded her and it quickly became apparent that they were not only walking down her old street, they were doing so during a different time period altogether. It was twenty years earlier and the same children, she had once gone to school with, were running past Mariah on the sidewalk as the same cars were driving down the street. The familiarity of everything made her feel nostalgic, as a pressure captured her chest and pushed through her body, causing such an intense emotional reaction that she had to stop walking. Curtis did the same. She let go of his hand.

"Was it always like this here?" Mariah finally found the words that caught in her throat. She spoke of the emotions that suddenly encumbered her soul, almost causing her to collapse on the very sidewalks she had walked on many times in her life. "Where is this coming from?" She spoke of the emotions that were stampeding their way through her body. "I don't understand what is going on, Curtis."

"You will see." He reached again for her hand, using the other to point in the direction of a house. It took her a moment to recognize it as her former childhood home. It now looked much smaller than she remembered it. Had it been so lackluster in appearance, so dismal and unmemorable?

Without saying a word, she allowed him to lead her up the path she had walked a million times before and enter the door of the small, irrelevant bungalow that she had once called home. Upon walking through the doorway, she felt crippled with emotion, an unexplainable sadness filled her body and brought tears to her eyes. There was a overpower sense of loneliness that was stronger than anything Mariah had ever known in her life. At the very core was an unmistakable sense of fear and isolation that was squeezed into an area that it never truly fit. It took a minute for her to regain her composure and when she finally did, her eyes were led to the other side of the room. There sat Polina Nichols.

Her mother was completely unaware that they were in the room. Still a young woman, she sat with a drink in hand and with tears in her eyes and although she said nothing, Mariah could feel every emotion that ran through her soul and it sent a powerful force that made her unable to move, but simply stands in that same spot and allow what started as a current and end with a riptide. Rather than the angry tyrant that she had experienced through childhood, she instead saw a defenseless woman, crippled by the world around her.

"Mariah, your mother came to this country with endless hopes, dreams and optimism. She thought her life would be better with the move and that she would not look back again." Curtis' words flowed over her and it took a moment for her to recognize the similarities to her own life but when she did, Mariah felt shame rather than a connection. "She didn't see herself as a Russian bride, sent here to fulfill a contract." He hesitated for a moment before continuing. "Until she arrived here, that is."

"She didn't feel like she was joining a family as she had hoped," Curtis continued and Mariah watched her mother on the other side of the room, continuing to drink in misery. "Your father was awkward once she arrived and reality hit him hard and unfortunately, your mother sensed that right away. The animosity between them only grew through time. He wasn't what she had expected, nor was she what he expected. Both had a pretty specific idea of what a marriage should look like and as you can imagine, everything from a different culture to age only complicated things even more and rather than attempting to find a viable solution, it just seemed that they both gave up."

"Why didn't she leave him?" Mariah asked.

"For many reasons," Curtis replied. "She was scared. You have to remember she was only 18 when she arrived and her parents told her that in order to obtain her Canadian citizenship, she had to marry this man. They also made another thing clear to her," Curtis stopped and Mariah turned to look into his eyes. "She couldn't return to Russia."

"Her English was limited and she struggled to learn it. Your father would often tease her if she misused a word and he did so with no ill intention, but she was very sensitive about her errors and would grow angry and self-conscious. It would make it hard for her to get work. Plus, she had a child almost immediately."

A smile curved Mariah's lips when she realized that he was speaking of Anton. She quickly wiped tears from her eyes and nodded in understanding. "She must've been so scared."

"She was and your mother didn't have much support. No friends in this country, she lost contact with almost everyone back in Russia." Curtis continued. "She felt very trapped with no way out."

Mariah stared at her mother as she sat her drink down and peaked out the window. Walking toward her, in hopes of seeing what was outside, she was stunned when a younger version of herself ran through the door, past her mother and down the hallway. Hurt filled the room and Mariah immediately recognized that it was coming from their mother. Rejection stung her like no other emotion and in a split second, Mariah immediately sensed why; her parents had turned their backs when she left their country, her husband rejected her upon her arrival in Canada and now her children were doing the same.

"You won't find him in there." Polina bluntly commented, feeling that it was the only way to reveal the truth. In hysterics, the younger version of herself was flying through the house, looking for her brother and finally returned to the living room. Tears were streaming from her face, her ponytail in a tangled mess and her mother suddenly felt resentment for the bond that her children had to one another. "He is dead to us."

The childhood version of Mariah misunderstood these words and collapsed to the floor in misery, believing with her whole heart that her brother was dead. Polina grew frustrated and attempted to explain the reality of the situation, but stubbornly refused to approach her daughter or show her any signs of comfort. She decided that her daughter would not be weak like her, not be naïve about the world that surrounded her and therefore, not be disappointed by the injustices that she would meet on her path.

Mariah intuitively dropped to the floor beside the childhood version of her and attempted to show comfort, even though she knew it was doing no good. The little girl merely dismissed her and cut herself off from everyone in the room - an invisible wall erupted and she refused to drop it, even for a moment. Her emotions ran deep and her maturity shone through as she worried that her brother was sad and alone, wondering what she could do to help him. Mariah felt pride that as a child, she was very intuitive and recognized the dangers of a teenage boy being alone and homeless. Why hadn't their mother thought of the same thing?

"Why couldn't my mother see it?" Mariah said the words out loud and rose from the floor. "Why didn't my mother see that Anton might've been in danger?"

"She did, but it was too late. He was already gone by then." Curtis replied, signaling toward a bottle of Vodka that sat on the kitchen counter, in the next room. "She reacted in a moment when she should've stepped back and thought, but it wasn't in her nature to do so. She was scared of what it meant when she found out that your brother was transgender. Your mother worried that she had somehow brought him up wrong and that all the times your father accused her of making him into a mama's boy that she had inadvertently affected his sexual orientation."

"That's ridiculous." Mariah pointed out.

"I know and eventually, your mother would figure that out, but it was too late when she did." Curtis barely whispered. "And she had many regrets."

Mariah turned to look at her mother once again, her eyes were detached but the room was filled with emotions that were a combination of both herself as a child and her mother in that same moment. There was no mistaken that what Curtis said was true. It was much more complicated than Mariah was able to see in those days and perhaps, hadn't considered since but stubbornly stuck to the version she knew as a child.

"I think it's time we leave." Curtis gestured toward her mother and Mariah noted that everything in the room appeared to be at standstill.

"Why has everything stopped?" Mariah asked as she walked toward the door, feeling sadness as she realized she would never be in that room again. She took a deep breath and walked out.

"That is all you need to see." Curtis replied and gently closed the door behind them. "I wanted you to understand that day and why it changed who you were and also, I thought you needed to see your mother through different eyes."

Mariah nodded apathetically. "You were right."

They silently approached the sidewalk and stopped. "Where to now?" Mariah asked, glancing in both directions.

"To see your brother."

Chapter fifty

T hings are often not as they appear to be. Just ask the little girl with the big brown eyes that grew up in the perfect family, in the perfect house, with the perfect brother. Most of what we see is an illusion and yet, we continue to believe that there is happiness behind every smile and sincerity in every voice. It gives us comfort to know that all is right in the world, even when nothing may be right at all.

Mariah Nichols assumed that she would live forever and gave little thought to the possibility of dying young. Most youth don't, even when forced to face death within their own lives because underneath it all, they have the misguided belief that it would never be them. It would always be someone else.

It isn't always someone else.

Before reaching her brother, Mariah and Curtis had to make a detour and she began to accept that she was no longer in the world of the living. This was not a dream that she would awake from nor a coma that was only temporary, she was gone. She had had her chance to make her dreams come alive, to resolve old issues and to live a happy, carefree life, but it was her choice to instead to walk the earth with a sense of arrogance that was never truly real at all. It was difficult to accept, but she had no choice and in that moment. Her tears were full of a million regrets.

"Why is it this way? Why did I not see this when I could've done something?" Mariah spoke in broad terms, but Curtis still knew what she was referencing. Although they had only made one visit she realized that human being were much more complicated than she would've believed when still alive. If she had been wrong about her mother, how many other things had she misunderstood? Many scenarios ran through her head and she grieved for the moments she could not explore from another point of view.

Curtis appeared apprehensive to answer and instead looked at the ground. "You did have opportunities, but you chose to ignore them."

"No, I didn't," Mariah insisted and Curtis didn't bother to argue with her. He knew that from her perspective, she hadn't the chance to see things as she did now and merely nodded in silence.

"I regret so much." Her voice was small, vulnerable, as her mind drifted over specific moments in her life and how she had a choice to assess them at the time. Had she ever been fair at all? Her snap judgments and assumptions were rarely given a second thought, but allowed to stand in time, as she walked away.

The people who had been a part of her life sprang through her mind; everyone from Emily Thomas, a friendship she ended abruptly and never looked back, to Alison Ruben in Montreal, whom she had broken her promise to keep in contact after moving to Vancouver. The men were numerous and there were many she couldn't even recall the names of but their faces were very clear in her mind, from meaningless one night stands to Teo, the man she had only chased to hurt her mother. Former coworkers like Jody. Oh Jody! She had been so terrible to her and now she saw her from a completely different light. A vision of the young woman holding a baby in the air flowed through her mind with the ongoing slideshow that she suddenly saw through different eyes. They were real people with feelings that she hadn't considered, not even for a moment.

"So now that we've reviewed that I'm a terrible person, now what?" Mariah was surprised to find that she was sitting on a park bench. She glanced at Curtis, who sat beside her, his emerald eyes observing her face, his divine, flawless lips pursed together. He was an image of perfection. She blinked hard and looked away.

"You're not a terrible person, Mariah." Curtis sternly intercepted. "Hey, this isn't why I'm showing you these things. I'm not here to shame you because if that were the case, we're all in the same boat. Very few of us die with no regrets or live a life that we deem to be perfect. We all make mistakes and misjudge situations. That's what makes us human."

"Then why?" Mariah asked, attempting to hold back fresh tears from escaping her eyes. "Why?" Her voice was weak.

"Do you remember when you were in school? Sometimes you would do a project or a presentation and the teacher would later go through the positive and negative? That teacher didn't do so to upset you, but to make you understand or see things you missed while you were in the process of working through the moment." Curtis explained and slid closer to her. "Life kind of works the same way. It isn't all bad Mariah, not by a long shot. I think there is something else you have to see."

He reached for her hand again. Hesitant to take his, Mariah eventually did and she was overwhelmed by the flashes of joy that ran through her entire being; it was every smile she had ever inspired, every moment that her actions and words made another person's heart sing with delight and every second of love she felt or created. It was unimaginable and it left her stunned for a moment, unable to move or speak. Had she had that kind of impact on other people's lives? It never would've occurred to her in a million years.

"Is this… is this true?" She stuttered through her words, as every syllable stuck in her throat. "I didn't even know some of the people. I don't know how I made them feel that way. I don't understand why."

"You don't have to know someone personally to make an impact." Curtis assured her. "It can be something as simple as a smile and a 'good morning'. Common courtesy, like holding a door opened for an overwhelmed mother or sometimes just being honest, when it would be easier to lie."

"I was probably too honest at times." Mariah considered this in brutal terms, while Curtis did not.

"Honesty can be harsh, but it is the most loving thing you can do sometimes." Curtis insisted. "It shows respect and it forces people to sometimes see things that are necessary."

Mariah slowly nodded.

"I think I'm ready now."

"Are you sure?"

"Yes."

Mariah was suddenly in a room that she recognized as her brother's apartment in Montreal. Everything was exactly the same. Her luggage was even piled in the corner as it had been in those days. The room smelled of the cheap body spray she used back then, a vanilla scent that was obtained at the nearby drugstore. Mariah slowly turned around, taking it all in and suddenly she felt herself freeze; unable to move or even blink her eyes focused on a short, slender woman that had the eyes of her brother Anton, in the body he had always wanted to be in.

"Oh my God!" She felt a rush of emotion that exceeded anything she had ever felt in her life – a combination of relief, gratitude and unconditional love that extended beyond the world she only briefly lived in. Mariah had an instant flash of her as a four-year-old child, telling her older brother that her love for him was bigger than the earth, the moon, the skies – it was bigger than 'everything, even an elephant'.

Her hesitation to hug Anton was only brief and soon she felt the comfort of his arms, as they tightly embraced her. She felt completely safe and fearless, for the first time since the accident and a sense of comfort that had not been a part of her mortal life. Mariah didn't cry, she was too astounded by the moment. A slight breeze alerted her attention and she turned to see Curtis walking away.

"Where are you going?" Mariah shouted out. "Curtis, I thought you were here. I thought you were one of-"

It was too late. He disappeared from the room.

"I don't understand." Mariah felt a loss fill her entire being. "I didn't get a chance to thank him. I didn't get the chance to say goodbye."

"You don't have to." Anton assured her with a feminine voice. "He already knows."

"I don't understand." Mariah whispered breathlessly.

"His job is finished." Anton continued to speak while stroking her hair. "He was only to bring you here."

"Where are we?" Mariah asked and finally let go of her brother to step back. "And do I call you… Ana now, I don't understand?"

"It doesn't matter here." Anton gestured to the room that surrounded them. "Here we are all the same and we are whatever we wish to be. It isn't about your body or your name; it's about your soul. It's truly beautiful. If only we had viewed each other this way in life, the world would've been a whole different place and such a truly amazing experience."

"Where are we?" Mariah repeated. "Is this heaven?"

"It's not really a place with a name." Anton insisted and sat on the end of the couch. "It's not like the heaven we learned about as kids. There are no pearly gates or angels flying around in the air. It's just a safe place where we reflect on our lives and learn from our mistakes. Some people choose to help others that are struggling on earth and others believe in reincarnation, so that is their path. It's really what you believe, Mariah."

"I don't know what I believe." She spoke hesitantly, almost in fear of what would happen as a result of her candor.

"It's fine. I was the same way when I arrived here." Anton smiled. "Death, just as life, is only what you believe it to be."

"I'm not sure what I believed when I was alive either."

"You believed you were a vampire." Anton's words shocked her and it surprised Mariah that she hadn't considered that aspect of her life until now.

"I did." Mariah asked nervously. "Are you suggesting that I was wrong?"

"I'm not suggesting anything but the mind is a powerful thing." Anton insisted. "Only coming second to your heart."

Mariah looked away and began to go over the facts that made her feel she was a mortal vampire. Had she been wrong all along? What about the people in her building? What about-

"Ava?" She heard her voice say the name as her face crossed her mind. "Ava? Is she.. I mean, does she know about me?"

"She knows that you have died." Anton nodded with an apologetic smile. "Your friends were devastated, Ava especially. This will be hard for her to overcome."

"Is there anything I can do? I mean, to make it… easier?" Mariah stumbled through her words. This was so foreign to her, so surreal.

"Many will do small things, gestures that let the living know that we are never far away, at least not in spirit." Anton replied. "You don't have to think about that right now, though."

Mariah nodded and felt dumbstruck by this information. She didn't know what was coming next. What if Anton disappeared just as Curtis had only moments earlier?

"Are you here to stay?" Mariah asked hesitatingly. "I mean, Curtis left."

"I'm here for now and you needn't worry about the future. We will talk much more about that later."

"Do we stay here?" She glanced around the small apartment.

"No, it was just our meeting place." Anton stood up and reached for her hand. "There's something that I need you to see."

The two walked out the door and Mariah found herself glancing back for a moment, then redirecting her attention as Anton continued to talk.

"It is important for you to know some things about our last days together." Anton led her to the elevator and they walked in. He hit a button. "I need you to know that I never meant to hurt you on those last days. I was in a very bad place and although that is no excuse, that is where so much turmoil stemmed from."

"I know." Mariah assured him. "I mean, you committed suicide-

"Mariah, there is something you have to see." Anton interrupted.

They were suddenly standing beside a window. "This is where I died." Anton spoke in a peaceful voice. "I fell so many floors and all the way down, I grasped on to those last few seconds in a way that I should've grasped onto my entire life. It is perhaps my biggest regret. But there is something else you should know."

Touching her arm, Mariah felt herself transported to that day. Anton was wearing a sweat suit; his matted hair pulled back in a ponytail and makeup was running down his face. He stood looking down, with tears dripping from his chin; She could feel his despair, as hopelessness flowed through his entire being. It broke her heart all over again, just as it had when he died and she attempted to shake his hand off her arm.

"No, you must see this." He firmly insisted and she felt like she was being punished further, when something in the picture changed. It was no longer Anton getting ready to jump, but her standing at the edge of the sidewalk earlier that day. The sun was shining down and for a brief moment, Mariah wondered if this was her opportunity to return to that time and regain her life, but this dream was quickly defeated.

She observed herself smiling, confident and strong in that instant and then a hand reached out and touched her back, caressing it gently, as if it were showing her signs of comfort. Mariah felt frozen still as she continued to watch herself, in those last seconds of her life. Trying to focus, she viewed the hand continuing to stroke her back, edging her toward the street and then with a sudden, abrupt move, Mariah watched as the hand suddenly shoved her in front of the bus. A horrified driver could be heard screaming through the confusion, which quickly became a collection of hysteria. Mariah was stunned by what she had just viewed, while her brother remained by her side, she felt his arm around her as tears rolled down her cheeks and yet, she couldn't move. It was unbelievable. It couldn't be real.

But it was real.

It hadn't been an accident. She hadn't tripped or unintentionally walked in front of a bus. She was pushed and by someone that Mariah never would've expected. It didn't make sense and yet, on some level, maybe it did.

"Anton? I was pushed? But why would..." She whispered and then was unable to speak, as the words caught in her throat. Beside her, he sorrowfully shook his head and pulled her into a tight hug. Feeling comfort in his embrace, Mariah felt herself break down, still in disbelief she was only left with one word. "Why?"

He slowly let her go and pointed toward the one who had ended her life, slinking through the crowd that was in too much of a frenzy to even notice.

"I think you know." His voice was suddenly so young, reminding her of the little boy Mariah grew up with and the innocence sparkled through his eyes. She felt herself involuntarily nodding.

She did.

Neither said another thing. They just stared into the horizons in a perfect world that they were never able to see before that moment.

Her name is Mariah.

This was her story.

To read more about Mariah Nichols,
check out *The Rock Star of Vampires.*
To learn more, go to www.mimaonfire.com